"The thought of people believing we are engaged is actually quite amusing."

"Yes," Caleb replied, his voice gruff, though his expression remained hidden from her.

This conversation was embarrassing enough without looking him in the face. He'd echoed her sentiments. Which was perfect. Excellent. Although none of her resolute thinking explained why she became instantly tongue-tied the instant he entered a room.

"Thank you, Mr. McCoy, for everything. Truly. I hope I haven't seemed ungrateful."

It's just that you tie me in knots, and I've never been the tied-in-knots-over-a-man sort of person.

He stuck his hands into his pockets and avoided looking directly at her. "Caleb." He cleared his throat. "I saved your life. I think that puts us on a first-name basis."

"I amend my apology. Thank you, Caleb. And you must call me Anna."

She tripped a bit over the last syllable.

"You have nothing to apologize for, Anna."

Her stomach fluttered. The use of her name lent an air of intimacy to the exchange. She'd never been particularly fond of her name. She liked hearing Caleb say it. She liked hearing him say her name very much.

Sherri Shackelford
and
Louise M. Gouge

The Engagement Bargain
&
Cowboy Seeks a Bride

LOVE INSPIRED
INSPIRATIONAL ROMANCE

LOVE INSPIRED®

INSPIRATIONAL ROMANCE

ISBN-13: 978-1-335-45671-7

Recycling programs for this product may not exist in your area.

The Engagement Bargain and Cowboy Seeks a Bride

Copyright © 2021 by Harlequin Books S.A.

The Engagement Bargain
First published in 2015. This edition published in 2021.
Copyright © 2015 by Sherri Shackelford

Cowboy Seeks a Bride
First published in 2015. This edition published in 2021.
Copyright © 2015 by Louise M. Gouge

This edition published by arrangement with Harlequin Books S.A.

For questions and comments about the quality of this book, please contact us at CustomerService@Harlequin.com.

Love Inspired
22 Adelaide St. West, 40th Floor
Toronto, Ontario M5H 4E3, Canada
www.Harlequin.com

Printed in U.S.A.

CONTENTS

Sherri Shackelford is an award-winning author of inspirational books featuring ordinary people discovering extraordinary love. A reformed pessimist, Sherri has a passion for storytelling. Her books are fast-paced and heartfelt with a generous dose of humor. She loves to hear from readers at sherri@sherrishackelford.com. Visit her website at sherrishackelford.com.

Books by Sherri Shackelford

Love Inspired Suspense

No Safe Place
Killer Amnesia
Stolen Secrets
Arctic Christmas Ambush

Visit the Author Profile page
at Harlequin.com for more titles.

THE ENGAGEMENT BARGAIN

Sherri Shackelford

Therefore if any man be in Christ
he is a new creature: old things are passed away;
behold, all things are become new.
—*2 Corinthians* 5:17

This book is dedicated to Shelley Miller-McCoy
and Renee Franklin, because some women
will always be ahead of their time.

Chapter One

Outside the Savoy Hotel,
Kansas City, Kansas 1884

"Remind me again why we're here." Caleb McCoy glared at the growing mass of people jostling into his space.

He didn't like Kansas City. There were too many people in too little area. A man could hardly breathe. He'd much rather be home. Working. The sooner they were on their way home to Cimarron Springs, the better.

His sister, JoBeth, flashed a wry grin. "You're here because my husband obviously forced you."

JoBeth's husband, Garrett, had been unable to accompany his wife to the suffragist rally in support of a sixteenth amendment to the constitution, an amendment for the women's vote.

Jo had been adamant on attending.

Fearing for her safety, Garrett had strong-armed Caleb instead. The opposition to the women's movement had been disruptive on more than one occasion.

The buildings surrounding the tiny grassy square

loomed over Caleb like brick-and-mortar sentinels. As the time for the suffragist speech neared, the mood of the crowd had shifted from lazy joviality into restless impatience.

His sister adjusted the gray knit shawl draped around her shoulders against the brittle fall breeze. "As you're quite well aware, *I'm* here for Anna Bishop's speech. This is the closest she's come in the year since we've been corresponding, and the best chance I have to see her in person again. If you'd met her when she traveled through Cimarron Springs last fall, you wouldn't be so surly."

"And yet she never replied to your telegram."

Jo pursed her lips. "It's possible she never received my message. She travels quite a bit."

Caleb mumbled a noncommittal response. Having been raised with five younger brothers, Jo was tougher than tanned leather. She was smart and independent, but vulnerable in the relationships in her life. Fiercely loyal, she naturally expected the same in her friends.

A good head taller than most of the women in the crowd, and several inches above the men, Caleb searched for any sign of dissention. "There's no trouble yet. That's a relief, at least. The sooner this speech is underway, the sooner it's over."

A faint, disgruntled snort sounded beside him.

While his sister had maintained an active correspondence with the prominent suffragist, the fact that Miss Bishop hadn't responded to Jo's most recent telegram had left him uneasy. "What do we know about Miss Bishop, anyway?"

"Well, she's the current darling of the suffragist movement, a sought-after speaker for the cause and an outspoken advocate for women's rights. You can't possibly find fault in any of that."

"An absolute paragon."

"She must be. You wouldn't believe the names people call her or the threats she receives. It's positively nauseating."

A grudging admiration for the suffragist's conviction filtered through his annoyance. His work as a veterinarian introduced him into people's lives during unguarded moments, and he wasn't naive to the injustices women faced. Men who were cruel to animals were just as apt to be violent toward the women and children in their lives. And yet a man who beat his horse was more likely to be censured or fined than a man who abused his wife.

Jo chucked him on the shoulder. "Even if Garrett forced you to accompany me, it's good for you to get out once in a while. You talk to animals more than people."

"That's my job," he grumbled. "Animals don't expect small talk."

Undaunted by his annoyance, she slipped her arm through the crook of his elbow. "I've been saddled with a male escort to an event celebrating the independence of women. You're lucky I'm not insulted."

"Then you should have mentioned that to your overprotective husband."

Jo sighed, her expression rueful. "And let you spend the day alone? Again? You're becoming too set in your ways. You're turning into a hermit. Everyone thinks you're still sweet on Mary Louise."

"I'm not—"

"Shush. Anna is about to speak."

Caleb lifted his eyes heavenward. He wasn't a man who sought attention. He wasn't a man who liked crowds. That didn't make him a recluse. He lived a good life. He had a thriving practice and he enjoyed his work. He'd tried his hand at romance once already. He'd been sweet on Mary Louise, but she'd chosen his younger brother instead. Since then he'd never had the desire to court anyone else.

With four brothers altogether, a confirmed bachelor in the family was hardly a great tragedy.

A smattering of applause drew his attention toward the podium. A nondescript woman in a gray dress took the stage and spoke a few words in a voice that barely carried beyond the first few rows of standing people.

Jo tugged her arm free. "I can't hear a thing. I'm moving closer."

She forged a path through the crowd, and he reluctantly followed. The scores of people pressing nearer had exhausted the oxygen from the space. Yanking on his collar, he sucked in a breath of heavy air. Bodies brushed against him, and sweat dampened the inside band of his hat. As the square had grown congested with late arrivals, the audience had abandoned their picnics and stood. He picked his way over the baskets and blankets littering the ground.

His heel landed in something squishy. Glancing down, he caught sight of the cherry pie he'd just decimated. No one cast an accusing glare in his direction, not that Jo paused long enough for him to apologize. He limped along behind her, dragging his heel through the flattened grass in a futile attempt to clean the sticky filling from his boot.

Near as he could tell, the gathering was an unequal mix of women to men. Judging from the expressions on their faces, the spectators were split between supporters and curiosity seekers. Jo charged ahead and found a spot near the barricades separating the makeshift stage from the audience. A young girl, no more than eight or nine years old in a bright yellow dress and white pinafore, scooted in beside Caleb. She rested her chin on the barricade and stared at the podium.

Caleb frowned.

While the onlookers currently appeared harmless, this wasn't the place for an unattended child. "Shouldn't you be at home? Or in school or something?"

Two dark blond braids rested on the girl's shoulders, and she blinked her solemn gray eyes. "She's the prettiest lady I ever saw." The girl's voice quivered with admiration.

"The prettiest lady *I've* ever *seen*."

"You like her, too?"

"No, that is…."

The woman on the stage announced Anna Bishop, and the girl's face lit up.

Caleb held his explanation. He'd been correcting his younger brothers' speech for years, and the habit was ingrained.

The girl in the yellow dress rose onto the balls of her feet and stared. Caleb followed her gaze and froze. He rubbed his eyes with the heels of his hands and looked again. Anna Bishop couldn't have been much older than her midtwenties or thereabouts. Her dark hair was smoothed away from her face and capped with a pert velvet hat decorated with an enormous teal plumed feather. Her skin was radiant, clear and pale, her cheeks blushed with excitement.

The cartoons he'd seen in the newspapers had depicted Miss Bishop as a dreary spinster with a pointed

jaw and beady eyes. Having expected a much less flam-
boyant person, he fixated on the vibrant details. Her
satin dress matched her feathered hat in the same deep,
rich shade of turquoise. Rows of brilliant brass buttons
created a chevron pattern mimicking a military style.
The material at her waist was draped and pulled back
into a modest bustle, the flounces lined with rope fringe.

She glanced his way, and he caught a glimpse of her
eyes. Blue. Clear, brilliant blue.

His heartbeat skittered before resuming its normal
rhythm. Miss Bishop marched up the stairs and exchanged a few words with the woman who'd made the
introduction, then faced her audience.

"I am here as a person whose opinions, according
to the laws of this nation, are of no merit to my community. I am here as a soldier in a great Civil War to
amend this gross injustice," she declared, her lyrical
voice pulsating with each word.

As she detailed the importance of the amendment,
her eyes flashed, and the passion in her voice swelled.
"We live in a country founded on the right of revolution and rebellion on the part of those suffering from
intolerable injustice. We cannot fail to recognize the
injustices heaped on one half of the population simply
because that half is female. The Fifteenth Amendment
was progress, but there is more to be done. If the question of race has been removed as a restriction, must
the question of gender stand between us and the vote?"

Caleb forgot the crowds, he forgot the little girl standing beside him. He forgot everything but the woman on
the stage. She was captivating. Her passion infectious,
her furor beguiling.

He leaned forward, his grip on the barricade painful. Loosening his hold, he studied the rapt audience. He wasn't the only person riveted. Jo appeared equally enthralled by the charismatic speaker, as did most of the folks standing near the front. With each subsequent declaration, Miss Bishop's enthusiasm held the audience in captivated silence.

Caleb exhaled a heavy breath and shook his head.

Just his luck. The one woman who'd caught his attention in the time since his childish infatuation with Mary Louise was a suffragist. A woman who, according to the newspaper clippings Jo collected, considered men an unnecessary nuisance and marriage a legalized form of bondage. If Jo hadn't been standing beside him, he'd have hightailed it out of there. The last time he'd noticed a girl, he'd wound up with his heart broken and a whole passel of trouble besides.

"Go home to your mother," a hoarse voice near his left shouted, jarring Caleb from his glum ponderings.

"I think her mother is here!" Another jeered.

"Yeah," a third man bellowed. "How about you do something useful? Find yourself a husband."

A chorus of titters followed.

Caleb yanked upright, blinking as though he'd been awakened from a dream. The growing hostility in the crowd sent a slither of apprehension up spine.

The dissenters remained buried in the confusion of people. Anonymous in their enmity. *Cowards.*

He glanced at the little girl in the yellow dress, then leaned down. "Where are your parents?"

She pointed at the Savoy Hotel across the crowded square.

Caleb tugged on Jo's sleeves and nodded toward the girl. "She shouldn't be here."

Jo's eyes widened, clearly noticing Miss Bishop's young admirer for the first time. "Is she all alone?"

"Near as I can tell."

His sister tightened her bonnet over her dark hair, tossed a wistful glance at the podium, then sighed. "The atmosphere here is growing hostile. We should take her home."

He stepped back and let Jo pass before him.

A gunshot sounded.

Someone screamed.

Miss Bishop's brilliant turquoise skirts disappeared behind the podium. In an instant the scene descended into chaos. A man tripped and slammed into his back, shoving Caleb forward, and he careened into Jo. They crashed over the barrier. He angled his body and took the brunt of her weight, knocking the wind from his lungs. His ears rang, and he shielded Jo with his arm, searching for the girl in yellow.

She stood in the midst of the stampede, her eyes wide, her hands covering her face. The crowd parted around her like water skirting a boulder.

Caleb pushed off and forced his way through the fleeing mob. A sharp heel dug into his foot. A shoulder knocked him off balance. With a burst of strength, he lifted the girl into his arms, turned and leaped back over the toppled barricade.

The mob pushed and shoved, scattering like buckshot away from the podium. A cacophony of deafening voices shouted as people were separated in the confusion. While disorder ruled, Caleb crouched behind the limited protection of the barricade with his sister and the girl, shielding them as best he could with his outstretched arms. He'd rather take his chances with a stray bullet than risk getting trampled beneath the fleeing spectators.

After several tense minutes that seemed to last an eternity, the ground ceased vibrating. The noise lessened. A gentle breeze stirred the hair at the nape of his neck.

He chanced lifting his head, astonished by the sudden silence. In an instant the square had cleared. Only a few people remained, looking dazed but uninjured.

Jo shoved her bonnet from her face. "Is everyone all right?"

The little girl nodded. She straightened and brushed at her yellow skirts, appearing no worse for wear.

A panicked voice shouted behind him. "We need a doctor!"

Caleb searched for the source of the frantic call. The dispersing crowd had all but emptied the grassy square, taking cover in the nearby hotels and businesses, leaving a mess of blankets and overturned baskets in their wake. Caleb pushed himself upright and reached for Jo.

She yanked her hand from his protective grasp. "Find out who needs a doctor, and I'll take care of this little sprite."

"I'm a veterinarian."

"You're better than nothing," Jo declared with her usual blunt edge. "Can you see Anna? Is she all right?"

"She took cover as soon as the pandemonium started. I'm sure she's fine."

His answer was mostly truthful. While his attention had been focused on Jo and the young girl, he'd caught a glimpse of Anna's turquoise blue dress near the podium.

"Help," the frenzied voice called. "We need help."

Though reluctant to lose sight of his sister, Caleb knew Jo better than most anyone. She wouldn't put herself in unnecessary danger. She was smart and resourceful. They had to separate.

He touched her sleeve. "Whatever happens, meet me in the lobby of the Savoy at noon. That's twenty minutes."

At his easy capitulation, Jo's expression lost its stubborn set. "Noon." She reached for the girl's hand. "We're going to find your parents. What's your name?"

The girl pressed her lips together, as though holding back her answer.

She shook her head, and her two long braids whipped around her neck. "I'm not s'posed to tell strangers."

Jo shrugged. "That's all right. You don't have to tell me. My name is Jo. Can I least walk you back to the hotel?"

The girl screwed up her face in concentration. "To mama?"

"Yes, to your mother."

The girl nodded.

Satisfied Jo had control of the situation, Caleb spun around and pushed his way through the knot of people toward the frantic voice. He broke through to the center, and his stomach dropped.

Anna Bishop lay sprawled on her back, a growing pool of blood seeping from beneath her body. Though ashen, she blinked and took a shuddering breath. The white banner across her chest was stained crimson near the point where the chevron ends met at her hip. The gray-haired woman kneeling beside her clutched Anna's limp hand in both of hers.

Caleb swallowed around the lump in his throat. "She needs a surgeon."

The woman's eyes filled with tears. "The streets are clogged with carriages. The hotel is closer. She's losing so much blood. I'm not strong enough to carry her." Her voice caught. "Help us, please."

"I'll do whatever I can."

He knelt beside Miss Bishop and took her limp wrist in his hand, relieved by the strong pulse thumping beneath his fingers.

Anna's stunned blue eyes stood out starkly against her pale, almost translucent skin, providing the only color in her pallid face. Even her lips were white with shock. At the sight of such a bold woman struck down in such a cowardly fashion, raw emotion knifed through him.

Who had such fear in their heart that they'd fight words with bullets?

A fierce protectiveness welled in his chest. Whoever had done this might still be near.

"Miss Bishop," Caleb spoke quietly. "I'm going to take you back to the hotel. I'm going to help you."

For a dazzling moment she'd appeared invincible. The truth sent his stomach churning. She was just as fragile, just as vulnerable as any other mortal being.

She offered him the barest hint of a nod before her eyelids fluttered closed, blotting out the luminous blue color.

"Don't give up," Caleb ordered.

Seeing her on that stage, he'd recognized a woman who didn't shrink from a fight. If she needed a challenge, he'd give her one.

"Don't you dare let them win."

* * *

The words drifted over Anna. She'd already lost. She was going to die for the cause.

At least her death would not be *ordinary*.

Clenching her jaw, Anna fought toward the surface of her consciousness.

Don't you dare let them win.

The opposition would not have the satisfaction of her death. She'd traveled to Kansas City alone, an unusual occurrence. The speech had started well. There'd been hecklers. There were always hecklers. Anna had learned to ignore them.

Then she'd heard the shot.

The truth hadn't registered until searing pain had lanced through her side.

For a moment after the disruption, the world had gone silent. Disbelief had held her immobile. She'd looked in horror as a dark, growing stain had marred her turquoise day dress. The ground tilted. She'd staggered and her knees buckled.

Her mother had advised her against speaking in such a small venue. Reaching a few hundred people wasn't worth the effort when crowds of thousands awaited them back East. Grand gestures were needed for a grand cause.

Two ladies from the Kansas chapter of the movement hovered over her, shouting for help. She'd met them this morning—Miss Margaret and the widow, Mrs. Franklin.

A dark-haired man knelt at her side and pressed his palm against the wound, stemming the flow of blood. Anna winced. The stranger briefly released the pressure, and she glanced down, catching sight of a jagged hole marring the satin fabric of her favorite teal blue dress. She always wore blue when she needed extra courage.

The man gently raised her hip to peer beneath her, and she sucked in a breath.

"It's not bad." The man's forest-green eyes sparked with sympathy. "The bullet has gone through your side. Doesn't look like it struck anything vital."

Her throat worked. "Are you a doctor?"

"A veterinarian."

Perhaps her death would not be quite so ordinary after all.

The absurdity of the situation lent Anna an unexpected burst of energy. "Will you be checking me for hoof rot?"

"I'll do whatever is necessary." The man glanced at the two women hovering over them. "If the hotel is our only option, we must leave. At once. You keep fighting, Miss Bishop."

She was weary of fighting. Each day brought a new battle, a new skirmish in the war for women's rights. Each day the parlor of her mother's house in St. Louis filled with women begging her for help. Though each problem was only a single drop in the oceans of people swirling around the world, she felt as though she was drowning. She'd given all her fight to the cause, to the casualties subjugated by an unfair and biased system. She didn't have any fight left for herself.

Mrs. Franklin lifted her gaze to the nearby buildings, then jerked her head in a curt nod. "It isn't safe for her here. I've sent two others to fetch a surgeon and notify the police. Someone else may be hurt."

"I'll see to Miss Bishop," the man said, "if you want to check for additional injuries."

"Maggie will stay here and coordinate with the authorities," she said, her expression stalwart. "I'll remain with Miss Bishop."

Anna nearly wept with gratitude. Despite his reassuring words, the man kneeling at her side was a stranger, and she'd never been comfortable around men. Her encounters were rare, often tied with opposition to the cause, and those men mostly looked at her with thinly veiled contempt. Or, worse yet, speculation. As though her call for independence invited liberties they would never dream of taking with a "proper" woman.

The man ripped Anna's sash and tied it around her waist as a makeshift bandage. All thoughts of men and their rude propositions and knowing leers fled. The pain in her side was like a fire spreading through her body. It consumed her thoughts and kept her attention focused on the source of her agony.

The stranger easily lifted her into his arms, and her head spun. Her eyelids fluttered, and he tucked her more tightly against his chest.

A wave of nausea rose in the back of her throat, and her head lolled against his shoulder. What reason did she have for trusting this man? Someone wanted her dead. For all she knew, he'd fired the shot. With only the elderly Mrs. Franklin as her sentry, there was little either of them could do if his intentions were illicit. Yet she was too weak to refuse. Too weak to fight.

"Who are you?" she asked.

He picked his way over the debris left by the fleeing crowd. "I'm Caleb McCoy. I'm JoBeth Cain's brother."

Her eyes widened. "Is Jo here?"

He nodded. "We're staying at the Savoy Hotel, same as you. Jo was hoping to see you."

Over the past year, Jo's letters had been a lifeline for Anna. Her glimpse into Jo's world had been strange and fascinating. Anna had been raised with an entirely different set of values. Husbands were for women who lived a mediocre existence. As her mother so often reminded her, Anna had been groomed for the extraordinary.

The cause was her purpose for existing.

Her mother had been fighting for women's rights since before Anna was born. There were moments when Anna wondered if her birth had been just another chance for her mother to draw attention to the suffragist movement. Women didn't need men to raise children. They didn't need men to earn money. They didn't need men for much of anything, other than to prove their point. Her mother certainly hadn't been forthcoming about the details of Anna's father.

He doesn't matter to me, why should he matter to you?

Why, indeed.

The pain wasn't quite so bad anymore, and Anna felt as though she was separating from her body, floating away and looking at herself from a great distance.

Mr. McCoy adjusted his hold, and her side burned.

She must have made a noise because he glanced down, his gaze anguished. "Not much farther, Miss Bishop."

An appropriate response eluded her. She should have answered Jo's telegram. When Jo had discovered Anna was speaking in Kansas, she'd requested they meet.

Anna had never replied. She couldn't afford to be distracted, and Jo's world held an undeniable fascination.

Pain slashed through her side. "Will you tell Jo that I'm sorry for not answering sooner?"

"You can tell her yourself."

Jo was intelligent and independent, and absolutely adored her husband. She had children, yet still worked several hours a week as a telegraph operator.

Anna had never considered the possibility of such a life because she'd never seen such a remarkable example. Marriages of equality were extremely rare, and if Anna let her attention stray toward such an elusive goal, she lost sight of her true purpose. Besides, for every one example of a decent husband, her mother would reply with a hundred instances of drunkenness, infidelities and cruelty. Unless women obtained a modicum of power over their own fates, they'd forever be at the mercy of their husbands.

Mr. McCoy kicked aside a crushed picnic basket, and Anna's stomach plummeted. Discarded blankets and the remnants of fried chicken and an apple pie had been crushed underfoot. "Was anyone else hurt?"

"Not that I know of."

Disjointed thoughts bobbed through her head. This was the first time her mother had trusted her with a speech alone. Always before, Victoria Bishop had picked and pecked over every last word. This was the first time Anna had been trusted on her own.

The concession was more from necessity than conviction in Anna's abilities. Her mother had been urgently needed in Boston for a critical task. The Massachusetts chapter had grossly underestimated the opposition to their most current state amendment vote, and the campaign required immediate reinforcement. More than ever, Anna must prove her usefulness.

Maybe then she'd feel worthy of her role as the daughter of the Great Victoria Bishop. The St. Louis chapter was meeting on Friday. Anna had to represent her mother. She'd arranged to leave for St. Louis tomorrow.

She'd never make the depot at this rate. "I have to change my train ticket."

Mr. McCoy frowned. "It'll wait."

"You don't waste words, do you, Mr. McCoy?"

A half grin lifted the corner of his mouth. "Nope."

The sheer helplessness of the situation threatened to overwhelm her. She wasn't used to being dependent on another person. She'd certainly never been carried by anyone in the whole of her adult life. She felt the warmth of his chest against her cheek, the strength of his arms beneath her bent knees. She was vulnerable and helpless, the sensations humbling.

Upon their arrival in the hotel lobby, Jo rushed toward them. "Oh, dear. What can I do?"

Though they'd only met in person the one time, the sight of Jo filled Anna with relief. Jo's letters were lively and personal, and she was the closest person Anna had to a friend in Kansas City.

"She's been shot." Caleb stated the obvious, keeping his voice low.

Only a few gazes flicked in their direction. The people jamming the lobby were too busy, either frantically reuniting with their missing loved ones or nursing their own bumps and bruises, to pay the three of them much notice.

Mr. McCoy brushed past his sister and crossed to the

stairs. "They've sent for a surgeon, but we're running out of time. Fetch my bag and meet me in your room."

"Why not mine?" Anna replied anxiously. Moving to another room was another change, another slip away from the familiar.

"Because we still don't know who shot you," Mr. McCoy said. "Or if they'll try to finish what they started."

Jo gave her hand a quick squeeze. "Caleb will take care of you. My room isn't locked. I'll let them know where to send the doctor, and I'll be there in a tick."

Panic welled in the back of Anna's throat. All of the choices were being ripped away from her. She'd always been independent. As a child, her mother had insisted Anna take charge of her own decisions. The idea of putting her life in the hands of this stranger terrified her.

Caleb took the stairs two at a time. Though she sensed his care in ensuring she wasn't jostled, each tiny movement sent waves of agony coursing through her, silencing any protests or avowals of independence she might have made. Upon reaching Jo's room, he pushed open the door and rested her on the quilted blanket covering the bed.

The afternoon sun filtered through the windows, showcasing a cloudless sky. The sight blurred around the edges as her vision tunneled. Her breath strangled in her throat. Her heartbeat slowed and grew sluggish.

Mr. McCoy studied her wound, keeping his expression carefully blank. A shiver wracked her body. His rigidly guarded reactions frightened her more than the dark blood staining his clothing.

"Am I going to die?" Anna asked.

And how would God react to her presence? She'd had

Corinthians quoted to her enough over her lifetime that the words were an anathema.

Let your women keep silent in the churches: for it is not permitted unto them to speak.

And since women were not allowed to speak in church, they should not be allowed to speak on civic matters. Were they permitted to speak in heaven?

Mr. McCoy's lips tightened. "You're not going to die. But I have to stitch you up. We have to stop the bleeding, and I can't wait for the surgeon. It won't be easy for you."

She adjusted her position and winced. "I appreciate your candor."

He must have mistaken her words as a censure because he sighed and knelt beside the bed, then gently removed her crushed velvet hat and smoothed her damp hair from her forehead. His vivid green eyes were filled with sympathy.

A suffragist shouldn't notice such things, and this certainly wasn't the time or place for frivolous observations, but he really was quite handsome with his dark hair and warm, green eyes. Handsome in a swarthy kind of way. Anna exhaled a ragged breath. Her situation was obviously dire if that was the drift of her thoughts.

"Miss Bishop," he said. "Anna. It's your choice. I'm not a surgeon. We can wait. But it's my educated opinion that we need to stop the bleeding."

Every living thing died eventually—every blade of prairie grass, every mosquito, every redwood tree. She'd been wrong before—death, no matter how extraordinary a life one lived on earth, was the most ordinary thing in the world.

Feeling as though she'd regained a measure of control, Anna met his steady gaze. "Are you a very good veterinarian?"

"The best."

He exuded an air of confidence that put her at ease. "Then, do what needs to be done."

She barely managed to whisper the words before blackness swirled around her. She hoped he had enough fight left for both of them.

Chapter Two

She'd trusted him. She'd trusted Caleb with her life. He prayed her trust wasn't misplaced because the coming task filled him with dread.

After tightening the bandage on Anna's wound, Caleb shrugged out of his coat and rolled up his sleeves. The door swung open, revealing Jo who clutched his bag to her chest. The suffragist from the rally appeared behind his sister. He'd lost sight of her earlier; his attention had been focused elsewhere, but she'd obviously been nearby.

The older woman glanced at the bed. "Where is the surgeon? Hasn't he arrived yet?"

"I'm afraid not." Caleb lifted a corner of the blood-soaked bandage and checked the wound before motioning for his sister. "Keep pressure on this." He searched through his bag and began arranging his equipment on the clean towel draped over the side table. "Unless the doctor arrives in the next few minutes, I'm stitching her up myself."

He'd brought along his case because that's the way he always packed. When his services were needed on an extended call, he threw a change of clothing over his instruments so he wasn't hampered by an extra bag. He'd packed for this trip the same way by rote.

Swiping the back of his hand across the perspiration beading on his forehead, he sighed. Perhaps Jo was partially right, perhaps he was growing too set in his ways.

The suffragist clenched and unclenched her hands. "You're the veterinarian, aren't you?"

Caleb straightened his instruments and set his jaw. Anna didn't have time for debate. "It appears I'm the best choice you've got right now."

"I'm Mrs. Franklin." The suffragist stuck out her hand and gave his a fierce shake. "I briefly served as a nurse in the war. I can assist you."

"Excellent." A wave of relief flooded through him. "I've got alcohol, bandages and tools in my bag. There's no ether, but I have a dose of laudanum." He met the woman's steady gaze. "I'm Caleb McCoy. This is my sister, JoBeth Cain."

Mrs. Franklin tilted her head. "I thought you must be related. Those green eyes and that dark hair are quite striking." The woman's eyes filled with tears. "Anna is tough. She'll do well." She pressed both hands against her papery cheeks. "I requested her appearance. I had no idea something like this would happen."

Jo snorted. "Of course you didn't. Assigning blame isn't going to stop a bullet. Caleb, tell us what to do." She lifted a pale green corked bottle from his bag. "And why do you have laudanum, anyway?"

"Got it from the doc when John's prize stallion kicked me last spring." Caleb rolled his shoulder, recalling the incident with a wince. John Elder raised horses for the cavalry, and his livelihood depended upon his horses' continued good health. Caleb's dedication had left him with a dislocated shoulder and a nasty scar on his thigh from the horse's sharp teeth. "I figured the laudanum might come in handy one day. I'll need the chair. You'll have to sit on the opposite side of the bed."

He uncorked the still-full bottle and measured a dose into the crystal glass he'd discovered on the nightstand. Jo rested her hip on the bed and raised Miss Bishop's shoulders. Anna moaned and pulled away.

Caleb held the glass to her lips. "This tastes foul, but you'll appreciate the benefits."

A fine sheen of sweat coated Miss Bishop's forehead. Her brilliant blue eyes had glazed over, yet he caught a hint of understanding in her disoriented expression. He tipped the glass, and she took a drink, then coughed and sputtered.

"Easy there," Caleb soothed. "Just a little more."

Jo quirked one dark eyebrow. "For a minute there, I thought you were going to say, easy there *old girl*."

Miss Bishop pushed away the glass. "This old girl has had enough."

"Don't go slandering my patients," Caleb offered with a half grin. "I've never gotten a complaint yet."

She flashed him a withering glance that let him know exactly what she thought of his assurances. "The next time you have a speaking patient, we'll compare notes."

He was heartened Miss Bishop had retained her gumption. She was going to need it.

After ensuring she'd taken the full dose, he rested the glass on the table and adjusted the pillow more comfortably behind Miss Bishop's head. "You'll be sound asleep in a minute. This will all be over soon."

"I have an uneasy feeling this is only the beginning, Mr. McCoy." She spoke hoarsely, her eyes already dulled by the laudanum.

"You'll live to fight another day, Miss Bishop. I promise you that."

Her head lolled to one side, and she reached for Jo. "Please, let my mother know I'm fine. I don't want her to worry."

While Jo offered reassurances, Caleb checked the wound once more and discovered the bleeding had slowed, granting him a much-needed reprieve. He desperately wanted to wait until the laudanum took effect before stitching her up. This situation was uncharted territory. He understood an animal's reaction to pain. He knew how to soothe them, and he took confidence in his skills, knowing his treatments were for the ultimate benefit.

People were altogether different. He wasn't good with people in the best of situations, let alone people he didn't know well. He never missed the opportunity to remain silent in a group, letting others carry the conversation.

Miss Bishop fumbled for his hand and squeezed his fingers, sending his heartbeat into double time. He wasn't certain if her touch signified fear or gratitude. Aware of the curious perusal of the other two women, Caleb kept the comforting pressure on her delicate hand and waited until he felt the tension drain from Miss Bishop's body. Once her breathing turned shallow and even, he gently extracted his fingers from her limp hold.

Satisfied the laudanum had taken effect, he doused his hands with alcohol over a porcelain bowl, then motioned for Mrs. Franklin to do the same. Without being asked, the suffragist cleaned his tools in the same solution, her movements efficient and sure.

Caleb breathed a sigh of relief. Mrs. Franklin knew her way around medical instruments. He put her age at midsixties, though he was no expert on such matters. Her hair was the same stern gray as her eyes and her austere dress, the skin around her cheeks frail. She was tall for a woman, and wiry thin. Her fingers were swollen at the knuckles, yet her hands were steady.

Jo cleared her throat. "Caleb, I never thanked you for coming with me today. I'm thinking this is a good time to remedy that."

They exchanged a look, and his throat tightened. A silent communication passed between them, a wealth of understanding born of a shared childhood that didn't need words.

A sudden thought jolted him. "Did you find the little girl's parents? Was anyone else injured?"

"One question at a time." Jo admonished. "Anna's youngest follower discovered her mother in the lobby, frantic with worry. As you'd expect, there was much scolding and a few tears of relief. I asked around, and, as far as anyone can tell, Anna was the only person hurt."

Relieved to set one worry aside, Caleb focused on his patient. "Most likely we'd know by now if someone else was injured."

Or shot.

The enormity of Miss Bishop's condition weighed on him. She'd placed her trust in him, and he wouldn't fail her. "If Anna comes around, you'll need to keep her calm. I've enough laudanum for another dose, but it's potent, and I'd like to finish before the first measure wears off."

He'd never been a great admirer of the concoction, and the less she ingested, the better.

Jo pressed the back of her hand against Miss Bishop's forehead. "Don't forget, I helped Ma for years with her midwife duties. I know what to do."

The irony hadn't escaped him. Of the three of them, Caleb was the least experienced with human patients, yet he had the most experience with stitching up wounds. After modestly draping Miss Bishop's upper body, he slid his scissors between the turquoise fabric and her skin and easily sliced the soaked material away from her wound.

He held out the scissors, and they were instantly replaced with a cloth.

His admiration for the suffragist grew. "How long did you serve in the war, Mrs. Franklin?"

"It was only a few months in '65. I'd lost both of my sons and my husband by then. Our farm was burned. There really wasn't anything left for me to do. Nothing to do but help others."

Caleb briefly closed his eyes before carefully tucking the draping around the bullet wound. "I'm sorry for your losses."

Mrs. Franklin lifted her chin. "It was a long time ago. I've been a widow longer than I was ever married. Would you like the instruments handed to you from the right or the left?"

"The right."

Her brisk efficiency brought them all on task. Caleb exchanged another quick look with his sister, and she flashed a smile of encouragement. Caleb offered a brief prayer for guidance and set about his work.

From that moment forward, he focused his attention on the process, certain the surgeon's arrival was imminent. While Caleb might be the best option at the moment, he was perfectly willing to cede the process to a *better* option. He wasn't a man to let false pride cloud his judgment.

Taking a deep breath, he studied the rift marring the right side of Miss Bishop's body. He'd seen his fair share of gunshot wounds over the years. It wasn't unheard of for careless hunters or drunken ranchers to miss their mark and strike livestock. Often the animal was put down, but depending on the location of the wound, he'd been able to save a few. His stomach clenched. Had the bullet gone a few inches to the left...

He set his jaw and accepted the needle and thread, his hands rock steady. While he worked, his pocket watch ticked the minutes away, resounding in the heavy silence. Though Miss Bishop wasn't anything like his normal patients, the concept remained the same. He watched for signs of shock, stemmed the bleeding, cleaned the area to inhibit infection, and ensured Jo kept his patient calm.

Once he was satisfied with his stitches on the entrance wound, he swiped at his forehead with the back of his hand. "We'll need to turn her to the side."

Jo grasped Miss Bishop's shoulder, and Caleb carefully tilted her onto her hip. Anna groaned, and her arm flipped onto the bed, her hand palm up, her fingers curled, the sight unbearably vulnerable.

Not even an hour earlier she'd held an entire audience enthralled with her bounding energy, and now her life's blood drained from her body, vibrant against the cheerful tulip pattern sewn into the quilted coverlet.

Impotent rage at whoever had caused this destruction flared in his chest.

He shook off the distraction with a force of will and resumed his stitching. With any luck they'd already apprehended the shooter.

Miss Bishop drifted in and out of consciousness during the procedure, but remained mostly numbed throughout his ministrations. For that he was unaccountably grateful.

Jo dabbed at Anna's brow and murmured calming words when she grew agitated, keeping her still while Caleb worked. Mrs. Franklin maintained charge of the instruments with practiced efficiency. Despite having only met the widow moments before, their impromptu team worked well together.

Caleb tied off the last stitch and clipped the thread, then touched the pulse at Miss Bishop's wrist, buoyed by the strong, steady heartbeat beneath his fingertips. He collapsed back in his chair and surveyed his work.

He'd kept his stitches precise and small. While he couldn't order his usual patients to remain in bed after an injury, he'd ensure Miss Bishop rested until she healed.

With the worst of the crises behind him, the muscles along his shoulders grew taut. Mrs. Franklin sneaked a surreptitious glance at the door.

When she caught his interest, a bloom of color appeared on her cheeks. "You've done a fine job. But I thought… I assumed…"

"You assumed the surgeon would be here by now." Caleb pushed forward in his chair and reached for the final bandage. "As did I."

He'd made his choice. Instead of walking away, he'd

stayed. That choice had unwittingly linked him to Miss Bishop, and he'd sever that tie as soon as the surgeon arrived. The two of them were worlds apart, and the sooner they each returned home, the better.

He sponged away the last of the blood and sanitized the wound. The instant the alcohol touched her skin, Miss Bishop groaned and arched her back.

Caleb held a restraining hand against her shoulder. "Don't undo all of my careful work."

She murmured something unintelligible and reached for him again. Painfully aware of his sister's curious stare, he cradled Miss Bishop's hand and rubbed her palm with the pad of his thumb. His touch seemed to soothe her, and he kept up the gentle movement until she calmed. The differences between them were striking. His hands were work-roughened and weather-darkened, Anna's were pale and frighteningly delicate. A callous on the middle finger of her right hand, along with the faded ink stains where she rested her hand against the paper, indicated she wrote often.

The ease with which she trusted him tightened something in his chest. He never doubted his ability with animals. For as long as he could remember, he'd had an affinity with most anything that walked on all fours... or slithered, for that matter. Yet that skill had never translated with people. An affliction that wasn't visited on anyone else in his family. The McCoys were a boisterous lot, gregarious and friendly. Caleb was the odd man in the bunch.

Once her chest rose and fell with even breaths, he reluctantly released his hold and sat back in his chair, then rubbed his damp fingers against his pant legs.

Her instinctive need for human touch reminded him

of the thread that held them all together. All of God's creatures sought comfort when suffering.

Voices sounded from the corridor, and Jo stood. "If that's the surgeon, I'm going to give him a piece of my mind."

Mrs. Franklin tucked the blankets around Miss Bishop's shoulders. "We should tidy the room and change the bedding. Perhaps Mr. McCoy should deal with any visitors we have."

Caleb took the hint. "If I'm unable to locate the surgeon, I'll check on Miss Bishop in half an hour."

He snatched his coat and stepped into the corridor, then glanced around the now-empty space. He caught sight of the blood staining his vest and shirt and blew out a breath. The voices they'd heard had not been the surgeon's, and he couldn't visit the lobby with such a grisly appearance. The telling evidence discoloring his shirt also placed him at the rally, and he wasn't ready to answer questions.

Or make himself a target.

He crossed to his room and quickly changed. Now that the immediacy of the situation had passed, exhaustion overtook him, and he collapsed onto the bed, clutching his head.

Of all the things that he'd dreaded when Jo had invited him to accompany her to Kansas City, he hadn't anticipated this dramatic turn of events.

He took a few deep breaths and raked his hands through his hair, letting the emotion flow out of him. This happened sometimes. Once the emergency had been dealt with, he often experienced a wave of overwhelming exhaustion. The greater the emergency, the greater his fatigue. He scrubbed his hands down his face and stood, then stepped into the corridor and made his way to the lobby. There'd be time for resting later.

A man in a loose-fitting overcoat brushed past him on the staircase.

"Say, fellow," the man said. "Were you at the rally this afternoon?"

"Yes. And you?"

Perhaps this gentleman knew if there had been any further injuries as a result of the shooting.

"Nope. I was supposed to be covering Miss Bishop's speech for *The Star* paper. Figured I'd slip in for the last few minutes. Who wants to listen to them ladies whine? Now I gotta figure out what happened or the boss will have my hide. There was some kind of commotion, right?"

Caleb measured his words carefully. "There was a disturbance. The crowd scattered."

"What kind of disturbance?"

Great. Now he'd gone and cornered himself into telling the whole of it. "A gunshot."

The man's eyes widened, and he gleefully rubbed his hands together, then splayed them. "I can see the headline now, Shot Fired Across the Bow of Suffragist Battle."

The man's elation turned Caleb's stomach. Brushing past the reporter before he said anything more revealing, Caleb loped down the stairs and paused on the balcony overlooking the lobby. A discordance of noise hit him like a wall.

Having survived the encounter at the rally, scores of people from the audience had obviously congregated at the hotel to share their dramatic stories. Voices were raised in excitement, and more than one gentleman clutched a strong drink.

Caleb sucked in a breath and made his way across the room. He couldn't have designed a better nightmare for himself. Twice in one day, he'd been forced into a crush of people.

Upon reaching the concierge desk, he waved over the gentleman in the bottle-green uniform he'd seen his sister approach earlier. "Did the surgeon arrive?"

The man lifted his hands. "Not that I know of. It's been like this since the rally. It's all we can do to keep the crowd contained in the lobby." The concierge glanced left and right and ducked his head. "I caught a reporter upstairs, and there are several policemen waiting to speak with Miss Bishop. I'll hold them off as long as I can."

Caleb rubbed his forehead. "That would be best."

The man cleared his throat. "I also took the liberty of removing Miss Bishop's name from the guest register." The man cleared his throat again. "I have your party listed in the register book as yourself, your sister and your fiancée."

Caleb's head shot up. "Say again?"

"I have a large staff. I can handpick the workers on the fourth floor. I cannot guarantee the characters of all my employees."

"But fiancée?"

The man lifted his hands as though in surrender. "The title seemed the least likely one for Miss Bishop to take. Since she's a, you know, she's a…"

"She's a suffragist. It's not a profanity."

"My apologies, sir. I can change the register."

Caleb pictured Anna, her turquoise dress ruined,

her bold speech silenced. Why would anyone want to live in the public eye? And yet he couldn't deny her obvious appeal, the way her vivacious speech had captivated the crowd. He couldn't imagine a better figurehead for the cause.

"No, you've done well," Caleb said. "Keeping her identity hidden is best."

As he surveyed the scene, voices ebbed and flowed around him. All of these people had come to hear her speak. He fisted his hands. Not all of them. For all he knew, the man who'd pulled the trigger was here. Waiting. Watching.

Caleb searched the faces of the spectators milling around the lobby. There was no way of knowing, no way of telling who held violence in their heart.

He raked his hands through his hair. Until they discovered the shooter, the less said, the better. What did it matter how Anna was registered? No one would know but the hotel staff.

After a few more words with the concierge about the new room arrangement, he returned upstairs and met Jo as she exited Miss Bishop's room.

Caleb checked the corridor, ensuring the space was empty of curiosity seekers before pulling Jo aside. "It's not safe for Miss Bishop. She needs a guard at her door. I've arranged for another room for you. Simply switching with Miss Bishop is out of the question. There are reporters and policemen. Not to mention whoever fired the shot is still out there."

His sister propped her hands on her hips. "She should come home with us."

Caleb had briefly thought the same thing, and had come up with a thousand reasons why the plan was not sound. "This isn't our concern. Surely she has family, friends."

A sweetheart, perhaps. The thought brought him up short. He shook his head. Nothing in the papers had ever indicated that Miss Bishop was linked with a gentleman—and that would certainly be newsworthy.

"I've corresponded with her for months. She doesn't have anyone close. Her mother lives in St. Louis, but she's in Boston for an extended stay. Besides, it's too far for Anna to travel in her condition."

Caleb sensed a losing battle ahead of him. This was the Jo he knew and admired. Given a problem, she immediately grasped for a solution and charged ahead.

He held out his arms in supplication and assumed his most placating tone. "Slow down. We don't have any influence here."

Jo slapped his hands away. "I'm not one of your animals. Stop speaking to me as though I'm a goat. Anna is my friend. She'll need a place to rest, a quiet place to recuperate. People who care for her."

"Jo, listen to me, even if you invited her back to Cimarron Springs, do you really think she'd accept your offer? She's not a country girl. She'd be bored in an instant." He indicated the elaborate appointed hallway with its hand-knotted rug and brass fixtures. "This is her world."

Though he knew the idea was ludicrous, he couldn't shake an impending sense of despair. He didn't want their paths to cross any more than necessary. Anna Bishop was beautiful and witty and captivating. In the brief time he'd seen her on that stage, he'd known she was different from anyone else he'd ever met. He was drawn to her, and those feelings were disastrous.

He was a veterinarian from a small town who loathed big cities. She was a nationally renowned speaker with a following. She had a calling. There was clearly no room in her life for someone like him. He'd grown emotional over someone who hadn't returned his affection once before. Only a fool made the same mistake twice.

His sister approached him and crowded into his space until they stood toe to toe. "She needs us."

"Why us?" Caleb stood his ground. "Why does she need us?"

Jo glared. "Until they discover who tried to kill her, Anna is going to need a place to hide. And you're good at hiding, aren't you?"

With that, she pivoted on her heel and stomped down the corridor.

His burst of fury quickly died, replaced by a bone-deep weariness. He wasn't hiding, he was simply a loner who should have stayed in Cimarron Springs where he belonged. And yet if he'd stayed at home, what would have happened to Anna? Who would have cared for her?

The answer troubled him more than he would have cared to admit. Which was why he needed as much space between them as possible, as soon as possible. Becoming embroiled in Anna's life was out of the question.

Chapter Three

A week following the shooting, Anna staggered from bed and took a few lurching steps, determined to reestablish her independence. Winded, she collapsed onto a chair before the window. She'd considered dressing, but even the simple task of standing had become a tiring battle in her weakened condition.

From this moment on she was taking charge of her life. No more depending on others, no more sleeping the days and nights away. Except her body had refused the call to action.

The bandage wrapped around her side restricted her movements, and the slightest agitation sent a shock of pain through her side. Near tears, she rested her forehead against the chilled windowpane.

A soft knock sounded at the door. She smoothed the front of her dressing gown and tucked a lock of hair behind one ear, relieved they'd had her trunk delivered to the room when she and Jo had switched.

"It's Mrs. Franklin," a voice called.

Anna sat up as straight as her wound allowed. "Please, come in."

As the door swung open, she recalled her embroidery and quickly shoved the evidence beneath her pillow. For reasons she couldn't explain, she kept the feminine hobby to herself.

The older woman took one look at Anna and tsked. "Why didn't you call for me? I would have helped."

The past week was a blur of disjointed memories. Between sleeping and waking, she recalled the visits from other suffragists. The room had erupted with flowers like a meadow after a spring rain. They crowded every available surface, perfuming the air.

"I managed well enough," Anna said. "I didn't want to inconvenience you."

"It's no trouble." Mrs. Franklin's gray eyes clouded over. "It's the least I can do."

As she crossed before her, Anna caught her hand. "This wasn't your fault."

"You can't blame me for feeling guilty." The older woman paused. "Will you at least let me help you dress this morning?"

"That would be lovely. I'm tired of lazing around in my nightclothes."

While Anna was eager to press her independence, she sensed the other woman's need to be useful, and remained docile beneath her ministrations. The widow was the opposite of everything Anna had been taught to hold dear. Mrs. Franklin seemed to revel in her role as protector and nurturer—character traits her mother abhorred. Victoria Bishop took great pains to surround herself with the like-minded. No action was ever taken without a purpose. Independence was prized in the Bishop household. Tutors and nannies who had coddled Anna as a child were quickly corrected or dismissed.

You are not here to care for the child, Anna recalled her mother's oft-repeated order, *you are to teach the child how to care for herself.*

After Anna donned her simplest outfit, a white cotton shirtwaist and brown plaid skirt, Mrs. Franklin spent several minutes fussing with her hair.

The older woman stood back and surveyed her work. "I'm no lady's maid, but you're presentable."

Having done her own hair for many years, the sensation was odd. Being pampered and cared for was not nearly as repellent as it should have been. In fact, Anna quite liked the relaxing sensation. Unbidden, her mother's fierce countenance popped into her head. Victoria Bishop had not raised her only daughter to be spoiled.

Anna took the brush from Mrs. Franklin and ran the bristles away from her temple, smoothing the wave created by her impossible curls. "It's lovely, really. I don't usually wear it this way."

The widow had pinned her loose hair in a cascade atop her head. When Anna perched her hat over the arrangements, the curls framed her face. The effect softened her countenance and made her look younger, more approachable.

Mrs. Franklin tugged one of the ringlets free and let it fall against Anna's cheek. "Oh, yes, I quite like that. You have lovely hair, my dear. If I'd had that hair back in '45, oh the trouble I could have caused."

Judging from the twinkle in Mrs. Franklin's eye, Anna guessed she'd broken more than one heart. "I have a feeling you caused plenty of trouble, no matter your hair."

"True, my dear. Quite true," the widow answered with unabashed pride.

Anna couldn't help but laugh with Mrs. Franklin's reflection in the mirror. When she turned away, Anna's smile faded.

Why was accepting assistance such a shameful weakness? If the situations were reversed, if Mrs. Franklin had needed help, Anna would have happily aided her. And yet each time she relinquished even the tiniest bit of her independence, she heard her mother's stern disapproval. Why was the desire to look attractive such an appalling offense?

If a woman's sole purpose in life was to attract a mate, then nature would not have given us the superior brain.

Anna patted her hair and recalled her manners. "Thank you, Mrs. Franklin, for your assistance. You've been absolutely indispensable. I don't know what I would have done without you this week."

"You must call me Izetta."

Mrs. Franklin—Izetta—straightened the horsehair brush on the dressing table. "There's a gentleman here to see you, if you're up for it."

"Mr. McCoy?" Anna's heartbeat tripped. "He's here?"

"No. A detective. A Pinkerton detective at that. Can you imagine?"

"Well, of course Mr. McCoy will have gone." Anna held out her hands and studied her blunt fingernails. She mustn't let her emotions turn at the mere thought of him. "I was only hoping for the chance to thank him properly."

"Oh, no, Mr. McCoy hasn't gone. He and his sister have been keeping the vultures at bay." Mrs. Franklin folded Anna's discarded nightgown and laid it on her trunk. "It's been a circus, let me tell you. I don't know what we would have done without those two."

Anna's memories of the past week were hazy at best. The police had questioned her briefly, but she had nothing to offer. She hadn't seen anything, and despite the ubiquitous protestors from the opposition, she'd never been threatened with bodily harm. Or shot at, for that matter. The police had pressed her for information until Mr. McCoy had ordered them away, but not before demanding they leave a guard at her door.

Mr. McCoy's soothing voice had been the one constant in a sea of confusion. She'd caught Jo teasing him, ribbing him for treating them all as though they were his four-legged patients, and yet she'd found the deep timbre of his reassuring voice a lifeline in the darkness. She'd been injured and out of sorts, that was all. Surely this curious fascination with the man would fade soon enough. Her fellow suffragists would not approve.

Love will ruin a woman faster than rain will ruin a parade.

Mrs. Franklin paused with her hand on the doorknob. "We kept your room number secret until that reporter grew weary of trying. After you speak with the detective, you'll have to make some decisions."

The door swung open, and Anna's breath caught in her throat. "Mr. McCoy! I was expecting the Pinkerton detective."

She desperately hoped he attributed the breathless quality of her voice to her recent injury. And surprise. Yes, she was simply surprised.

He jerked his thumb over his shoulder. "That'd be him."

Her eyes widened. If she didn't know better, she'd

have thought the other man was derelict. The detective appeared to be in his late forties with a curiously rounded middle and stick limbs. As though all of his weight had congregated in his belly, starving the fat from his arms and legs. He wore an ill-fitting coat in a nondescript shade of brown which matched the shock of disordered, thinning hair covering his head.

Anna swept her arm in an arc. "I'm afraid I don't have enough seats for all of you. I wasn't expecting company."

Mr. McCoy propped his shoulder against the door frame. "I'll stand."

How did he manage to pack such a wealth of meaning into so few words?

The detective huffed.

Annoyance radiated from Mr. McCoy's stiff demeanor. There was obviously no love lost between the two men.

The detective straddled a chair and rested his arms on the back. "The name is Reinhart. I'm here on another case."

A sharp ache throbbed in her temple, and Anna pressed two fingers against the pain. "I don't follow."

"When I'm working on a case, I pay attention to things. To everything. You never know what you might hear."

"I see," Anna replied vaguely, though she didn't see at all.

Reinhart shrugged. "Anyway, I'm from St. Louis. Moved to this office last May."

Caleb pushed off from the wall. "Just get to the point. Tell her what you told me this morning."

The detective rubbed the salt-and-pepper stubble on

his chin. "I've been doing some digging and I've heard a few things. Mind you, if you want to find the shooter, that's a separate job. Like I said this morning, that'll cost you extra."

Mr. McCoy cleared his throat.

The man glared over his shoulder, his movements twitchy and nervous as a rat. "Anyway, I've been doing some digging, and I ain't found nothing."

Oddly deflated by his vague speech, Anna tilted her head. "That's what you came here to tell me?"

"Don't you get it? No one has claimed responsibility. No one seen nothing. Nothing."

"I still don't follow."

"This is personal. Someone with a grudge against women voting wants his voice heard. He wants attention. Someone with a personal vendetta is going underground. He doesn't want to get caught. Leastways not until the job is done right."

While the man's clothing and grooming might lead one to believe he was not educated, his speech let slip his intellect. Clearly playing the bumbling fool suited his work.

He glanced meaningfully at her side and Anna pressed her hand against the bandages beneath her clothing.

She sat up and winced. "Someone wants me dead. Just me?"

"That's the way I see it."

Blood roared in her ears. Somehow she'd pictured the act as random. A lone, crazed shooter with a grudge against women who was bent on causing an uproar. Someone determined to halt the rally.

In the back of her mind, she'd even wondered if

the whole thing had been an accident. Years ago, their neighbor in St. Louis had inadvertently discharged a firearm while attempting to clean the weapon. He'd shattered the parlor window and taken a chunk out of the porch railing.

This was no accident.

This was more focused. This was *personal*.

As the realization sank in, her heart thumped painfully in her chest, leaving her light-headed.

The twitchy man shrugged. "That's the problem. That's *your* problem. My guess is, he's going to try again."

Anna searched the expectant faces staring at her. What was she supposed to do? What was she supposed to say? She glanced at Izetta who remained at her vigil near the window.

"I've asked the others." The widow offered an apologetic grimace. "There's been no great trouble with our local chapter. We've gotten the usual threats, of course. The occasional brick through the front window and painted slurs. But no one has taken responsibility for the shooting. Perhaps they wanted the notoriety of targeting a suffragist with a large following."

Though no hint of censure showed in Izetta's voice, Anna's ears buzzed. "I'm only well-known because of my mother. I'm hardly worthy of notice otherwise."

She thought she heard mutterings from Mr. McCoy's direction, but when she caught his gaze, his face remained impassive.

Jo sidled through the doorway and exchanged a glance with her brother.

Anna welcomed the interruption. "Have you heard anything new?" she asked Jo.

With any luck the criminal had been found and all this conjecture was pointless.

"Nothing. But there's a telegram from your mother. I've been keeping her informed of your progress. I did as you requested, I brushed over the details so she wouldn't worry. Perhaps I blunted them too much." Jo glanced at the curious face of the detective and cleared her throat. "Never mind. We can discuss that later. Alone."

Anna exhaled slowly, gathering her thoughts, following Mr. McCoy's lead by keeping her face bland. Perhaps they *had* kept the details too blunted. Thus far her mother had been sympathetic, but impersonal. As though she was commiserating with a distant acquaintance instead of her only daughter. Not that Anna expected her to come charging to Kansas City. Victoria Bishop had never been one for nursing the sick. She considered any weakness, even ill health, an inconvenience.

There was no need to involve anyone else in this mess, especially if the shooting was targeted at her. Anna might have been injured, but she was no victim.

Bracing her left hand on the seat, she suppressed a grimace. "Then I shall return home. To St. Louis."

She'd been sitting upright too long, and the injury in her side had turned from a dull ache into a painful throbbing.

"Nah." The Pinkerton detective grunted. "I don't think that's a good idea either. You're known. You're not hard to find. I ain't that smart. Other people could do the same."

He was plenty smart, Anna had no doubt of that. Studying the faces turned toward her, she had the distinct sensation they wanted something from her.

That she was the only person in the room who hadn't been apprised of the predetermined plan. "What do you propose I do?"

Caleb held up his hand, silencing Reinhart. "Come to Cimarron Springs. Stay with Jo."

A thread of anxiety coiled in her stomach. She wasn't helpless. She wasn't a victim. She wouldn't be delivered onto someone's doorstep like an unwanted package.

"And how will that attract any less attention?" Anna gritted her teeth against her clouding vision. "I do not mean to sound arrogant, Mr. McCoy, but my name is not unknown. I have dealt with reporters before. They are far wilier than one supposes. It won't take long for them to discover where I am."

Jo stepped forward. "Not if we give you a new name. You can be Anna Smith or something. Caleb and I will keep in touch with the detective. Cimarron Springs is quiet. You'll have a chance to recuperate."

A chilly perspiration beaded on her forehead. Anna couldn't shake the sensation she was missing something in the exchange. "It's very kind of you, but I am not unfamiliar with small towns either. Gossip is rampant, and curiosity is lethal to your plan. We're bound to slip up sooner or later."

The excuse sounded weak even to her own ears. She'd been a controversial figure since before she was born—the illegitimate daughter of heiress Victoria Bishop. Her mother had been singularly remorseless in her infamy. Senior ladies in their chapter had regaled Anna with stories of her mother's brazen disregard for convention.

Anna had eventually grown old enough to hear the harsher opinions of her mother's behavior, and suffer for them. For a time she'd ignored her notoriety. Then the parents with children attending Miss Spence's Boarding and Day School for Girls had demanded her removal. They didn't want their daughters' reputations sullied by association.

Victoria Bishop had marched into the school, her heels click-clacking along the marble floors. Anna had waited outside the office, her buttoned leather boots swinging to and fro, while her mother told Miss Spence exactly what she thought of Anna's expulsion.

A succession of tutors proficient in various subjects had followed. A more focused education, if a touch lonely. Training for solitude had served her well. Despite all the women she met in her travels, most of her time was spent alone. Traveling. Writing letters. Organizing the many separate chapters into a united front.

Proving herself worthy of her mother's legacy.

"You'll be there as my friend," Jo said. "A friend who had an accident and needs some quiet."

"It could work." The detective spoke. "Remember, though, if you show up out of the blue with someone they ain't never heard of before, people will talk. You gotta give them something to talk about or else they'll make up the missing pieces on their own."

Anna's side was on fire, and she wasn't opposed to resting. After her near-failed attempt at dressing herself this morning, she'd admitted the gravity of her wound. She was exhausted. Mentally and physically. Though she'd never admit her weakness, she was still grappling with the realization that someone wanted her dead.

Dead.

Jo planted one hand on her hip and drummed her fingers on the dressing table. "The last page of the *Crofton*

County Gazette has a listing of visitors with each edition. You know the stuff, 'Mrs. Bertrand's two grandchildren are visiting from St. Louis. The Millers have gone to Wichita for the wedding of their niece.' That sort of thing. How would we print Anna's visit in the paper? That should give us some ideas."

Caleb reached into the side pocket of his bag. "You're brilliant, Jo. I've got a copy right here."

Anna surveyed their enthusiasm with a jaded eye. A small town was simply Miss Spence's School for Girls all over again. She'd be a pariah once the townspeople uncovered her true identity. Already, too many people knew their secret, and the McCoys didn't strike her as proficient in subterfuge. Sooner or later someone was bound to discover the truth.

While she didn't think the townspeople would stalk her with pitchforks and torches like the beast in Mary Shelley's *Frankenstein*, there was bound to be awkwardness. Most small communities she'd frequented had narrower rules of propriety than larger cities.

Flipping over the paper, Caleb frowned at the last page, his eyes scanning the columns. "It's all family visits. We're too well known. If we dig up another McCoy cousin, they'll figure out we're lying soon enough. What about Garrett? Could she pretend to be a relative of his?"

"No," Jo spoke emphatically. "Garrett's family is quite off-limits."

The sorrow in her voice gave Anna pause.

Caleb didn't seem to notice. "All right then, let's see what else." A half grin lifted the corner of his mouth. "Here's something interesting. 'JoBeth Cain and her brother, Caleb McCoy, will attend the suffragist rally in Kansas City calling for an additional amendment to the constitution allowing for the women's vote. Daughter of the renowned suffragist, Victoria Bishop, is set to give the keynote speech. Garrett Cain is escorting a prisoner to Wichita.'" Caleb shook his head. "I guess we did make the news."

"It's a small town." Jo shrugged. "Everyone makes the newspaper."

Mr. McCoy folded the paper and squinted. "Well, I'll be, here's something I didn't know. 'Mr. Frank Lancaster has brought his fiancée, Miss Vera Nelson, for an extended visit with his family. A mail-order bride advertisement was recently listed in *The Kansas Post* by a woman with the name of Miss Vera Nelson. Mr. Lancaster declined to comment on the happenstance.'" Caleb rubbed his chin. "I spoke with him two weeks ago when his dog had the mange. I had no idea he was considering taking a wife."

"I suppose if you sent away for a bride like a pair of shoes from the Montgomery Ward wish book," Jo said, "you wouldn't want that to be common knowledge."

Mrs. Franklin crossed her arms. "There's nothing wrong with doing what needs to be done. I'm sure the girl had her reasons. For a woman, sometimes marriage is the only answer."

"Wait," Jo snapped her fingers. "That's perfect. Marriage is our answer, as well. Anna can come to visit as your fiancée."

"My fiancée." Caleb's eyes widened.

Anna started. "What?"

"You two can pretend to be engaged."

Shocked silence filled the room. Anna recalled the scores of letters her mother had received over the years from desperate women. All of them had one thing in common—they had pinned their hopes on a man.

"No!" Anna and Caleb replied in unison.

Chapter Four

Anna leaned more heavily on her left arm. "Absolutely not. I mean no disrespect, Mr. McCoy, but I will not hide. I'm not going to change my name or pretend to be something I'm not. That goes against everything I stand for."

She wasn't relinquishing her independence. Killer or no killer. If the shooting had been caused by the opposition, then such a concession meant they'd won.

Jo's arms flopped to her sides. "We can say you had a whirlwind romance."

Caleb laughed harshly. "No one would believe it."

"You're right." Jo appeared crestfallen. "Of course you're right."

"You're missing the point," Caleb said. "No one would ever look for anyone in Cimarron Springs. She might as well wear a banner and parade down Main Street."

"True enough. Remember Elizabeth Elder's first husband? The bank robber? He hid all his loot in a cave by Hackberry Creek. No one ever suspected a thing. You didn't suspect him, did you, Caleb?"

"He didn't treat his livestock very well."

"Or his wife." Jo's voice strangled. "This may have escaped your notice, but people are just as important as animals." She pinched the bridge of her nose. "People are *more* important than livestock."

"I was making a point. There were obvious signs of bad character."

Caught up in the tale of the loot hidden by the creek, Anna made a noise of frustration at the sudden change of subject. "What happened to the bank robber and his poor wife?"

"He's dead now, God rest his soul." Jo's voice was stripped of remorse. "Elizabeth remarried and she's doing fine. She's living in Paris now."

"France?"

"Texas."

"I see," Anna said. "At least I think I understand."

A little dazed by the turn of the conversation, Anna considered Mr. McCoy's earlier denial. Why would no one believe they were engaged? The idea didn't seem far-fetched enough to incite laughter. Disbelief, certainly. Skepticism, perhaps. But outright mocking laughter?

She studied the fidgety detective and knitted her forehead. "All we have are rumors and speculation. For all we know, they've captured the man responsible, and this conversation is all for naught."

Reinhart's continued presence, especially considering his fierce demand for payment if he provided information, struck her as suspect. What had he said before? Something about cataloguing everything he saw and heard. Why the sudden interest in an injured suffragist if no one had offered him compensation? She had the distinct impression the detective never made a move without an ulterior motive. He certainly hadn't moved from his chair during the entire conversation.

"This isn't your case, Mr. Reinhart," she prompted. "You indicated that a moment before. Why are you here?"

"Because it suits me."

He shot her a look of such naked disgust that Anna inhaled a sharp breath. The sudden effort sent a shaft of agony tearing through her side.

She'd seen that reaction before, a curious mixture of disdain and resentment. "You're not an admirer of the women's movement, are you?"

"A woman's place is in the home. Not squawking out in public and making a spectacle of herself. Women are too emotional for politics."

Izetta gasped. "How dare you!"

Mr. McCoy pushed away from the door frame, plumping up like a gathering thundercloud. Anna gave an almost imperceptible shake of her head. The Bishop women were not victims.

They did not need to be saved like milquetoast princesses from a Grimm's fairy tale. "A woman's place is wherever she chooses."

The detective made a great show of rolling his eyes. "If the woman wears the pants, what's the man supposed to wear?"

"Short pants," Izetta declared. "Especially if they insist on acting like children."

"Say now!"

"That's enough," Caleb growled. "You're not here for your opinion."

"I don't work for you." The detective rested his fisted

knuckles on his thighs, elbows out, one bony protrusion jutting through a hole in his sleeve. "Either way, you got a problem, Miss Bishop. A big one. This wasn't a warning. Whoever took that shot meant to leave you dead."

Stomach churning, Anna shifted to the edge of her seat. She'd underestimated the limits of her endurance, but she wasn't about to let that infuriating little man witness her frailty.

Mr. McCoy's sharp gaze rested on her ashen face. He motioned toward the detective. "You've had your say. If you hear anything else, let us know."

"For a price."

Widening his stance, Mr. McCoy fisted his hands beneath his biceps. The posture was uniquely male, a declaration of his authority.

He might be a quiet man, but she doubted anyone who knew Mr. McCoy well would readily cross him.

He leaned toward Reinhart. "For a fellow who says he's not very smart, you seem to do all right."

Mr. McCoy was far too perceptive by half. Hadn't Anna thought the same thing only moments before?

Reinhart stood and tugged his ill-fitting jacket over his rounded stomach. He tipped back his head since Mr. McCoy was a good foot taller, and waved his bowed and skeletal index finger. "You know my rate. Pay or don't. Don't make me no never mind."

Once he'd exited the room, Anna's flagging reserve of strength finally deserted her. Desperate to alleviate her discomfort, she pushed off from the chair and stumbled. Mr. McCoy was at her side in an instant. He hooked his arm beneath her shoulder, carefully avoiding her injury.

"I'm quite well," she said, and yet she found herself leaning into the bolstering support he offered.

Her stomach fluttered. This was what her mother had warned her about. Victoria Bishop had declared men the ruin of women, turning perfectly sensible ladies into churning masses of emotions—robbing them of the ability to make sensible decisions. Sheltered from even the most banal interactions with gentlemen her own age, Anna had inwardly scoffed at the exaggerated tales.

Occasionally older men had flirted with her over the years. Once in a while, a stray husband of one of their acquaintances decided that charming a suffragist was a sign of virility. She'd been singularly unmoved by the obvious ploy. Their honeyed words had sluiced off her like raindrops off a slicker.

With Mr. McCoy near, a whole new understanding dawned. This wasn't the forced regard she usually deflected. His touch made her restless for more. There was an unexpected tenderness within him, a compassion that drew her nearer, tugging at the edges of her resolve.

"You're not well at all." He gingerly assisted her to the bed. "You're exhausted. We've overdone it. I'll fetch the doctor."

"No," Anna said, crumpling onto the mattress, too tired to care about detectives and gunshots and unassuming veterinarians who surprised her with their fierce protectiveness. "I simply need to rest."

To her immense relief, no one argued. Instead, in a flurry of pitying looks and murmured orders to repose, Izetta and Jo reluctantly exited the room.

Only Mr. McCoy lingered, one hand braced on the doorknob, the other on the wall, as though propelling himself from the room.

Was he that eager to be free of her?

He briefly glanced over his shoulder. "Rest. We can discuss what needs to be done later."

At least the change in position had temporarily alleviated the worst of her pain. If only her troubled thoughts were calmed as easily.

She desperately searched her memory for the events preceding the rally. A little girl had handed her a bouquet of flowers. Yellow flowers. Anna had recalled the color matched the child's dress.

My mama says you're a hero.

Anna was no hero. She was hiding in her room. Once she stepped out the door, she'd have to face reality. Just the idea sent a wave of fatigue shuddering through her.

You two can pretend to be engaged.

How did one simple sentence cast her emotions spinning? Disparate feelings pummeled her senses faster than she could sort them all out. She should have been more outraged by the suggestion. Her injury had obviously sapped her strength. For all her uncharacteristically mild response, she knew she *should* have felt as horrified as Mr. McCoy had appeared.

A lowering realization. She might be a suffragist, but she was also a woman. Not a bad-looking woman either. Anyone would have believed they were engaged. He could do worse. Anna wrinkled her nose. His opinion was of absolutely no concern.

Or was she reading him all wrong? Was he uncertain of his own appeal? No. That couldn't possibly be the case. Certainly there were plenty of ladies in Cimarron Springs eager for the attentions of the handsome veterinarian. While she may have been relatively isolated from the normal courting and machinations of men and women, she was not completely ignorant. If she trailed him through the crowded lobby, no doubt she'd observe more than one lady casting him a second glance. Which meant he couldn't possibly believe the problem rested with him.

Why on earth was she debating with herself?

She was wasting all sorts of time and energy on an absolutely worthless endeavor. None of her speculations mattered. The only way to navigate this mess was with facts—identify the difficulty and solve the problem. Mr. McCoy wasn't a problem. He was simply a diversion.

A diversion who'd soon be out of her life.

Another thought sent her stomach lurching. "How did he find me, anyway? The detective. Could someone else do the same?"

"He saw me. The day of the rally, carrying you. You're listed in the hotel register as my…as my guest."

Long after he was gone, Anna stared at the closed door. Something about how he'd said *guest* piqued her curiosity.

Mr. McCoy was hiding something.

Caleb caught up with his sister and blocked her exit. "What were you thinking?"

"I don't know what you're talking about."

"Yes. You do."

"Fine." She sniffed. "I saw the register. You're already listed as her fiancée. The engagement seemed like an excellent idea."

"No. It's not."

What if Anna discovered his deception in the guest registry, as well? With Jo spouting off about fiancées and his own collusion with the hotel, she'd never believe the two occurrences were not connected.

What would she think? He didn't even want to contemplate the answer.

"At least everyone would quit assuming you're mooning over Mary Louise," Jo said.

While that idea did hold some appeal, he wasn't letting her off the hook that easily. "Stop pushing, Jo. This is Anna's decision."

"Anna?"

"Miss Bishop is an intelligent, independent woman. She will make her own decisions regarding her life. If she wants help, she'll ask."

He kept thinking about her trunk. The week before, when they'd switched rooms, he'd carried the trunk himself. While he trusted the hotel staff, the fewer people who knew her whereabouts, the better.

The trunk had been expensive. A sturdy wooden affair with brass buckles and leather straps. Even the stack of books she'd plunked on her side table were leather bound. Her clothes were exquisitely tailored, there was nothing ready-made about Anna Bishop. Nothing at all. He'd traveled far enough away from Cimarron Springs, and he understood that even in the United States, a land built on equality, a class system prevailed. The McCoys had always been a hardworking lot who eked out a humble existence.

Judging from her wardrobe and her luggage, Anna had probably never cooked a meal for herself. He'd read the newspaper clippings Jo collected. Anna's mother was not just Victoria Bishop; she'd been nicknamed "the heiress." He might not know much about women, but he didn't figure an heiress would cotton to the kind of living in Cimarron Springs.

She was above his touch, both in wealth and in her ideology. And while his brain understood the implications, he feared his heart was not as wise.

Jo rubbed her thumbnail along her lower teeth, a sure sign she was worried about something. "Did you think Anna looked pale?"

He'd thought she was stunning. His heart picked up its rhythm, and he absently rubbed his chest. The first few days he'd corralled his wayward thoughts. When he caught himself staring at her lips, he closed his eyes and pictured the day of the rally. He pictured the blood staining his shirt and his hands. Anything that prevented him from thinking of her in a romantic fashion.

With her sitting up and dressed, her hair swept up in a tumble of curls, smelling like cherry blossoms, her lips rosy, he'd found himself staring at those lips once more. Wondering if she'd ever been kissed. While the detective had been talking, he'd been aching to run his hand over the soft skin at the nape of her exposed neck.

Jo pinched him back to attention. "I said, didn't you think she looked a little pale?"

Come to think of it, he'd noticed the lines around her mouth had deepened and the skin beneath her eyes had taken on the bruised look of fatigue.

"I noticed." He dragged the words from his throat. "It's my fault. I shouldn't have brought the detective."

Jo's expression softened, and she touched his arm. "No, you were right."

When the hotel staff had let him know the detective wanted to speak to Anna, he'd vetted the man first. "I'll ask Anna if she wants me to fetch the doctor."

"She'll say no," Jo said. "You know she will. She doesn't want to be a bother. I can tell."

"Then I won't give her a choice."

Jo didn't hide her triumphant expression fast enough.

"It won't make a lick of difference," he said. "If she refuses our help, we can't force her."

"We can show her we care."

Some of the steam went out of him. "Sure."

"I'll check the train station for times. We can give her the information. She can make her own decision after that. We're doing the right thing." Jo insisted.

Were they? Were they truly? Anna was in danger, and he was a country veterinarian. Were they really the best choice for her protection? He did know one thing—after seeing her that first day, the blood pooling beneath her, something primal inside him had broken free. He'd do anything to protect her, he knew that much for certain.

Jo rubbed her thumbnail on her bottom teeth once more. "I'll try and be back by the time the doctor comes. No promises, though."

"I'm sure Mrs. Franklin will be available if you're not."

At least fetching the doctor gave him something to do, something besides thinking of how Anna had looked at him when Jo had suggested the engagement. The look was the same one Mary Louise had given him when he'd asked to court her.

She'd looked at him with shock and derision.

At least this time his heart hadn't been involved. Not yet, anyway. He didn't plan on staying around long enough for any more damage to be done.

He'd go to the grave before he let anyone know he'd been playing her fiancé behind her back.

After a fitful nap that left her no more rested and no closer to a solution, Anna awoke more determined than ever. Her path ahead was clear. Her best hope at ending this turmoil was finding the person who wanted her dead or proving the whole thing was a mistake. Then she could go home.

There was every chance the police would discover that someone had accidentally shot out their parlor window like her inept neighbor, nearly killing Anna in the process. Either way, she'd go back home. Back to traveling during the week and corresponding with other suffragists over the weekends. Back to a future that looked remarkably like her past.

There was nothing unsatisfying about her life, was there? And yet her mind rebelled at the notion. The nagging feeling lingered. A sense that something was missing.

A knock sounded at the door and Anna groaned.

Was it really too much to ask for a moment's peace? The guard at her door announced Mr. McCoy, and her agitation intensified. She wasn't ready to see him again. Her thoughts and feelings were too jumbled, too confusing.

She considered refusing him entrance, then dismissed the idea as churlish. "Come in."

The door swung open, and Mr. McCoy entered with another, shorter, gentleman in his later years with a smooth-shaven face, a bulbous nose and prominent ears.

The second man tipped his hat. "I'm Dr. Smith. You

probably don't remember me, but I checked in on you a few days ago."

Anna glared at Mr. McCoy. "As I stated earlier, I'm fine. I simply need rest."

"I'm quite sure you do," Dr. Smith said. "I recommend several weeks of light activity. A visit to the country would do you good."

Anna huffed. She was usually quite reasonable, but this constant interference was unacceptable. "Did Mr. McCoy put you up to this?"

The doctor washed his hands in the basin. "No. Can't say that he did. It's simply a treatment course recommended for my gunshot victims. I must say, my gunshot victims are usually men, but the convalescence procedure is the same. These are modern times, I suppose. Not sure I like all the change. Let's have a look, shall we?"

Deciding it was easier to concede than argue, Anna lifted her arm and tugged her shirt loose, exposing her bandaged side.

She glanced across the room to where Mr. McCoy had suddenly discovered an intense fascination for the flocked wallpaper. Staying annoyed with the man was impossible. Which annoyed her even more.

Dr. Smith perched on a chair near the bed, peeled away the bandage and squinted. "You're excellent with a needle, Mr. McCoy. Your talents are wasted on livestock. Sorry I missed the excitement firsthand but I was paying a house call on another patient when they came to fetch me after the accident." He reached for his bag. "While I hate to unravel all your fine work, it's time we take out the stitches. Might hurt a bit. Can I send for someone?"

Caleb glanced around as though searching for help. "Jo had an errand. Can I fetch Izetta to sit with you?"

"No. She's home. She's been running herself ragged."

"I should leave," he said brusquely.

"Stay," she blurted, immediately regretting her outburst. "Talk with me," she added quickly, covering her embarrassment. "Tell me a story. I've read Jo's letters, the McCoys must be excellent storytellers."

What on earth was she blubbering about? A little pain was nothing. She didn't need her hand held like a child.

"I'll stay," he said, a wealth of reluctance in his voice.

Though she'd had plenty of visitors, she'd also had too much time alone. She clung to him because he was the one constant in all her confusion, which was understandable.

That wasn't exactly true. He and Jo and Izetta had become her salvation.

All the logic in the world failed to ease her fear. She didn't want her independence right then. She wanted someone to hold her hand and tell her everything was going to be all right.

The doctor clipped the first stitch, and Anna hissed a breath, closing her eyes. Caleb's hesitation said everything. She'd pushed their relationship beyond the boundaries he'd established. A forgivable mistake.

The situation had forced them into a false intimacy, and that state was temporary. She'd do well to remember the distinction. Except she'd lost all of her usual soft landing places. Normally when she was feeling alone or out of sorts, her work filled in the desolate spots. Here there were only four walls decorated with that abysmal olive-colored flocked wallpaper. She much preferred looking at a pair of kind, forest-green eyes. That was her downfall. Those infernal eyes.

Once she was home, certainly she'd forget all about him. Here there was too much time for thinking, too much temptation to read more into a kind gesture or a caring word.

Too much time for realizing that she'd almost died.

Chapter Five

She'd asked the wrong McCoy for a story, but he'd do his best. She'd been through a rough time, and Caleb wanted to infuse her with some of his own strength.

The bed depressed beneath his weight. "I'll tell you about the time my cousin nearly got himself killed at the husking bee."

He watched as the doctor lifted the first stitch free, then adjusted his position on the edge of the bed. The doctor studied the wound, humming softly, ignoring their exchange. With the doctor claiming the only chair, Caleb was left with a sliver of the bed for sitting on the opposite side. He plumped one pillow against the headboard and pushed up straighter, his right leg stretched out on the coverlet, his left knee bent and his foot braced against the floor so that he didn't take up too much room.

"What's a husking bee?" Anna asked, her head turned toward him, her expression curious and devoid of the fright he'd seen earlier.

Despite the pain and the forced confinement, she'd not complained, not once that he'd heard. She'd soldiered on through the worst of conditions. Caught in her trusting gaze, the last of his reluctance melted away.

He might not be the storyteller in the family, but for Anna, he'd give his best effort. "Back in the day, a farmer put up his corn in the barn before winter came and husked it at his leisure during the cold months. But old farmer Bainum had a better idea. He figured if all the ladies gathered every Saturday for a quilting bee, then all the fellows could hold a husking bee. He figured if he disguised the work as a party, he'd get a lot of help. That first year, he rolled out a barrel of his best hard apple cider, and every able-bodied man in the county showed up. Except Bainum cider is strong stuff. Only half the husking was finished before the boys decided they were having more fun drinking than husking."

The doctor muttered something unintelligible.

The groan that came from Anna's lips died in a hiss. His heart clenched at the sight of her distress. He'd never felt so helpless, so utterly inadequate.

Her grimace eased and she said, "Liquor has never been conducive to work."

"Not even in the country," Caleb babbled, desperate to keep her mind off her hurts. "Old Mr. Bainum was stuck husking the rest of the corn himself, and he'd given up a whole barrel of apple cider for his trouble. The next year he had an even better idea. He'd invite the ladies. Even though he'd been widowed longer than he'd been married, he knew enough from family gatherings and church picnics to realize a thing or two about ladies. A wife never showed up at an event without a covered dish, and they always kept an eye on how much cider the men drank."

"Sounds like more work for the women." Anna hoisted a disapproving eyebrow.

"He thought of that, as well. Once all the corn was husked, old farmer Bainum decided to throw a barn dance. Around Cimarron Springs, the ladies always like a good dance. Mr. Bainum made a game of the husking, too. He threw in a couple of ears of red corn. When a young man discovered an ear of red corn, he was allowed one kiss with the lady of his choice."

The doctor lifted another stitch free.

For a brief moment, Anna's face contorted in pain. "What if a lady found the red ear?"

"Then she made certain that red ear made its way into the stack of the fellow she was sweet on."

"Did you ever find the red ear?" she asked, then winced.

The doctor murmured an apology.

Maintaining his perch on the opposite side of Anna, Caleb touched her shoulder. "Don't get ahead of the story." Though she was clearly uncomfortable, his tale was distracting her, and for that he was grateful. "This is about my cousin Gus. You see, one particularly memorable husking bee, we were all sitting around on stools, shucking the corn and throwing the ears onto the floor in the center, when my cousin Gus found the first red ear and asked Becky Bainum for a kiss."

"Mr. Bainum's daughter?"

"The one and only."

"How outrageous. What did Mr. Bainum think?"

"Old farmer Bainum was not happy about Gus's selection. You see, the Bainums fought for the Confederate Army during the War Between the States. The McCoys, being of good, strong Irish stock and having arrived at the Castle Garden Depot as fast as the County Cork could send them, lived in the North and fought for the North. Sometimes voluntarily, sometimes by order of President Lincoln. One thing you have to know around these parts, the war never really ended for some folks, especially old farmer Bainum."

"Poor Gus."

"Don't feel bad for him just yet. Gus found three more red ears in less than an hour."

Anna grimaced. "How did Becky feel about all those kisses? Could she refuse if she wanted?"

"She didn't mind a bit." Caleb grinned. "Old Mr. Bainum was another story. A man who'd gotten his neighbors to husk his corn and bring all the food for the party afterward is no fool. He knew well enough the McCoys didn't have that kind of luck. No Irishman does. That's when Mr. Bainum decided to fire up the pot-bellied stove."

The doctor blotted the wound with an alcohol soaked pad, and Anna sucked in a breath. Her skin grew ashen. "Isn't a fire in the barn, even in a stove, dangerous with all those dry husks lying around?"

"Old farmer Bainum took the risk." Though he kept his voice even, Caleb battled the guilt swamping him. Seeing her in pain invoked a fury he'd never experienced before, along with a deep sense of tenderness. The two disparate emotions raged a battle within him. "Mr. Bainum stoked that stove until it burned hot. Soon enough, everybody took off their coats and rolled up their shirtsleeves. Everyone except Gus."

A knowing smile stretched across her strained and pale face. "How long did he last with his coat on?"

Caleb's stomach dipped. He shouldn't be staring at

her lips while talking about kisses. This was hardly the time or place for amorous thoughts. "Through two more kisses. Finally got too hot. Gus pulled off his coat, and six more red ears of corn fell out."

Anna chuckled. The movement didn't seem to bother her, an excellent sign for her continued healing. While he preferred leaving the stitches in for longer, the doctor was right, Anna was young and healthy and healing fast.

She brushed the hair from her forehead. "The McCoys don't need any luck. They make their own."

"That they do."

Caleb sneaked a discreet glance at her side. The doctor had finished removing the row of stitches from the front of the wound. The skin was healthy, the scar puckered, with no sign of infection. He breathed a sigh of relief. A septic wound was often worse than the original injury.

The doctor motioned with one hand. "On your side and I'll take a look at the exit site."

Anna reached out her arm, and Caleb grasped her fingers; together they carefully rolled her toward him onto her left side, her left hand tucked beneath her cheek. Her fingers were icy cold, and he longed to infuse them with his own warmth. All too quickly she was settled, and he reluctantly released his hold.

The color deserted her cheeks, and her lips pinched together, a sure sign of pain. He touched her shoulder. "Should I stop?"

"No. I'm fine," she said, although they both knew she was lying. "I want to hear how the story ends. What happened with Gus and Becky?"

"Gus borrowed a Confederate coat and a Union Jack from a fellow in town. He marched right up to Mr. Bainum's door and told him he was there to enlist in the Confederate army."

"He did not."

"He might have." Caleb shrugged. "A fellow will do odd things when he's in love."

"You almost had me fooled. What really happened?"

The exit wound was larger than the entrance wound, meaning Caleb better stretch out the ending of his story. A difficult task since his concentration kept slipping. He loathed the marring of her beautiful skin. He hated her suffering.

"Mr. Bainum kept them apart, even though everyone told him that he was a crotchety old fool for doing so. My uncle, Gus's dad, even tried reasoning with him, but he wouldn't listen. All the while Becky kept those six ears of red corn wrapped in an old flour sack. She didn't hum when she gathered eggs in the morning, she didn't whistle while she churned the butter. She didn't take the long path around the pond and cut lilacs for the table."

Sorrow darkened Anna's brilliant blue eyes. "My mother always said love ruined a woman faster than rain ruined a parade."

A deep tenderness welled within him. "Your mother is wrong."

He'd seen the redeeming power of love lift even the most shattered soul from the darkness.

"Victoria Bishop is never wrong," Anna stated matter-of-factly.

"Of course she is. Nobody is right all the time."

"Don't let her hear you say that."

Another tick mark against the elder Miss Bishop. While Anna's expression held no rancor, his own feelings were clear. How had such a rigid woman raised such a compassionate child? Did the elder Miss Bishop scorn all love or merely the love between a man and a woman? She'd certainly poisoned her daughter with her attitude.

What of Anna's father? From what Caleb had read in the papers, Anna's mother had never revealed his name. Had the man taken advantage of her? Was that what had shaped her attitude? He doubted Anna even knew. Her convictions were too innocently stated. Was her mother hiding something? Victoria Bishop didn't seem the sort to protect a man, but what did he know? Seeds of hate were just like any other seeds; they started small and, with careful tending, grew into massive things.

Anna stared at him expectantly, and he forced his attention back on the story. "It wasn't love that took the skip out of Becky's step. It was keeping that love hidden away. Mr. Bainum had already lost his wife, and he realized soon enough that he was losing his daughter, as well. He could remain a stubborn old coot, or he could put the song back in his daughter's heart."

"I suppose they lived happily ever after?" Anna asked, her voice dripping with sarcasm. "Isn't that always the way?"

"You've read too many fairy tales. This is real life."

"You're wrong on that account. Fairy tales were strictly forbidden and considered frivolous except for educational purposes. I was allowed to read Peter Parley, but only because his adventures were deemed educational. Although I did smuggle a copy of *Little Women*. I still have the book."

"What's wrong with *Little Women*?"

Not that he'd read the book, he was simply curious of

the reasoning behind the ban. Jo had a copy dog-eared from multiple readings.

Anna's expression turned wistful. "Miss Alcott considered true love a necessary facet of a woman's identity. My mother disagreed. Vehemently. Fairy tales and love were frivolous and unnecessary."

He opened his mouth, a scalding retort for the elder Miss Bishop on the tip of his tongue, but he couldn't say the words. What did he know of raising children? He pictured Anna as a child, her wide blue eyes alight with curiosity. What other activities had been deemed frivolous? Why was something as innocuous as true love vilified?

Clamping shut his lips, he sucked in a breath through his nose. He wasn't here for debate. He was here to take Anna's mind off the pain. "Nobody lives happily ever after, near as I can tell. My ma and pa love each other, but I've seen them go at each other like a couple of raccoons fighting over the same bone." He grinned at her shocked expression. "They're married, Becky and Gus. Most days are good, some days are bad. Same as everyone else."

"What happened to old farmer Bainum? Did he die a lonely death after his daughter left?"

"You can't jump the ending." He brushed the stray lock of hair from her forehead once more. "Mr. Bainum got used to the idea of having a Yank for a son-in-law, especially after he saw his first grandbaby. Gus and Becky have four boys, and he's got his hands full teaching them all to fish and farm."

Anna tucked both hands beneath her cheek. "Does he still host the husking bee?"

"Every year. And since he only has one daughter,

he doesn't care how many red husks the other fellows smuggle in."

"I knew it!" She scowled. "You're just as bad as Gus."

"I didn't say I snuck a red ear into the batch."

"But you did."

"I did. I just didn't say it."

"It's the same thing and you know it. Shame on you." She rubbed her cheek against the back of her fingers. "Who did you kiss?"

The years rushed away, and he was a green youth again, all of his tender hopes pinned on a girl who didn't love him. "I didn't kiss anyone. My brother David got the girl before I did."

She touched his hand, and he started. "I shouldn't have teased you."

"Nah. It's all right. That's the thing about being young. You think if you love someone enough, you can love them enough for both of you. But that's a self-ish love."

He'd never thought about Mary Louise's feelings, only his own. He'd been young and self-centered, too wrapped up in his own feelings to think about her, to notice she was only using him to make David jealous. He'd forgiven her by and by. They'd all been little more than children.

The doctor removed the last stitch. The area around the wound was pink, and the edges holding together nicely. Caleb might have waited a few more days, considering the placement of the stitching, but the skin had already healed over some of the sutures, causing her discomfort as they were removed. There were no signs of infection on this side either, and for that he was grateful.

Anna tugged on his hand for his attention. "I bet there were plenty of other young ladies who wanted your attention."

"Too many to count. There's not a stalk of red corn in the county before a husking bee. By the end of the night, I have a whole pile at my feet."

"That's the only part of the story I believe." Her eyes shimmered with laughter.

There was no use telling the truth. He'd never kissed a girl. The desire had been long dormant.

Until now. He feared she was his undoing.

Anna kept her attention on Caleb's bent knee, finding his eyes far too distracting.

The doctor pulled up the blanket and sat back. "All finished. No strenuous activity for the next few weeks. Don't lift anything heavy. No horseback riding or bronco busting."

"I'll pull my name from the rodeo lineup."

Mr. McCoy stood and took a few steps away, his attention focused on the olive-green flocked wallpaper she'd grown heartily sick of staring at from morning till night.

She'd embarrassed him with her request, though she'd enjoyed his story. Whether or not the tale was entirely true was suspect. In any event, the distraction had worked, she'd hardly noticed the doctor's painful poking and prodding. Her glum mood had also lifted.

The interlude was over, and she'd best place their relationship back on normal footing. Show him that he needn't fear another lapse. She wasn't a clingy helpless female hoping for a boy to kiss her.

Well, she wasn't a clingy, helpless female, at any rate.

The thought of Caleb kissing someone else hit her in the chest like a cannon ball. She did not like the idea one bit.

"I'd recommend staying put for the next several days," Dr. Smith said.

The delicate start of her lighthearted mood fled. The walls closed in on her, and the air in the room thickened. She'd been resting because of the stitches. She hadn't thought much past the future. She'd harbored the naive belief that once the stitches were removed, she'd skip out of her room, down the corridor and out the front door to freedom once more.

She'd never been confined to bed. Not even when she'd had the chicken pox as a child. The rest of the household, including her mother, had been too busy with their own chores and affairs to pay her any mind. After the few first days she'd been up and about. Until the spots went away, she'd had the run of the house. She was used to being independent and spontaneous, not lolling about in her room.

Being ordered to stay put sparked a burst of restless energy and an immediate urge to escape. The guard outside her door had her feeling more like a prisoner than protected.

Mr. McCoy continued his study of the raised pattern on the wall covering, tracing his fingers along the edges. "How soon can she travel by train?"

"Yes. I'd like to travel as soon as possible."

There'd be no more talk of Cimarron Springs. She wouldn't be foisted on Jo's family like an impoverished relative. The detective was obviously mistaken, and after a day or two of quiet, they'd all realize his error. There was absolutely no reason for someone to want her dead. She had few friends in her solitary life, let alone enemies. The bullet had been meant as a warning to the suffragists. Or an accident. No one had considered that likelihood. They still hadn't ruled out the possibility that this was all some horrible mistake.

"Hmm, travel by train." The doctor smoothed his thumb and forefinger along the edges of his mouth. "Anytime, really, if she's up to it. As long as the trip isn't too lengthy." The doctor snapped shut his bag and stood. "Try and sleep. Rest will do you the best good. If you have any problems, send for me."

As the doctor exited with a tip of his hat, Mr. McCoy cleared his throat, then stared at the floor. "I'm sorry about what Jo said earlier. I don't know what she was thinking. I'm sure they'll find the shooter and this will all be over soon. Jo and I are in the two rooms across the way. If you need anything, just holler."

The tips of his ears had reddened. Obviously he'd regretted his sister's impulsive suggestion.

He kept edging toward the door. Most likely he was frightened she'd insist he tell her another story.

Anna plucked at the stitching of her coverlet. "We have the word of one man. There's no need for everyone to descend into a dither. We should have taken Jo's suggestion for what it was—a light moment during a tense situation. The thought of people believing we are engaged is actually quite amusing."

"Yes," he replied, his voice gruff, though his expression remained hidden from her.

He took another step toward the door.

She fixed her gaze on the coverlet. "They'll be no need for me to burden your sister with a houseguest."

Another step.

"Likely not."

Yet another step.

This conversation was embarrassing enough without looking him in the face. He'd echoed her sentiments. Which was perfect. Excellent. Although none of her resolute thinking explained why she became tongue-tied the instant he entered a room.

That was a problem best solved at another time. In another place. Perhaps safely ensconced at home in St. Louis.

Her mother's home, more accurately. Perhaps it was time she sought living arrangements of her own. A spinster's residence. Anna nearly gagged on the word. Unmarried men were "confirmed bachelors," treated with mild admiration by other men, as though they'd achieved some sort of higher standing by remaining unattached. Women were spinsters.

Yet another distinction she abhorred. No matter how they referred to her, she was looking into moving out of her mother's home once she recovered. She had a modest trust from her grandfather—a man who'd died before she was born. Anna was never quite certain why he'd provided for her since he didn't seem the sort of man who would have approved of his daughter bearing an out-of-wedlock child. Whatever his thoughts, the money was there and she was a fool not to make use of it.

Having a goal strengthened her flagging reserves of energy. "Thank you, Mr. McCoy, for everything. Truly. I hope I haven't seemed ungrateful."

It's just that you tie me in knots, and I've never been the tied-in-knots-over-a-man sort of person.

He stuck his hands in his pockets and avoided looking directly at her. "Caleb." He cleared his throat. "I saved your life. I think that puts us on a first-name basis."

"I amend my apology. Thank you, Caleb. And you must call me Anna."

She tripped a bit over the last syllable.

"You have nothing to apologize for, Anna."

Her stomach fluttered. The use of her name lent an air of intimacy to the exchange. She'd never been particularly fond of her name. She liked hearing Caleb say it. She liked hearing him say her name very much.

He straightened and smoothed his jacket. "Rest. We don't need to decide anything right now."

She opened her mouth with a protest, then quickly changed her mind.

Later she'd tell him that all of her decisions had been made. She'd go home as soon as the train schedule allowed. Most likely they'd never see one another again. She'd only hear of him through Jo's letters.

The vague headache she'd been fighting all morning throbbed into life. "I'm certain we'll discover this is all some mad mistake. I'm hardly important enough to have attracted an enemy."

"I think you're quite attractive." Caleb's face flamed. "That is, you gave a very impassioned speech. I was quite moved. The crowd was quite moved. In any case," he rushed on, "I'm certain this will all be resolved soon."

He spun out of the room so quickly she half expected a plume of smoke in his wake.

He'd called her attractive.

The frantic beating of her heart didn't signify anything. Reacting positively to a compliment, whether deliberate or accidental, was human nature. Though the admission had been a slip of the tongue, his mortification had lent the unintentional admission truth. Not that a woman's looks defined her worth. Quite the opposite.

She studied the bright sunlight streaming into her room. Soon he'd be part of her past, a diverting memory mixed in with the pain and fear of this past week.

The sense of relief she expected never came.

Feeling beneath her pillow, she located her embroidery and finished stitching the edges of a red poppy. Truth be told, she'd been intrigued by the idea of concealing her true identity. Assuming a new identity meant she'd be invisible. There would be no expectations. No comparisons to the Great Victoria Bishop.

How liberating, to be anonymous. There would be no living up to her mother's reputation.

An envelope on the table caught Anna's attention, and she reached for the forgotten telegram. Her mother's familiar clipped speech greeted her in bold capital letters. Her worry was evident, the concern apparent. It was the last line that gave Anna pause. She read and reread the words.

BEST YOU RECUPERATE IN KANSAS CITY STOP YOU MUSTNT RISK THE JOURNEY STOP

For some inexplicable reason, tears sprang in her eyes. Despite all the solitude she'd endured during her life, she couldn't recall a time when she felt more utterly or completely alone.

Chapter Six

Upon returning to the hotel after a brief walk the following day, Caleb took the steps two at a time. He didn't know why, the closer he got to Anna, the greater his sense of urgency. He'd been fighting an inexplicable sense of anxiety all day.

A woman blocked his path on the landing, and he nearly toppled over her, stopping short just in time. The other hotel guest was in her midtwenties, dressed in an expensive burgundy brocade jacket with a fur muff, even though it was only early fall.

"Pardon me," he said.

"No need for pardon." She patted the side of her brassy blond hair, her eyes glittery blue chips against her powdered cheeks. "Are you staying at the hotel long?"

"Checking out soon," he answered, his voice clipped.

He wasn't in the mood for polite small talk. Occasionally people mistook his silence for interest, and the woman standing before him appeared the sort who'd have plenty to say.

She shrugged and continued on her way, glancing once over her shoulder.

After nearly a week cooped up at the Savoy Hotel, it was time he returned home. He'd left his younger brother, Maxwell, in charge of his animals while he was gone, but there was no one available to take over his practice. Truth be told, he wanted some space between him and Miss Bishop. She held an undeniable draw, and he was going to make a fool of himself if he didn't leave soon.

His face flushed. He'd gone and called her attractive. He'd always been reticent around women, and Anna exacerbated his condition. His first instincts had been correct—the longer he was around her, the likelier he was to make a fool of himself. A bigger fool, he silently amended.

His purpose here had been served. Miss Bishop—Anna—had a guard outside her door. The suffragist women had kept up a steady stream of visitors. They'd brought enough flowers to blanket a meadow. Even now the scent of roses perfumed the corridor.

He didn't consider himself an intuitive man; more often than not he missed the signs other people assured him came from women. With Anna he felt a definite sense of distance, as though she kept a protective space between them, like a wounded animal, skittish of contact. A part of him longed to challenge that distance.

Which was precisely why he needed to find Jo and arrange their departure. Certainly Garrett, Jo's husband, was growing impatient by now. She must miss her children.

Upon arriving at Jo's room, she waved him in. "Where have you been?"

Her obvious annoyance took him aback. "I'm sorry, was I supposed to leave a note?"

"You might have told me where you'd gone. I was worried."

"I didn't mean to worry you. I was looking at some plumbing fixtures."

"Plumbing fixtures?" She paused, then planted her hands on her hips. "You were looking at plumbing fixtures with all that's going on?"

"There have been some amazing improvements in indoor plumbing. Kansas City is the closest place to find the modern equipment."

"If you weren't my own brother, I'd think you were being deliberately obtuse."

"Why are you so cranky? We're sitting around the hotel waiting for Miss Bishop to be well enough to travel. I'm going crazy. Besides, yesterday you bought taffy for the kids, and I didn't lecture you."

She'd gone and left him alone with Anna. Every encounter had him craving more. If he was staying away from the hotel, avoiding more encounters with Anna, his decision was none of Jo's concern.

"When I said I was going for taffy, you rolled your eyes."

"That is not a lecture." Best he changed the subject. They were all on edge. Torn between oppressive fear and crushing tedium. "Have you heard anything from Anna's mother?"

"No. And I'm tempted to give the woman a piece of my mind. Anna's never said a cross word, but what kind of mother leaves her daughter all alone, in a strange town? Injured. I've been away from Jocelyn for a week, and I'm already crawling up the walls with worry. And she's fit as a fiddle. If she were hurt…" Jo grimaced. "If she were hurt, I'd be by her side in an instant."

His thoughts had run along a similar vein. "Anna's an adult. I have a feeling her mother values independence. I have a feeling they both value independence."

Yet another reason he needed space between them. He didn't hold her background against her, though he recognized plenty of others did. He knew enough about himself to realize he was more traditional. Back when he'd been interested in courting, he'd always pictured a marriage similar to the one his parents shared. A wife and children, a quiet life in Cimarron Springs. Another reason he and Anna didn't suit.

"The Bishops are a unique pair," Jo said. "From what I've read, Victoria is one of those rare individuals who seems larger than life in any setting, no matter how mundane."

"Like mother, like daughter on that account."

Anna certainly had the ability to draw in a crowd. He'd been singularly transfixed the moment she stepped behind the podium. While he might have chalked up the experience to his own attraction, he'd seen Jo respond the same way.

"They are similar in that way, I suppose," Jo said thoughtfully. "Anna possesses much the same appeal, but there's a gentler, more compassionate aura surrounding her."

Caleb's gaze sharpened. "Don't let Anna's mother hear you say that. I have a feeling that *soft* is a word she abhors."

Life with Victoria Bishop must surely have been anything but conventional. Their own upbringing had been completely ordinary. What must childhood have been like for Anna, living with such a forceful personality? What expectations had been laid at her feet? Did she ever feel the weight of responsibility crushing her?

Judging from her dedication to the cause, most likely not. She already had her own legacy in the making. Probably why she kept her distance. Anna had a calling.

Anna.

Her name whispered at his conscience. He should have kept their relationship on a more formal footing. Calling her Miss Bishop kept him detached. First, Jo had gone and said they should pretend to be an engaged couple. Then, he'd blurted out that he found her attractive. Anna must have thought their whole family was daft.

No doubt she was ready to see the last of them both. The longer they stayed in Kansas City, the more he worried about their deception, of Anna discovering she'd been hiding out as his fiancée. He and Jo had offered their assistance, and she'd refused. There was nothing more to be done.

Another knock sounded, and Jo scooted past him to admit a young, uniformed maid clutching a handful of bedding.

The girl bobbed her head. "Fresh linens, miss."

"Thank you," Jo replied distractedly, then turned toward Caleb. "We should talk with Anna. Make some decisions about what to do next. I don't want to abandon her, but I can't be away from the children any longer."

Her obvious longing for her children reinforced his own plans. "If Miss Bishop refuses our help, there's not much else we can do. This was never our responsibility in the first place."

The maid straightened from her crouch beside the

bed. "You know Miss Bishop? Did her relatives find her? Her uncle seemed quite concerned."

Caleb and Jo exchanged a confused glance.

Jo touched the girl's arm, halting her exit. "Are you certain the man was looking for Miss Bishop?"

"Oh, quite certain."

His sister frowned slightly. "I don't recall Anna ever mentioning an uncle."

Caleb sprinted into the corridor, relieved to see the guard stationed before Miss Bishop's door. Taking a slow deep breath, he stilled his racing thoughts. For all any of them knew, she had a whole bevy of aunts and uncles and cousins. No need for panic. He'd speak with Anna before charging off in a frenzy. Then he'd alert the hotel staff as an additional precaution.

A commotion snapped him upright. A shrill scream sounded from Anna's room. Glass shattered. A male voice shouted.

The guard whipped around and kicked open the door. In a blaze, Caleb raced after him and tripped over the maid's linen basket. He cracked his knee on the floor. A flurry of movement caught his attention. From his awkward crouched position, he managed to grasp the man's leg as he raced by. The assailant went down hard. Caleb scrambled upright and the man kicked out with his free leg. The blow glanced off the side of Caleb's head. An explosion of pain burst behind his eyes.

He lost his hold and his vision blurred. Staggering upright, he braced one hand against the wall. Someone shrieked. Squinting, Caleb made out the hazy form of the maid. He blinked a few times, unable to clear his vision.

The man shoved the maid forward and she careened

into Caleb. The collision tipped him backward and they slammed into the wall.

Bracing his hands against the maid's shoulders, he caught only the blurred image of her pale face in a halo of blond hair because of his impaired vision. "Are you all right?"

"Shaken, that's all."

He set the woman aside and staggered toward the stairs. Feeling along the banister, he managed his way to the lobby. By the time he reached the front doors, his vision had mostly cleared, but the improvement was too late.

The assailant had disappeared. He spun around and searched the surrounding streets. People hustled to and fro. There was no sign of the intruder.

He turned back to the hotel and nicked something with his foot. Bending, he caught sight of a knife, blood still visible on the blade. His heart seized.

He took the stairs two at a time and burst into Anna's room a moment later.

Miss Bishop leaned over the guard who lay writhing beneath the broken window, his hands clenching his face as blood seeped through his fingers.

Caleb's pulse thundered in his ears, adrenaline still coursing through his body. "Are you hurt?"

He knelt beside Anna and grasped her shoulders, turning her toward him. He kept his arms rigid, resisting the urge to crush her against his chest. Her scream had taken a decade off his life. The vision of the bloody knife was still forefront in his thoughts.

Seconds before, he'd been making plans to leave her. Now he couldn't let her go. His fingers remained clenched on her upper arms, his arms shaking. She was safe and nothing else mattered. Nothing else mattered except finding the man responsible.

"I'm fine," she replied, a tremor in her voice. "This poor man took the brunt of it. The intruder had a knife. He must have thought I was sleeping."

Caleb released her, tearing his fingers away, hoping she didn't notice his reluctance. Jo caught his stricken gaze, and he quickly looked away, afraid she might read the raw emotion behind his actions.

After quickly ensuring the guard's wound was superficial, he stood and crossed the room.

While Anna and Jo plucked glass from the floor, Caleb leaned out the broken window and briefly searched the roofline and the ground three stories below. A flash of silver pipe caught his attention. No other movement flickered in either direction. The intruder had obviously swung in from the fire escape attached to the adjoining room, a dangerous endeavor, but obviously not impossible. Even if Caleb made the jump as well, the man already had a head start, he was no better off than before. He'd never find him.

With a muttered curse, he snatched a towel from the washstand and pressed it against the guard's face. "This isn't as bad as it looks. Facial wounds, well, they tend to bleed more."

He should have been with her. He should have alerted the guard instead of lingering in the corridor like an inept fool. He should have done a lot of things differently. Anna might have lost her life because of his hesitation.

From that moment on, he wasn't letting her out of his sight. "What happened? Did you see who did this?"

Anna swiped the hair from her face, inadvertently

smearing the guard's blood across her forehead. "I was resting and I heard a noise. A man broke through the window."

A desperate act. Though the room faced the much-less traveled alleyway, it was broad daylight. The man had climbed the fire escape three stories and navigated a narrow ledge, probably holding the pipe Caleb had eyed below in order to break the window. The guard outside the door had thwarted any attempts of gaining entrance through the hotel, forcing the ill-fated break-in attempt.

Reality slammed into him. The man had been mere feet from Anna. Shooting someone from a distance was impersonal. Stabbing or bludgeoning someone at close range was far more heinous.

Jo turned toward the stricken maid cowering near the door. "Fetch the doctor. He should know the way by now."

Anna's jaw tightened. "This has gone too far. I'm going to hire that fidgety Pinkerton detective and find out who's responsible before someone gets killed."

"The offer still stands." Jo crouched beside them. "You can come to Cimarron Springs with us. Whatever you decide, we'll support you. Won't we, Caleb?"

"Of course."

Anna didn't answer immediately, and neither of them pushed her for answer. Not that her reply mattered. He'd talk her into coming back with them, no matter how long it took.

Caleb caught his shirt cuff over his wrist and anchored the material with his fingers, then lifted his arm, gently wiping the blood from her face with his sleeve. The events of the previous week came rushing back. How close they'd come to losing her. Not once but twice.

When the last evidence of the blood had been wiped away, he realized his hands were shaking. He'd let Anna say her piece, but he planned on arguing their case until she saw reason.

She lifted her lashes and met his steady gaze. His breath caught in the back of his throat. She had the most fascinating, expressive eyes. A blue so deep and pure, he was drawn into the exquisite pool of color.

She tugged her lower lip between her teeth. "I'm wondering... That is..."

Her rare hesitation had his attention. He edged closer.

Close enough that if he leaned just a little farther, he might touch his lips to the curve of her ear. "You were saying."

His breath whispered against her cheek.

Curiosity overcame him. Her unspoken words became paramount.

"I'm wondering if we should..."

The guard sat up between them with a grunt, bumping them apart, the reddened towel pressed against his face. "Hey, now, what's wrong with you people? I'm bleeding to death here."

Caleb bristled at the interruption. "It's only a scratch."

The guard lurched upright, and Caleb hooked his arm beneath the man's elbow, pulling them both into a standing position.

He reached for Anna, but she'd turned away. Disappointment knotted in his stomach. The moment was gone. She'd lost her courage. Whatever she'd been about to say was lost to him forever.

With a startled gasp, Mrs. Franklin appeared in the

doorway. "For goodness' sake. I only left for a moment and it's chaos."

Guiding the injured man toward a chair, Caleb motioned for the widow. "Can you see to him? He's been cut on the cheek. It's not deep. It looks bad, though. You know how these facial wounds are."

She studied the wound with an expert eye. "I saw plenty of those from my boys growing up."

A sorrowful shadow passed over her eyes. She cleared her throat and dusted her hands, as though brushing away the troubled memories of her lost sons. "Let's see what's to be done."

Caleb held out his hand and reached for Anna. Her fingers clasped his, trembling.

His momentary annoyance at the interruption fled. "You've had a fright. Would you like to lie down?"

A delicate shudder swept through her. "I've had enough of lying about to last a lifetime. Besides, I believe the bed is otherwise occupied."

The guard had slumped from the chair onto the bed. Flat on his back, he clutched his face and stared at the ceiling, moaning.

Mrs. Franklin reached between Anna and Caleb. "Just amongst us," she spoke in a harsh whisper, "I've tended children with stronger constitutions than this one."

In a scene eerily reminiscent of the one that had played out only a week before, the room descended into a flurry of controlled pandemonium. The doctor arrived, his chest puffing with exertion, and the guard was stitched up with much groaning and complaining before he was hustled away.

Once the four of them were alone again, Anna

perched on the edge of the bed. Jo continued gingerly plucking the shards of glass from the floor, and Caleb took the only chair.

Mrs. Franklin paced the room, her hands behind her back. "Mr. McCoy, you're a far better surgeon than Dr. Smith, and Anna is a far better patient."

Jo paused in her work and scrunched up her nose. "You'd have thought he'd been cleaved in half with all that whining."

"Let's not be so quick to judge." Anna hid a grin. "We all experience pain differently."

Mrs. Franklin straightened the plain white collar adorning her serviceable gray dress. "It is becoming increasingly clear that the detective was correct. This is the second attempt on Miss Bishop's life. She cannot possibly stay in Kansas City, and St. Louis is equally unsafe. There is an obvious solution to our problem."

When Mrs. Franklin failed to complete her thought, Caleb rolled his hand forward. "And what solution is that?"

"I shall accompany Miss Bishop to this town of yours. What was the name?"

"Cimarron Springs," the three other occupants of the room spoke in unison.

"I shall accompany you to Cimarron Springs. While one person might raise a few eyebrows, the two of us will attract less attention."

"Sounds good to me," Jo offered cheerfully.

Anna shook her head. "I couldn't possibly ask that of you."

"You're not asking. I'm offering. This is the best solution. You need care. Jo has her own family."

Caleb's sister, normally eager to add her opinion to any conversation, remained oddly silent.

"I took the liberty of making a few inquiries while the three of you were foiling murder attempts," Mrs. Franklin continued brusquely. "There is a property owned by a Mr. Stuart for rent."

Caleb slanted a glance at Jo. "Surely you don't mean that shack at the end of Main Street. It's hardly habitable."

"Idle hands make the devil's work." The widow paused once more in her pacing. "I shall enjoy the challenge."

"It's very kind of you," Anna sputtered. "But why would you do such a thing? I don't know how long I'll be staying. Won't you be missed here?"

"I'm a widow. I go where I please. And I want to help. Isn't that enough?"

Jo broke in before Anna voiced another objection. "I think it's a good idea. The Stuart house is on the same side of town as ours. And it's right across the way from Caleb. You'll practically be neighbors.

"Neighbors," Anna said weakly. "This all seems a little too neat and tidy. I sense collusion."

Jo had the decency to look abashed. "I might have mentioned the availability of the house and its convenient location over breakfast with Mrs. Franklin."

"The location is fine." Caleb made a mental note to strangle his sister once they were alone. "It's the condition of the place."

Not to mention Anna would be a stone's throw away. Every day. Even if he wanted to ignore his longing for her, how could he? The more time they spent together, the harder it would be to forget her.

She looked at him then, and for the first time he realized she'd done something different with her hair. Her appearance was softer somehow. She'd donned a blue dress this morning, almost identical to the color she'd worn that first day. The shade suited her. One silky, dark curl rested against her flushed cheek. His fingers ached to touch the loose strands.

"Caleb." She spoke his name softly. "What do you think?"

If she'd called him Mr. McCoy, his answer might have been different. He might have been stronger.

But she hadn't.

She'd called him Caleb. He knew at that moment he'd do just about anything to hear her speak his name again. He'd do just about anything to see her like she was that first day—shaking her fist at the crowd, bullying them all into action.

He'd give her the answer he dreaded most, because even if her presence scraped at his resolve, he'd rather have her near. For an hour, for a day, for a week. For whatever amount of time God deemed fit.

He'd rather spend this little time with her than never see her again.

"I think it's an excellent idea."

All he had to do was avoid her for the next few weeks. She'd be living a stone's throw away from him. In Cimarron Springs. A town with more cows than people.

Avoiding her shouldn't be a problem at all.

As long as he never left his house.

Chapter Seven

"If you're certain." Anna exhaled her pent-up breath.

For reasons she didn't want to explore, his opinion mattered. If he'd offered any dissent, any sign of reluctance, she'd never agree.

He'd spoken without hesitation. Her fate was decided.

"I still have absolutely no idea who would want me dead. This all seems a little ridiculous," she said.

She was not the Great Victoria Bishop. She was only the *daughter* of the Great Victoria Bishop. There was no reason for anyone to want her dead.

Caleb remained pensive. He'd moved from the chair and stood with his shoulder propped against the door, his arms crossed. The pose was already familiar. Comforting.

"There's something else." Anna stared at her folded hands. "The guard was hurt today because he was protecting me. You must consider the safety of your families. Mrs. Franklin, you have your own well-being to consider."

"I survived the War Between the States," Izetta said. "Nothing can frighten me off after that horror."

"My husband is the town marshal," Jo said in exasperation. "You can't get much safer than that."

Caleb spoke last. "I can take care of myself."

They'd offered their friendship and protection, though she had nothing to give in return. The realization humbled her even as a nagging sense of unease lingered. This was not the sort of arrangement her mother would approve of. Quite the opposite. Victoria Bishop would stand fast. Face the problem dead to rights. She'd never scuttle to the countryside like a startled crab cowering beneath a dark ledge.

The three impersonal telegrams her mother had sent rested on the night table. Boston was a world away. If Victoria Bishop didn't like her daughter's choices, then she could tear herself away from the cause and help Anna instead.

For once Anna didn't want to be the new rising star in the suffragist's movement. She didn't want to be the illegitimate daughter of Victoria Bishop. She wanted to be herself, not a figurehead or, worse yet, a legacy. Mostly, though, she didn't want to see the censure in the townspeople's eyes.

And there was always censure. The women's movement brought change, and change frightened people. Men and women alike. They'd thrown eggs and rotten tomatoes at her. Often before a picketing, her knees quaked and her heart pounded. The trick wasn't gathering courage like seashells along the beach; the trick was trusting that courage would come when one needed it most. This time she wasn't waiting on nerve.

She was hiding.

Every fiber of her being rejected the notion of running; every lesson taught during her rigid upbringing rebelled.

She might have been raised for daring, but the lessons hadn't taken. Nothing silenced the terror of that man bursting through the window. She was a coward through and through.

"I'll come," she said. "On one condition."

"What's that?"

"I should definitely have a new name. My middle name is Ryan. Anna Ryan should do quite nicely. It's not far from the truth."

She wasn't taking a chance that someone might recognize the name Bishop. Not only for her safety and the safety of those around her, but because the idea of having a name separate from her mother's had taken root. For reasons she refused to examine, the idea was exhilarating—and terrifying. If she was taking the coward's way out, she might as well see the game through.

Caleb stuffed his hands in his pockets. "What were you going to say earlier? You know, when the guard was injured, you started to say...*we should.*"

Oh, dear. Must he recall that moment of weakness? She'd been scared. In shock. Not quite herself. "It's the silliest thing." She laughed. The sound hollow and false even to her own ears. "I was going to say that we should consider Jo's idea. Since Mrs. Franklin is accompanying me, there's no need to go to such extreme lengths."

"Which idea?" Caleb straightened. "The pretend engagement?"

Jo pushed off from the window seat and slapped her palms against thighs. "If we're leaving, I'll inform the hotel staff."

Izetta crossed to the door. "I had better start packing. I'll be back around six for suppertime in the dining room."

After they'd exited the room, Anna raised an eyebrow. "Was it something I said?"

A wry grin spread across Caleb's face. "They're not very subtle, are they?"

"No." Anna shared in his amusement. "As I was trying to explain before, with Mrs. Franklin coming along, there's no need to go to such desperate lengths."

"I wouldn't say *desperate*."

"Although, if we did pretend an attachment," she continued thoughtfully, "once this business is resolved, you'd be the jilted suitor. You could turn that to your favor. I'm sure you'd cut quite a romantic figure as the injured party. No doubt you'd find plenty of ladies to comfort you."

"Being the jilted suitor isn't nearly as romantic as you'd suppose."

The tone of his voice wiped the teasing smile from her lips. "Oh, dear, I've done it now, haven't I? I've said the wrong thing."

"I'm embarrassed to admit this," he said, heaving a breath, "but I've already played the part. I won't bore you with the particulars. Let's just say, a few years ago, I had a crush on a certain young lady named Mary Louise Stuart."

"Forget what I said." Embarrassment heated her cheeks. "I was trying to lighten the moment and doing a poor job of it."

"Her name is Mary Louise McCoy now."

The realization took a moment to sink in. "Oh."

"Yes. Oh."

"She's married to one of your brothers?"

"David."

Anna searched her memory for mention of David in Jo's letters.

"Mary Louise is having a baby," Anna blurted.

"Yep."

"Oh."

"Everyone thinks I'm still sweet on her."

"Are you?"

The question was rude. She didn't care. She needed his answer. A few days ago she'd nearly died. A lapse in polite conversation hardly seemed noteworthy after that event. Since the accident, she'd been living in a constant state of worry. Now she was running off to the country. She needed to recapture a modicum of her courage.

"No. And the worst part is, I don't know that I ever was." He raked his hand through his hair. "She was pretty."

"Pretty?"

"I liked her because she was the prettiest girl in town."

Something twisted in Anna's chest. "I see."

All of her mother's warnings came rushing back. Men only sought out women because of their looks or their station. They wanted either a trophy or a business arrangement, a way to unite dynasties or a prize. She'd thought Caleb was different.

"I was young," he said. "I wasn't thinking about much of anything else. David and I fought. Words were said. I went away for a while after that. I trained as a veterinarian. I've always been better with animals than people."

"I think you do quite well."

"You won't find many folks who agree. You were

right about one thing. People felt sorry for me after David and Mary Louise were married. I even got an extra slice of pie at the Harvest Festival that year. And some ice cream, as well."

"You're incorrigible."

"Yep."

"How are things between you now? Between you and David and Mary Louise?"

The question was too personal, and she was rude for asking. None of that stopped her. She'd come this far, there was no going back.

"Things between us are good. Real good. I mean, here's the thing. Every time I see Mary Louise, I'm glad she didn't choose me."

At the look of astonished joy on his face, Anna stifled a burst of nervous laughter.

Caleb dropped his head, his shoulders shaking. "That wasn't what I meant." He fisted a hand against his own amusement. "I only mean that we wouldn't have suited."

"I think I understand." Anna wrestled with uncharacteristic jealously. She'd never met Mary Louise, and already she'd had enough of the woman. "Isn't it strange, the ideas we have about ourselves? I wanted to be a nurse when I was young. It all seemed very exciting and adventurous. Then I realized that what I really loved were the uniforms."

"The uniforms?"

"They looked so neat and tidy and efficient."

"I can see how that would appeal to a young girl."

Anna palmed her cheek and shook her head. "It does seem a little silly now that I'm admitting it to someone."

"Don't worry. I wanted to be the town sheriff because he had a tin star. I thought it must be the bravest thing to wear a tin star and carry a gun."

"Did you ever have your own tin star as a child?"

"I cut one from card stock."

"It sounds quite impressive."

"Not when it rains. Card stock melts in the rain."

"Then you must have made a very good sheriff on sunny days."

"David is a deputy sheriff now."

An unexpected sorrow tugged at her heart. "He got your job and your girl."

What a pair they made, and yet they were no different from everyone else. The world was filled with lost dreams and missed opportunities. Why should the two of them escape unscathed? He wasn't upset by the losses. Instead he appeared relieved. Though he didn't have a shiny tin star, he'd discovered something better. He'd found his calling.

Had he found another sweetheart, as well? A shaft of pain pierced her somewhere near the region of her heart. But, no, his sister never would have suggested the engagement charade if he was courting someone else.

Sensing the shift in mood, he offered a sad smile. "Maybe I should have asked for two free slices of pie at the Harvest Festival." He idly checked his watch, then flipped shut the lid. "Don't go painting me as some tortured hero. I'm happy with the way things turned out for me. Sometimes we have to wait for God's plan and not our own."

There was something she'd never understood: God's plan. If there was a benevolent being plotting out their lives, He was doing an awfully poor job of things. Not to mention the statement stripped all responsibility from those helpless souls on earth, providing a convenient excuse for setbacks and failures. A convenient excuse for quitting. *I suppose it wasn't God's plan.*

Responsibility and faith were far too tangled in organized religion. The contradiction had been an oft-debated topic amongst the more ardent suffragists.

She recalled something she'd read not long before. "Susan Anthony once said, 'I distrust those people who know so well what God wants them to do because I notice it always coincides with their own desires.'"

He didn't blink at her contrary rejoinder. "Would faith in a higher power be more acceptable if God were to want the opposite of our desires?"

A thousand heated words balanced on the tip of her tongue. If God had a plan for her, He should have left some instructions. A rudimentary map. At the very least, an arrow pointing in the right direction. Often in her own life she felt as though she was swimming upstream against her desires. What she truly wanted didn't always match what she had been groomed for, what she had a talent for, what was expected of her.

She was a good speaker. She recognized her own power over a crowd. She acknowledged the responsibility that accompanied such an influential talent. Yet she'd never felt as though she belonged on the stage. The only time she sensed a calling was when she wrote the words on paper. Planning and writing the speeches enthralled her with passion and purpose. Giving those speeches filled her with trepidation.

"It must be a comfort," she said. "Believing in something outside of yourself. Believing in a higher power."

There was no mollycoddling in the Bishop household. Personal responsibility was paramount. One did not place one's destiny in the hands of deities created by men for the continued subjugation of women. While even Victoria Bishop acknowledged there were other, more beneficial aspects of religion, she was quite clear on what she considered the most egregious offences.

Anna braced for Caleb's subsequent shock and disappointment. She'd noticed an almost identical sequence of actions when someone of faith encountered someone of doubt. First came shock, then came disappointment, then came proselytizing. She was adept at deflecting the arguments.

No condemnation appeared in his thoughtful expression. After a long moment he said simply, "What do you believe in?"

"I've never been asked that before."

"Then it's high time someone did."

Most people were eager to spout their own beliefs, bullying one into submission. No one had ever asked her about her own thoughts. The question was candid, sincere.

Since she'd quizzed him about his relationships, she supposed she owed him some honesty in return. "I don't know what I believe. I've seen the words in the Bible used for great good and great evil. I have seen the words used to justify a multitude of charity, as well as a multitude of offences."

She readied herself for a barrage of reproach. If his overzealous response caused him to sink lower in her estimation, all the better. This strange fascination she was developing for the man must stop. No good could ever come of it. They were from two different worlds. Their paths led in opposite directions.

He'd no doubt marry a nice girl from the neighboring farm who would never dream of questioning the veracity of a supreme being. Which suited her just fine. To each his own.

Annoyed by his continued silence and determined to goad him into revealing himself, she spoke more sharply than she'd intended. "How do you justify the evil men do? Is that God's plan, that we should fight amongst ourselves? Is it God's plan that a woman be beaten by her husband with no recourse? Does God condone the subjection of women and children?"

He remained infuriatingly impassive beneath her barrage. Exhausted by her uncharacteristic temper, Anna fell silent.

"We are, all of us," he said thoughtfully, his voice quiet, "capable of both good and evil. It's too easy to slip into indulgence, assuming that because one man is capable of great evil, his actions refute all the light in the world. If the limits of evil are endless, then so must be the limits of good. God may have a plan, but He has also given us free will. We have a choice. We struggle toward the light or we drift toward the darkness. The secret is ensuring we're always moving in the right direction. That we stay on the side of righteousness."

Suddenly exhausted, Anna abandoned her argument. "It sounds like a great deal of work."

"Every relationship in our lives requires work. Even our relationship with God."

He replaced his hat and ran his fingertips along the brim. A habit, she supposed, judging by the wear marks in the felt.

He was a man of faith, and she was a woman consumed by doubts. Together they made a poor match.

A poor match indeed.

Chapter Eight

Caleb dreaded the task ahead of him. This time he'd keep his resolve. He'd keep his emotions in check.

A thread of cigar smoke led Caleb toward the cramped parlor horseshoed into the end of a corridor. Reinhart glanced up from the sheaf of papers he'd been studying. "Can't say I'm surprised to see you, Mr. McCoy."

Caleb touched his breast pocket. "I have the first payment. The amount you requested. We'll see how things progress from there."

Anna had insisted on paying, but she wasn't able to visit the bank herself. He'd tell her the truth one day, that he'd paid the fee himself, if the question ever came up. He doubted she'd appreciate his interference. Independence was one thing, bullheadedness was another.

"Fair enough." Mr. Reinhart smoothed a palm over his dark, thinning hair. "Found something."

They'd chosen to meet the detective at the hotel before their train departed. They'd moved Anna's room yet again, a location with an undamaged window far from the fire escape.

Caleb straightened. "Already?"

"Miss Bishop's name was familiar. It stuck with me. That's what got me thinking about this case in the first place. Asking questions. Then I realized why. Somebody was looking for Miss Bishop before."

"Who?" Caleb asked, then shook his head. "No. We'd best wait for Miss Bishop. This concerns her most of all."

"She's late."

"She's not late. There's still five minutes until nine o'clock."

The detective seemed to take great satisfaction whenever he thought Anna had failed in some regard. As though lack of punctuality might somehow justify the lack of vote. As though if Reinhart put enough ticks in one column he justified his prejudices.

Caleb grunted. As if anything in life was that simple.

Anna appeared at the end of the corridor and Caleb automatically stood, his pulse quickening. Reinhart remained stubbornly ensconced in his seat. She glided toward them with her inherent grace, her feet barely whispering over the carpet runner. Only a slight hitch in her step indicated her injury.

She wore an elegant dress in a deep shade of green, the trim black. She carried herself with instinctive elegance and an economy of movement. There was nothing clumsy or rushed about Anna Bishop, and her natural confidence drew him forward.

Even Reinhart started to rise before thumping back down on his seat again. "Don't s'pose these ladies appreciate civility."

"Civility is the whole point."

Reinhart grunted and rolled his eyes.

Caleb held a chair for Anna. She swept her skirts aside and sat. "You said in your note that you'd discovered something. I hadn't expected news quite this soon."

"This is old news," Reinhart said. "That's what's been bothering me. I was telling Mr. McCoy here, your name was familiar. I figured it was because I'd heard about you from the papers. Then I remembered something. Months ago, in St. Louis, a solicitor was looking for you."

"A lawyer? What was his name?"

"Don't remember the name." Reinhart punctuated his sentence with one of his quick, tight-lipped smiles. "It wasn't my case. I sent a message back to St. Louis. The telegrams are costing me a pretty penny already, I can tell you that. Telegrams ain't cheap."

"The cost is included in your fee." Anna smoothed her gloved hands down the armrest. The only sign of nerves Caleb had seen thus far. "Can you at least tell me why this lawyer was looking for me?"

"Your father hired him."

Anna blanched, half stood, then caught herself and sat back down. "You must be mistaken. The man must have used that as an excuse."

"Mebbe. But I don't think so."

"If the inquiry was a hoax—" Caleb placed his hand on the back of Anna's chair "—do you think the shooting was planned that far in advance?"

His suspicions had finally been validated, though he took no satisfaction in the victory. Anna clearly didn't think the threat was personal. This information proved her wrong.

Reinhart leaned forward. "The shooter might have been planning something, but not what happened at the rally. How could he? They only arranged the speech three weeks ago."

As much as it galled him to admit, the unkempt detective had a point.

Anna's booted foot beat a steady tattoo on the carpet near his own foot, the tufted covering on the armrest compressed beneath her fingers.

Caleb pressed against his forehead with a thumb and index finger. "How can you be sure the man wasn't lying? How can we know he was really Anna's father?"

"I figured he was on the up and up because Miss Bishop's mother agreed to meet with the fellow last April," Reinhart said. "The solicitor met with Victoria Bishop."

Anna rose from her chair and faced away from them. "No, that can't be. Surely she'd have said something to me."

Her distress cut him to the quick. Caleb approached her, keeping his body between her and the detective, then spoke low in her ear. "There's no easy way to ask this, but do you know your father's identity? We'll be able to tell easily enough if Reinhart is lying."

He'd rather risk alienating her than be led astray by falsehoods.

She pressed both hands against her pale cheeks. "I don't know. I asked my mother. Of course I asked. She'd only ever say, 'He doesn't matter to me, why should he matter to you?'"

An instant dislike for a woman he'd never met took root. What kind of answer was that for a child? The vague reply smacked of the self-indulgent excuse of a spoiled heiress accustomed to having her way.

A cold rage settled low in his belly for both the detective and Anna's mother, stripping away at his vow to remain impartial. Caleb faced the detective.

Reinhart drummed his fingers on the table. "When the Pinkertons sent me out here, they said I'd starve for lack of work. I knew they were wrong. People come out West for a reason. Most times that reason ain't too savory, if you get my meaning. Makes for plenty of work for a man like me. Had to get me an assistant to help out."

Caleb remained silent. He wasn't revealing any information Anna wasn't sharing first. "Last spring a solicitor talked with Victoria Bishop, but she never said anything to her only daughter. Perhaps it was a mistake."

Anna resumed her chair and smoothed her skirts over her knees, wrestling back her control. The revelation had been a shock. He'd known there was a scandal connected with Anna's mother. The paper clippings Jo had saved took great delight in splashing Victoria Bishop's unmarried status across the headlines.

He'd assumed Anna knew more about her parentage. She hadn't appeared beneath a cabbage leaf, after all.

Either way the declaration by the detective had been deliberately provoking. Had Reinhart been studying her reaction? Caleb had been too focused on Anna, and he hadn't been watching the detective.

Caleb rested his hand on the armrest of her chair, and she covered his fingers with her own. Her touch was cautious, whisper light, and he kept his attention rigidly forward. He sensed her conflict with these lapses, these moments when she needed the bolstering support of another person.

She sat up straighter, her back stiff, her face so impassive her profile might have been carved from marble. "If this man was my father, why didn't he come for me himself?"

"Because he was sick. Dying."

Anna hid her distress well. Only the tightening of her fingers on his hand and the two spots of color appearing high on her cheeks revealed her true state. "Where is my father now? Do you have a name?"

"His name was Drexel Ryan."

Anna leaned forward. "Where is he? Give me that much at least."

The detective looked away, and Caleb sagged back into his seat. The detective had spoken the name in the past tense, a telling slip. A dying man had sent his solicitor searching for Anna last April, five months ago. Anna clearly hadn't made the connection, and his heart ached for her.

Her eyes flashing, Anna gripped the arms of her chair. "I am in no mood for games. Where is my father?"

"In Omaha," Reinhart grumbled. "Buried in the Forest Lawn Cemetery."

"That can't be." Anna reared back. "It's not true. None of this is true."

Caleb reached for her and she flinched away. Her rejection cut him to the quick. She adjusted in her seat and winced, unconsciously touching her side.

With no place to vent his rage, he turned his anger on the detective. Furious, he faced Reinhart. "You might have softened the blow."

"She didn't even know the man. What does she care if he's alive or dead? He's nothing to her."

"That's not for you to say."

"Enough," Anna spoke. "This is all a game for you, isn't it? Have you humiliated me quite enough? Are you satisfied I'm not worthy of the vote or your time?"

"You don't pay me to play nursemaid. You pay me for information. I gave it to you."

This time when Caleb covered her trembling fingers with his own, she didn't pull away. "Let's hear him out."

At that moment, he loathed the detective. He loathed him for his clumsy handling of the situation and his obvious disdain. They were trapped. The realization kicked his anger from a slow simmer into a full boil. Reinhart had information they needed.

Right then he had the overwhelming desire to punch something. The detective wasn't a bad choice, but he was off-limits until they had all the information. Which left Caleb ensnared. He was entirely inadequate. Surely there was something more he should say, something more he should do. In less than a week she'd had two attempts on her life. She'd discovered her father had been looking for her, and now he was dead. Buried in a cemetery in Nebraska.

Anna reached out and with her right hand fingered the edges of the lace curtains, keeping her left hand motionless beneath his. The shades had been drawn for safety, and privacy, blanketing the parlor in perpetual gloom.

When was the last time she'd stepped outside? Seen the sun? A week at least. The confinement must have been maddening.

She drew in a breath, keeping her face averted. "Last spring my mother received a large envelope. I normally take care of all her correspondence. She wouldn't let me touch the envelope. I believe she took it to the bank.

I know she keeps a safe deposit box. Do you think the envelope had something to do with the man looking for me?"

"Mebbe. If your father was dying, he may have left you something. People get sentimental that way." Reinhart shrugged. "I'll ask around. See if I can find the lawyer. He's probably from Omaha. Can't be that hard to find. Only your mother can answer that question."

Her expression hardened. "I see."

Caleb's heart ached for her. "You told us about Anna's father. Did you discover anything about the shooter?"

At least they finally knew what had sparked the detective's interest in the beginning, though they were no closer to finding the shooter.

"That's the thing about this job. Things ain't always the way you think. You gotta be ready. You can't force the pieces to fit. A puzzle doesn't work that way."

Reinhart reached for his cigar and pinched it between his teeth, then took a long draw. He kicked back in his chair and blew the smoke toward the ceiling.

What had the detective said before…if you give people a puzzle, they'll fill in the blanks by themselves? Reinhart could fill in his own puzzle.

"Strange thing, families," the detective said. "They can be the making of a man, or they can be his destruction. Loyalty is just a step away from delusion."

"That's an odd thing to say."

"Just something I've been thinking about lately. See, all of my cases are about finding someone. Most of my cases are about finding someone who doesn't want to be found. That's the thing, see, everybody is hiding from something. From the past, from the future, from themselves. Everybody is hiding something."

The detective leaned forward and replaced his cigar in the tray, then tipped back in his chair and threaded his hands behind his head. "You're leaving Kansas City. That's good. When Miss Bishop disappears, he'll move. That's when I'll catch him."

"Then I guess you've got some work ahead of you."

Though it galled him, Caleb needed the detective. He couldn't stay in Kansas City any longer, and he couldn't leave without ensuring someone was looking for the shooter. The police had already lost interest, and his dependence on the man rankled. Needing someone's help and liking it were two different things. Reinhart already knew more about Anna than Caleb did.

"I'll find him. Mark my words." Reinhart tapped the ashes from the end of his cigar onto the mountainous pile, spilling some on the marble surface.

Anna stood and touched her temple, her gaze distracted. "Catch him. I'll be in my room if you need me."

Caleb stood and reached for her, then let his hand fall. She'd revealed something very personal. He doubted she wanted more of her past aired out before the detective. Pride held her back straight. If she felt humiliation or sorrow, she didn't show it either. A week together and he was no closer to reading her than that first, eventful day.

Sometimes he thought he knew her, then she surprised him. He was always guessing around. The feeling left him edgy and off balance. Lamps flickered along the corridor, throwing her shadow into relief. Her steps never faltered, her back never stooped. She was a proud woman. Proud and independent.

Having grown up around a large and boisterous family, he was finally catching a glimpse into Anna's world. How lonely her life must have been. Nothing in the memories she'd shared hinted at lightness or frivolity.

She was skittish of affection, reaching out and pulling back at the same time, confused by her own needs. There was nothing weak about seeking comfort. He doubted Anna shared his thoughts. Especially considering her past had been exposed before the detective. Perhaps his blunt attitude had been for the best. He'd inadvertently given her the upper hand. She had taken the news with grace and dignity, denying Reinhart a reaction.

As she reached her door, the guard stationed beside it stood and let her into her room.

Behind him, Reinhart grunted. "You be careful with that Miss Bishop. She ain't for the likes of us."

Caleb set his jaw. "Take the job or don't."

Anna hadn't given the man a reaction; neither would Caleb.

"Women like that. Getting ideas in their heads." Reinhart puffed the tip of his cigar into a cherry-red flame. "Next thing you know they'll be slugging whiskey and swearing. No good can come of that. It's men that should be in charge."

"Your ignorance has me doubting your ability." Caleb fisted his hands and rested his knuckles on the back of the tufted chair. "You want me to take my money and leave? Or do you want to keep your opinions to yourself?"

Reinhart's remarks came from a place of fear. The man's argument didn't fit the fight the suffragists had undertaken. How did the desire to vote and control one's destiny translate into trousers and swearing? What did any of that matter, anyway? How did one suffragist threaten Reinhart?

The detective chuckled, but the fine shine of sweat visible beneath his thinning hair belied his good humor. With a sudden burst of insight Caleb realized he wanted the case. Mr. Reinhart enjoyed a puzzle. He also liked money.

Reinhart mopped his brow with a dingy handkerchief. "Fair enough. But never say I didn't warn you."

His assistance, along with whatever meager inquiries the police made, were the best options Caleb had without remaining in Kansas City, and he'd already been gone from home too long. Reinhart might be a confirmed woman-hater, but according to the inquiries Caleb had made, he was one of Pinkerton's best detectives. He'd gotten his teeth sunk into a puzzle, and he wouldn't quit until it was solved. Of that Caleb was certain.

"You know where to find me," he said. "Send word if you have news."

Reinhart was right about one thing. Anna wasn't for the likes of him. With each day that passed she grew stronger, and as she regained her strength, she pulled further away from him. There'd be no more storytelling, of that he was certain.

Which left him wrenched in two separate directions. He'd prayed for her life, for her continued health. His prayers had been answered.

He'd lectured Anna on trusting in God's plan, and no part of their separate lives meshed. There was no common ground to build on. They were opposite people moving in opposite directions.

No outcome he envisioned ended with them together. Turned out swallowing his own advice was a bitter pill. Worse yet, he doubted the medicine would help. With each day that passed, he feared he was growing too far gone.

He'd double his resolution from here on out. He wasn't letting his heart take the upper hand. Even if she did have the most beautiful blue eyes he'd ever seen. All those years ago he'd thought Mary Louise the prettiest girl in the county. She was a pale comparison to Anna.

With sudden insight he realized the difference wasn't in their features, the difference was in their hearts. When Mary Louise smiled all those years ago, she'd done it for a calculated response. A flirt or a giggle. When Anna smiled, her whole heart shone through her eyes.

From here on out, he was tripling his effort. Especially since he couldn't rest until he checked on her.

This time he'd keep his resolve.

He'd keep his resolve after he took care of one last little problem.

With Anna gone, he decided on a less diplomatic way of dealing with the detective.

Reinhart stood, and Caleb shoved him against the wall, his elbow holding the man's shoulder, his forearm pressing against the detective's throat. "I don't like the way you do business."

His pupils dilated, Reinhart smacked his lips.

Caleb pressed in slightly, his jaw set. "The next time we meet, I'll expect you to use your manners."

"S-sure," the detective stuttered.

"Then we understand each other?"

His bluster gone, the detective raised his hands in supplication. "Y-yes."

Caleb released his hold and turned away. He strode down the corridor, tugging his sleeves over his wrists. "Good."

Chapter Nine

Anna took the seat by the window and waited. He'd come. Of course he'd come. Caleb had seen through her façade. He'd seen her distress. She'd only known him a week, and she knew he'd check on her.

At least he hadn't looked at her as Miss Spence had looked at her all those years ago, with a curious mixture of pity and disgust. Her parentage wasn't her fault, why should she be blamed? More often than not, she was. As though she had any choice in the matter.

Much to her disgust, there was a very provincial side to her. A side that envied regular families who did regular things and had children that were only expected to be ordinary. Families that were building a life together instead of a legacy for the ages.

A knock sounded not fifteen minutes later. She didn't even ask, only stood and opened the door.

He glanced toward the empty chair. "Is Mrs. Franklin here?"

"She's home, packing her things."

There was another relationship she'd grown far too dependent upon. Why hadn't she refused Izetta's offer? What was she thinking, retiring to the country with someone she'd only known a week? Once again she blamed the false intimacy of the situation. They'd all been through something harrowing. They'd been thrown together under traumatic circumstances, stripping away all the polite maneuverings taken over time in normal friendships. She'd only known the widow a short time, and yet their days together had been a lifetime.

"Would you like me to stay?" Caleb asked. "To call for her? I'll sit with you. I know the detective's revelations came as a shock to you."

"There's no need." Anna glanced toward the curtained windows of her room. She'd grown heartily tired of pulled shades and perpetual twilight.

Her days had lost their rhythm, and she desperately craved something normal. A change in the routine. Anything but the endless monotony of sitting around and waiting for another attempt on her life. "It's not as though I knew the man. I suppose I always assumed he was dead. Life was easier that way."

What must Caleb think of her? A woman who didn't even know the name of her own father. She might have passed him on the street a thousand times and never known the difference. The idea was odd, unsettling. She'd pushed it to the back of her mind and piled a thousand excuses on the mere idea of him.

He didn't matter. She was fine without him. Thousands of girls had lost their fathers during the war. All of the lectures her mother had given came rushing back. But she was different from those other girls. They knew the names of their fathers, they had stories, they had love. Without even a name to attach to her father, she'd kept even the idea of him distant.

Finally hearing his name had thrust him back into her life, into her thoughts. He might be dead, but the feelings lingered. All the thoughts she'd shoved aside and buried rose once more to the surface. There'd been too much upheaval in her life recently. Old memories broke through all the walls she'd erected.

Her mind drifted back over the years. "When I was a little girl, I thought of him all the time. Children are not always kind to one another, and everyone knew my parents were never married. They knew I didn't have a father. Not a father who was in my life, anyway. I imagined he was a ship's captain. Sometimes I pictured him as a pirate. Not very original, I know, but those professions seemed very romantic, and they explained all the questions a child knows to ask."

"His absence must have been difficult for you."

"It's odd. I never thought he mattered much to me. I'd been told often enough he didn't. He didn't matter until that one brief moment when I realized he was looking for me. At that moment he mattered very much."

"Reinhart is an idiot." Caleb spoke harshly.

She was grateful for his defense of her, but there was no need.

"I'm glad he was tactless. It's easier to be angry than sad. I've been one or the other for quite some time. I suppose as children there's always a part of us that believes we've done something, that it's our fault they're gone. I thought if I'd been a boy, he might have stayed. We might have been a family."

"You don't believe that now?" His green eyes shimmered with sympathy.

She didn't need his pity. "Of course not. I'm all grown-up now."

She'd shoved her father into a darkened corner of her soul, and someone had kicked open the door. There was no shutting out the pain, and somehow that realization was worse. She'd kicked open the door of an empty room.

"We'll find out what we can about him," Caleb said. "Find out why he was looking for you."

"She knew he was looking for me." Anna's words were barely a whisper. "Why didn't my mother say anything?"

Her thoughts should not have been voiced. She had a few theories, although none of them were suitable for sharing quite yet. The news was too raw, too immediate. She needed time. She needed distance.

Caleb kept his vigil near the door. Seeking a chance for escape, no doubt. She smothered a sigh. Even if he wanted to, he wouldn't leave her alone. He'd stay even if remaining made him uncomfortable. Because staying was the right thing to do, and Mr. McCoy always did the right thing. She mustn't read anything deeper into his actions.

"Perhaps she was protecting you," he said.

Anna scoffed. "If you knew Victoria Bishop, you'd know what a preposterous suggestion that is. She manages both her personal and professional life by rigid standards. She had a reason. She always has a reason. My middle name is Ryan. At least she left me a clue."

"Your mother must be quite an imposing woman," he said, then held up his hands. "I'm sorry. I shouldn't have said that."

"No, you're right." He'd hit upon the truth. The man

was far too insightful "There is no one quite like Victoria. I remember sitting on the footstool in her room, watching her dress for meetings. I never saw her hurry. Not ever. And she didn't tolerate people who were tardy. Once, I had a nanny who was always late. It was such a shock, all that running around and panic. The nanny did not last long."

Dr. Smith was correct, Caleb's talents were wasted on animals. He inspired her confidence, and she sensed he'd never betray her trust. He'd have made an excellent country doctor, moving from household to household, listening to his patient's woes with that steady, compassionate gaze. Keeping their secrets and sharing their sorrows.

"That must have been difficult," he said.

"I grew accustomed to the changes. Life was very busy for my mother. She was always needed. There were so many people who wanted her time. Looking back, I've often thought I was raised by everybody and nobody at the same time." He must think her a melancholy fool. She forced a smile. "I make my childhood sound very lonely. It wasn't. Not at all. There were always people around."

"Any children?"

There he went again, asking the simplest questions and invoking the most complicated answers.

"Sometimes, yes. Despite what the newspapers would have you believe, many suffragists are married women. I had plenty of children to play with. I told you, there was nothing solitary about my upbringing."

"A person can feel most isolated in a crowd."

Her eyes burned and she blinked rapidly. "I'm tired lately. Healing is much more exhausting than I expected." She rubbed a hand over her forehead. "I think I overestimated my stamina."

Life had suddenly lost its sense of urgency. Away from the cause, away from the correspondence and the meetings and the demands, life had slowed. Without the bustle of activity, she'd lost track of her routine. Her days had lost their meaning. Who was she, if she wasn't Victoria Bishop's daughter?

She'd built a pedestal of activities and proudly stood at the top. Her support had crumbled, leaving her vulnerable and exposed. In St. Louis, fighting for the vote was immediate and crucial. Away from the cause, women and girls went about their daily business, singularly unaware of the battle being waged in their honor.

"You've had a busy few days," Caleb said. "Rest. I'll make all the arrangements."

Despite her exhaustion, annoyance flared. "If someone orders me to rest once more I'm afraid I might scream. I'm quite able to take care of myself."

She didn't want rest. She wanted her energy back for fighting. She wanted to do something. She wanted to be something. Someone besides a victim.

"A strong person takes care of herself. A stronger person asks for help."

"Who said that? Some wise philosopher?"

"I did. Just now."

Anna laughed in spite of herself. "Then by all means, purchase my train tickets and make all of the arrangements. I'll finally prove to you what a strong person I am."

"You don't have to prove anything to anybody."

Anna reached for a rose dangling from a vase of flowers. The fragile petals broke free the instant she touched the stem, fluttering onto the floor. She'd been proving herself for as long as she could remember; there was no stopping now. Her mother was building a dynasty, and Anna was an integral part of that heritage. If she wasn't fighting for the greater good, then what was the point of her existence? No one raised outside the Bishop household understood the expectations heaped upon her, and there was no use explaining.

Little girls with fathers and mothers were ordinary. Anna was different, and that difference was extraordinary. Or so she'd been told. The childish explanation no longer soothed her adult heart.

She glanced at her packed trunk. "The wonders of transportation by train. We'll be in Cimarron Springs by suppertime. You must be relieved."

He must have been chafing at the bit to run as fast and as far as he could from her and the problems she dragged behind her like leaded weights.

"There is no feeling quite like the joy of coming home," he said. "You stopped there once when you met Jo. I know our little town is only a jumping-off place, a lunch rest on the way to somewhere better, but what do you remember about Cimarron Springs?"

Once he was home, she'd never see him again. There'd be no reason. A perfectly sensible outcome. Except lately she wasn't feeling quite as sensible as she used to.

"I don't remember anything. Not really." She caught herself and smiled. "That must sound insulting, but I travel through so many towns, they all blend together. My stay in Cimarron Springs was brief. I sent a telegram, and Jo was working that day. We've been friends since that moment."

"I hope—" he paused, as though struggling for words "—I hope when you see Cimarron Springs again, you like our town."

She plucked the now bare-stemmed rose from the vase. Whether or not she liked the town hardly mattered. She wasn't staying long, and both of them knew that. His words were only polite conversation, a way of passing an awkward moment.

"I'm sure I'll find your town quite lovely," she said.

Actually she hoped it was dreadful and smelly and filled with insufferable people. She didn't want to be drawn into his world any more than she already had.

Her life was in St. Louis. Everything she knew, everything she stood for was a lifetime away from Cimarron Springs. Gaining the vote for women was vital. Someone had to struggle for those who couldn't defend themselves.

Someone had to fight, and Anna had been chosen the moment she was born. Her mother lived as though victory was around the corner, a vote away, a state away, an amendment away. Anna had her doubts.

She often wondered if any one of them would live long enough to see the day when men and women were treated equally under the law. They'd made great strides, but there were more and bigger challenges ahead.

She never doubted her importance to the cause. In one afternoon in Kansas City, she'd spoken before hundreds of people. How many people could she influence in Cimarron Springs? A handful at best.

Susan Anthony, Elizabeth Stanton and so many others had given much of their lives already, and Anna was privileged to have known them. She needed grand gestures for a grand cause.

Caleb cleared his throat, and Anna realized he'd been trying to gain her attention. "What were you thinking about so intently?" he asked.

"I was wondering how history will remember any of us, or if we'll even be remembered at all."

"That is a question for the ages."

She was changing, losing track of herself, and she desperately wanted her purpose back. Only one thing was certain, her purpose was not in Cimarron Springs, and they both knew it.

Chapter Ten

Cimarron Springs was love at first sight. Well, love at *second* sight, she hastily amended. She'd made that brief stop before.

Leaning heavily on the railing, Anna exited the train and glanced around the crowded platform. Clouds had covered the afternoon sun, chilling the air. The depot sat at the far end of town, framed between the rows of buildings lining either side of Main Street.

False fronts advertised the mercantile, the haberdashery, a blacksmith shop. All of the usual trappings of a small town. Picturesque covered boardwalks, the railings and eves painted a crisp white, contained the hustle of shoppers taking advantage of the temperate fall weather.

She'd stopped here a year ago and hadn't spared a glance at Main Street. She'd been in a hurry, her head down. She'd sent her telegram, and Jo had struck up a conversation. All too soon the train whistle had blown, and she'd boarded once again, never looking back.

This time she drank in the scene, inhaling the scent

of baking bread and admiring the yellowed leaves of the cottonwood trees.

She'd been living with a vague sense of unease and fear for the past week, holed up in her guarded room. Having her first taste of freedom in a week was delightful.

Izetta surveyed the platform and touched Anna's arm. "I'm going to freshen up. Every time I travel by train I feel as though I'm covered in soot by the end of the journey."

"I'll wait here," Anna said, dreading another step. "Looks as though the porters are already unloading the baggage car."

She'd thought her wound mostly healed. The constant sway of the train had exacerbated her injury, and the incessant ache had become a frustrating nuisance.

A tall man separated from the crowd, and Jo dashed around her. She launched herself at the man, and he caught her easily. Her husband, Anna hoped.

Jo stood on her tiptoes and bussed his cheek, flipping off his hat in the process. The gentleman returned her enthusiastic embrace. Unused to such boisterous displays of affection, Anna's cheeks warmed, and she glanced away. Jo pulled back and led her husband toward Anna. Without pausing in his stride, he reached down and snatched his missing hat.

"I've brought us a visitor," Jo said. "This is Miss Anna. Anna, this is my husband, Garrett Cain. Most folks around here just call him Marshal Cain."

The marshal offered a warm smile. "I realize this is the first time we've met in person, but I feel as though I know you from Jo's description."

Anna held out her hand, and he clasped it, his palm

calloused, his handshake firm but not brutal. "A pleasure to meet you, Marshal."

Mr. Cain reminded her a bit of Caleb. They were both
tall and dark-haired, but that's where the similarities
ended. Jo's husband appeared older, more jaded by time.
His features were more angular and his eyes dark and
guarded, not nearly as striking as Caleb's green eyes.

He wore a silver star stamped with the word *Marshal*.

Caleb followed her gaze and winked, both of them
remembering his childhood love of tin stars. Another
gentleman tugged on Caleb's sleeve, and Anna turned
her attention back to the marshal.

Though Jo's husband was talking with her, Anna
sensed that his focus remained on his wife. He held
his arm wrapped around her waist, his fingers resting
on her hip. The gesture was protective and sweet. If he
resented Anna's appearance in his life, he hadn't let
on, though she sensed a hint of wariness in his gaze.

Anna pressed her hand against her bandaged side.
"I hope you don't mind a bit of upheaval on such short
notice."

"Not at all. There's always room for one more in Cimarron Springs," the marshal said.

"Where are the children?" Jo demanded. "Where are
Jocelyn and Shawn? Where's Cora?"

"Coming along shortly. David is showing them his
new horse."

"JoBeth!" a voice called. "There you are."

A stout woman charged ahead and elbowed the marshal aside, grasping Jo's shoulders. "You had me worried sick."

"I'm fine, Ma." Jo lifted her eyes heavenward. "You
didn't have to meet me at the train station."

"Of course I did. I had to make certain you were well with my own two eyes. You can never trust the menfolk with details. The newspapers aren't much better either. *The Kansas Post* only said there'd been a disturbance at the rally. As though shooting someone was a disturbance. What's wrong with the newspapers these days, do you suppose?"

"Ma." Jo leaned closer. "Remember what Garrett told you?"

"Oh, right. Yes. Well. All's well that ends well. I'm only glad you weren't injured in the *disturbance*. Your Pa thinks they didn't have more details because they were worried there'd be too much sympathy for the cause." She huffed. "They certainly gave enough space for the editorials opposed to the woman's vote."

"As you can see, I'm no worse for wear." Jo splayed her arms as proof. "I'm fit as a fiddle."

Jo's mother looked her up and down, a deep wrinkle between her brows, presumably deciding for herself whether or not her daughter was the worse for wear.

Jo pulled away and indicated Anna. "This is Anna. Miss Ryan."

Mrs. McCoy started. "We've left the poor thing standing while you and I chatter." She hooked her arm through Anna's and tugged her toward a narrow bench. "Have a seat. I can't tell you how exciting it is having a celebrity in town."

"Ma," Jo pitched her voice in a warning. "I just reminded you."

"Yes, but your other poor…friend. That poor Miss Bishop person." Mrs. McCoy widened her eyes at Anna, demonstrating how well she was holding to the deception. "A single injury was reported. That's all the newspapers said. As though a woman nearly dying was no more important than the weather."

Anna touched her side. She'd been curious about the lack of interest in her injury, and yet she'd never considered the paper had failed to report more extensively on the shooting. Of all the outcomes she'd anticipated, she hadn't expected this one. They'd trivialized her. They'd relegated her to the last page alongside the news of robberies and quilt patterns.

A single injury was reported.

She'd been shot, for goodness' sake. There was a murderer on the loose. Well, an attempted murderer. Certainly that was cause for concern. While she'd never enjoyed the notoriety of her cause, the incident warranted more than a few lines. Without a single mention of the violence she'd experienced, they'd marginalized the cause, they'd marginalized her injury. They'd marginalized *her.*

"At least everyone is safe." Mrs. McCoy plunked down beside Anna and patted her hand. "After such an experience, are you certain you want to stay in that tiny little cottage Mr. Stuart calls a house? He hasn't done a lick of work on it since his mother-in-law passed away." She lowered her voice. "His mother-in-law lived there alone until she died. Not that Mr. Stuart didn't like his mother-in-law, he just liked her better when they weren't living beneath the same roof."

Anna searched for the question in Mrs. McCoy's rapid-fire speech. "We'll be fine. Mrs. Franklin and I are quite looking forward to fixing up the place."

Her suspicions were correct. Her secret was as good as out. How many more "slips" from Mrs. McCoy before the whole town knew she was staying here? Though she'd been shocked by the lack of newspaper coverage at first, the lack of interest worked in her favor. At least the papers hadn't picked up the news, and for that Anna was grateful. If the reporters would rather suppress her shooting than risk sympathy for the Right to Vote movement, all the better for her.

"Let's hope your enthusiasm doesn't wane after you've seen the place," Mrs. McCoy said. "It's quite a job. I wish I'd known sooner. I'd have gotten the ladies together and cleaned the house for you."

"No, no. You mustn't put yourself out. We're quite capable of caring for ourselves."

"Of course you are! We simply want to leave you with a good impression of our little town. What do you think so far?"

"Ma?" Jo planted her hands on her hips. "How can she think anything? She's only seen the train depot."

"She's had her first impression. Didn't you, dear? First impressions are important."

"Your town is absolutely lovely."

The exact opposite of what she'd been hoping for when she'd decided on her stay in Cimarron Springs.

Mrs. McCoy flashed a triumphant smile at her daughter. "*Lovely* is an excellent first impression. You'll be coming for supper tonight, won't you?"

"Well, I, uh, I hadn't thought that far ahead."

Although the idea of meeting more of Caleb's family intrigued her. There was Jo and three other brothers. She was interested in how such a large family worked.

"Then it's settled. You're a guest. Don't bring anything. We sit for dinner at six."

"All right," Anna replied.

She hadn't realized she'd accepted the invitation, but it was too late now.

Mrs. McCoy stood and glanced around. "Jo, have you seen your father?"

"Not in the last five minutes since I stepped off the train," Jo said, clearly exasperated.

"If you do, tell him I've stopped by the mercantile. Picking up a housewarming gift. We want you to feel welcome."

"That's very kind of you."

Caleb had finished his conversation and faced his mother. She grabbed him in a quick, fierce hug. "I'm so glad the three of you are home and safe." She glanced over her shoulder. "Anna, if I can call you Anna, don't forget to invite your friend for supper, as well."

"I'll tell Mrs. Franklin."

"Mrs. Franklin. That's an easy name for remembering." Mrs. McCoy released her son and patted the marshal's cheek. "I won't expect you and Jo. You two need some time alone after being apart. I will see you on Sunday, though, right?"

"Wouldn't miss your fried chicken for the world," the marshal said.

Mrs. McCoy waved over her shoulder and set off down the street, her pace clipped.

Caleb tossed Anna an apologetic smile. "I hope you don't mind. She won't be satisfied until she knows we're well fed."

"Her concern is quite endearing."

"Don't worry. You get used to it after a while."

Anna stifled any comparisons. Her own mother had never been affectionate, and she had never picked up Anna at the train station. A waste of time when there was important work to be done. Victoria Bishop had far more vital tasks than meeting her daughter at a train station. Anna was far too independent to care. She was a grown woman, for goodness' sake.

Her mother simply had a different way of showing her love.

Jo caught sight of something in the distance and clapped her hands. "There they are!"

She knelt and held open her arms, and two toddlers and her oldest child rushed into them. Jo made a great show of collapsing beneath the weight of the three squirming children and smothered them with kisses. Anna's heart ached a bit. This was exactly the sort of scene she'd pictured reading Jo's letters. The yearnings in her chest were exactly what she'd been avoiding.

No, that wasn't right. She enjoyed her life. She relished fighting for something larger than herself. She knew her place in the scheme of things. She had the honor of working with women who'd carved a place in history for themselves. She had the luxury of joining a legacy already in process. Small gestures were wasted when Anna had no doubt Susan and Elizabeth would be heralded long after they were gone.

After much giggling, Jo rose and clasped hands in a row and towed them toward Anna.

"I have someone very special I'd like you to meet," Jo said. "This is Miss Anna."

A lovely little girl, no more than four years old, offered a quick bob of her dark head. "Hello, Miss Anna. I'm four. My name is Jocelyn."

"That's a very pretty name."

Though young, Jocelyn enunciated each word slowly and carefully. She was a petite version of her mother with two dark braids slung over her shoulders and expressive green eyes.

Instantly charmed, Anna smiled. "It's nice to meet you, Jocelyn. That's a very unusual name."

"It was my great-grandpa's name."

"Well I think it's a very bold name for a girl."

The younger child, a blue-eyed boy with a shock of dark hair, stuck his pudgy fist in his mouth.

Jo patted his head. "This is Shawn. He's two. He doesn't talk very much."

"Horse!" Shawn pointed a dimpled finger toward the street. "Horse."

Jo hooked him beneath the arms and hoisted him onto her hip. "He's mad about horses these days."

The oldest girl, who appeared to be about ten or twelve, was the last to speak. She had blond hair and blue eyes, and she was definitely not the natural child of the dark-haired parents standing before her. Though Garrett's niece, Jo spoke warmly of Cora as her "oldest child." More recently Jo had fretted that Cora was taking on too much responsibility for the younger two children, and Jo worried Cora was missing out on her own childhood. Seeing the obvious affection surrounding the family, Anna didn't think there was much to fret about in that regard.

Cora was simply mature for her age, a product of losing her parents young, no doubt. Grief had a way of aging people, even children.

"I'm Cora," the girl said.

"I'm pleased to meet you, Cora."

The marshal took his niece's hand. She smiled up at him, her face adoring. "Can we have ice cream?" she asked.

Jocelyn circled around to his opposite side and took his free hand. "I want ice cream, as well."

"First we have to find your mother's trunk," he said. "Then we'll have lunch. Then ice cream."

Jocelyn resisted her father's change in direction, digging in her heels. "Are you eating with us, Miss Anna?"

"That would be nice," she said, unable to recall the last time she'd eaten. The whole day was a blur. "I'm famished."

"Me, too," Jo said. "We'll find the trunks and stow them in the telegraph office while we eat. I'll sit with you while Garrett gets the trunks," Jo continued, though she gazed longingly at her husband. "I can't leave you alone, and Caleb can't escape his conversation. It's Mr. Patterson. He can talk the ears off a whole field of corn."

"You two go," Anna replied. Clearly husband and wife had missed each other, and Anna didn't need tending. "I'll wait here. I could use the rest."

A lie. Since her initial discomfort from traveling had passed, she'd rather do anything but rest. She wanted a hot meal and brisk walk after her time on the train, but she also sensed the couple needed time together.

Marshal Cain linked his free hand with his wife's, and together they meandered toward the pile of luggage the porter had retrieved from the train. Jo pressed her forehead against his shoulder, and Anna turned away. The gesture was too personal, too heartfelt.

She caught Caleb's gaze and he leaned away from Mr. Patterson. His inattention didn't appear to bother the man as he continued speaking.

Caleb rolled his eyes, clearly unmoved by the tender moment. "Nearly four years they've been married and you'd think it was yesterday."

The wistful tone of his voice was at odds with his exasperated expression.

He shook hands with Mr. Patterson and tipped his hat. "I'll get back to you on that."

The man looked as though he wanted to prolong the conversation, but Caleb didn't give him the chance, smoothly turning away without being outright rude.

"Stay here," he said, facing Anna. "I'll help Garrett with the luggage while Mrs. Franklin is freshening up."

Anna sagged. "I miss my good health. Only a moment ago I was ready for a long walk after sitting for so long." She collapsed back onto the bench with a weary grin. "But I've changed my mind. I don't know how sitting on a train doing nothing could have exhausted me so."

These swings in her health were annoying at best, debilitating at worst.

"You're healing. It takes time."

"I'd argue with you, but I'm far too drained."

He flashed another of his grins. The kind that curled her toes and sent a flutter through her belly. She rubbed a hand over her eyes. Exhaustion was taking its toll.

She took the opportunity to study the crowd. People raised their voices to be heard over each other. Someone brushed against her skirts. Sitting up, she caught the gaze of a gentleman standing near the train. He was plainly dressed in a dark suit and hat, with nothing to distinguish him from the other men milling about. Like any other banker or businessman, he naturally blended into the crowd. He surveyed the people around him, his gaze intense, as though he was searching for someone.

A shiver of apprehension raised gooseflesh on her arms. She might be anonymous, but so was the person who'd made an attempt on her life. Anybody could have shot her. Any one of these people jamming onto the platform.

Anna glanced around, searching for either Jo or Caleb. Two men hoisted an enormous steamer trunk between them and blocked her view of the spot where Caleb was giving instructions to the porter. Jo and her family had disappeared into the cramped shop attached to the depot. The telegraph office, she presumed.

The man near the train kept his steady vigil of the crowd. He lifted his pocket watch and checked the time. A young woman in a smart burgundy dress, her hair a shade of blond that defied nature, approached him and touched his sleeve. The man grinned and stuck out his elbow. Smiling in greeting, the woman hooked her hand over his bent arm.

Anna blinked.

Good gracious. The gentleman was simply waiting for his companion, and yet she'd read something sinister into his innocent actions.

Chagrined, she realized he'd been looking behind her, and yet she'd been certain he was looking *at* her. Studying her.

Her heart thudded against her ribs, and she rubbed her damp palms against her skirts. As the passengers departed for the extended break, the platform grew crowded. Footsteps shuffled, vibrating the bench, dozens of conversations melded together in boisterous confusion.

A woman in a violet dress stomped on her foot and muttered an apology. Anna's breath came in short gasps, and her head spun. Tears sprang behind her eyes, and she pressed a fist against her mouth. There were people everywhere. Closing in, brushing against her, looking at her. She wanted to run, but her legs remained paralyzed.

She'd been shot in a public square during a speech. Why was a crowded platform any different? What if the killer fired into the crowd? With her side stitched and her stamina gone, she'd never survive another stampede like the one on the day of the rally. And where would she run? A hysterical giggle bubbled in the back of her throat. Her gaze darted toward the train and then toward the street. She couldn't breathe.

A violent shudder traveled all the way down the length of her body. Clamping shut her jaw, she fought to regain control of her shaking. Despite her efforts, the shivering continued. She wrapped her arms around her middle, her teeth chattering. Nothing helped.

She had to escape.

Leaping from her seat, she clawed at the ribbons of her bonnet, desperate to escape the tunneled vision. She lurched away from the squeeze of bodies. A hand touched her shoulder, and she jerked away.

"Anna," a familiar, soothing voice said close to her ear. "It's all right. Just take a deep breath and hold on to my arm."

Her vision swimming, Anna clutched his sleeve and stared into Caleb's vivid green eyes. "I can't breathe."

She was suffocating. The edges of her vision turned hazy. In another moment she feared she'd faint dead away before the crowd of people. Her heart would hammer right out of her chest.

"You can breathe. You can. Relax."

His fingers worked the ribbons of her bonnet, brushing against her neck. He flipped back the brim, and the hat fell down her back, anchored by the loose ties at her neck.

"You're not trying." He sucked in a breath, and she automatically mimicked his movements.

"That's it," he said. "Just keep breathing."

As the air filled her lungs, her vision focused and her heartbeat calmed. He kept his fingers wrapped around her forearm for support. The voices swirling near her came into focus. She wasn't suffocating. She wasn't dying. The odd interlude had left her disoriented and exhausted.

With a muffled sniff she pressed her free hand against her forehead, unable to meet his eyes.

What must he think of her? "I don't know what's happening to me."

"It's anxiety." His deep timbered voice was soothing and free of censure. "To be expected, considering what happened to you."

Anna tipped back her head and chanced a peek at his face. "I don't know what's wrong with me. All at once I felt as though everyone was looking at me, talking about me. I knew it was silly, but I couldn't stop the panic."

"It's a common reaction," Caleb said after a long pause. A certain hesitancy in his voice sharpened her attention. "Did you feel as though your heart was about to leap out of your chest?"

"That's exactly right," she said, blinking in astonishment. "How did you know?"

Caleb considered the consequences of admitting the truth and tossed his pride aside. "It's happened to me before."

"Really?"

"I don't like cities." He sighed. "I avoid closed-in spaces. When I was growing up, everyone else was fascinated by the caves along Hackberry Creek. Especially after it turned out we had a real live outlaw hiding his loot in those caves. My brothers sold tours for years after that. I never went along."

"It's a good thing you became a veterinarian instead of a bank robber. You'd have no place to hide your ill-gotten gains."

"I'm not much good at giving cave tours either."

"I'm glad you found your calling."

A bittersweet note crept into her voice.

He tilted his head. "As have you. We both found our place."

Her expression turned wistful. "Yes."

There was no conviction behind the word. He'd seen her fire, though. He'd seen her on the stage. From Jo's letters and the stories he'd read in the newspapers, he knew the power she wielded in the suffragist movement. She had a natural presence that drew people toward her. She reminded him of the fireflies he'd captured as a child, beguiled by their light. Fireflies died in captivity.

That's what they'd done by bringing her out here, they'd placed her in a jar for safekeeping. He knew well enough that safety didn't last long before it became smothering. She'd been pacing her hotel like a caged animal. He had no doubt she'd soon find the town oppressive.

"Caleb McCoy," a voice called. "Glad to see you're back in town."

The interruption was like a frigid dunk in the rain barrel. Caleb and Anna sprang apart. Hiding his annoyance, Caleb spun around and discovered the mercantile owner's wife from Cimarron Springs.

"Mrs. Stuart." Caleb hid his scowl. "How are you?"

Probably filled with gossip. The woman delighted in spreading the "news" of the town.

He'd much rather finish his conversation with Anna. There were things about her that none of them understood. Even Jo, who probably knew Anna better than anyone, didn't have all the pieces. Had they been making false assumptions, making the mistake Reinhart had warned them about, filling in the missing pieces of the puzzle? Forcing the edges together to make a whole?

"Good to see you, Caleb," Mrs. Stuart said coyly. "I hear congratulations are in order."

"Congratulations?"

"Well, of course you know my sister and her husband live in Kansas City. When I heard what happened at the rally, and then your stay was extended, well, I simply had to ask her to check on you." She leaned closer. "All this time I thought you were still sweet on Mary Louise when you'd transferred your affections elsewhere."

Anna was staring at him as though he'd grown a second head.

"I'm sorry," Caleb said. "I don't follow."

What was the woman blabbering about?"

"You know." She gave an exaggerated wink.

Anna had taken the opportunity to replace her bonnet, securing the ribbons beneath her ear with a large bow. He found the bonnet as annoying as she did, especially since the rounded brim blocked his view of her expression. He'd sensed her panic even before he'd seen her face. He was attuned to her, though he didn't know quite how or why.

After everything she'd been through in the past week, he was surprised she hadn't had a lapse sooner. She'd been injured in a city far from home, far from everything and everyone she knew. They were no closer to catching the man who'd shot her than they were the day of the rally. Even with the Pinkerton detective, Caleb was skeptical of finding the man before he tried again.

He moved nearer to Anna. They'd brought her back here for her safety.

A duty he took seriously. "What were you saying?"

Mrs. Stuart elbowed him. "You know."

"No, I do not know."

The day had started too early and gone on too long. He was grateful to be home at last. While he wanted Anna settled, he also wanted to check on his house and make his rounds. There'd be other needs, as well. Anything anyone had put off in his absence would gain a new urgency now that he'd returned.

Mrs. Stuart crossed her arms over her chest and opened her mouth to speak. The two men carrying the trunk grimaced and walked between them. Whatever had been packed must have been heavy. The two burly men had unloaded an entire stack of baggage without incident.

One of the men muttered. "Biscuits and beans, what's she got in this thing—rocks?"

"Bricks more like it," the second man replied.

The first man caught his toe on an uneven footing. He lurched forward, and his hand slipped. The trunk toppled to one side. The second man's arms twisted beneath the teetering weight. He released his hold and sprang away. The trunk crashed to the ground, and the top flipped open.

Two things happened at once.

Mrs. Stuart said, "Your engagement, of course. I know all about it."

And a limp, pale hand flopped out of the overturned trunk.

Chapter Eleven

Anna blinked and looked again. Caleb knelt before her, blocking her from the grizzly sight.

He chafed her cold fingers between his. "It's all right," he said. "Don't look."

"I couldn't look if I wanted."

A crowd of people had quickly circled the trunk, pointing and gesturing.

Caleb glanced over his shoulder and recognition lit up his face. "Here comes Tony. You'll like her. She must be going on seventeen or eighteen now. She reminds me of Jo. You'll see why once you meet her. Smart as a whip and unshakable. She's good with animals, too."

A young girl marched across the platform toward them. The resemblance to Jo was uncanny, although Tony was much taller and more angular. She wore trousers and suspenders over a button-up chambray shirt. As she approached, Anna noted her eyes were blue, another difference between her and Jo. And yet her carriage, the way she cut a path through the crowd without saying a word, reminded Anna of Jo's forthright manner.

The girl's hands were stuffed in her pockets, and

she bypassed them on her way toward the commotion. The crowd parted in her wake. Clearly Tony was a well-known character around town.

Upon reaching the trunk, Tony bent at the waist and tilted her head. "There's a dead fellow in there."

Marshal Cain jogged the distance from the telegraph office and gently moved the girl aside. "Thank you for the assessment, Tony. I'll take care of things from here on out."

Caleb waved the girl over. "Tony, this is Miss Anna. Can you sit with her a moment?"

"Sure. 'Cept she looks like she can sit alone fine enough."

Anna immediately liked the young girl. "You don't have to stay with me."

"Oh, I'm staying. I can see and hear everything from this spot. We've got the best view of the hullabaloo. Not much goes on around here. When something does happen, it's best to stay put and take in the show."

Well, at least Tony wasn't being forced on Anna as a companion. That thought had her feeling positively ancient.

Caleb chucked Tony on the shoulder. "Told you she was like Jo."

"It's a pleasure to meet you, Tony. I'm Anna."

Tony plunked down beside her, stretched out her legs, and crossed her ankles. "How do you suppose a dead man winds up in a trunk? Someone must have put him there."

Anna shivered. "Who would do such a thing?"

"The marshal will figure it out. He's smart."

Caleb surveyed the growing circle of curious spectators. "I'd best see if he needs any help."

"We'll be fine," Anna said, knowing he'd be concerned about leaving her alone.

If nothing else, the marshal needed help controlling the crowd.

Caleb crouched before her and tilted his head. "That is absolutely the most atrocious bonnet I've ever seen. I feel as though I'm talking with the brim and not you."

"Once I unpack my things, I promise I'll burn it." Anna loosened the strings and flipped back the brim.

"That's better."

The wind whistled through the trees overhead, sending leaves drifting over them. Anna shivered. Caleb shrugged out of his coat and draped the heavy material over her shoulders.

"Do you want to sit inside?" he said. "You'll catch a chill on top of everything else."

Anna glanced up and realized the dead body wasn't the only spectacle attracting attention. More than one person stared at her and Caleb with open curiosity. Surely a town this large saw more than its fair share of strangers. Judging by the rapt interest, the two of them were as much of a curiosity as the dead body. They weren't in Kansas City anymore, and she'd do well to remember the distinction.

What had Mrs. Stuart been saying before the disruption? Anna recognized a gossip when she saw one. Someone had gotten engaged, and the news was obviously noteworthy. She'd ask Tony about it later. Right now they were creating a spectacle.

People around here knew the McCoys, they knew Caleb. "I'm fine. I was simply surprised. One does not expect a body to fall out of a trunk. Despite the circumstances, I'm enjoying the fresh air. I've been cooped up for days."

Caleb lifted one corner of his mouth in a wry grin. "How do you like small-town life so far?"

"It's rather more exciting than I had anticipated."

"Sit tight. I'll be right back."

After circling around the trunk, he stopped dead and met Anna's eyes over the lid. "He's familiar. I think I've seen him before."

"From where?" the marshal asked.

"Kansas City. I think. Can't say for certain."

Curious, Anna pushed off from the seat and sidled toward the men, carefully keeping the trunk positioned between her and the body.

Marshal Cain looked up. "You can't think of anything more specific?"

Caleb rubbed his chin. "No, except, well, there's something familiar about him. It's right on the edge of my memory. It'll come to me."

"What about you, ma'am?" The marshal caught her gaze. "Do you know this man?"

The stern edge in his voice sent a flush of color creeping up her neck. The marshal was no fool. Someone wanted her dead, and now he had a body sprawled before him.

Anna gingerly peered over the side. The dead man stared with unseeing eyes. In his thirties with dark hair and a full beard and mustache, he might have been anyone. Judging from the position of his body, he was neither tall nor short, fat nor thin.

Her stomach lurched, and she pressed a hand against her lips. "I've never seen him before."

Anna leaned forward once more, then jerked back. "Perhaps he was a guest at the hotel."

With so many people milling about, she might have passed him on the stairs or seen him in the lobby before the accident.

The marshal hoisted an eyebrow. "We'll need to talk."

"I assumed as much."

Anna returned to the bench where Tony waited. "Can you see Jo?" she asked.

Tony stood and tented her eyes with one hand. "Nope. She must be in the telegraph office. Probably staying put since she's got the young'uns with her."

"I'm sure that's best." Though there'd been nothing gruesome about the sight, seeing a dead man was unsettling. "Can you help keep an eye out for my traveling companion? Mrs. Franklin? She's tall and slender with gray hair, midsixties or so."

The press of curious townspeople closing in around the trunk and the dead man had left the platform a confusing mess.

"I'll keep a lookout." Tony remained standing, searching the faces of the crowd. "Nothing yet."

Curious about the younger girl, Anna asked, "Do you have any brothers and sisters, Tony?"

If Tony was an example, she wanted to meet the rest of the family.

"Sort of. I live on the Elder place with my uncle. He's the wrangler there. He's the cook, as well. Kind of. I think he cooks more than he wrangles these days. The Elders have two children of their own, and then there's Hazel and Preston."

"Hazel and Preston?"

"Hazel came on the cattle drive with us. Her and Sarah and Darcy. Sarah lives in town. She's sweet on Brahm McCoy. Darcy is Preston's mother. She's been staying with the Elders since Preston's pa died."

The names buzzed around her head like a swarm of bees. "Where did Hazel come from exactly?"

"The orphan train."

"I thought she was from the cattle drive."

"That, too."

"Tony, I might need a pen and paper to keep this all straight."

"Did you hear about the outlaw who hid his loot in a cave out by Hackberry Creek?" Tony asked.

"I heard that part of the story." At least they were once again in familiar territory.

"We live in his old homestead. John Elder is Jack's brother."

"And who is Jack?"

"Jack married the outlaw's widow," Tony said.

"Ah, yes, the infamous outlaw of Cimarron Springs. And they live in Paris."

"Texas."

A few of the confusing people in the jumbled explanation fell into place. "Then you live by Hackberry Creek."

"That's the place," Tony said. "Say, if you ever want to see the cave where he hid the loot, I can show you."

"That's a lovely offer, but I've heard the description enough I feel as though I've been there already." Anna couldn't help but think of Caleb and his fear of closed spaces. "Sounds like quite a place to live."

"Mr. Elder asked me to meet the train. He sells horses. Mostly to the cavalry. I guess word about his stock has got out. There's a fancy couple interested in starting a horse farm down South. They're looking to buy a whole passel of horses. Mr. Elder sent me on ahead to fetch them."

Tony tapped her chin and squinted at Anna. She glanced at the telegraph office and back. "Jo was exchanging letters with someone named Anna. Are you…." She searched the space around them and lowered her voice. "Are you one of them suffragists?"

By now Mrs. McCoy was probably at the haberdashery swearing the proprietor to secrecy about the recipient of her housewarming gift. Which meant that by this afternoon, the news of her identity would blanket the town like fluffy seeds from the cottonwood trees.

"I am," Anna admitted, knowing her "secret" was anything but. By tomorrow, the whole town would know. So much for remaining anonymous.

"What do you do? I mean, is it like a job being a suffragist?"

"It's more of a calling than a job."

This was precisely why coming to Cimarron Springs was not a waste. There was always an opportunity for changing someone's mind, for educating someone about the cause. She'd have another recruit, another person who spread the word. They needed all the soldiers they could muster. The cause depended upon the next generation. While her mother believed the fight was winding down, meaning they didn't need the younger generation, Anna disagreed. There was always another mountain ahead, always a need for fresh troops. Not every gesture need be grand.

"Then, how do you make money? What do you live on?"

"My mother is comfortably set, as am I."

Tony nodded sagely. "You mean she's rich."

Anna sighed. In for a penny, in for a pound. "She doesn't have to worry about money, that much is true. She gives speeches around the country and organizes other chapters. Right now she's working on a sixteenth amendment to the constitution. She's in Boston meeting with another chapter about a state amendment. Some people think we should target the states, others think we should target the federal government. Some members favor a militant approach, some members favor a peaceful approach. The chapters split over the direction of the movement after the War Between the States. It's a job all on its own keeping everyone together in a united front."

"Why didn't they put the women's vote on the fifteenth amendment?" Tony braced her hands on her knees. "You know, after the war when they gave the black man the vote? Never could figure that one out."

"The process is complicated," Anna continued more slowly. "The fifteenth amendment is another case where people didn't agree. I think most people felt that the black man deserved his day in court without anything else clouding the waters. But I was just a baby back then. I don't really know for certain. You'd have to ask one of the older members."

"Do you think Mrs. Franklin will know?"

"She might."

If someone had told Anna two weeks ago she'd be sitting on a train platform with a tomboy telling her the history of the suffrage movement while waiting for her escort to clear the crowds away from a dead body, she'd have laughed at the absurdity. Life had a way of changing in a flash.

"I'm glad we talked," Tony said. "This stuff is interesting."

"If you ever want to know more, you can stop by. We're staying in the old Stuart house."

Tony patted her knee. "I'm sure all those stories about how Mr. Stuart's mother-in-law haunts the place are false. You should be fine."

"Uh. I don't believe in ghosts."

"Neither do I. That thumping and chatter people hear at night, probably just bats or raccoons taking up residence. There's nothing a raccoon likes better than an abandoned building."

"Bats?" Anna said weakly.

Perhaps she should have been more open to Mrs. McCoy's offer of cleaning help. Small-town life was definitely more stimulating than she'd expected. The next time someone bemoaned the sluggish pace of country living, she'd tell them about her first hour in Cimarron Springs.

Word of the body had spread like wildfire. Everyone within a mile of town must have arrived by now. A string of wagons stretched down Main Street. Children fought their way past bustled skirts to get a better look, while scolding mothers held them back.

The storefronts along Main Street soon emptied, signs reading Closed had been flipped into view. A gentleman scooted past the bench, a bit of foam from the barber visible behind one ear.

The body was hoisted onto a makeshift litter, and a hastily salvaged sheet draped over the macabre sight, much to the disappointment of a group of school-aged children huddling on the fringes of the gathering.

The boys jostled for a better view, shoving one another forward and ducking back until Tony marched over, her hands on her hips. Without saying a word, her presence sent the boys scattering.

The town's deputy, Caleb's brother, David, was fetched.

With all the commotion, Anna had a clear opportunity to study the McCoy brother who'd gotten Caleb's job and his girl. They shared the distinctive McCoy coloring, dark hair and green eyes. They were both tall and broad shouldered. Yet there was something softer about David. A certain rounding of the chin and plumping of the cheeks that lent him a boyish quality, making him appear younger than his years.

He was wider around the middle, as well. It wasn't simply his physique that differentiated the brothers. David's gaze lacked the sharp inquisitiveness of his sibling's. Though she'd never met this Mary Louise, Anna found her taste lacking. Caleb was clearly the better choice of the two men.

Mrs. Franklin emerged from the depot, took in the scene, and marched toward the commotion. She glanced at the sheeted body and fought her way toward Anna.

"For goodness' sake, is there a dead body beneath that sheet?"

Anna threw her a resigned glance. "He fell out of a trunk."

"He was on the train? With us?"

"I believe so."

"I left for one moment. One moment. I'm afraid to turn my back on you. We're probably lucky the train didn't derail on the way here."

"Ma'am," the marshal said. "If you were on the train as well, would you like to take a look? See if you recognize the fellow?"

Izetta tugged on her collar. "If it will end this non-sense sooner, then absolutely."

The marshal lifted an edge of the covering and Izetta leaned closer, wrinkling her nose. "I don't know him. Although, I must say, there is something familiar about him."

Disappointment flickered across the marshal's face.

He searched the crowd milling about the platform and faced his deputy. "Let's have the passengers take a look. It'll make my job easier if we can figure out his identity."

Returning to the bench, Izetta wrapped her hand around Anna's shoulder. "This is shaping up to be a rather odd day." She leaned away, pulled a handker-chief from her reticule and pressed the embroidered fab-ric against her nose. "Excitement trails you, my dear."

"I don't know if *excitement* is the term I'd use." Anna indicated Tony who'd been watching the exchange with unabashed curiosity. "This is Tony. She's been filling me in on the local legends."

Not to mention ghosts, bats and raccoons. She'd save those particular tidbits for later. She hoped Izetta didn't harbor any superstitions.

Tony bobbed her head in greeting. "I didn't know suffragists were married."

"Widowed. We come in all shapes and sizes, as well as marital statuses."

"Have you ever met the president?"

"I have not had the pleasure. Although I have penned him several letters in support of the cause."

The two struck up a lively conversation, and Anna let her attention drift. The train was delayed, much to the agitation of the conductor and the grumbling passengers who streamed onto the platform. David lined them up and scratched careful notes of their names and descriptions.

At a lull in the conversation, Izetta glanced around. "Where are Jo and Mr. McCoy?"

"Jo is keeping the children away from the commotion, and Caleb is managing the crowd."

"This has turned into a spectacle."

A flash of yellow caught Anna's attention. "It's the little girl from the rally."

"Where?"

Anna pointed, and Izetta shook her head. "I don't recall seeing her."

"She was definitely there that day. She gave me a bouquet of yellow flowers. Jo and Caleb saw her, as well."

Her last chance of remaining anonymous splintered into a thousand icy fragments. They knew her.

Anna tightened Caleb's coat around her shoulders. The wind had picked up, tugging at her hair and biting her ears and cheeks. She cupped her hands over her face and blew a puff of air, warming her chilled nose.

The marshal searched the now-empty trunk and read the name inscribed on the domed surface. "Is there a Mary K. Phillips here?"

The girl from the rally tugged on her mother's hand. "That's your name, mama."

Chapter Twelve

Anna stifled a groan. The marshal wasn't going to appreciate this turn of affairs one bit. Once again the coincidences were piling up. The little girl had been at the rally the day of the shooting. Mother and daughter had been staying at the same hotel. Now a body had rolled out of their trunk.

Clearly agitated, the mother stepped forward, clenching her daughter's hand, her chin set at a defiant angle. "I am Mrs. Phillips."

The woman was young, not much older than Anna. Her dress was expensively made, though a season or two out of fashion judging by the size of her bustle, a distinction Anna doubted anyone else noticed. She'd always had an eye for fashion, a useless trait in the Bishop household.

The woman was pretty, though clearly exhausted. Dark circles surrounded her hazel eyes, and the corners of her lips tugged down as though in perpetual frown. Tendrils of chestnut hair had escaped the tight bun at the nape of her neck. Neither mother nor daughter wore a coat against the late fall chill.

The marshal nudged the trunk with one booted foot. "That's the trunk you stowed in Kansas City."

"That is my trunk." The woman's frown deepened. "But I can assure you that is not what I packed."

Someone in the growing crowd tittered.

The marshal held up a hand. "This is a man's life. Show a little respect."

Several people ducked their heads. No one left the platform. They were all transfixed by the show playing out before them. No one wanted to hear about this event secondhand.

The marshal waved Mrs. Phillips over. "Why don't we let your daughter have a seat for a moment, ma'am, while we sort this out?"

The woman offered a reluctant nod. She caught sight of Anna, but no recognition flared in her gaze. Expelling a breath, Anna caught the little girl's eye. She patted the seat beside her, and the child skipped over. The mother hadn't known her identity, which was something. Her secret was much safer with the little girl.

"My name is Anna. I remember you from the rally. Would you like to sit next to me?"

"My name is Jane. You're the prettiest lady I've ever seen. That man—" she pointed at Caleb "—he said you were the prettiest lady he'd ever seen, as well."

Anna's eyes widened. "Oh, my. That was a nice thing for him to say."

"When you were giving your speech and everyone started running and pushing, he protected me."

Why was Anna not surprised? Of course Caleb had come to the rescue. "That was very kind of him."

"He stayed behind to help someone who was hurt."

The marshal and Caleb flanked the girl's mother, parting the crowd as they approached the draped body.

Caleb knelt and pulled back the cover, revealing the man's face.

The woman's hand flew to her throat.

"Do you know this man?" the marshal asked.

"Yes and no. I saw him before. In Kansas City. At the Savoy Hotel. He was always lurking around."

"Name?"

"I don't know. I never actually met him."

The marshal gestured toward the trunk. "I assume the last time you checked your trunk was at the hotel?"

She offered another hesitant nod. "Yes. The porter took the trunk from our room and made the arrangements."

"Which hotel?"

"I told you already. The Savoy. In Kansas City."

The marshal shot another look at Caleb. Anna sighed. None of this boded well for her welcome. Not only had she brought danger, she'd come accompanied by a dead body. The marshal was clearly protective of his family. How long before he decided Anna's presence was a risk that wasn't worth taking?

She was dangerous and notorious. A lethal combination. They might have forgiven one of those offenses, but not both. She had her doubts.

"How long was the trunk out of your sight?" the marshal asked.

"Not more than hour," Mrs. Phillips said.

"Time enough for killing."

The color drained from her face, and her eyes rolled back.

"She's fainting," Caleb called, catching the woman before she hit the ground.

He gently lowered her the remaining distance. Izetta leaped up and whipped off her shawl. Caleb bunched the material and tucked it beneath the woman's head.

The marshal rubbed the back of his neck. "Well, that's a fine kettle of fish."

"She's had a shock," Caleb said. "Is Doc Johnsen here yet?"

"On his way," the marshal replied.

The little girl clutched Anna's hand. "What's wrong with mama?"

Anna wrapped her arm around Jane, carefully averting her face. "Your mother will be all right. She's had a bit of a fright."

Anna glanced around the crowded depot. All eyes were pinned on their odd tableau. Sweat beaded on her temple. She recalled the girls at Miss Spence's Academy, how they'd stared at her as though she was some exotic animal. Their curiosity an odd mixture of fascination and disgust.

Once her identity as the illegitimate daughter of the famous heiress had been exposed, the other girls had kept their distance, whispering behind her back and pointing. In the week before her expulsion, they'd tossed her shoes onto the roof and hidden her nightgown. Offences which had gone unpunished.

While she assumed her shoes were safe among adults in Cimarron Springs, it was only a matter of time before their attitudes shifted. She'd leave well before that happened. Well before the McCoys were affected by her notoriety.

Jane squeezed her hand. "Is mama sad because of that man in our trunk?"

"Yes. I know this must all seem very strange and confusing."

"I saw him before, at the hotel."

Anna narrowed her gaze. "Are you certain?"

"He was watching us."

Anna pulled back from the little girl and studied her face. "When?"

"At the hotel yesterday. He made mama sad. That's when she said we had to leave."

Anna's heart sank. Mrs. Phillips had said she didn't know the man. Her daughter just revealed they'd talked. How were those two involved? Worse yet, she'd have to disclose her suspicions to the marshal.

With every new revelation, the news grew more tangled. "Don't worry, Jane. The marshal and his brother-in-law will take good care of your mother."

What would happen to the little girl if her mother was accused of murder? Anna shoved the thought aside. Simply because the man had been watching them didn't mean Mrs. Phillips was involved. Perhaps Jane was mistaken.

Not for the first time, Anna noted that Jane was wearing the same yellow dress from the rally. Memories assaulted her senses. The pungent scent of burning fuel from the fires set against the frigid wind, the sunlight bouncing off the windows of the buildings around the square. The sound of the shot. Caleb lifting her into his arms.

Calming her ragged breathing, she focused her attention back to the present.

Already Mrs. Phillips was coming around. Jane's mother struggled upright, her hand pressed against her forehead.

The conductor approached, his watch chain swinging from his fingers. "I can't hold up this here train all day. I've got a schedule to follow. If I'm late, everyone on down the line is late."

The marshal gestured for David. "Allow everyone back on the train once you've taken down their names. Did you search the rest of the luggage car?"

"Yep. Nothing suspicious. This seems to be the only body."

"Then let 'em go. Not much more we can do."

The woman stifled a sob, and Caleb helped her into a sitting position.

She gasped and frantically searched the crowd. "Where's Jane? Where's my daughter?"

Caleb placed a hand on her shoulder and pointed. "She's with Miss Anna. Safe and sound."

The woman visibly relaxed, and Caleb assisted her to her feet.

Her face pale, she approached the marshal. "Am I under arrest? This isn't our stop. We must get back on the train."

"Where are you headed?" the marshal asked.

The woman paused. "Texas."

The hesitation was only a tick, but enough that Caleb and Garrett exchanged a glance. Anna shook her head.

Whatever her involvement, the woman was only making matters worse for herself and her daughter by lying.

Mrs. Phillips must have sensed her error. She glanced at her clenched hands, her face ashen.

The marshal flipped over the tag on her trunk. "According to this, you were going to Cimarron Springs."

"There must have been a mistake. We're, uh, my daughter and I, are bound for Texas."

The marshal rocked back on his heels. "Why don't you stick around town for a day or two instead? Until we get this all sorted out. We'll put you up in the hotel. I'll even buy you both another train ticket when everything is sorted."

Judging from her stricken expression, the woman had caught the subtle undertone in his words. The question was not *when*, but *if.* The body had been discovered in her trunk. According to her daughter, she'd spoken with the dead man the day before. She'd been afraid of him. The little girl had been at the rally. None of the pieces of the puzzle were particularly damning, but taken together, they aroused suspicion.

Anna rubbed her arms.

Jane unfurled a length of string. "Do you know Cat's Cradle?"

"No. But maybe you can teach me."

Mrs. Phillips pressed her hands against her cheeks. "Are you forcing me to stay? Do I have a choice?"

The marshal's gaze was sympathetic but unwavering. "I can arrest you and force you to stay. Or you can remain here voluntarily."

Her back stiffened. "Then I suppose we'll be staying." She whipped around and marched toward her daughter. She snatched the girl's hand. "Come along."

Jane reached for Anna. "Where are we going?"

"We're going to stay in town for a while. We're going to have a little adventure."

"Can I see Miss Anna again?"

"Maybe. I don't know."

The girl glanced over her shoulder, and her look resonated with Anna: the loneliness, the isolation. Something had gone wrong in their little family. Something that had scared her mother. While Anna didn't want to believe the woman was capable of killing a man, there was a good possibility she had.

Mrs. Phillips caught Anna staring and pursed her lips. "I don't know. We'll see."

Tears welled in the girl's eyes.

Sensing her distress, Caleb rested his hand on Anna's shoulder. "Don't worry, the marshal is a good man. He'll do what he can."

Two men lifted the litter holding the dead man's body and set off down the street. The group of boys trailed behind in an odd parade. Now that the show was over, the passengers filed back onto the train.

Another thought chilled her to the bone. Jane had been at the rally. Mrs. Phillips had been conspicuously absent.

Had Mrs. Phillips been involved in Anna's shooting? They all assumed a man had shot her. A woman was just as capable of murder as a man was.

No. Anna violently shook her head. Shooting her put Jane in danger, and Mrs. Phillips clearly loved her daughter. Besides, she'd shown no recognition of Anna.

A sharp gust whipped her skirts around her legs.

At her reassuring smile, Caleb had resumed his conversation with the marshal.

She'd left one set of worries behind, only to pick up another set.

The marshal glanced at Mrs. Phillips and her daughter and back at Caleb. "How much do you know about them?"

"Nothing. Jo and I saw the little girl at the rally. She was alone. After the shooting, Jo took her back to the hotel and found her mother."

"What about Anna? How much do you know about her?"

A flush of anger crept up his neck. "She's not involved, if that's what you're thinking. We've been with her the whole time. There was a guard at her door. There's no way she could have done this. Besides, you're better off asking Jo about Miss Bishop."

"I'm asking you."

"Why?"

"Because Jo admires her. Because I like to take care of my family."

Caleb lowered his hackles. Marshal Cain was simply protecting his wife. He'd do the same. "I only know what I've seen the past few days. She's tough. She's loyal."

The marshal hitched his fingers into his gun belt. "Jo said the same thing."

"I haven't seen anything that would make me question her loyalty. You weren't there. You didn't see what happened when she was shot. She's the victim, not the aggressor."

The challenge disappeared from the marshal's expression. "That's another thing. Jo asked me to look into the shooting. Didn't discover much. They think the shooter hid out in a building across the way. The window on the second floor was unlatched. I don't get the feeling the boys up north are putting much into the investigation. They figure it's all wrapped up with the suffragists' movement. They don't think it's personal."

"They're idiots. There were two attempts on Anna's life."

A muscle ticked along his jaw. They'd been standing mere feet away from Anna while the man had waited and watched. They'd been entranced by the speech while the killer had taken aim. He'd been one door away from her when the second attempt occurred.

The marshal squinted. "And you don't know of any other reason why someone would want Anna dead?"

"She's a suffragist, you know that much. Her mother is famous. I'm sure Jo has filled you in on the family. Anna is on her way to overtaking her mother's fame. After hearing her speak, I don't have any doubt she can lead the movement."

"Then, you think this has to do with the suffragists, as well?"

"Partly, sure, but it's personal. The man tried again. He might have succeeded the second time if there hadn't been a guard at the door."

"What a mess. But if this is about the cause, why target Anna alone?"

"She's a powerful asset. Don't know if that's worth killing over, but people get odd ideas."

The marshal made a noncommittal sound in the back of his throat. "Someone wants Anna dead. Then a body shows up in Cimarron Springs. Mrs. Phillips was staying at the hotel. You saw her daughter at the rally."

"I know Anna." Caleb glanced up sharply. "She had nothing to do with any of this."

"I didn't say she did. There's a lot of bodies piling up around your Miss Bishop. A lot of the same people are circling around, winding up in the same places. You think it's a coincidence those two women were on the train with a dead man?"

"I don't know how. We were careful. No one saw us leave the hotel."

Caleb recalled Mrs. Stuart's earlier declaration and groaned. "There's something else. Before. At the hotel. The desk clerk registered Anna as my fiancée. Mrs. Stuart's sister lives in Kansas City. Evidently she visited the hotel, put two and two together, and made five."

The marshal adjusted his hat over his eyes. "The Stuart sisters are fond of a good piece of news. Especially if they have it first. It's not such a bad idea."

"I don't think Anna would agree."

"She might not have a choice." The marshal nodded in the direction of Mrs. Stuart. "Gossip spreads faster than maple syrup on a hot day around here."

Perhaps the discovery of the body had distracted Mrs. Stuart. There was time, time for setting the rumor to rest.

"I'll think about it."

"Think about this, as well. This town is full of good people. They'll do right by Miss Bishop, I don't doubt that. But if people think the two of you are engaged, she's part of the family. The McCoys are well respected around here."

"She's a friend of Jo's. Isn't that enough?"

"Everyone knew Jo was in town for that rally. Might be better if they think the rally was a convenient excuse for you to do a little courting. A little misdirection buys us time."

The idea made sense if there weren't so many other problems. "What happens if people discover that we've deceived them?"

"You gotta give people credit. If they feel like they've helped save someone, they'll forgive soon enough."

"Anna is the last person that needs saving," Caleb said. Mostly he was worried about his own hide. She'd made her feelings about an engagement bargain abundantly clear already. "She's smart and independent. She'd rather meet this problem head on than hide behind a lie."

The marshal lifted one shoulder in a careless shrug. "You don't have to explain to me. My wife once shot me."

"To save you."

"See. It's all about intent." The marshal flashed a grin.

Anxious to leave the conversation behind, Caleb offered a greeting as Mr. Lancaster, the blacksmith, approached them with a young woman whom Caleb assumed was his new bride. "Caleb, I wanted you to meet my wife."

She was petite and shy, her head down, her two blond braids wrapped around her head like a coronet.

"This is Helga."

She offered a few murmured words of greeting, her quiet voice heavily accented.

"We've just seen her mother off." Mr. Lancaster hid

his relief well, but not well enough. "We'll be seeing you at the Harvest Festival, won't we?"

The marshal touched the brim of his hat. "Our family will be there."

"Excellent. Helga hasn't had the chance to meet too many people yet." He gazed adoringly at his new bride. "Best be getting home. Looks like it might rain."

Caleb tipped his face toward the sky. Sure enough, the horizon appeared hazy and dark. Mr. Lancaster clasped his wife's hand and led her toward their wagon.

The marshal followed their progress with a slow shake of his head. "We're going to need a new blacksmith."

"Are they moving?"

"Mr. Lancaster may not know it yet, but they're moving, all right. You should have seen the tears when his wife's mother left."

"That doesn't mean he's leaving."

"Mr. Lancaster is smitten, and his wife is unhappy. You don't need to be a Pinkerton detective to put those two pieces together."

Caleb glanced at where Anna was sitting. She tilted toward the left, her hand braced on the bench, her lips pinched and white. Her suffering touched off a fierce protectiveness, and he understood what the marshal was saying. He'd wrestle a grizzly if his actions alleviated her suffering.

"I'd best see to Miss Bishop," Caleb said. "They're staying at the Stuart house. Is it fit for them?"

"Mr. Stuart had some of the boys over yesterday to patch the roof and fix the door on the back. Still needs a lot of work, but it'll be good for tonight if the ladies aren't too picky."

Caleb wasn't certain. After the Savoy Hotel, what would Anna think of the tiny, neglected house? It was a far cry from Kansas City.

Yep, he'd do whatever it took to make her happy. Even if that meant ensuring she was back in St. Louis, far away from Cimarron Springs.

He adjusted the brim of his hat lower over his eyes. "Can anything else go wrong today?"

"Ask and you shall receive." The marshal pointed down the street toward the man marching their way.

Caleb frantically searched for an escape.

Chapter Thirteen

Caleb backed away from the man charging toward him. He glanced at the marshal for help, but Garrett only grinned and turned his back.

Caleb groaned. If he backed up any farther he'd be sitting in Anna's lap.

Mr. Aaberg thrust a squirming bundle of bleets and hooves into his arms.

Caleb fumbled with the distraught goat. "This isn't a good time, Triple A."

They'd called Avery Aaberg Triple A for as long as Caleb could remember. The man was ornery and disagreeable, more so since his second wife had died the past winter. Most folks avoided the cantankerous farmer, but Caleb didn't mind him as much. Triple A kept his barns clean and his animals tended, he never waited until it was too late to save an animal before he came calling and he didn't expect Caleb to stay for coffee and gossip after a visit.

Caleb fumbled with the goat, and Triple A crossed his arms over his chest, then stepped out of reach.

"That one there is a runt," the man declared. "The

others are going to kill it. I can't look after him all the time. You'll have to take him."

"Find someone else."

"Why?"

"Because I'm otherwise engaged. This is Miss Anna, she's—" A loud bleat interrupted his words. "We've just gotten back into town and Anna—" Another bleat drowned out his explanation. "Bring the goat around to the house later."

Triple A grinned and slapped his shoulder. "Good to hear. I thought Mrs. Stuart was just gossiping again."

Caleb gaped. He'd never seen the man smile. Not once. And he'd known him all his life. In twenty-six years he'd never seen Triple A's teeth full on. Not that he was missing much. They were yellowed and uneven with a large gap down the center two.

The farmer stuck out his hand toward Anna. "Nice to meet another *a*, Miss Anna. I'm Avery Aaberg. That's two *a*'s in Aaberg. Folks around here call me Triple A."

"It's nice to meet you, Mr., ah, Mr. Triple A."

"Just Triple A. We don't stand on ceremony in these parts. Especially now that you're one of the family."

Anna kept her head facing forward, but her eyes swiveled toward Caleb. "Family?"

Biscuits and gravy. He was too late. The rumor had started.

"And now you have a goat." Triple A clapped his hands together. "Everything is settled."

"Wait," Caleb demanded. "I do not have a goat. You have a goat."

He needed time with Anna. Surely she'd understand his explanation. How things had gotten out of hand. How he'd never intended for this to happen.

"He's got his ear bit," Triple A said. "Might be an infection. Thought you better take a look at it."

The animal was definitely a runt, about half the size of a normal goat, with light gray fur that turned darker at the tips.

One hoof dug into Caleb's side, tearing his shirt and scratching his stomach. "I can take a look at his ear, but then he's going home with you."

"Can't. Told you. He's the runt."

"Yes, but why is it my responsibility to find him a home?"

"Do you have any goats?"

"No. You know that. Three horses, a lame cow and the occasional stray cat."

"Then you have room for a goat."

"I don't want a goat."

"You're the vet. You must know someone who needs a goat. He might be a runt, but he eats well enough. He'll keep the yard cleared. Just mind you don't have any roses. He likes roses."

Triple A turned his back, and Caleb limped after him, the goat impeding his pursuit. "This isn't a good time. I told you."

"If I take him back, the others will trample him," Triple A said solemnly. "His death will be on your hands."

Triple A pinned his mournful gaze on Anna. A muscle ticked along Caleb's jaw. Triple A was doing this on purpose. The old blackmailer knew exactly what would happen.

Anna gasped. "Really? They'll kill him?"

Triple A scratched the stubble on his cheek, and Caleb shot him a scalding glare. Of course she'd hear that little tidbit.

"Happens sometimes," the farmer said. "With these little ones. The other fellows weed out the weak one. It's a shame, but that's life on the farm."

Anna stood and rested her hand on the goat's back. "That's terrible." She appealed to Caleb. "Couldn't you find him a home?"

Triple A shook his head and Caleb glared. The farmer had gone and done that on purpose. Now Anna was looking at him as though he was a black-hooded executioner sending the goat off to the gallows.

"Tomorrow," Caleb spoke through gritted teeth.

"Has to be today." Triple A was grinning again with that big annoying gap-toothed smile. Right then Caleb missed never seeing the man's teeth. He didn't appreciate his sense of humor. "I'm cutting hay first thing in the morning. I won't be around. I'd hate to come and find him trampled."

Anna sucked in a breath.

"That is blackmail." The goat kicked him in the gut. "Oomph. Could we talk about this tomorrow?"

He was stuck with the goat. No amount of arguing was changing that.

"He won't last the night."

Caleb groaned and set down the squirming animal. Triple A tipped his hat toward Anna. "Pleasure to meet you, Miss Anna." Then he stuffed his hands in his pockets and set off toward town.

Caleb angled his head. "Is he whistling?"

Anna stifled a grin. "Yes. I believe he's whistling 'The Battle Hymn of the Republic.'"

"That old coot. What am I going to do with a goat?"

Anna leaned down and cupped the goat's face in her

hand. "I think he's just precious. Why, he's smaller than a collie. Will he get much bigger?"

Caleb squinted at the goat. He was barely more than six weeks old, with that curious shade of gray that darkened at the tips of his fur. "Probably not."

The goat bleated and tipped its head. One ear hung at an odd angle, a bit of dried blood matting its gray fur.

Anna stared up at him, her gaze appealing. "Can you fix his ear?"

There was no help for it, the animal needed medical attention. At the very least, Caleb was finally back in his element. Finally taking care of something he understood.

Since this detour also gave him a reprieve from telling Anna about the engagement rumor sweeping through town, he'd forgive Triple A. For the moment.

"That ear needs tending," Caleb said. "I'll have to get him home for a better look."

Mrs. Franklin appeared again, fording her way through the crowd like a steamship through rough waters. "I have secured our baggage. I had to suffer the indignities of opening each trunk and box, proving that no additional bodies had been secreted in our baggage." She sniffed. "As though a grown man could fit in a hatbox. Perhaps they assumed he'd been chopped up and distributed equally amongst the tissue paper and bows."

Anna blanched.

Caleb fought a grin that tugged at the edges of his mouth. While there was a certain absurdity to the situation, a man had lost his life.

Mrs. Franklin pulled at her collar. "I suggest we continue on to the hotel. I could use a strong cup of coffee. This has already been an eventful day."

The goat nibbled on her skirts.

Mrs. Franklin leaped back. "Why do you have a goat?"

"He's injured," Anna said. "He's the runt. The other animals have been bullying him."

Mrs. Franklin took another cautious step back, her wary attention focused on the goat. "It appears Mr. McCoy has his hands full for the foreseeable future. We'll save him a seat."

"Much appreciated."

Caleb hoisted the goat into his arms once more and nodded. "My home, I mean my office, well, my home and my office are just down the street. A block or so after the hotel." He raised the goat a notch and pointed. "The Stuart house is a couple doors down and across the street. I'll tend to his ear and meet you. Jo should be around here somewhere."

"Don't worry." Anna scratched behind the goat's good ear. "We'll manage."

Caleb offered a serene smile, pivoted on his heel and grimaced. He'd just gotten home and already there'd been a dead body, a goat and an engagement rumor. Not exactly a good first impression. What did any of that matter, anyway? She wasn't staying long.

Only her opinion did matter. Her opinion mattered too much. He just hoped she'd forgive him once she realized everyone in town thought they were engaged.

Anna stared wistfully after Caleb. While she wanted lunch, she wasn't quite certain if she was up to the task of meeting more people.

Izetta dusted her hands. "Dead man or no dead man,

goat or no goat, I've a mind to see this house where we'll be staying. I want to see what needs to be done."

She marched toward a wagon and a man leaning against the baseboard, and Anna realized she must be arranging for their luggage.

She glanced down and discovered Caleb's familiar battered leather satchel resting on the bench. She stuck her arms through the sleeves of his coat and stood.

Catching up to Mrs. Franklin, she hoisted the bag. "Mr. McCoy may need this. Why don't I meet you at the hotel later?"

"I'm not surprised he forgot it in all the confusion. I shall have this gentleman deliver our bags and meet you at our new home."

"Perfect." Anna blew out a relieved breath. "If you see Jo, tell her where I've gone."

The day had been too full of surprises and unexpected news. She needed quiet. The idea of making small talk with a group of strangers sounded exhausting at that moment. Any excuse for escape was welcome.

Clutching Caleb's bag against her chest, she set off down the boardwalk. Though carrying the heavy bag tugged at her wound and had her side aching, the wind on her cheeks had revived her flagging reserves of energy.

She reached the end of the boardwalk and searched the street. There were three houses on the left side, spaced well apart, each featuring a barn and an outbuilding.

A gentleman passed her, and she caught his attention. "I was looking for Mr. McCoy's home?"

The bearded man paused. "Which Mr. McCoy would

that be? There's a whole passel of them around these parts."

"Caleb McCoy." Anna indicated the bag she carried. "I came with him from Kansas City. He forgot his bag."

A wide grin spread across the man's face. "Of course, of course. Second house, the one with the porch swing."

Anna smiled her thanks. My, but people were friendly around here.

She walked the distance and paused before the tidy little house. The home was a perfect square with steeply pitched pyramid roof. A wrought-iron weather vane with a stamped rooster perched on the peak. From the direction of the rooster's tail feathers, the brisk fall wind was blowing from the north.

A bricked walkway flanked by two towering elm trees bisected the yard to the front porch. Though the burnt orange leaves were already falling, the trees must have shaded the whole yard in summer. She pictured sitting on the porch swing, cooled from the dappled sunlight.

One of the crisp leaves fluttered to the ground, and she caught the papery edges in her fist. This was most definitely a bachelor's residence. Painted white, there were no feminine adornments visible anywhere. No flowers lined the area below the porch railing, no colorful curtains hung in the window. Only the porch swing smacked of anything domestic. Though plain, the home was neat and tidy, the native grasses none too tall.

Three wide steps led to the porch. The door was open, leaving only the screen door in her way. She knocked on the wooden edge.

"Come in," a voice called.

Suddenly shy, she winced at the loud creak of the

hinges. Inside, the house had been portioned off into another perfect square. A parlor to her left, and on her right, an area sectioned off with double doors, she presumed to be Caleb's office, with what must have been a kitchen and a bedroom behind them. From her vantage point, the corridor stretched through the center of the house, leaving a line of sight out the back door toward the barn. The design would allow a refreshing cross breeze.

She turned toward the glass double doors on her right and cautiously pushed one open.

"Watch your feet!" Caleb shouted.

The goat had broken free of his grasp and dashed toward Anna. She scooted into the room and slammed the door behind her.

Caleb sat back on his heels. "That is an incredibly stubborn goat who does not want my assistance."

"Can I help? I brought your bag and your coat."

She extended her hand, and he took the bag from her, his knuckles brushing against her fingers. The simple touch was sweetly intimate. Anna shivered and stepped back.

"I'm sorry there's no heat," Caleb said, misinterpreting her reaction. "I haven't had time to start a fire."

"That's quite all right." She rubbed her arms.

His brief touch had caused the reaction, but there was no need to tell him that.

The air was a touch chilly. "Is there something I can do to help?"

"There's a garden patch out back. I think there's some late potatoes growing. They should distract this little guy while I'm tending him. Unless you'd rather stay with the goat."

"I'll fetch the potatoes."

While Caleb held the goat, Anna slipped out the doors once more. She navigated the corridor, pausing before the kitchen door. The space was bare, and if she didn't know better, she'd have thought the house deserted. There were no pictures on the walls, no tables holding decorative objects. The place was scrupulously clean, and she admired his efforts in that regard at least.

Except the house felt lonely. Caleb clearly preferred the simplicity, and yet he struck her as a family man. A man who wanted a wife and children.

Her heartbeat skittered. Children. They'd have green eyes and dark hair. Or blue eyes. Anna reared back. If she didn't cease thinking about Caleb in terms of the future, she'd be asking for heartache. She wasn't the sort of wife he needed, and they were both well aware of the obstructions.

After passing through the screen door at the back of the home, she imagined once again the lovely breeze that must come through the house in the spring and summer. There was something inexorably peaceful about the setting.

The two garden patches were laid out in precise rows, mirroring the tidy efficiency of the house. A path led through the center to the barn, and she followed the bricks. Each square on either side of the pathway was protected with a short mesh fence. Having never had a garden, she wasn't quite certain what she was looking for.

She tapped her front tooth with one finger. "If I were a potato, where would I be?"

"In that patch on your left."

Anna shrieked and whirled around. An identical copy, albeit a younger version, of Caleb stood behind her.

He lifted an eyebrow. "Although I don't know why you'd want to be a potato."

"You must be one of Caleb's brothers."

"Yep. Abraham. People call me Brahm."

"I'm Anna. I was just getting a potato."

"I figured that."

She mentally slapped her forehead. The poor man must think her a dolt. "For Caleb."

Oh, yes, that helped. He definitely wouldn't think of her as an imbecile anymore.

He glanced at the door behind her. "Does this mean Caleb's home?"

"Yes."

"Good. Maxwell's supposed to be doing his chores, but he went into town and left them for me today."

"I'm sure Caleb is grateful for your assistance."

He stepped over the wire mesh fencing surrounding the garden patch and stared at the tufts of green, then leaned down and dug in the dirt for a moment. He straightened, turned toward her and held out his hands.

She cupped her fingers together, and he dumped three potatoes the size of eggs into her outstretched palms.

"There's been a frost," Brahm said. "That's the best you'll get this late in the season. Hope you weren't planning on a big meal."

"This should be enough. They're for a goat."

"Yep."

Oh, dear. This was not going well at all.

"I'll just—" she jerked one shoulder toward the back door "—go back inside now."

He stepped around and grasped the handle, swinging open the screen door. Anna blushed. With her hands full, the task was impossible on her own.

"Thank you. Would you like to come in?"

"Nah. Tell Caleb I changed the dressing on the milk cow's foreleg and cleaned out the horses' stalls."

"I'll tell him." She stepped into the house and glanced over her shoulder. "It was nice meeting you."

"You, too. Hope everything turns out well with the goat."

Anna flapped her elbow in what she hoped resembled a wave. So much for making a good impression on Caleb's family. She returned to the double doors and called out.

Caleb pushed open the door a slit. She twisted sideways and scooted through the narrow opening. Her skirts brushed his pant legs, and her knuckles skimmed his white shirt, leaving a streak of dirt.

Anna glanced up into his green eyes. "Oh, no. I've ruined your shirt."

He didn't reply, only stared down at her, his gaze intense. Her mouth went dry, and she swayed forward, bracing her knuckles against his chest, the potatoes still fisted in her hands. Heat from his body spread through her fingers, and her heartbeat quickened.

He rested his hand on her waist, his touch separated by layers of clothing and bandages.

She stared at the buttons on his shirt, tension coiling in her belly. "I met your brother."

"Which one?"

"Abraham."

"Maxwell must have talked Brahm into doing his chores."

"He looks like you."

"We all look alike."

"Not really. You're much more…"

He tucked his knuckles beneath her chin and urged her head up until she met his eyes. "Yes?"

The goat tangled in her skirts and dashed through the open door into the parlor. Anna tripped forward and splayed her hands for balance. The potatoes landed on Caleb's sock foot, and he grimaced, staggering backward. Off balance, Anna followed him, her hands fisting in his shirt. Caleb yelped.

She realized her hold on him was causing the pain and instantly released her fingers.

He sat down hard on the chair behind him and grasped her waist, keeping her upright. "Mind your side."

Anna stepped back and slipped on a potato. Caleb lunged upright and caught her around the waist.

They stared up at each for a long moment. A curious sense of anticipation filled her.

He angled his head and leaned down. The touch of his lips was featherlight, barely more than a whisper. His fingers held her waist loosely, giving her every chance for escape. She pressed closer. She slipped her hands around his neck and felt the bare skin at his nape.

Footsteps sounded from the parlor.

She leaped away from Caleb, blinking rapidly. Caleb appeared equally stunned, breathing as though he'd run a great distance.

Brahm entered the room, the goat cradled in his arms. He glanced between the two of them and lifted an eyebrow.

Caleb released Anna and fisted his hand in front of his mouth, then cleared his throat. "Hey, Brahm."

"Hey, Caleb. Figured you lost this."

As Brahm handed his brother the goat, Anna took another step back and ducked her head.

"You coming by for supper tonight?" Brahm asked.

"Yes."

"Are you bringing your friend?"

"Yes."

"You know I mean Anna and not the goat, right?" Brahm burst into laughter, and Caleb shoved him none-too-gently out of the room, securely latching the door behind his brother.

He raked his hands through his hair. "Sorry about that."

"I didn't make a very good impression on your brother."

The goat remained between them, snuffling along the floor for the lost potatoes.

Anna gestured over her shoulder. "I should go now."

"Let me walk you. The Stuart house is just across the way. It's white with blue shutters. You can't miss it."

"I'll be fine on my own."

She fumbled with the latch. Caleb brushed her hands away and completed the task. She raced out the front doors, down the stairs and struggled with the latch on the gate. Why were there latches everywhere? Why must they be difficult?

She'd kissed him. She'd kissed Caleb McCoy. Well, he'd kissed her. She didn't know if there was a difference. They'd kissed and she liked kissing.

She'd liked kissing him a lot.

Chapter Fourteen

A few small improvements had made an enormous difference.

Two days following her arrival, Anna stood in an exact replica of Caleb's house. The only difference being the dining room was actually a dining room and hadn't been cordoned off with glass doors for an office. The trees outside were oak instead of elm, and the garden behind the house had obviously been used for flowers instead of vegetables. Izetta had immediately fallen on the overgrown space and attacked the suffocating vines with an almost giddy zeal.

Anna had been more interested in the interior of the house. She'd used housework as her excuse for avoiding a dinner with the McCoys. The thought of looking Caleb in the eye after what had happened had been more than she could bear.

The Stuarts had kindly donated a few old pieces of furniture. There was a square wooden table in the dining room that had seen better days flanked by two mismatched chairs. Neither of the painted chairs quite fit the table, which meant one either chose to sit slightly above the optimum table height or slightly below. Given their size differences, Anna had chosen the tall chair and Izetta had chosen the shorter chair.

The whole experience was very much like playing house. Until setting her trunk in the second bedroom, she hadn't realized she'd been living her life as a guest in her mother's home. Chairs were not there to be moved, pictures were not rearranged, rugs were left where they were placed.

One particularly memorable Christmas, Anna had been given a dollhouse. Two stories high with a vaulted attic and hinges that opened the whole house down the middle. The miniature house was fully stocked with furniture and rugs and a family with painted porcelain faces dressed in their Sunday best—a mother, father, a boy and a girl. There was even a yellow tabby cat with real fur.

In the year after receiving the gift, Anna had kept the furniture straight. The second year she'd set about moving the chairs around, then the rugs, then she painted tiny murals on the walls with her oil paint set. On her sixteenth birthday her mother had declared dollhouses childish, and since Anna was no longer a child, the dollhouse had disappeared.

Surveying the tiny, well-laid-out cottage, Anna crossed her arms and studied the plaster wall in the dining room. She pictured a mural with a babbling brook lined by trees.

Voices sounded outside, and she turned away from her musing. She opened the door, surprised to find Mrs. Phillips standing on the covered front porch. Jane stood at her mother's side wearing the same yellow dress, the hem darkened with dirt.

"Miss Bishop," the woman said. "I wondered if I might have a word with you?"

Anna waved them inside and indicated the mismatched chairs. "Have a seat. May I bring you a cup of coffee?"

"Yes. Please. I was hoping Jane might play outside while the two of us are speaking."

The circles beneath her eyes had darkened since the last time Anna had seen her, only two days before. Having reached the end of her endurance after the shooting, Anna recognized the signs in others.

"Izetta is out back pruning the roses. Follow me." Anna led the girl toward the kitchen and rummaged around for the empty tin can she'd seen earlier. "If there are any good blooms left, would you make me an arrangement?"

"Yes, ma'am." Jane spoke solemnly.

Whatever sadness gripped Jane's mother was obviously taking a toll on her daughter, as well.

Anna opened the door and found Izetta hunched over a rambling hedge rose. "We have a visitor."

The older woman caught sight of Jane and smiled.

Anna leaned against the doorjamb. "Jane's mother and I are having a chat over coffee. May Jane help you in the garden?"

"I can always use a helper."

Grateful for her easy acceptance of the situation, Anna ushered Jane outside, then poured two cups of coffee into the recently washed chipped mugs, and carried them into the dining room.

Mrs. Phillips had taken the taller seat. Anna recalled her thoughts at the train depot—that Mrs. Phillips had been involved in her shooting. Seeing the woman now, her suspicions vanished. Mrs. Phillips appeared too beaten down by life to plan a murder.

She wore a different dress this morning, and Anna caught the faint whiff of camphor, as though the dress had been in storage.

Mrs. Phillips cupped the mug with both hands. "Thank you for speaking with me. Especially, well, especially after what happened."

"You don't look like the sort of woman who'd kill a man and stuff him in her trunk."

"Evil never appears the way we imagine."

Anna sucked in a breath at the stark sorrow in the woman's eyes. "Why don't you tell me what's troubling you?"

"It's a long story, and not very pretty."

"I have all the time in the world."

Mrs. Phillips flashed a grateful smile. "I married Jane's father when I was very young. My mother had recently passed away, and I'd barely turned seventeen. Clark was the son of one of my father's business associates. I never even questioned our marriage. That's the way I was raised."

Tears sprang in Mrs. Phillips's eyes, and she gripped her coffee mug. "He wasn't a kind man. After Jane was born, well, things took a turn for the worse. The business was failing. He couldn't accept the humiliation. My father died, and he left me a bit of money." She pursed her lips. "Not much, mind you, but enough to give Jane a good start. I wanted the money for Jane. I didn't want him to have it. He'd always spent too much money on his…hobbies…his activities outside the home."

She choked off a sob, and Anna laid her hand over the woman's trembling fingers. "You needn't go on."

"No, no. I have to finish. He was enraged after that. Cruel. I tried to take Jane and leave, but he discovered us. He had a mistress. I asked for a divorce." She paused, her mouth working. "He had me committed to an asylum."

"Oh, my."

Anna had heard similar stories before. The practice was more common before the war, but tales of such incarcerations still abounded. Often the practice was done by men who wanted to live openly with their mistresses, or wanted control of their wives' money since divorce was taboo.

"He couldn't obtain control of the money. My father must have suspected something of his true nature. He'd left the portion in my name only. I'd hoped Clark would release me once he realized his mistake. The business improved. He didn't need the money after that. He came one day as though nothing had happened." Her jaw tightened. "He assumed we'd simply pick up where we left off. As though he'd done nothing wrong. I took Jane and we ran. I knew the family who owned the Savoy Hotel, they were friends of my parents. They offered to let me stay. But then a man came around, asking questions. I knew he'd found us."

"What did the man look like?"

"Older. Dark hair, graying. He had an unusual build. Thin arms and legs with a rounded stomach. Jane noticed him first. Children, they're more observant than adults, I think."

"Reinhart."

"What?"

"I believe the man who was following you was a Pinkerton detective named Reinhart."

Mrs. Phillips pressed her hands over her face, muffling her words. "I didn't know what to do. I didn't know where to go. I think that's how he found us. I ran out of money. I had to wire the bank. That's when that man, the Pinkerton detective, appeared."

Anna stared into her coffee cup. "What about the gentleman yesterday? The man in your trunk…"

"The dead man? I don't know. I think they knew each other, him and that other gentleman, Reinhart, you said. I saw them talking once."

Anna frowned. Reinhart had mentioned something about hiring an associate, about needing more help. Was the dead man his associate? The marshal needed that information.

Mrs. Phillips drew her hands down her face and shook her head. "I used the money for train tickets. Your fiancé was ahead of me in line. Cimarron Springs sounded like a nice name. A nice town. I figured we'd stay a while and plan something else."

Anna held up her hand. "I'll do what I can. Although I don't have the resources my mother has, I can always ask for her assistance." She cleared her throat. "Although you must be mistaken, I don't have a fiancé."

"It's all right. Everyone knows about you two. About you and Mr. McCoy."

Anna gaped. "He's not my fiancé."

"You don't have to pretend with me." Mrs. Phillips patted her hand. "I can imagine what a quandary this is for you. Jane said you were one of the suffragists. You only have to pick up a newspaper to know how suffragists view marriage. But I'm a woman, too, and I know how powerful love can be. Even though my story did not have a happy ending, I always have hope for others."

"I don't, uh, we're friends. I know Mr. McCoy's sister. That's all."

"I'm afraid your secret is out. Everyone in town is talking about it. How you came through town last year and the two of you have been corresponding ever since. How he was so smitten, he went to Kansas City and asked you to marry him. How you were injured at the rally and he never left your side. I think it's all very romantic."

"The whole town, you say?"

"Yes. Apparently Mrs. Stuart's sister lives in Kansas City. She was quite impressed that Mr. McCoy brought his sister along as a chaperone."

"And when did you hear this?"

"At the train depot yesterday."

"I see."

"And then Mr. McCoy's brother saw you visiting his house."

"I don't know how I missed all the news."

"Because you're not staying at the hotel. Jane and I have become something of a local sensation. Everyone wants to see the trunk."

Stupefied by the turn of the conversation, Anna asked dumbly, "The trunk?"

"Yes, the trunk where the body was found." Mrs. Phillips shrugged her shoulders. "Whoever killed that man tossed out most of our clothing in order to make room for the body. Jane has been wearing the same clothing for two days now."

"I can sympathize." Anna had packed for a brief trip, and she'd lost one her outfits already. "You should speak with the marshal. Tell him what you told me. He's a good man. He'll do whatever he can to help."

As much as she craved pursuing this business of her engagement, Mrs. Phillips had a problem. A much larger problem. She'd set her own worries aside for the moment.

"No." Mrs. Phillips pushed back from the table. "Absolutely not. I saw the way the marshal looked at me yesterday. He thinks I'm guilty already. I promise you, I did not kill that man. Even if I had, why would I put the evidence in my own trunk?"

Anna took a fortifying sip of her coffee. Cases such as Mrs. Phillips's were difficult, though not impossible. "I'll do what I can. I can offer you some money."

"No. I won't take charity."

"A loan, then. It's not wise for you to use the bank. If your husband found you that way once, then he can find you again."

Mrs. Phillips offered a curt nod. "A loan. Please, believe me, I don't know how that man wound up in my trunk. I know how it looks. If he was working on a case for my husband..."

There was a chance the man in the trunk had no connection with Reinhart. Either way, Mrs. Phillips didn't strike her as a killer. And if she was, why ask Anna for help? Why not simply run again? Cimarron Springs wasn't a prison. The marshal had requested she stay, a request only. Mrs. Phillips could leave anytime she chose.

"I'll do what I can. But if the marshal—"

A shriek sounded from the back of the house. Anna pushed out of her chair and dashed out the rear door, Mrs. Phillips close behind.

Izetta stood with her hands on her hips while Jane chased a very familiar-looking goat around the hedge roses.

Anna sighed. "I know the guardian of that terrifying little beast."

Jane clapped her hands, and the goat leaped into the air. "Mama, look. He's dancing."

Mrs. Phillips held out her hand. "We must be going."

Jane appeared crestfallen, though she didn't argue with her mother. They linked hands. "I'll show myself out," Mrs. Phillips said.

Anna glared at the goat nibbling the tall grasses near the fence. "You are a troublemaker."

Plastering a serene expression on her face, she turned to her guests. "I'll visit with you tomorrow. About the subject of our earlier discussion."

Anna kept her words deliberately vague, respecting the woman's plea for privacy. Mrs. Phillips appeared quite opposed to accepting charity. And while Anna trusted Izetta, she'd also learned how quickly stories spread.

Pinching off her gloves, Izetta approached. "That poor woman looks as though she hasn't slept in a week."

"She probably hasn't." The two exchanged a glance filled with a wealth of meaning.

"I hope she confided in you," Izetta said.

"She did. Although I doubt I can help very much."

"Sometimes a shoulder to cry on is help enough." Izetta's head snapped around. "Shoo, you little beast. That animal is chewing on my roses."

Anna considered her choices. Mrs. Phillips was her chance to prove once and for all that small differences were as important as grand gestures. She'd help Mrs. Phillips and the cause at the same time.

She snapped her fingers, and the goat lifted its head. "Come with me this instant. You're going home."

Sooner or later she had to face Caleb, and the goat had forced her hand.

She circled around the house, and the goat trailed behind her. Since she and Caleb were practically neighbors, the trip didn't take long.

She reached Caleb's gate in short order and lifted the latch. "Come along, then," she ordered. "In you go."

Though reluctant, the goat followed orders. Anna stepped inside the yard and latched the gate. If Caleb was home, it was best he learned of their problem sooner than later.

The whole town thought they were engaged.

They had kissed.

She inhaled a fortifying breath, stepped onto the front porch and knocked sharply. When no one answered, she circled around the house toward the barn. She'd come all this way, after all.

She reached the double doors and heard the low timbre of his distinctive voice. Once again the day of the rally came rushing back. Anna gripped the edge of the wooden door and rested her forehead against the rough surface.

As her heart pounded, she closed her eyes and pictured the flowers behind their little cottage. She imagined the garden in spring, in full bloom, the bushes filled with roses and peonies blossoms bending their stalks. After a moment, her heartbeat slowed and her breath evened out.

Satisfied she'd gotten ahold of herself, Anna stepped into the barn and waited as her eyes adjusted in the dim light. She followed the sound of Caleb's voice and discovered him in the last stall, kneeling before a milk cow. He'd removed his coat and rolled his shirtsleeves over his corded forearms.

Anna cleared her throat, and he lifted his head. When he half rose from his seat, she held up her palm. "No need to stand."

His gaze flicked toward her and quickly away. "How is the house? How are you settling in?"

This was going quite well. Not awkward or uncomfortable at all. Well, mostly not. "The whole place needs a good scrubbing. Izetta's fallen in love with the garden."

"I forgot about that. Mr. Stuart's mother-in-law planted the flowers."

"You will be happy to know that the rumors of her hauntings are grossly exaggerated. I haven't seen a single specter."

He chuckled, and the cow glanced around at the disturbance.

Soothing the animal with a gentle pat on its neck, Caleb smiled. "You must have talked with one of the local children."

"I was warned, yes. And to answer your earlier question, the house and garden are fine, though poorly tended. There are quite a few volunteer plants still making a go of it." She indicated the tuft of fur hiding behind her skirts. "We had an unexpected visitor today. Your goat is quite fond of roses."

Caleb pinched the bridge of his nose. "Was there any damage done?"

"No, thankfully. We caught him in the nick of time. I rescued him this go-around, but I can't vouch for his safety if he storms the garden again. Izetta is quite militant."

"I'll check the fence." He wrapped a length of bandage around the cow's leg. "I haven't found the little guy a home yet. Haven't had time."

Entranced, Anna followed Caleb's nimble fingers. He accomplished his task with an economy of movement, murmuring soothing words all the while.

This was the first time she'd seen him in his element. From Jo's teasing and her own observations, his dedication had been apparent. And yet only this moment did she truly understand his calling. His actions were deft and practiced, his concentration absolute until the bandage was in place.

"How was she injured?" Anna asked.

"Barbed wire. Her name is Golden." He chuckled. "Fitting somehow. She's lucky to have survived. She'll go back home in a week or two."

"Then she was too injured for her owner to look out for her?"

He lifted one shoulder in a careless shrug. "It's harvest time. That's about all folks can handle."

"Which means you're caring for her instead."

Caleb sat back and blotted his forehead with a square of white cloth. "Farmers around here can't survive without their animals. A good milk cow can cost a season's pay for some folks. It's a small thing to do."

A small thing, and yet his simple sacrifice might save that family, should something else happen.

"There's something more," Anna blurted.

Unless she planned on standing out here and making chitchat about goats and cows and chickens and whatever other farm animals she could think of until suppertime, she'd best get this over with.

"What's that?"

"Everyone in town thinks we're engaged."

That got his attention, although not the way she expected.

Not a hint of surprise showed on his face, only a sort of weary resignation. "I know. I'm sorry. I should have told you yesterday. Mrs. Stuart's sister lives in Kansas City. She…well… It's a long story. I was hoping if I didn't say anything, the rumor would go away."

"I don't think your plan worked." The goat nibbled at her hem, and she snapped her fingers. The nibbling ceased. "How did Mrs. Stuart's sister get the idea in the first place?"

"It's my fault." He braced his fisted hand on his knee. "The desk clerk registered you as my guest to keep your identity a secret. He listed me as your fiancé. We were worried about you, after the shooting. Worried about another attempt." He scoffed. "As much good as that did."

She waited for her reaction. The outrage, the betrayal, a hint of annoyance at the very least. He had lied to her, after all. Perhaps not lied, but there was a large omission on his part.

Snippets of conversation from the past few days suddenly made sense. "That explains a lot."

He rested his forehead against the cow's rounded side. "Are you very angry?"

"No." She couldn't help a grin at his mortification, especially considering she'd felt the same way only moments before. "Not at all. I was actually more concerned about you. The jilted suitor and all that."

"Don't mind me. I'll survive." He straightened. "You do realize this will be a difficult rumor to stop. The more we deny the engagement, the more people will think it's true."

"I know. Perhaps your first idea was correct. We say nothing. Simply let the whole thing blow over on its own. Once I'm gone, none of this will matter, anyway."

"I'm not making any guarantees." He rolled his shirtsleeves down his arms. "The marshal thinks it's a good idea. The engagement. Gives people something to talk about. Makes them protective of you."

"Maybe."

This was a close community of people, and yet she wasn't one of them, no matter what he said. She was a stranger.

The goat head-butted her leg. "My goodness. You are a persistent little fellow, aren't you?"

"I think he likes you. Animals are very perceptive."

Her throat constricted. He'd paid her a great compliment.

Dust motes swirled in the shaft of light slicing through the half-open door. A combination of hay and feed and animal filled the air. As he slipped into his jacket, her gaze lingered on his broad shoulders. She longed for the warm comfort of his arms, the quiet thud of his heart against her ear, the scratch of his wool jacket against her cheek.

Did he ever sit on the porch swing and watch the setting sun, his heel braced against the floor, gently rocking?

She grimaced. Of course he didn't. He was a man, not some romantic fool. Had she become the one thing she'd been warned against? A romantic ninny with nothing but fluff in her head?

If she didn't change the subject soon, she feared she'd say something entirely inappropriate. Something along the lines of…*are you sorry you kissed me?*

She was sage enough to know that one did not ask questions if one did not want the answer.

She wasn't sure which answer she feared the most—yes or no.

Instead she asked, "How is Jo?"

"Happy to be home."

A spark of guilt dampened her mood. "I'm sorry I missed supper the other evening. I hope your mother wasn't upset."

"You were tired. Everyone understands."

She considered telling him about her visit from Mrs. Phillips, then discarded the idea. The woman had taken her into confidence, and Anna honored her trust. She'd speak with the marshal instead—pointing him in the right direction was for the best. He seemed fair and open-minded. Jo obviously adored him.

"You didn't miss much at dinner, anyway," he said. "Mostly the boys gossiped about Mrs. Phillips and the dead man. I imagine she wishes she could change her identity right now. For a little peace."

Finding peace was not easy as people supposed.

"You know, it's odd. I thought I'd like to be someone else. Even for a day. I think I miss being myself."

The visit from Mrs. Phillips had reminded her of her true purpose. This was an interlude, a brief stop along the tracks. There were greater fights ahead of her. There simply weren't enough soldiers in the battle. If she bowed out, they'd lose one more.

If anything good was to come of her injury and her subsequent absence from her scheduled speaking engagements, she'd make a difference. She'd make a difference in the life of one person, and she'd prove that small changes were just as good as grand gestures.

Caleb kept his gaze fixed on the ground. "About the other day."

The moment she'd been avoiding. Clutching her hands together, she breathed deeply. Here was the reckoning. There was no reason for either of them to linger over a lapse that had most certainly been quite out of character for both of them.

Anna held up her hands. "Don't worry, it will never happen again."

A swift kick of disappointment socked him in the gut. She'd said the words on the tip of his tongue. Then why did he suddenly feel such a crushing loss?

"I'm sorry," he said. "I don't know what came over me."

Actually, I know exactly what came over me. You're beautiful and funny and smart and kind, and every time you're near I want the seconds on the clock to tick slower.

He'd altered their easy camaraderie with his careless actions. He'd kissed her, and she'd practically run from his house. He'd ruined things between them, and he had only himself to blame.

Her face grew thoughtful. "We've been thrown together in odd circumstances. I had a lot of time for thinking in Kansas City. Because of what we went through that day, I believe we feel a false sense of intimacy."

Well, that was one way of saying it. "Yep."

"About the engagement rumors."

"What about them?"

"You're all right if they stick?"

"Like I said, the marshal thinks it's a good idea if we

keep up the front. People around here look out for one another. If people think we're engaged, well, it explains a lot of things. Gives them something else to talk about besides why you're here in town."

He and his brothers had played outlaws and lawmen down by Hackberry Creek for years. This wasn't all that different. They didn't even have to lie. As long as neither of them confirmed nor denied the rumor, everyone else would fill in the pieces.

Pretending to love Anna was far easier than pretending he was a lawman.

"I think you're right."

The air whooshed out of his lungs. "Really?"

"Yes. Don't worry. You needn't be concerned about any false intimacies." Her cheeks flamed. "You needn't worry I'll misconstrue the established boundaries of our relationship."

He gave a crooked grin at her obvious discomfort. "I'm not worried."

A little flattered, but definitely not worried. Perhaps he'd read the situation all wrong. Her flustered speech had him hoping she wasn't as immune to him as she'd declared.

He allowed himself a moment to simply admire her. She should have been out of place, standing in a barn, her soft leather boots scuffing across the hay-strewn floor. Instead she appeared perfectly natural. Perhaps it was the way she approached every situation with an innate curiosity and a genuine interest that was so delightfully appealing.

"I have two conditions of our engagement bargain," she continued briskly.

Yet another interesting turn in the conversation he hadn't been expecting. "What are those?"

"First, your mother must know the truth."

"Agreed," he said.

As though he could keep the truth from his mother.

"Second, when this is all over, I want you to jilt me."

"Why is that?"

Nothing had gone the way he'd expected with this conversation—why should her second demand be any different?

"Because I don't want everyone in town feeling sorry for you. If they think you're that unlucky in love, you'll gain ten pounds during the Harvest Festival with all the free slices of pie and ice cream."

Despite her teasing smile, he fought an inexplicable burst of anger. He wasn't an object of pity. He wasn't a pathetic schoolboy with his first crush.

The cow shifted and lowed. Caleb patted the animal's side before standing.

"I'm not one of your causes, Anna," he spoke gruffly, his anger simmering just below the surface. "You don't have to rescue me."

Her expression transformed slightly. The change was so subtle, he might have missed the difference a week ago.

"I know that. But I owe you. You saved my life."

She'd sensed his anger, and the realization had hurt her.

"Anybody would have done the same."

"They didn't." Her voice was barely a whisper. "You did."

The last of his fury ebbed away. "Jo made me do it."

Anna only smiled. "Either way, I owe you. No one

is going to feel sorry for you or treat you like the jilted suitor."

She hadn't been pitying him at all. Instead, she thought she was protecting him.

"You aren't going to give up until you save me, are you?"

"Nope."

His gaze drifted toward her lips. How did he tell her he was already too far gone?

A scuffle sounded, and he peered around Anna. A young boy stood in the doorway of the barn, a dripping burlap sack in his hands. The bag moved.

Anna gasped and Caleb stepped forward. "You're Jasper, aren't you?"

The boy gave a hesitant nod. Caleb stifled a sigh. He was too thin for his age, his clothing barely more than rags. Caleb had heard through his sister that Jasper wasn't allowed to attend school more than a few months a year, which put him behind the other kids. When they started teasing him for the difference, he'd stopped going to school altogether.

Jasper's dad was a great bear of a man with a fierce temper, and his mother was little more than a shadow.

Caleb motioned with his hand. "What you got there?"

"Kittens."

Anna clutched her mouth.

Caleb gently extracted the squirming bundle from the boy and crouched. He rolled back the soaking edges of the bag, revealing two tiny squirming kittens, both of them orange tabbies. The boy snuffed and wiped his nose with the back of his hand. "Pa said we had enough cats around the farm, so he figured he'd drown them. Triple A fished 'em out of the pond. He said you'd maybe help."

"I'll help." Caleb stood and crossed the barn, snatching a blanket draped over one of the stall doors.

Caleb gave each of the kittens a quick exam. They'd been weaned too early; he noticed that right off.

Anna hovered near his shoulder, offering assistance when needed, handing over a prettily embroidered handkerchief for their bedding.

The kittens would require constant attention for the first days. After drying them off as best he could, he snatched the pail of milk from outside the stall and measured a portion onto the plate he'd set over the top as a lid. The kittens lurched the distance and lapped up the treat. Once sated, their bellies full, they curled up on the blanket.

How can someone do such a cruel thing?" Anna asked Caleb, out of earshot of Jasper.

The boy had taken up vigil near the kittens and didn't show any signs of moving.

A myriad of emotions flitted across her expressive face—anger, sorrow and frustration. She held up her shaking hands as though she wasn't quite certain what to do with them.

He clutched her chilled fingers and stilled their trembling.

She blinked rapidly. "I'm furious. I have a few choice words for that man."

"Let me deal with him." The thought of her confronting Jasper's father sent a cold chill through his heart. "Stay away from him."

All that she'd been through the past few weeks had finally caught up with her. He tangled his hand in the hair at the nape of her neck, and she pressed her forehead into his shoulder. He'd seen worse, he'd seen far worse.

He'd spoken more harshly than he'd intended, and by way of an apology he added, "I'll find good homes for the two kittens."

After a moment she straightened. "I'm not usually such a watering pot."

She reached for her handkerchief and realized her error.

He gestured toward the kittens. "You've given up your embroidery for a good cause."

A fat tear rolled down her check. He'd deal with Jasper's father, all right. If he could fix this, he would. If he thought he could make her happy, he'd never let her go.

He retrieved his own handkerchief, a plain starched square with no lace and no embroidery. This time he realized his own hands were trembling.

She accepted his offering and swiped at her eyes, then gave a delicate sniffle. "What about that little boy's parents? He doesn't appear any healthier than those kittens."

"I don't know much. The father is a drinker. He has a bad temper. The mother is little more than a shadow. She's lost two babies to stillbirth. I think she's too worn down."

Her chin tilted into a determined set, as though she'd come to a decision about a problem he hadn't known existed. "That's who I fight for. That's who I'm trying to save. That's who I'm trying to give a voice."

Something they had in common. He stayed in Cimarron Springs because of the small differences he made each day. For Jasper. For Triple A. For the animals that provided labor and even those that simply provided companionship. Except nothing he did would ever amount to much or make a great difference. He was content with his contribution. He trusted in the Bible. He trusted that those who had faith in the small things would also have faith in the large ones.

Anna needed a much larger stage. She deserved a larger stage. He ran his thumb around the curve of her ear and cupped her neck, hair and shoulder. This was a woman who needed a fight, who needed a cause.

He'd been lying to himself, clutching onto a hope that didn't exist. He'd been lying because a part of him wanted her near. He admired her, he liked her. The feelings she invoked were a far cry from those he'd felt for Mary Louise. Those had been insignificant and childish by comparison. He finally understood love. He finally understood loss.

"You already make a difference," he said. "There's nothing you can't do."

She smiled, and the last vestiges of his doubts faded. Everyone lost their way once in a while, and Anna had lost hers. He'd be doing her a great disservice if he didn't set her back on the path she'd chosen, the path that brought her joy and gave her life meaning.

Too bad he'd done a poor job of protecting himself in the process. He'd done the one thing he'd promised himself he'd avoid. He was falling for a girl who could never love him in return.

"You make a difference to everyone you meet, whether you know it or not."

Chapter Fifteen

At the pounding on the door, Anna raised her head from the floorboard she was vigorously sanding. Her hair was piled atop her head and covered with a handkerchief. Dirt streaked her hands and arms. She'd only planned on scrubbing a stain in the corner, but the task had grown. Once one part of the floor shone, the other parts appeared even duller.

While the structure was sound and Mr. Stuart had assured them the roof didn't leak, the inside had been neglected. A family of mice had taken up residence in the kitchen cupboard, and they'd had to relocate a Lark's nest built over the back door. The evidence of the birds was a touch harder to remove.

She sat back on her heels and surveyed her work. She'd sanded the floors in the entry by hand, and they were ready for a fresh coat of lemon oil.

The pounding sounded once more, and she pushed off her knee and stood. She hoped her visitor didn't stay long because there was too much work to be done and she wasn't exactly dressed for company.

She opened the door to a beaming Mrs. McCoy.

"Thought I'd better check up on you since I'm going to be your mother-in-law."

This certainly didn't bode well for the floor waxing.

Anna gaped. She was going to strangle Caleb if this web tangled any further. "But you know the truth, right? Caleb…uh…your son promised me he'd tell you."

"Of course, dear." Mrs. McCoy leaned closer. "I'm playing along."

The woman bustled past her and set her basket on the counter, then busied herself with removing jars and wrapped parcels from its interior.

"Really," Mrs. McCoy said. "I wish I'd made up the rumor myself. It's quite romantic."

"I'm not certain *romantic* is the term I'd use."

Anna was thinking more along of the lines of *harebrained* or *ill conceived*.

"You and Caleb and your whirlwind courtship. How you're fixing up your house so Izetta will be all settled before the two of you get married. You've gained the admiration of the whole town."

"But it's not true." How had such a simple bargain spun out of control? "Any of it."

"Well if it were true then it would be news, wouldn't it? News is boring. Filled with all sorts of facts and figures. We're talking about gossip."

Right now, Anna would much prefer a weather report. Something simple and boring and not all connected to her. "You're not even a bit alarmed by any of this? I hadn't expected such a furor."

"Don't you worry. This will all blow over soon. With any luck, there'll be another dead body off the five-fifteen train. Not that I wish ill on anyone. I mean to say that something else will take the place of this rumor.

Are you feeling better this morning? You looked a might peaked the other day. Course that was probably all the fuss at the train station and the bustle of settling into a new town. We've had our share of excitement here in Cimarron Springs, but that dead fellow was a new one. Well, mostly new."

Pressing a hand against her head to still the spinning caused by her unexpected visitor, Anna said, "I'm feeling much better. I tire more easily than I used to."

"That's to be expected, I'd imagine. Never been shot myself, though." Mrs. McCoy appeared thoughtful, as though searching her memory, ensuring she hadn't taken a bullet at some point. "This engagement gives us the excuse to get to know one another. I'm absolutely fascinated by your work, my dear. Jo has done nothing but sing your praises for the last year. You've made an admirer out of Tony, as well. She's all set for a protest during the presidential election. That's next Tuesday. Or is it a week from next Tuesday? My, but doesn't time scoot by?"

"That's very brave of Tony."

Here was another example in her arsenal. Tony had taken up the cause. After only a brief conversation, she'd set about staging a protest. Small gestures built into something bigger than all of them.

"You'll find things are different out here in the country," Mrs. McCoy stated. "Women's rights are a matter of necessity. When there are only two of you doing the work, sometimes you both wear the pants on the farm. And I mean that quite literally, my dear."

Another knock sounded.

Mrs. McCoy shooed her away. "Don't mind me. Go

and answer that. I thought I saw your friend Izetta working on the lilac bush out behind the house."

"It's overtaken the roses."

"Lilacs are aggressive that way. They'd be a weed if they didn't smell so sweet in the spring. My mother always kept a tincture of lilac water on her dressing table. To this day, the smell brings back memories of her. What were we talking about?"

"Izetta," Anna prompted. Mrs. McCoy had an endearing way of sliding off topic.

"Oh, yes. I wanted to ask her about the Harvest Social. You'll be coming, won't you?"

"I don't know. When it is? I don't know how long I'll be staying."

"Next Monday. Or is it a week from next Monday? It's around the corner, anyway. Certainly you'll be here that long."

The knock at the door grew more insistent.

"Oh, and call me Edith." Mrs. McCoy hustled into the kitchen. "Don't let me keep you. Seems like I've come on visiting day."

Anna patted her scarf-covered hair. Leaving a card and observing calling hours were obviously not customs of Cimarron Springs.

She returned to the door and discovered Caleb on the porch holding a bunch of flowers. Her heart beat an odd rat-a-tat-tat in her chest.

She whipped off her scarf and smoothed her hair.

"I thought you'd like an update on my unexpected guests," he spoke cheerfully. "You'll be happy to know the two kittens are fit and feisty."

Her cheeks warmed at his thoughtfulness. "I admit

I was a touch worried. They had quite a traumatic time of it."

"I believe I've found them a new home and names, as well."

"You work quickly," she said.

"I had to visit the Elder ranch, and Jasper had already told them about our heroic rescue. They were immediately adopted by Hazel and named Viola and Sebastian."

"A Shakespeare reference. I must meet this young Hazel one day."

"I hope you do."

Had she imagined the note of longing in his voice? Glancing down at her dirt-streaked apron, she sighed. Was there any chance he'd simply leave and let her freshen up?

"A job well done," she said.

"Your handkerchief played a pivotal role."

Anna rolled her eyes. "In any event, thank you for keeping me apprised."

"I brought you a housewarming gift." He handed her the bunch of purple asters. "There isn't much selection this time of year."

He doffed his hat and ducked beneath the low door, crowding into the entry. Why hadn't she considered he'd visit this morning? Why had she worn her most unbecoming dress? Why was she fretting about something so mundane, so entirely feminine and frivolous?

Anna clutched the flowers against her chest and gazed into his emerald-green eyes. My, but he had the most beautiful eyes. Even that first time she'd met him, with all the commotion, she'd been entranced by those eyes. The allure hadn't faded.

He stared at her expectantly, and she started. "Do

come in. And thank you, they're quite lovely. Your timing is fortunate. Your mother is here. She's around back talking with Izetta."

Caleb grimaced. "She's probably escaping the boys. All Maxwell talks about these days is the dead body."

"Apparently he's the only one interested in something as mundane as a murder. Everyone else is discussing our engagement."

"Don't blame me." He quirked an eyebrow. "You'd think a dead man was more interesting than an engagement."

"One would suppose."

"Our plan of saying and doing nothing has been wildly successful. If we never spoke again they'd probably have us married by spring."

"I'm developing a worry over the future of mankind."

Anna stepped aside and placed the flowers in a pitcher of water on the dining room table, fanning the blooms.

She returned and accepted his hat, absently running her hand along the worry spot on the brim, then hung it on the hook near the door. "You must tell me more about this Harvest Festival. When you spoke of the social in Kansas City, I had assumed you were exaggerating."

"I never exaggerate. However, I do sometimes lie outright."

Anna laughed in spite of herself. "You are incorrigible."

Her carefully constructed walls were eroding by the moment. Why hadn't nature granted him with pale blue eyes? Or boring brown? Or dismal gray? No. He'd been given the eyes of a charmer. Worse yet, he didn't even know his own attraction. A dash of arrogance might have blunted his hold on her.

"You already know about the shucking bee and barn dance," he said. "It's a bit of a marriage market, as well. A lot of the ranchers and farmers don't get to town very often, and it's a good chance to check out the local stock."

"The local stock? Isn't that a bit crude?"

"Sorry." He had the grace to blush. "That's what it feels like, though."

"Will you be attending?"

"Wouldn't miss it. There's a whole bevy of McCoy cousins there. If I didn't go, they'd never let me live it down. It's practically a family reunion."

"How many McCoys are there?"

"As many as the County Cork in Ireland could send."

The twinkle in his eyes sent a flutter of butterflies in her stomach. "Where are my manners? Can I get you something to drink?"

"No, thank you. I can't stay long. I need to check on the Elder's stallion again this afternoon. I thought I better check on my fiancée in the meantime."

Her cheeks flushed. "I guess Mr. Reinhart was correct. We gave the town a puzzle, and they filled in the pieces."

Caleb hesitated. "You don't mind, do you?"

Actually, she was rather enjoying the wonders of everyday living. She no longer felt as though the weight of the world rested on her shoulders. She'd stepped away from the cause, and nothing had happened. They sky hadn't fallen. The sun still set in the evenings.

She'd been infused with the wonder of everyday beauty. Oddly enough, polishing the floor had given her the same sense of accomplishment as giving a speech. There was pride in a job well done, no matter what the job.

She rested her hands on the back of her hips. "Admit the truth. If this was happening to someone else, we'd both find the situation terribly funny."

"Especially since half of Cimarron Springs knows who you are." Caleb offered an abashed smile. "It's the worst-kept secret in town, that's for certain. All the McCoys know, the Elders know, Jo's family knows, so that's the Cains, as well."

"Is there anyone left?"

"Not a lot."

"Should we simply tell everyone the truth?"

"And ruin everyone's fun? I don't have the heart. The last excitement this town had was when Jo shot her husband."

"On purpose? I've never heard the whole story."

"Of course, on purpose," he said, as though she'd asked a silly question.

The answer didn't seem as obvious as everyone around her assumed. "Did she mean to kill him?

"Just wound him. If Jo had wanted him dead, he'd be dead."

The one part of the story she had no trouble believing. "That does sound exciting."

"Someone was holding the marshal hostage. Jo took the shot as a distraction, then John Elder killed the man."

"The same John Elder that married the widow whose husband hid his loot in a cave by Hackberry Creek?"

"That's the one."

"I'm starting to like this town more and more."

"The past few years, there's been a dry spell. Now there's a dead body and a false engagement. You can't beat that kind of excitement."

"I wouldn't want to."

"How are you settling in, anyway?"

"I've been invited to a quilting bee."

"I hope you can stitch better than Mary Louise."

Anna couldn't hide her decidedly feminine emotions. She'd yet to meet this paragon, Mary Louise, but she took an unhealthy, an uncharacteristic, pride in the fact that she could sew.

Before she could reply, yet another knock sounded on the door.

Anna fumbled with strings on her apron. There was no use fighting the tide. She was going to host everyone in Cimarron Springs with her hair mussed wearing her oldest and most worn dress. "The knocking hasn't stopped since this morning."

"Don't expect the visitors to stop anytime soon. They usually allow you a day or two to get settled. After that they release the barrage."

"Exactly how long do you think this barrage will go on?"

When her mother had moved townhouses in St. Louis, they'd received a basket of muffins from the neighbor on their right and a polite but firm note from the neighbor on their left informing them of her allergy to Russian sage, and could they please not plant any.

"The visits will continue until everyone has satisfied their curiosity," Caleb said.

She caught sight of a streak of dirt on her forehead in the oval mirror hanging on the wall. "You mean to say, indefinitely?"

"Indefinitely. Welcome to life in a small town."

The knock sounded again, and they both laughed. Caleb fanned his arm. "Please, don't let me stop you from answering that."

She opened the door and gazed upon yet another, younger version of Caleb. The boy standing on her step was tall and gangly, his arms and legs equally proportioned. She supposed he'd eventually fill out and assume his older brother's build. She cast a sidelong glance at Caleb. Lucky boy.

"I'm Maxwell McCoy," he said. "People call me Max."

"I had a feeling you were a McCoy. You and your brother and sister are remarkably similar in appearance."

"People say we look alike. But all the McCoys look alike. Except for ma. She has blond hair." He scratched his head. "I guess it's mostly gray now."

"We'll stick with blond. Ladies don't always like to be reminded of their age. Not that age denotes ability or worth. It's simply the polite thing. Are you looking for your brother?"

He appeared a touch bemused by her speech. "Nah. I came to meet you."

"That's very nice." Anna held out her hand for a perfunctory shake. "I'm Anna. It's a pleasure to meet you."

"Maxwell McCoy." A violent blush colored his cheeks. "I said that before, didn't I?"

"Quite all right."

"Did you see the dead body? I tried asking Caleb about it, but he wouldn't tell me. Tony said she got a good look, and he was waxy and pale. Is that true?"

"Um. I suppose it must be correct. I only took a peek at his face. Mostly I only saw his hand."

"Was there any blood?"

"Not that I saw."

The enthusiasm drained from his expression like air from an overfilled balloon. "No blood, huh? That's what Tony said. I guess I'll have to take her word on the rest."

"The rest of what?"

"She said his eyes were all bugged out, like he'd been choked or something."

Max wrapped his hands around his throat and stuck out his tongue, making a strangling sound in his throat.

Caleb crossed his arms over his chest. "That's enough, Max. No more talk of dead bodies. There's a lady present. It's time you learned how to behave. No more talk of bugged eyes, or blood or strangling to death."

"Mary Louise says she's not a lady, she's a suffragist."

Anna raised her eyebrows. "A woman can be a suffragist and a lady, as well."

"I don't get it."

Caleb playfully cuffed him on the back of his head. "You don't have to understand. You simply have to use your manners."

"You're worse than Ma," Max grumbled.

"What was that, young man?" Edith McCoy's voice sounded from the kitchen.

Max blanched. "Ma is here, too?"

Anna sighed. "Pretty soon everyone will be here."

A knock sounded at the door, and Anna grinned ruefully. "See what I was saying?"

She opened the door to Jo's husband. "It's a pleasure to see you again, Marshal Cain, you'll be pleased to know several of your in-laws are here."

"Not surprised. Mind if I come in?"

"Not at all. The more the merrier. I was hoping to speak with you."

Mrs. McCoy returned to the sitting room, belaying the marshal's reply. "Hello, Garrett. Wasn't expecting to see you." She turned to Anna. "Well, it's all settled. You and Izetta are coming to the quilting bee on Friday at the church."

"If you're certain the other ladies won't mind an extra."

The thought of sharing her skill held a certain thrill. If the legendary Mary Louise didn't share that skill, than so much the better. Sewing was women's work, and strictly prohibited in the Bishop household. The only reason she embroidered was because one rebellious nanny had taught Anna the basics out of spite. Serving as Victoria Bishop's employee was never easy.

During the summer of '74, Anna's mother had traveled through England meeting with other women in the movement. Her strict instructions for Anna's care had been largely ignored by the nanny, and with no one there to oversee her, the revolt went unnoticed until her mother's return. Anna certainly hadn't confided the rules broken in any of her letters. Her mother must have suspected the rumblings of a rebellion. She'd returned unannounced and discovered Anna helping with the laundry. The poor nanny had been fired immediately. Anna still kept in touch.

Undaunted, Edith forged ahead. "What about embroidery? That's a lovely piece you're wearing now."

She indicated the stitching on Anna's collar where Anna had embroidered a trail of ivy into the linen.

"Yes." She fingered the raised stitching on the collar. "My embroidery is quite up to par."

"That'll be perfect. David's wife has been doing all the piecework, but the poor girl simply doesn't have the patience for detail. Now we have a quilt full of stems without any blossoms. She has a tendency to begin with the easy stitches first, and never quite gets around to the harder work. I've got a quilt full of stems and leaves for Mr. Lancaster's bride. You think you can finish up the flowers?"

"I, uh, I can try."

Mrs. McCoy squinted at Anna's collar. "Judging by the work you've already done, you should be quite up to the task."

"I look forward to helping?" Anna raised the end of her sentence in a question, unsure whether she'd be asked or ordered into work.

"Excellent. The roses will finally have blooms. This day just keeps looking up. Come along, Maxwell. I hope you haven't been pestering Anna with questions about the dead body."

"He's no bother."

"That's a yes, then. I've raised five boys, and every one of them the same. Oh, and I'll expect you for supper after church on Sunday. Do you like fried chicken?"

"Yes."

"Then it's settled."

Slightly confused by the rapid-fire instructions, Anna asked, "Is there anything I can bring?"

"What is your specialty?"

Anna thought for minute. "Toast."

Edith chuckled. "Then just bring yourself and Mrs. Franklin. We'll have the rest. Mary Louise isn't much for cooking either, so I'm used to fixing extra for the family."

She patted Marshal Cain on the arm. "Tell Jo to make an extra batch of rolls."

"I will," the marshal replied, clearly accustomed to taking orders from his mother-in-law.

Edith tugged a reluctant Maxwell toward the door, leaving Anna alone with the marshal and Caleb.

The marshal patted his stomach. "That's one thing about the McCoys—you never go hungry."

She'd nearly forgotten she asked the marshal over for a reason. "I wanted to talk with you about Mrs. Phillips."

Caleb lingered by the door. "Is this conversation private? Should I go?"

"Stay," Anna spoke impulsively.

His expression softened and she knew immediately he was recalling the last time she'd asked him to stay. Already they were building a past together, sharing memories of events they had in common.

She'd been taught to view affection as a destructive force. A lightning bolt or a raging inferno. Instead this gathering fondness for Caleb was more like tree roots, branching out, seeking a foundation built over time and shared experiences.

"I can't break Mrs. Phillips's confidence, but something she saw at the hotel may shed light on the identity of the dead man."

Since the conversation looked to expand past a few polite sentences, Anna glanced around the room. "I'd offer you a seat, but we don't have much furniture yet. I can pull a chair from the kitchen."

"Don't put yourself out. I can tell by the line of

people filing in and out your door it's been a busy morning."

Anna glanced at the muddy footprints marring her freshly scrubbed floor. Actually, she didn't mind so much. She'd rather have friends than a clean floor any day.

Anna rubbed her temple. The girl's words returned in a rush. *My mama says you're a hero.*

"Mrs. Phillip's daughter, Jane, was at the rally." Anna grimaced; how did she speak without revealing too much? "Mrs. Phillips saw the man discovered in her trunk speaking with another gentleman. From her description, it sounded like Reinhart."

"Reinhart?" the marshal tilted his head.

"He's a Pinkerton detective looking into my case. He had, uh, he had some information for me."

She hadn't thought about what he'd said in days. She'd pushed the information aside. Since her father had never been in her life, losing him hadn't quite sunk in yet. He was where he'd always been, hidden away like a box of photographs she planned on looking at one day, but never quite found the time.

"Then it's possible that fellow was a Pinkerton detective, as well," the marshal said.

"He's a strange man, Mr. Reinhart. But he did say something about hiring extra help. He was working on another case. I think it's worth looking into."

Caleb remained silent, his arms crossed over his chest, his gaze intent. What was he thinking?

"Did you find out any more about the man?" she asked. "About…about what happened to him?"

"The doc thinks he was strangled. Probably happened in Kansas City. Then he was stuffed in the trunk."

The marshal considered the hat he held in his hands. "Do you have any idea what other case Reinhart was working on in Kansas City?"

"I think it's possible he was looking for Mrs. Phillips." She pictured the bunch of yellow daisies the little girl had given her. Probably Jane's father had hired the Pinkerton detective. "I can't say any more without betraying her confidence."

"I've been in this business for a while now, Miss Bishop. I can make a few guesses. That woman is mighty scared about something."

"Her fear was there already."

"I figured that much."

"How can I help?"

"She trusts you, that's good. While she may not have killed the man in the trunk by herself, I can't rule out the possibility that she knows who did. She's hiding from someone. And while I've got a fair guess who and a fair understanding of why, I have to remain cautious. Keep the lines of communication open. She may say something else."

Caleb stepped forward and held up one hand. "I don't like this at all. You want her to talk with a woman who may or may not be a murderer? That doesn't sound wise."

"It's probably the safest place for Anna. If this Mrs. Phillips is somehow involved, then this is the best thing. She's here where we can keep an eye on her. Something is troubling that woman, and I think she'd feel better if she had someone to talk with."

Anna stood up straighter. "I know what's troubling her, and I can assure you that I'm perfectly safe."

The marshal replaced his hat. "Mrs. Phillips is as

jumpy as a mouse in a room full of cats for a reason, which means we all have to watch our backs. I'll have to let her go in a day or two. In the meantime, I'll see if I can run down this detective of yours. Find out if there's a connection."

"I don't want you alone with her, Anna," Caleb said.

"I appreciate your concern, but I can take care of myself."

He assumed a mask of contrition that didn't fool her a bit. "What sort of man would I be if I didn't protect my fiancée?"

"You two sort out the details," the marshal said, a twitch of a smile appearing at the corner of his mouth. "Let me know if you discover anything. Anything at all, even if it doesn't seem important right off. You never know what might make a difference."

As she ushered him to the door, her annoyance blossomed.

Her feelings over Caleb's protective attitude were conflicted. On the one hand, she appreciated his concern. On the other hand, she resented his interference. She was independent. Used to doing things on her own without a protector. Then again, the last thing she'd done on her own, she'd wound up shot. Maybe having a companion wasn't such a bad thing after all. Not that she wanted him to put his life at risk for her. She most definitely did not appreciate him questioning her judgment.

After the marshal left, Caleb lingered. "I'll pick you up on Sunday. For church. Just after ten. People will expect that you'll sit with my family."

The change of subject left her unsatisfied. "First, I need to set a few things straight."

He hooked his thumbs in his pockets. "All right."

"I'm perfectly capable of making decisions about whom I should and should not associate with."

He sucked in a breath, and she glared.

"I am not chattel. Do not use our engagement as an excuse."

"I wasn't going to."

"Then what were you going to say?"

"I'm sorry."

Her suspicions flared. "No one says they're sorry."

"I did. Just now."

She sidled nearer and narrowed her gaze. "Do you mean that?"

No one in the Bishop household ever apologized. Ever. An apology was a sign of weakness. Which meant he obviously had an ulterior motive. "Why are you giving up so easily?"

"I'm not giving up. I'm admitting that I was wrong. There's a difference."

"What difference?"

"This isn't a war, Anna. We're having a conversation, not a battle. I said I was sorry, and I am."

"Thank you," she said, humbled by his admission.

"You're welcome." Though a crinkle appeared between his brows, he didn't question her further, and for that she was grateful. "We're set for Sunday, then?"

As easy as that. This was not at all how she'd been taught to argue. A disagreement was absolutely a war. Battle lines were drawn, troops were mustered for the opposing sides. Words were fired like gunshots, aimed to inflict the most damage. Even the vaguest of half-hearted apologies was treated as a surrender, as an excuse to humiliate the enemy.

Anna realized the true folly of what she'd been taught all her life.

Refusing to apologize was a sign of cowardice and not a sign of strength. Caleb McCoy was no coward.

Speaking of cowards, she focused on his invitation. "Um, about that. I've never been to church."

"Ever?"

"Ever. My mother doesn't approve of organized religion."

"I don't suppose that makes any difference. But you don't have to go, if you don't want to."

Anna stared at the floor. She'd stick out like a sore thumb. "I don't know what to do. I don't know when to sit or when to stand. I don't know any of the words to the hymns."

"Nobody knows all the words." He chuckled. "That's why they give us all a hymnal."

This visit gave her the opportunity to explore new things. To expand her horizons. "I'd like to go. At least I think I would. I'm fairly certain."

"You can change your mind. I promise I don't mind either way. If you still want to go on Sunday, I will walk you there myself."

"There's no need. I'm hardly likely to get lost." She'd have found a refusal much easier had he been even the least bit judgmental. "Your mother has invited me back to the house after church. I feel as though I should bring something. Since I don't cook, I thought I'd visit the General Store. Is there anything she enjoys? Preserves or the like?"

"You don't cook?" he asked, appearing shocked. "At all?"

"No."

"Nothing?"

"When I said nothing, I meant nothing."

A hint of annoyance crept into her voice. He'd wanted to court Mary Louise and she didn't cook. Edith McCoy had said as much. What was the big deal?

"How do you get along?"

Anna heaved a fortifying breath. "My mother employs a cook and a housekeeper."

He let out a low whistle. "Does this mean Mrs. Franklin will be doing all the cooking and you'll be doing all the cleaning?"

"I suppose that's all that women are good for? Cooking and cleaning?"

"I live alone. I do both."

"Oh, fine." She'd been too long without a fight. The lull was wearing on her. "You cook and clean."

"Yes."

"Point taken." She swiped at a smudge on her sleeve. "Can you teach me how to cook?"

"Uh…"

The idea was inspired. While Izetta hadn't complained, Anna knew her lack of assistance put extra work on her.

She'd surprise Izetta with her new skill. Anna immediately warmed to the idea. "I don't need to know everything. Just a few basics to get started. Mrs. Franklin can show me the rest. What with cleaning the place, I don't want to ask any more of her."

The more things she learned, the more she strengthened her own independence.

He snatched his hat from the hook and backed toward the door. "Jo is the cook in the family. I'll talk with her."

"Perfect," she said, keeping her tone cheerful.

"She likes a schedule," he said, fumbling for the door. "She makes noodles every other Friday."

"How do you know that?"

"Because I always make certain to drop by for dinner."

With a tip of his hat he spun on his heel and strode down the stairs.

She'd gone and done it again. She'd assumed a familiarity that didn't exist. Would she ever learn? It was far too easy to slip into the fictional world they'd created and forget the real one.

She closed the door and leaned back.

A shriek sounded from the back garden and she dashed through the house. Anna emerged into the garden in time to find a red-faced Mrs. Franklin chasing a very familiar goat.

"Look what he's done!"

Gleefully unremorseful, the goat galloped toward Anna, a half-eaten red rose in his mouth.

She reached down and patted the animal on the head. "Shall I return him?"

"No," Mrs. Franklin spoke firmly. "This time I shall have the honors. I don't know what this little beast likes more—you or the rosebushes."

The goat butted Anna's leg and bleated. "He does seem awfully fond of me."

"He's positively smitten."

Watching Izetta walk the recalcitrant goat back home, an uncharacteristic bout of melancholy swept over her. She couldn't shake the feeling that this was all just a dream, that she'd wake up back in her home in St. Louis the same Anna Bishop. Which was foolish, of course.

She'd never be the same. Her injury and her stay here had eroded everything she believed about herself. Yet the process had been more enlightening than corrosive.

Leaves rustled above her head and she wrapped her arms around her middle. They'd better find the killer soon, because the more time she spent in Cimarron Springs, the harder it was going to be to leave.

Chapter Sixteen

The following days passed in relative peace. All of the leaves fell, and the first frost blanketed the prairie. She'd studiously avoided any contact with Caleb and found her new strategy had failed. With each passing day he filled a greater portion of her thoughts. Today she waited for Izetta at the door.

The older woman lifted an eyebrow but didn't say anything. The church bell clanged in the distance, heralding the service. As they stepped onto the dirt-packed street, they met the Stuarts. Then Mr. Lancaster and his wife, then a whole group of other people she'd never met before. Everyone they passed smiled a greeting or offered a friendly handshake.

The engagement bargain had worked. The people in town accepted her without question, without censure. The notion left her almost giddy.

Upon approaching the church, the crowds parted and Caleb stood there. He was wearing a suit she'd never seen before, black trousers and a close-fitting black jacket. He smiled a greeting, and her heartbeat tripped, then took up a frantic rhythm. She was drawn toward him against her better judgment, longing for just another moment more in his company.

People stepped aside and let him pass as he approached them. "Will you sit with us?"

She glanced at the McCoy clan and nodded. "Are you certain?"

He frowned and tilted his head. "What's the matter?"

Leaning closer, she whispered, "Remember what I said before."

"Remember what I said before." He spoke in an exaggerated whisper. "Follow my lead."

Silly, but she'd faced hordes of people armed with rotten fruit with less trepidation than this simple Sunday service. As though the congregation might suddenly discover her a fraud or declare her a heretic before the whole church.

His stuck out his elbow, and she hesitantly looped her hand through his arm, her fears calming.

A snuffing sounded from the bushes and she paused, certain she'd spied a glimpse of gray fur. "Did you lock the gate?"

"I don't follow."

"That goat of yours is remarkably ingenious."

"His name is Pipsqueak," Caleb said. "I needed something to shout when he escaped."

"And you're certain he hasn't escaped today?"

"Positive."

Practically the entire town was present, which meant nothing could go wrong this morning. This might be a fake engagement, not to mention absolutely the worst-kept secret in town, but she wasn't letting the Mc-Coys down. They'd been kind and welcoming, and she wouldn't embarrass them. Or Caleb. Mostly Caleb.

He led her a few feet away and she heard the sound again.

Whipping around, she glared at the bushes. "He's here. I know it."

"I'm not saying you sound crazy—" Caleb tugged on her arm "—but others might."

She glanced around to ensure no one was watching them, then pointed at the dense green foliage lining the base of the church. "Stay out of Izetta's rosebushes."

"Now that did sound crazy."

"Crazy or not, that goat has a passion for roses. And me."

"Something we have in common." His face suffused with color. "The roses, of course."

"That's odd," she said, her voice teasing. "I don't recall any roses around your house."

"It's a recently discovered passion."

Feeling absurdly shy, she abandoned her search for the mischievous goat and let Caleb lead her up the stairs. Besides, what could possibly go wrong on such a beautiful day?

The church was delightful. The sort of picturesque building depicted on Christmas cards with smiling cherubs and seraphim. The building wasn't terribly large or ornate, a white clapboard frame with a modest steeple. Plain glass panes let in sunlight from both sides, and a stain-glassed window cast colorful patterns over the altar. The effect of such simplicity in design was charming.

They filed into the sturdy, polished pews with Anna on the aisle. The first half went well. She stood when Caleb stood, she sat when Caleb sat. He held the book and pointed out the hymns, his baritone voice reverberating beside her. He had quite a lovely singing voice. She let her eyes drift closed and simply enjoyed the sound.

When her inherent skepticism reared its head during the homily on forgiveness, lightning did not strike.

All in all her first foray into religion had not been a disaster.

Until she heard the noise.

A familiar bleating sound came from the back of the church. Her stomach knotted. Heads swiveled. She kept her attention rigidly forward. The sound of hoof beats scuffling across the wood floors neared. Someone tittered. A wave of whispered voices rippled through the church. The scuffling stopped. A snout nudged her arm.

Oh, no. That little troublemaker was not ruining her morning.

Assuming her fiercest countenance, Anna confronted Pipsqueak and snapped her fingers. "Outside. Now."

Pipsqueak ducked his head and backed away.

"I do not feel the least bit guilty. You know the rules. Outside."

The animal turned and wearily trudged toward the exit.

Anna glanced up and caught the wide-eyed stare of Reverend Miller. Her heart turned to lead and dropped into her stomach. So much for making a good impression.

Beside her, Caleb's shoulder trembled against hers. From the corner of her eye she caught his merry grin. She elbowed him in the side. The shaking only grew worse.

Reverend Miller smothered a grin and fisted his hand

on the pulpit. His face grew red. He searched his breast pocket and dug out a handkerchief, then mopped his brow.

A full minute went by while the reverend composed himself and began speaking once more.

Anna clenched her teeth.

The next twenty minutes passed in agony. If she could have followed the goat out the door, she would have. Except fleeing the church now only added more fuel. As soon as the congregation was released, she shot out of her seat and collided with Triple A.

He grinned at her and winked. "The missus had some mighty fine embroidered aprons. Since she passed, they ain't doing me no good. Can I bring them by your place?"

For gracious sake what was that all about? "Of… of course."

He pivoted on his heel and melted into the swirl of people.

Anna searched behind her. The aisle soon crowded with McCoys, and Mrs. McCoy planted her hands on her hips. "Land sakes. That's more words than I've heard Triple A speak in a month of Sundays. I didn't think anyone could win that man over."

She squeezed Anna's shoulder as though she'd gained a great victory instead of embarrassing herself in front of the entire congregation.

Brahm scooted past and chucked her on the shoulder. "Will you be here next week?"

"I suppose."

"I can't wait."

"I don't…uh…that is…"

Maxwell gave her two thumbs up. "Can you teach me that?"

"What?"

"Can you teach me how to train a goat?"

"I don't, that is, I didn't..."

His father gently shoved him forward. "If you can figure out how to turn that charm on children, you let me know."

Jo and the marshal appeared next, little Shawn perched on her hip, Cora and Jocelyn in matching pink dresses.

"I second that," Jo said. "You have a way with animals."

The marshal only grinned.

By the time they emerged into the late morning sunlight, Anna was swamped with people who wanted her attention. She received three invitations to supper and one offer of another goat, which she politely declined.

Pipsqueak spent the whole time chewing on a patch of nettles near the corner of the church, seemingly unaware of the excitement he'd stirred up.

Bemused, Anna let the conversation swirl around her. Mrs. McCoy must have realized her confusion.

"That's the thing about small towns," she said, "All newcomers to a small town need a story before they're fully accepted into the fold."

"A story?"

"Yep. I remember when Triple A came to town before he even married his first wife twenty years ago. Got himself stuck up on the roof when his ladder fell over. He was too prideful to call for help. He spent the whole afternoon sitting on that roof hollering hello until my husband, Ely, came walking by. Poor Ely couldn't figure out what kind of fool sat on his roof yelling hello. Figured the man must have gone daft. He helped him down and told him that if a man needed help, he was better off asking for it than letting his vanity stand in the way. Anyway, you see how it is."

A small seed of pride took root in her chest. Sure, she'd gone and made a fool of herself in church, but no one seemed to mind. She'd established her place in town. She had her own story. While it wasn't the story she might have chosen, it was a story nonetheless.

Reverend Miller tipped his hat and grinned. "We'll be seeing you next week."

Her pride increased tenfold. She'd gotten the approval of Reverend Miller. No one held any grudge for the untimely interruption in the church.

Her steps were lighter and heart happier on the way home. Caleb walked them down the hill and around the corner toward their street.

A carriage and two horses stood outside the house. A gentleman Anna remembered from town held their lead.

Izetta frowned. "Who can that be?"

As they reached the wagon, the blood drained from Anna's face. She recognized the trunk.

Her mother was here.

Caleb sensed Anna's reaction immediately. She'd gone deathly pale, her hands gripping her reticule, her lips devoid of color.

His stomach clenched. "What is it?"

"My mother is here."

Caleb stopped his jaw from dropping in the nick of time.

The man standing near the horses' heads flagged Caleb over. "Give me a hand with the trunk, will you?"

"Sure, Berny."

Uneasy, he kept Anna in his peripheral vision. He didn't know what reaction he expected, but he sure hadn't expected her obvious dread.

As Izetta and Anna made their way into the house, Caleb and Berny followed along behind them with the trunk. The impressive piece of luggage was an almost exact replica of the one Anna possessed with the same leather straps and the same brass fittings.

After reading about Victoria Bishop in the newspapers and hearing Anna's anecdotes, he wanted to see the woman for himself. He needed to understand the forces shaping Anna's life.

They stepped into the parlor, and he struggled with the heavy trunk. Was the lady carrying another body in there? He glanced and paused, then jerked forward since Berny was still moving. An imposing-looking woman sat in the chair, one hand braced on a walking stick.

Berny stopped in the doorway. "Where do I put this?"

"Back in the wagon," the woman declared sharply. "I shall be staying in town at the hotel."

Caleb chanced a glance at Anna. All the sparkle had left her eyes. She was a shadow of the woman he'd seen only moments before. Her mother had dimmed her spirit, and the result was visible.

"I wasn't expecting you, Mother," Anna said. "What a pleasant surprise."

"Not pleasant at all. The townhouse has burned to the ground."

"Our house?"

Anna sat down hard on one of the sturdy dining room chairs.

"Yes, our house. Whose house do you suppose I meant? The grocer?" She sniffed. "The houses on either side received significant damage, as well." She patted the side of her head. "Not that the Smith place was any great loss. I never did trust that man."

Anna gripped the arm of her chair. "Was anyone hurt?"

"I didn't ask. It didn't seem relevant."

Caleb's forearms strained against the weight of the trunk. Neither he nor Berny moved.

Anna spread her hands. "Do they know how the fire started? Were you there?"

"Arson. The fire was deliberately set. I received word in Boston. I returned home immediately."

"You returned for the fire?" Anna's voice was heartbreakingly quiet.

"I had to see what was salvageable." The elder Miss Bishop scowled. "You cannot trust the help to make those decisions."

The hurt on Anna's face cut him to the quick. Victoria Bishop hadn't come when her daughter had been shot. She'd been too busy, the work in Boston too important. He snorted softly. She'd found time enough when her precious belongings had been damaged.

Victoria glanced around and gathered her skirts closer, as though worried they might be sullied. "I had hoped to stay with you until things were settled. I can see now that won't be possible."

At Anna's crestfallen expression, a cold fist tightened around Caleb's heart.

She held up her hands then let them drop to her sides.

"There's a hotel in town. Perhaps you'd be more comfortable there."

Her distress cut him to the quick.

"I can't imagine being comfortable anywhere this far west of the Mississippi." Victoria flicked at a bit of lint on her sleeve. "I told Elizabeth that Kansas City was a waste of time."

"That's enough, Mother."

With the sound of Victoria Bishop's sharp intake of breath, he jerked his head toward Berny, who took the hint. Together they hauled the trunk back out to the wagon. Nothing about seeing Anna's mother had changed his initial impressions of her.

At least Anna had regained some of her fire. She needed it with that woman.

Berny mopped his brow. "You could store that lady in an icehouse. I've never seen the like." He braced his hand against the wooden slats of the wagon bed. "I don't think she likes our town very much either. She kept sniffing and covering her face."

"I was thinking the same thing."

Caleb had the feeling Victoria Bishop didn't like much of anything that didn't go according to her plans. She was treating all of them as though they were somehow involved in her great inconvenience. Was that how she treated Anna? As an inconvenience? She didn't appear the sort of woman who'd have a sense of humor about their engagement either. He doubted she had much of a sense of humor about anything.

The door swung open, and she marched down the bricked pathway toward the wagon. Mrs. Franklin had arrived by then and offered a friendly greeting.

Miss Victoria Bishop stared down her nose. "Pleasure," she said, though her voice remained hard.

Anna hovered behind her mother and motioned toward him. "This is Mr. McCoy. He saved my life in Kansas City."

He touched the brim of his hat. "Pleased to meet you, Miss Bishop."

"You are the veterinarian." Once again she managed to coat her words in disdain.

"I am."

Anna shot him an apologetic look and he returned what he hoped was a comforting smile.

"Then I suppose thanks are in order. My daughter appears to be in fine health."

She didn't wait for a reply, but rather circled around the wagon toward the passenger side.

Berny scooted past and rolled his eyes. "Glad it's a short way back into town. She's a scary one."

Caleb didn't doubt the assessment.

With everyone on the opposite side of the wagon, no one saw exactly what happened next. They certainly heard what happened.

Pipsqueak bleated. The horses startled and lunged forward, yanking on the wagon. The set brake held them at bay. Anna's mother shrieked.

Caleb sprang forward and snatched the horses' lead, murmuring soothing words. Anna and Mrs. Franklin dashed around the wagon.

Berny peeked around the corner and his eyes widened. "Well she ain't looking so high and mighty now, I'll say that."

Anna's mother wailed. "That infernal animal has broken my ankle."

* * *

An hour later Doc Johnsen stood next to the bed. "The ankle isn't broken," he said. "It's a bad sprain. I recommend staying put this evening."

The news did not please her mother. Anna cringed.

"Return me to the hotel this instant," Victoria demanded.

"We'd have to put you on a litter and carry you the distance. You won't be able to put weight on that foot until tomorrow at least."

Anna watched as her mother weighed the options. She clearly wasn't interested in remaining in the Stuart house along with her and Miss Franklin. The indignities of being carted down Main Street on a litter obviously held less appeal.

After a long silence, she sniffed. "Then I shall remain here and make do. I insist you slaughter that goat and serve him to the dogs."

Anna started. "Your fall was an accident. You can't blame Pipsqueak."

"I most certainly can."

"Can I get you a cup of coffee?" Mrs. Franklin interjected.

"Tea is better."

"I only have chamomile. Will that suffice?"

"I suppose it shall have to do then, won't it?"

"You are a guest, Mother." Anna heard the tremor in her voice and hated herself for the telling weakness. "I'm quite sure you'll be happy with anything Mrs. Franklin has to offer."

"I am a guest because this town is teeming with barnyard animals. That is hardly my fault."

"Neither is it the fault of Mrs. Franklin."

Anna was mortified, humiliated and downright furious. From Berny to Doc Johnsen, everyone in town had been nothing but solicitous. Her mother, on the other hand, had been absolutely insufferable. The strain of the fire had obviously shortened her temper.

Victoria Bishop glanced around the room. "I will need a sturdy side table along with my pens, papers and correspondence. Between your injury and the fire, it is time for another campaign. We must capitalize on these events before interest grows cold."

"What do you mean? Capitalize?" Anna hadn't yet recovered from the idea that her mother was here. Staying. For an extended length of time. Confined to her bed.

If Victoria Bishop loathed weakness in others, she abhorred weakness in herself. The next twenty-four hours were going to be miserable.

"This is our chance for front-page coverage. I saw nothing about your shooting in the pages of the newspapers back East. Absolutely nothing. Since two events of violence have occurred against our family, the papers will be obligated to report the story. I shall demand they do so."

"You're using this for the platform?"

"Do not be naive, dear. Passing up such an excellent opportunity is foolish. As soon as my leg heals, we shall return to St. Louis. Nothing can be done from this isolated location."

Her mother was wrong. There were plenty of ways one made a difference, even in a small town. The cause wasn't simply about making a change in Washington. If they made grand speeches and forgot the individual stories, then they gained nothing. They had traveled the country and focused on getting the vote, all the while forgetting the very people they were fighting for. That was Victoria Bishop's mistake.

Anna exhaled her pent-up breath. This was not the time to change her mother's mind. There were other, more pressing matters. Anna wasn't a child anymore, easily distracted by her mother's verbal sparring. She wanted answers. Needed answers. There were questions still hanging between them—about her past, about her father, about everything.

"Actually, Mother," Anna began, "I think this convalescence will give us the opportunity to clear the air between us."

"I wasn't aware the air had been polluted."

A knock sounded from the front parlor, and Izetta crossed the room, no doubt using the distraction as a polite way to leave them in privacy.

"I spoke with a Pinkerton detective named Reinhart," Anna said, studying her mother for even a hint of reaction. "He said someone was looking for me in St. Louis."

Victoria Bishop plucked at a loose thread in the tufting on the arm of her chair. "What on earth are you babbling on about?"

"I think you know."

Izetta interrupted Anna's next words, her gaze apologetic. "You're needed in town, Anna. It's Mrs. Phillips."

The look on Izetta's face indicated bad news. "Oh dear, what's wrong?"

"Her husband has arrived."

Why did everything always happen at once? She'd spent a week here with hardly more than a breeze to stir the leaves, now a veritable tornado of activity was brewing.

Anna snatched her shawl from the peg near the door and leaned into the parlor. "I shall return shortly." She pinned her mother with a stare. "You and I are not finished speaking."

"Of course not, dear. I need your assistance with a speech for the Boston chapter," her mother said.

Anna gritted her teeth. She'd finish this talk later, whether her mother liked it or not.

Her mother told women like Mrs. Phillips to wait for change. Mrs. Phillips didn't have the luxury of time.

Everything jumbled together in her mind. This was her chance to prove she wasn't a child, to prove she deserved answers, to prove she was more than simply Victoria Bishop's daughter. She understood things her mother couldn't comprehend, about people, about their heartaches.

When she arrived at the hotel, Mrs. Phillips was tugging her gloves over her wrists. Jane sat solemnly beside her mother wearing a fresh pink dress with several layers of lace flounces.

Her feet swung, and Anna returned to her own youth, recalling her vigil outside Miss Spence's office all those years ago.

Mrs. Phillips didn't meet her eyes. "We're going home with Clark."

Panic gripped Anna. "But you can't. After what he's done. How can you?"

"We had a long talk. He's said he's changed."

Anna felt as though the ground beneath her feet had crumbled away. "Mrs. Phillips. This isn't a matter of leaving one's dirty clothing on the floor or working too many hours, or even of drinking too much. This man had you—" She caught sight of Jane and held back the words. "You know what he's done."

"I'm not like you. I'm not independent. Clark handled all the decisions, all the bills. Jane needs a stable home."

"Do you really think that's what your future holds? A stable home life? You must think about Jane."

"I am thinking about Jane. This is what's best. Clark can guarantee a comfortable life for her. I cannot."

Anna caught the slight change in her tone. "Has he done something? Has he threatened you? Is he blackmailing you?"

Her expression hardened. "I'm doing what's best for me. For Jane. I don't expect you to understand that."

The extent of her failure stole the breath from Anna's lungs. She'd lost the battle. She'd done nothing for Mrs. Phillips. She'd done nothing for Jane. She'd thought she'd understood but she was just as naive and self-absorbed as her mother. She'd been fighting for a personal victory, as well.

"Will you stay in touch?" Anna begged, grasping for any thread of hope. "Will you write and let me know how you're faring?"

"I don't think so. Perhaps it's best if we don't remain in contact."

Anna glanced between mother and daughter. She'd failed. There was nothing left. No more arguments. By the set of her jaw, Mrs. Phillips had made up her mind. Nothing Anna had done had made a difference.

Her anger burned unchecked and she knelt. "Goodbye, Jane," she said.

The younger girl stared. Anna wished she had more time. She wanted to tell her that she didn't have to continue the pattern. She needn't grow up and make the same mistakes as many children seemed to do. Mrs. Phillips had entered into an unhealthy marriage because she hadn't known the difference. Jane was destined to do the same. The chain of suppression continued from one generation to the next, unchecked unless someone took a stand.

She'd so hoped Mrs. Phillips had the strength. Jane deserved a better life.

As she stared into Jane's pale gray eyes, she willed her understanding.

Victoria Bishop had been right all along. The only way of breaking the chain was from a position of power. They needed the vote. They needed a say in the politicians elected for office. They needed laws to protect women like Mrs. Phillips.

"You're the prettiest lady I've ever met," Jane said.

"There's more to being a girl than being pretty," Anna replied.

"You're pretty here," Jane said, touching her hair. "And pretty here." She touched Anna's chest over her heart.

"When you're older." Anna blinked rapidly. "You can write to me."

"Where will I find you?"

"Here," Anna said impulsively. "Write to me in Cimarron Springs."

Mrs. Phillips yanked Jane's hand and glared. "Time to go."

With helpless rage Anna watched them go. Anything she said or did now only made matters worse. For her. For Mrs. Phillips. For Jane. For all of them.

She hadn't made one bit of difference.

* * *

Caleb kept the porch swing moving with the heel of his boot, his eyes on the street. Anna had to pass by on her way home. They hadn't talked about her father once since that day in Kansas City. The subject was too private. With Anna's mother in town, he wondered if Anna was thinking about him.

He almost didn't recognize her. Always before when he'd seen her, her shoulders were back and she walked with purpose, her steps brisk. This afternoon her head was down, her back stooped, her steps lagging.

He leaned forward and rested his forearms on the whitewashed porch rails. "Penny for your thoughts."

She glanced up. "Where's Pipsqueak?"

"In the barn. Under lock and key. And chains. And whatever I could find to keep him from causing more mischief."

"My mother was hoping you'd feed him to the wolves."

"That's funny. Berny thought we should give him a medal and name him honorary mayor of the town."

Anna hid a grin behind her hand. "I would attend that ceremony."

"Ah, well. We rarely get everything we wish for, do we?"

Anna turned toward the gate, remaining just outside the fence. "No, we don't."

She was only fifteen feet away, yet he sensed the gulf separating them. "I heard Mr. Phillips arrived on the same train as your mother."

"He did."

"The marshal talked with him."

"Good."

"She's making the best choice she knows how."

"Why do we cling to things that hurt us so?"

He stood and crossed the distance, standing on the opposite side of the gate. "Animals are creatures of habit. Look at the buffalo. They followed the same trails for so long, they cut divots into the earth. Then the wagon trains came along and did the same. Because people aren't much different, I suppose. Taking chances means taking risks. Not everyone has the stomach for change."

"We all simply stay with the devil we know?"

"Rather than risk greater pain."

"What a sad state of affairs."

"Except sometimes, on very rare occasions, someone comes along who's willing to make a change," he said. "Someone who's willing to stand on a stage in front of hundreds of people and risk everything for what they believe in."

Her smile was tinged with sadness. "I didn't make a difference, though."

"You don't know that. No one truly knows the changes we make on people. Look at Jane. She's met you. She's seen a different way of living, of thinking."

Anna had changed him. He'd been careless of the life he'd built, of the friends and family surrounding him. He'd been complacent with their love and affection. He'd even been dismissive of their relationships, rolling his eyes at Jo's fondness for her husband.

No more. He had something rare and precious, something he wasn't going to take for granted anymore. He had a family who loved him, a community who supported him and a job that fulfilled him. There were pieces missing, a wife and a family. He'd always mourn that loss. After knowing Anna, he'd never settle for anything else. Instead, he'd appreciate the things he did have.

"Maybe." Anna shook her head. "I'm not certain anymore. My mother works in grand gestures. I get caught up in the details. In the people and their stories."

The two kittens they'd rescued frolicked in a large crate near the porch. "Would you like to see the boys? They're doing well. Should be on their own in a week or two."

"No." She tilted her head toward the sky. "I don't want to grow attached."

She kept her distance, and he sensed her purpose. She was separating from him, from the town, from everything. She was going home. He'd known she'd leave, he'd always known. He just hadn't considered how soon. With her mother here, they only had a few days at best.

"I lost sight of everything," she said. "I was impatient. I wanted to see a change. I wanted to know I was making progress."

"Haven't you?"

"I don't know anymore."

He chose his words carefully. "Everyone has different gifts. You see the human side of each story, and you are moved by the individual stories. Use that strength."

"How?"

"I don't know. That's for you to discover." A deep, abiding sadness filled his heart. "Are you coming to Harvest Festival tomorrow night?"

"I shouldn't. My mother. I shouldn't leave her alone."

"You'll miss the husking bee."

"I did want to see Gus and Becky. I've been here one week already, and I've never even seen your Mary Louise."

"She isn't mine. She's simply a girl who caught my fancy a long time ago."

A thousand reasons for her to stay remained locked away. There was only one reason for her leaving. She was better off without him. The very thing that drew him toward her was the very thing that stood between them. She craved independence and reveled in the public eye. He was a man who preferred a quiet life. She defied convention. He embodied convention.

She twisted the filial atop the gate. "After we left church, I felt such a sense of peace."

"Have we made a believer out of you?"

"It's too soon to tell, but I believe you have. I hadn't expected the sense of grace. I keep thinking about what you said before, how all relationships require work, even our relationship with God. I've never put in the effort before, but I'm willing to try."

"Then I wish you peace on your journey."

They had developed a friendship, which was something. A rare gift he was grateful for. Eventually, though, they'd tear each other apart. If they tried building a life together, there was no way of avoiding a terrible rift. They were each moving in opposite directions. For a moment in time they'd crossed paths. He'd known the truth all along, only he hadn't counted on the pain.

She started to turn and he called out, "Wait. Come to the Harvest Festival. Only for an hour. Surely your mother will be fine for a short length of time? One last memory of Cimarron Springs."

"I'll come," she conceded. "But only for a short time."

He didn't know why the concession was important, but her acceptance of the invitation was vital. "I'll take you there myself. It's only a mile down the road. I'll take you and Mrs. Franklin," he added quickly.

He rested his hand over hers. Their fingers entwined. She sighed, and he pressed his mouth against her temple, the soft beat of her heart beneath his lips. They stood that way for a long time, neither willing to break the moment. There was nothing more to say, he'd spent all his words.

He swallowed thickly and stepped away, his feet crunching over fallen leaves. It seemed fitting they'd met in autumn. A fiery end before a long, cold winter.

She turned and smiled wistfully over one shoulder. "Will you save a dance for me?"

"Of course."

He wouldn't burden her with words of love. His heart, so painfully empty before, was replenished. He'd hold these feelings close through the coming years. They weren't courting. They weren't engaged. They were neighbors. They were acquaintances. Nothing more, nothing less.

He was a selfish man. He'd begged her to come not because he wanted her to remember Cimarron Springs, but because he wanted his own memory of her.

One last dance before they said goodbye forever.

Chapter Seventeen

The evening of the shucking bee arrived with a brisk wind from the north. Winter was well on its way. Any lingering fall blooms had died with the frost, and most of the leaves had fallen, leaving only the oak trees with their crown of browned leaves.

Anna had worn her shirtwaist and plaid skirt, though she'd conceded she must don her navy velvet wrap against the chill. She had nicer clothing, but she wanted to blend in with the other girls, and her fine silks set her apart. She'd never realized before, but clothing was another form of armor. Tonight she was shedding her reticence and enjoying herself.

Her mother cast a disapproving glare from the parlor. "I hope nothing happens while the two of you are gone. I shall be quite all alone."

Izetta tossed Anna a sympathetic smile before saying, "Why don't I wait for you outside?"

"I'll be right there." Anna turned toward the parlor. "I know how much you value your independence. I'll only be gone an hour or so. The solitude will help you concentrate."

Her mother grimaced and set down her quill, pushing aside the paper covering her makeshift desk. "Must you attend this provincial gathering?"

"These are good people. They've been kind to me. I don't like you speaking of them with such derision."

She'd known her mother was a snob. Of course she'd known. She hadn't realized the extent of her prejudices.

"Yes," her mother drawled. "Good people. They won't miss you any more if you attend their little social."

She thought of Caleb and those eyes. Those entrancing forest-green eyes. "I will miss them."

"Will you at least say your goodbyes this evening? I don't want a scene on the train platform tomorrow. You know I detest scenes. You always were too softhearted. Makes a woman weak."

"I'm well aware of your preferences. I will not make a scene."

Her anger took root and grew. Like a living, breathing thing it took hold of her. She wasn't weak for having feelings. She wasn't weak for growing attached to the town and the people. She wasn't weak for falling in love.

Her anger crystalized and shattered.

Her mother grasped the spectacles hanging around her neck and perched them on her nose. She studied the paper before her, effectively dismissing Anna.

Caught up in the depth of her revelation, Anna barely spared her a glance. She'd missed the signs because she'd been taught to see love as a destructive thing. A crushing force. Her love for Caleb was as light as a thistle on the breeze. As bright as a blanket of stars of a moonless night.

She was halfway through the door before her mother called, "Can you bring me my tea before you go?"

"No time," Anna called in return. "I'm already late."

She slammed the door behind her, blocking her mother's ferocious mutterings.

"That was awful," Anna said to Izetta. "I should go back."

Izetta took her elbow in a firm, though not painful grip. "You will do no such thing. You should be in the annals of sainthood by now, dealing with that woman. I don't know how you manage."

"You've been extremely patient with her, and I'm grateful."

Over the past twenty-four hours, they'd done little more than fetch and carry for her mother. With no thanks besides. The tea was never hot enough, the biscuits never light enough, their service never quick enough. Anna had an hour reprieve, and she was going to enjoy herself.

"Your help has been indispensable," Anna said, hoping her apology was enough. "I'm afraid my mother has never had much patience for the weak or the sick. Being helpless is frustrating for her. She's never been home much. This is the most time we've spent with each other. Ever."

Again that morning she'd almost broached the subject of her father, only to stop herself. He was dead, what did digging up the past matter? Curiosity lingered despite all her good intentions. Tomorrow, tomorrow on the train, when they were alone, she'd ask her. After all these years, she deserved something of an answer. Even if that answer wasn't satisfactory.

Izetta patted her hand. "There's no need for apologies. I've quite enjoyed my stay in Cimarron Springs. In fact, I believe I'll stay."

Anna started. "You're staying?"

"Why not? As I said before, I'm a widow with a pension. I make my rules."

"But what about your work in Kansas City?"

"I'll still fight, never doubt that. I'll simply find another way."

Anna held her tongue. Izetta's plans were not up for debate. A tinge of jealousy caught her by surprise. Izetta had choices. Another reason Anna must return home. In St. Louis, she made a difference.

Tonight, though, she was forgetting all about the vote. Tonight was her last night with Caleb, her last hour, her last stolen moment, and she planned on enjoying their evening.

A tingle of anticipation danced along her nerves. After hearing about the Bainum farm from Caleb, she was anxious for her first view.

When she caught sight of him, her soul filled with tenderness. Caleb halted the wagon, set the brake and hopped down.

He circled toward the front and her. His gaze caressed her, and a shiver went down her back. He wore a crisp white shirt, dark trousers and a dark close-fitting coat. His hair had been brushed till it gleamed, his face freshly shaved. As he approached, she caught the faint hint of bay rum. She leaned closer and inhaled the scent, committing the sensation to memory.

Izetta urged her forward. "You sit in the middle. I'll feel claustrophobic if I have to ride squashed between the two of you."

Anna blushed. Caleb looked her up and down, his gaze slow and lingering, his eyes showing his appreciation. She fought the urge to dash back into the house and change into her blue taffeta dress. This was the last evening they'd spend together, and she wanted to look nice. Blue always gave her courage. She wanted him to remember her fondly. But no, she didn't need courage. She just needed to be herself for once.

He slipped his hands around her waist and easily lifted her into the wagon. If his fingers lingered a bit, she didn't call him out.

When he reached for Izetta, she held up her palm. "I'm too old to be lifted into the air. Just give me a foot up."

Caleb dutifully bent and threaded his finger. Izetta stepped into his outstretched hand and hoisted herself onto the seat beside Anna. Caleb circled the wagon and swung up on her opposite.

Claustrophobic was not the word Anna would use to describe the situation. The arrangement was cozy. Caleb's body pressed against her left side, shielding her from the worst of the wind. Izetta blocked the right. Each bend and dip in the road threw her more tightly against Caleb. If she didn't know better, she'd have thought he'd aimed for a few of the divots.

With a lingering sense of disappointment she alighted at the Bainum farm. Izetta hopped out on her own, sprightly despite her age. Caleb once again wrapped his fingers around her waist.

"Are you sure this doesn't hurt?" he asked.

She doubted she'd notice if his touch exacerbated her wound. All she thought about were the gold flecks around his irises and how the setting sun behind him haloed his dark hair. Pausing a moment, she memorized his features, locking away each line in his forehead, the tiny scar near his ear, the way his hairline flared at his temples.

She forced her thoughts back to Jane. A little girl without a voice. A little girl who would grow into a woman without a voice. Jane deserved better. She deserved a champion.

Their gazes held for a long moment, each realizing this was their last evening together. He looked as though he might say something, but the moment was lost.

Another wagon had arrived. One of the boys from town dashed over and grasped the lead lines, promising he'd take good care of the team.

Caleb made a show of escorting Izetta, and Anna appreciated the courtly gesture.

The Bainum barn was a rambling succession of buildings tucked against a hill, banked by shrubs and trees. The barn had been painted red at one point, although weather had faded the siding almost pink.

Music and laughter spilled from the open barn doors. With the setting sun, the men scrambled for lanterns, turning the inside of the barn a warm yellow glow.

The shucking had already begun, with a dozen men seated on low stools, a pile of corn in the middle.

A low table held an assortment of covered dishes along with an enormous jug of cider.

Caleb fetched them both a glass. At Anna's hesitation, he said, "Don't worry, it's not hard cider. The old farmer learned his lesson."

She gratefully accepted the glass. A shout sounded from the men seated behind her, and a gentleman proudly raised his ear of red corn. The man was married, and his wife made a great show of looking put out before bussing him on the cheek. A few of the single men grumbled at the loss of a stolen kiss.

Anna spotted Jo and the children. "There's your sister. This will be the last chance I have to thank her for everything she's done."

"I'll join the others," Caleb said.

Anna met up with Jo, and they made great study of the delectable desserts and pies lining the food table. Shawn snatched a crinkle cookie and stuffed the sugary mess into his mouth quick as a flash.

He chomped through his mother's scolding and reached for another before she finished her lecture.

Jo was faster this time and caught his arm. "No more until after supper."

Shawn blinked his reluctant agreement. Anna figured Jo better not turn her back—the little sprite looked as determined as Pipsqueak staring down a rosebush.

The marshal motioned her aside. Frowning, Anna followed him toward a quiet recess.

He glanced around. "I don't mean to bother you, but I have some information that might interest you."

"Please, I'd rather hear it now."

"Reinhart is in town. He came a few days ago. We figured it was better if his visit stayed quiet."

"I understand."

"Turns out he discovered a few things about your father." He paused. "Are you sure you're okay to hear this?"

Anna clenched her hands. "I'm certain. Just don't say his name quite yet. I'm not ready to make this personal. I only want the details."

If the marshal thought her request odd, he didn't say

anything. "He was an architect. Wealthy. Married and widowed once. A pillar of the community."

Another cheer went up from the crowd, and Anna turned with a smile, wondering who'd get the next kiss. Her gaze clashed with Caleb's, and she realized he held the prize.

The marshal touched her elbow and urged her forward. "We'll talk about this more tomorrow. Come by my office at lunch. I'll make certain Reinhart is there."

She nodded and caught sight of Caleb once more. Her cheeks warmed. He made a great show of rubbing his chin and searching the room. He passed before several giggling girls, his progress leading him steadily in her direction. Her heart clattered against her ribs. He paused before her and crouched.

Anna started.

He bent and kissed Cora's forehead, then planted another kiss on Jocelyn's, then hugged them close. "My two best girls!"

Jocelyn and Cora giggled, and the crowd roared its approval.

If she hadn't loved him before, she would have fallen hard right then.

She caught his eyes; those bewitching forest-green eyes were filled with a promise of more to come.

His breath whispered against her ear and sent her whole body trembling. "I'll have my boon later."

After all the corn was husked, the ears were loaded into wheelbarrows and dumped into the enormous grain stalls at the end of the barn. The stalks were bagged for kindling, and the floor swept clean for the dance.

The men relinquished their low stools and many of

the ladies claimed them. A violin began playing a low, mournful tune.

"Ah, c'mon, Berny!" Maxwell yelled. "Play something happy."

A gentlemen with a guitar joined Berny and his violin. Soon a lively rendition of the "Farmer in the Dell" had several couples on their feet.

Maxwell appeared before her, his hair slicked back, his suit pants only slightly too short. He sketched a bow and held out his hand. "Dance?"

"I don't know the steps."

One of her many nannies had taught her the waltz amidst much laughter and teasing, but she'd never danced with a gentleman before. Dancing was another one of those frivolous activities her mother deplored.

"Don't worry," Maxwell urged. "You'll catch on soon enough."

He twirled her onto the dance floor, and before she knew what was happening, she'd joined in the merry jig. After that her feet never stopped moving. First one McCoy brother, then another joined her in the dance.

She watched as Sarah joined Brahm on the dance floor, his ears a vivid shade of red, a shy smile on her face. Just when she thought she'd collapse from all the activity, the music slowed.

Caleb appeared before her. "May I have this dance?"

She rested her left hand on his shoulder, her gloved right hand clasped in his. Behind them, the small band strummed out the mournful tune of the Tennessee Waltz.

Caleb swept her around the dance floor, his expression admiring. "I wasn't sure if you waltzed. I didn't know if Victoria approved."

"I don't always listen to my mother."

"Scandalous, Miss Bishop."

"One of my nannies taught me."

"Remind me to thank her."

The soothing cadence of his voice sent a warm glow through her. "That was a very sweet thing you did, giving your kiss to Jocelyn and Cora."

"They weren't my first choice."

"Oh," said Anna coyly. "And who was your first choice?"

"Mrs. Franklin."

Anna burst out laughing. "Are you ever serious?"

The light in his eyes dimmed. "I'm going to miss you."

The music cocooned them, the dancers swirled around the floor, everyone caught up in their own conversations. He was the more sensible of the two of them. The time for kisses was over. She was leaving the following day. Weak, feminine tears welled in her eyes and she didn't care a whit.

"We can write," Anna said.

"I don't think that's a good idea."

"Why not?"

"Because I love you."

She jerked away from him and dashed toward the exit. If anyone noticed her hasty departure, no one said anything.

There were people everywhere, people in the barn, in the house, wagons lining the drive. She walked away from all the noise and commotion, seeking a moment of solitude.

Why had he gone and said he loved her? She'd just discovered her own feelings, and her emotions were too chaotic. Somehow, believing only her heart had been broken had made the whole situation more palatable. Except she'd been lying to herself. Of course she'd known his feelings were deepening, of course she'd known they were both drawn to each other. She simply hadn't wanted to acknowledge his part, as well.

Leaving was much easier when she didn't know his feelings ran as deep as her feelings for him. He was a good man, a kind man. This was his home. He wasn't going to leave, and she wasn't staying. The situation was impossible, and both of them had known the truth.

Only one of them had been brave enough to state their feelings outright. She bent her head and tugged her wrap tighter around her shoulders. The coward among them was plain. She'd rather face an angry mob than the one man who held her heart.

She was so preoccupied that she nearly ran into the gentleman. In fact, he had to reach out to stop her from colliding with him.

"Mr. Baker?" she said hesitantly.

"Mr. Bekker."

She'd been introduced some time earlier. "Yes, sorry. You're here for the horses, aren't you? Visiting with Mr. Elder."

"Actually, no."

Something in his voice had her glancing behind her. "I should be going."

"Don't you want to know why I'm really here?"

She felt a twinge of alarm. She was too far from the barn. The music was loud. People were dancing and clapping, their feet stomping on the wooden stage. Away from the light, she was vulnerable. Mr. Bekker knew it as well, she could tell. A spark of fear raced along her spine.

She spun away, and his arm snaked around her waist. With a startled cry she slammed into his chest. Summoning up all her strength, she stomped on his toe. The man yelped and released her.

She dashed toward the barn, toward the people. A heavy weight socked her from behind, knocking her onto the ground. Pain shot through her side. She sucked in a breath to scream, and his hand clamped over her mouth.

"You're a difficult woman to kill, sis."

Her world went black.

Caleb stumbled off the makeshift dance floor and into the night air. Why had he said that? He'd destroyed what little rapport remained between them. He'd destroyed any chance of maintaining even a sliver of friendship.

People milled about, talking and laughing. Triple A sat on an overturned washtub, smoking a pipe, the smell pungent and familiar. The night was crisp, the moon bright. What kind of fool ruined such a beautiful evening?

Caleb stuffed his hands in his pockets and stared into the darkness.

Triple A let out a low whistle. "How are things going with the goat? Found him a home yet?"

"Pipsqueak is staying with me."

Caleb kicked at the dirt. They had something in common, he and that goat. They both loved Anna; they might as well stick together. Beyond the circle of light glowing from the open doors, the night turned pitch.

Clouds drifted over the moon, dimming the light and blocking the stars.

The patter of running feet brought him around.

Jasper dashed forward and grabbed his hand. "They took her."

Caleb crouched, and the boy grabbed his hand. Touching the boy's wrist, he felt the rapidly beating pulse. "Slow down. What's going on?"

"They got Miss Anna. Some man knocked her down. I followed him. I figured I couldn't help unless I knew where he was going. He tossed her into the back of the wagon, and that other lady joined him."

His heart twisted painfully. "What other lady? Who were they?"

"That couple from back East, the ones after Mr. Elder's horses."

Caleb had seen the couple around town, though he hadn't given them much notice. "Which way were they headed?"

"Toward town."

His blood ran hot. A sudden memory burst into his head. He'd seen the woman before, Mrs. Bekker. He'd seen her on the stairs in the hotel. He'd almost run into her, then Anna had nearly been killed. They hadn't come for the horses, they'd come to kill her.

He grasped Jasper by the shoulders. "Fetch Marshal Cain. He's inside. Tell him what you told me."

Someone had tethered their horse near a tree, and Caleb snatched the reins. He tightened the cinch on the saddle and swung into place. Kicking the horse into a gallop, he set off down the darkened road.

They were in a wagon, going slower than a man riding alone. He had the advantage; they didn't know he was following. As he reached town, ambient light from the saloon and hotel lit the street. The wagon was nowhere in sight.

His stomach churned. Whoever had taken Anna was hampered by the conveyance. He reined his horse and quickly scanned the street. The only other place they could take a wagon was near the houses on the edge of town. He kicked the horse into a lope once again and had nearly reached town when he caught sight of the wagon.

They were in his house.

He swung down and cautiously approached. Voices sounded from inside. The marshal was a smart man; if Caleb had found the wagon, Garrett wasn't far behind.

He made for the stairs, and someone grabbed his shoulder. He cocked back his arm.

"Wait!" a familiar voice grated harshly. "It's me. Reinhart."

Caleb lowered his arm. "They've got Anna."

"I know. I'll explain everything later. You'll get yourself killed if you storm in there."

At least with two of them they had a fighting chance. "How many are there?"

"Just two. A husband and wife. You got a gun?"

"Inside."

"Can you get to it?"

"If I go in around back."

"Good," Reinhart said. "You take the back. Once you're inside, I'll come in the front. We'll trap them."

Satisfied with the plan, Caleb ducked beneath the window. The voices grew louder.

"They'll think it was a crime of passion," the man said.

"You always complicated things." The woman, presumably Mrs. Bekker, spoke. "We should have shot her and dumped her body in the woods."

His fingers shook with rage and he fisted them a few times, clearing his head. Scooting on his hands and knees, he made his way toward the back door. He always left his bedroom window unlatched. If the husband and wife continued arguing, he and Reinhart had the advantage.

He eased open the window and hoisted himself over the sill. Creeping through the house, he made his way to the center corridor.

A woman blocked his view of Anna.

"Why are you doing this?" Anna asked, a quiver in her voice.

"Money. Your father left you a lot of money, and I want it."

"Then take it, there's no need to kill me. I'll do whatever you want, I'll sign over the money."

"It's too late for that now. You should have died in Kansas City. Everyone would have assumed you were killed because of your mother."

"How did you find me?" This time her voice was stronger.

"We followed your mother. The Great Victoria Bishop. Mummy must not love you very much. She didn't come until we burned down her house."

Caleb sneaked a glance and whipped back again.

"You're lying," Anna said. "Why would my father leave the money to me? He's never even met me."

"He tried, but your mother turned him away. One word—" Mrs. Bekker's voice dripped with frustration "—one word in his will shut me out. He left all his money to his *natural* heir."

"Then you're not really my sister."

"Of course not. I was three years old when my mother married your father. She died the year I married Harvey. Your father didn't think we deserved any money after that. Said he only took care of us for my mother's sake." Her tone turned shrill. "Your father owes me."

There was more to the story than what she was saying, of that Caleb was certain.

"What do you hope to accomplish by this?" Anna implored. "You'll be murderers. Living on the run."

"No one will ever know what happened here. When your lover returns, we'll kill him, too. People will think it was a lovers' quarrel." She smoothed her eyebrow with one gloved pinkie. "I am accustomed to a certain manner of living. Crime doesn't pay as well as it used to."

"You lied to Mr. Elder," Anna continued. "You were never here to buy horses."

Excellent. She was keeping them talking, keeping them distracted.

The man chuckled. "You're finally catching up. The wife here is next in line for the money, and I've a mind to settle down."

Caleb moved quietly through his bedroom. He retrieved his gun and checked the chamber, then returned to the hallway. He'd heard enough, and Reinhart should be in position by now. With the marshal on his way, so much the better.

Pulling back the hammer, he stepped into the light. "Let her go."

Mrs. Bekker spun around. "You'll have to shoot me first."

This was the same woman from Kansas City, all right. The same unnaturally blond hair and glittery cold eyes. He shifted his gun a notch to the right. "No one wins here. Turn around and go, and we'll forget all this ever happened."

He had no intention of keeping that promise, but the Bekkers didn't need to know that.

Anna sat awkwardly on the edge of her chair, her face pale. Caleb tore his gaze away from the distraction. "C'mon, Bekker, you strike me as a gambling man. You've played the odds before. You know you can't win this."

Mr. Bekker aimed the gun at Anna. "I don't have to win. I just have to eliminate the competition."

Husband and wife exchanged a glance and Mrs. Bekker lunged. Caleb fired. Another shot sounded. Then another. Gunpowder smoke filled the room.

He coughed and stumbled toward Anna.

Mr. Bekker lay on his back on the floor, his eyes sightless. Mrs. Bekker backed away from his lifeless form, her gaze skittering toward the door.

Reinhart loomed over the body. "I hope you're a good vet, because you're a terrible shot."

He jerked one thumb over his shoulder and indicated the hole in the window. "I think you hit the tree out front, if that's any consolation." The man tipped his hat at Anna. "You have my vote the next time."

Anna launched herself at Caleb, and he caught her against his chest.

Mrs. Bekker dashed for the door and collided with Marshal Cain on the porch.

He grasped her around the upper arm and guided her back into the house. "Not leaving so soon, are you?"

She shot him a look of pure loathing and flounced back to the chair Anna had abandoned, not even glancing at her husband.

The detective nudged Mr. Bekker's still body with his booted toe. "He killed my partner. I owed him one. I asked poor Owen to help me out, to ask a few questions while he was working on the Phillips case. They killed him for it."

"He knew," Mrs. Bekker snarled. "He saw us that day—the second time we tried killing that tramp. We knew he was watching Mrs. Phillips. We stuffed him in her trunk. Figured he could fail at both cases. Served him right."

The woman was clearly mad, her eyes wild and unfocused. Caleb tucked Anna against his chest and turned. "We'll be out back if you need us."

The marshal rubbed his chin. "We'll be busy for the better part of the night, that much is certain."

Caleb left Anna for a moment while he lit a lantern, then led her out the back and into the barn.

She glanced around and rubbed her shoulders. Caleb draped his coat over her and unlatched the barn door. Pipsqueak leaped out of the darkness as though he'd been shot out of a cannon.

Anna laughed and patted his head. "I missed you, too."

She half turned. "How did you find me?"

"Jasper saw them take you."

"And you rode to the rescue."

"Something like that." He flashed a grin. "I have a feeling you'd have rescued yourself. I just simplified things."

She tugged her lower lip between her teeth. "I've been thinking about what you said...."

"Forget it."

"No, I won't. What if I stayed? We can...we can try. See how things are between us."

He pushed off and crossed the distance, sweeping her into his arms. "That's a nice idea. I'll tell you what— why don't you go back to St. Louis? Stay a while. Sort things out with your mother. If you still feel the same way in six months, you can come back."

She hugged him more tightly, and he prayed she never saw through his ruse. She'd never return. Once she acclimated to her own life again, she'd forget all about him.

She'd had a scare this evening. They all had. Her feelings were confused, jumbled. She was mistaking her fear and gratitude for something more. He wasn't going to take advantage of that.

"What if...what if I go for a few weeks? If you're feelings are the same..." Her voice trailed off.

He perched on a bale of hay and tucked her against his side. Pipsqueak clambered up and rested his head on her knee.

"Have you ever read *Black Beauty*?" he asked, changing the subject to something neutral, something he hoped she'd understand later.

"Everyone has."

"That story is the real reason I became a veterinarian. Anna Sewell wrote that animals do not suffer less because they have no words. That idea stuck with me. Words have power. I grew up on a farm. I never thought much about the treatment of animals beyond their general welfare. But Anna Sewell showed me empathy, and that changed me. Your words changed me."

"You've already got the vote," she scoffed. "Why would you care what I have to say?"

"Because I care about what you care about. Because your passion is infectious, because you have a way of sharing your empathy with others. Whatever you do, whatever path you choose, never forget that."

She rubbed her cheek against his shoulder and yawned. "This has been a very long day."

She hadn't understood what he was trying to say. Maybe she never would. Caleb held her away from him. "I'll walk you home. You're dead on your feet. It's been a long night, and you have a train to catch tomorrow."

"Is that tomorrow already?"

He walked her back to her home, each caught up in their own thoughts. Izetta was waiting on the porch; she caught sight of them and quickly closed the distance.

"What happened? I turned around and you two were gone. Then the marshal dashed off, and Caleb was no-where to be found. I feared the worst."

"It's a long story, and you'll need a strong cup of coffee."

She shrugged out of Caleb's coat and handed it to him. He fisted the material in his hands. "I'll see you tomorrow."

She kept hold of the coat and he ran his index finger down the back of her hand.

"Do you know what I remember from *Black Beauty*?" she asked, her eyes luminous in the pale moonlight.

He shook his head.

"'It is good people who make good places.'"

Izetta urged her inside, and he waited as the door closed behind them.

Six months, six weeks, six years. What did time matter? She was never coming back. She'd forget all about him soon enough.

He'd gone and done the one thing he'd promised he'd never do. He'd gone and fallen in love with a woman who could never love him in return.

He was a fool and he didn't care. His brief time with Anna was worth a lifetime of suffering.

Chapter Eighteen

After Anna had finished her tale, Izetta rose, sensing Anna and her mother needed time together.

As soon as they were alone again, Anna turned toward her mother. "Tell me. Tell me about him."

"This isn't the time. All this fuss and shooting. Things like this don't happen in St. Louis."

"Mother."

Victoria Bishop heaved a great sigh. "You don't understand. You can't. It was the war. People were dying every day. They were dying faster than we could bury them. My own brother joined up. He was only fifteen, and lied about his age. I assume the army knew full well he was too young, he was little more than a boy. By that time, no one cared. There weren't enough men, there weren't enough volunteers to replace the dead. He was killed within a month. They didn't even inform my parents. We read his name in the papers, we read his name along with all the rest."

Anna shook her head. "I never knew. You never told me."

"That's when I finally understood my purpose, that's

when I knew I had a calling. If women had the vote, there'd be no wars, there'd be no more dead bodies."

Anna had her doubts. Mrs. Bekker had seemed perfectly willing to kill without a second thought. Anna kept her views private, not wanting to interrupt her mother.

"Your father was born under a lucky star." Her mother snorted delicately. "He was one of the few who survived, and I hated him for it. He came home on leave, after I'd discovered I was pregnant. He no longer looked at me as a woman after that. I was a mother. A wife. All of our grand plans for the future were dashed. We were going to travel Europe, see the world, to have adventures. He was done with all that after the war. All that death had changed him. I gave him his freedom because I wanted my own. I wasn't going to raise a passel of brats because he'd suddenly decided to settle down."

A kick in the chest could not have hurt worse. Anna was a person, not a nuisance. And yet her mother's attitude toward her finally fell into place. Victoria Bishop would not play at domesticity. Anna was little more than an experiment for her mother, a tool for notoriety. Miss Victoria Bishop was not shackled by the conventions of motherhood.

Her mother rested her elbow on the arm of the chair and cupped her chin. "I agreed to keep his name out of the papers, and he agreed to stay out of my life."

Anna flinched from the bitterness in her mother's voice. "He simply walked away?"

"A lowering realization, isn't it? The male is a fickle species. His heart must not have been too broken. He was married within the year. Look what it got him. A stepdaughter who hated him and nearly killed his own flesh and blood."

Yet he'd left her an inheritance. He'd tried to find her. Somewhere along the way he must have questioned his choices. Anna collapsed onto a chair.

"Still, you proved useful," her mother said. "Bearing an out-of-wedlock child kept me in the news. Kept the cause in the news."

"I'm glad I was of service to you."

"Don't be peevish. You're not naive, you know how this works."

Her mother replaced her glasses and began scribbling out her correspondence, effectively dismissing Anna.

The fog that had enveloped her since the shooting cleared. She didn't want to believe that Caleb loved her because she didn't believe anyone could truly love her. Not without conditions. Not unless she brought some purpose, some value to the relationship, and she had nothing to give him.

She stepped outside and stared at the moon. A few moments later, Izetta joined her.

"How are you holding up?"

"Well enough I suppose."

"What are thinking?"

Anna studied the night sky. "I'm wondering about God. I'm wondering about forgiveness. What does it even mean, and why does any of this matter?"

Izetta walked a few paces into the garden. "I don't think I know anyone who hasn't struggled with forgiveness. After the war, we all had to forgive. There was so much pain, so much suffering. People think of forgiveness as chopping away at something, hacking at a suffocating milkweed vine until you are sweaty and exhausted and there is nothing left, not even the roots. An afternoon's work followed by a cold lemonade on the back porch.

"I always thought of forgiveness as a seed, something you plant in the best spot in the garden. A place with neither too much sun nor too much shade. A delicate seedling you fertilize and water and protect from an early frost. A plant you nurture through drought and flood, carefully guarding the first fragile blooms from encroaching weeds and voracious rabbits.

"Until one day you realize your patient labor has borne fruit, the roots have grown deep enough, and the stem is stout enough to survive the strongest wind.

"Even then you must tend forgiveness through the seasons, through harsh winters and dry springs. Like any garden, forgiveness is something you must never neglect for long."

She wasn't a legacy, she was a person. A person who had the right to choose her own future.

"Thank you," Anna said. "Thank you for everything you've done. For your friendship, for your advice. You have become very dear to me."

"And you to me." Izetta passed Anna on her way back inside and caught her shoulder in a brief embrace. "If my sons had grown and married, I hope they would have picked someone like you. I would have been honored to have you as a daughter-in-law."

Izetta stood and dusted her hands. "Don't stay up too long, you've a busy day tomorrow."

A busy day. A busy day of sitting on a train. She was returning home to a burned-out hole in the ground. All of her possessions except the ones she carried with her were gone. At the very least, she had nothing left to lose, which left her a certain freedom.

She stared at the sky and another line from *Black Beauty* drifted over her, the words resonating in her heart.

"My troubles are all over, and I am at home; and often before I am quite awake, I fancy I am still at the orchard at Birtwick, standing with my friends under the apple trees."

Where would her memories drift when her troubles were over? Anna feared she already knew the answer.

The following morning, she woke to the rain, packed to the rain and watched as two men loaded the wagon while rain sluiced off her umbrella. She'd said her good-byes to Izetta in the rain, both of them promising to write often.

Her mother had limped through the process with considerable grumbling about everything from the men's handling of the baggage to the hard bench seat.

Anna stared at the town and thought of the past few weeks. She'd been shot, nearly stabbed, she'd discovered she had a father and lost him in the same instant. She'd discovered she had a stepsibling when that woman had tried to kill her.

All in all it had been a momentous month.

She'd forgotten that is was the second Tuesday in November until she saw the bunting outside the post office. Another election gone by, and still women were denied the vote.

She was doing the right thing by leaving. A few weeks away and both of them could sort out their feelings. They'd been through a lot together. They needed space, they needed quiet. She'd test the waters in a few weeks. A letter to Jo with a few dropped hints should suffice. If Caleb wanted to see her in a few weeks, they'd see what happened from there. No need to rush things. Her mother required her assistance. This was the perfect time for them to separate. Anna would buy her own town house, and perhaps she and Caleb would strike up a correspondence.

Everything neat and tidy and devoid of the melodrama that had plagued her life these past few weeks.

One of the wheels of their carriage became stuck in the mire, forcing them out of the conveyance and into the mud. Anna assisted her mother onto the boardwalk, and they traveled the rest of the distance on foot.

She reached the train depot and found a knot of women huddled beneath the eves of the telegraph office.

One of the blurred forms broke free and dashed through the rain toward Anna. On closer inspection, she realized the woman was Jo, and she wore a Votes for Women banner across her chest.

"We're giving you a proper send-off," she said. "We're protesting as the men vote."

She grinned as though it was the Fourth of July and not a damp and drizzly November afternoon.

Tony joined her. The younger girl didn't hold an umbrella; instead she let the rain drip off her Stetson hat.

Anna did a quick head count and realized more than half the women from the town were staring at her, all of them wearing banners.

She turned to Jo. "You did this for me?"

"Mostly for you. Plus, it's good for the men around here to stand up and take notice sometimes. We can't have them taking us for granted."

"But it's raining."

Tony tipped her head forward, and a river of water trickled from her hat. "A little rain never ruined a good parade."

Her mother took in the display with a curt nod. "How quaint. Come along, Anna. I'll catch a chill in this rain."

She trudged toward the waiting train, her walking stick splashing through the puddles.

The porter assisted her onto the train while Anna remained rooted in place.

Her mother gestured. "Come along."

"No," Anna called over the rain. "I'm staying."

"Don't be absurd." She shook her head. "Come over here this instant."

Anna walked the distance, then paused. "I'm staying here."

"Do you think that countrified veterinarian can make you happy?"

Anna blinked.

"I saw how you looked at each other. I'm not an idiot. He'll saddle you with a half dozen children and a miserable existence."

"Maybe that doesn't sound miserable to me."

"You don't know what you're saying. I groomed you for something better. I raised you for something more."

"No. You raised me to be independent. That's what I'm doing. I'm asserting my independence."

"If you choose that man over me, I will never speak to you again."

"You know what I just realized?" Anna said. "Caleb would never make me choose. That's why he asked me to leave. He wanted me to know I didn't have to choose between him and the cause. Besides, I am in charge of the flowers at the quilting bee and a Bishop does not shirk her duties."

"You're babbling now. I will not speak to you when you're in this…this emotional state." She banged her walking stick against the train deck.

"A man will ruin a woman faster than rain will ruin a parade."

"That's the difference between you and me," Anna said, turning away. "I never did mind a little rain."

The train whistle blew, and Anna didn't look back. She strode into the crowd of women, and they let up a cheer. Jo caught her around the shoulder. "You're missing your train."

"I'm not leaving!" Anna shouted. "I love your brother."

Jo whooped and did a little jump. She slipped in the mud and lost her balance, careening into Anna. Anna slid backward and bumped into Tony. They all fell into a heap in a chilly mud puddle, laughing.

For the first time in a long while, the future was rife with possibilities.

Caleb stepped into the barn and handed Pipsqueak a stem of roses. "I figure you're feeling just about as rotten as I do right now."

"I hope those roses didn't come from Izetta's garden," Anna said.

He froze. "You should be gone by now. I heard the train whistle blow."

"I decided to stay."

Pipsqueak trotted past him, the roses forgotten.

"Why?" he asked, wondering if this was all a dream.

"Because of something somebody said to me about the power of words."

He turned toward her and gaped. "What happened to you? You're covered in mud."

She smiled, her face smudged, her clothes streaked with dirt, looking a bit like the bedraggled kittens they'd rescued and more beautiful than he'd ever seen her.

"Jo and I had a slight accident."

He fished his handkerchief from his pocket and approached her. "I have a feeling this isn't the only trouble the two of you will cause."

"You're probably right."

He rubbed a smudge from her forehead. "How about I move to St. Louis? I hear it's a beautiful city."

"And why would you do that?"

A spot of dirt near her temple caught his attention and he dabbed at the mark. "To be near you."

"Then you would be terribly disappointed, because I don't have any plans to return."

"Why is that?"

"Because St. Louis is far too boring. Cimarron Springs is much livelier. There are caves for hidden treasures, and the finest Harvest Festival in the state."

"Anything else?" A bit of dirt on her ear needed tending.

"There are good people here. I read in a book once that good people make good places."

He leaned back, creating some distance between them. "You don't have to do this, Anna. I don't mind moving. Your work is important. I won't have you give that up."

She placed a finger over his lips, silencing him. "I won't be giving anything up. The cause will always be a part of my life, a part of who I am. That will never change. I don't have all the answers yet and I don't know quite how things will turn out, but I know that this is where I need to be. With you."

He remained steadfast, hardening his resolve. "You were meant for something better than this."

Her lips tightened. "I'm not a legacy. I'm a person with thoughts and feelings and hopes and dreams. All my life someone else has told me what I should do, how I should live my life. I don't know who I'm meant to be, and I need the space to find out."

A silent war raged within him. "I can't let you do this."

A shadow passed over her eyes. "Would you love me if I was ordinary?"

"Of course. How can you even ask such a thing?"

"Then let me decide my own future. Even if that future is very ordinary."

He cupped her cheek and ran his thumb along her chin, dislodging another speck of dirt. "You will never ever be ordinary."

"I've never saved a life," she said. "And that is a very extraordinary thing indeed."

His expression softened. "That's the most amazing thing I've ever done."

"Life with me will always be challenging."

"What if you grow bored here? What if you find married life unsatisfying?"

Her lips parted. "Who said anything about marriage?"

The teasing glint in her eye gave her away. "I'm very conventional. I demand you make an honest man out of me."

"I'm not very conventional at all. I still haven't learned how to cook. I can only make eggs and toast."

"I'm a very good cook."

She brushed the hair from his forehead. "I'm dazzled by your looks and enthralled by your kind heart."

"You do have a way with words, Miss Bishop. Have you ever thought of being a writer?"

"Actually, I've given that thought quite a bit of consideration. I want to write about women, about their struggles, about their pain. I want to make a very small difference in a very big way."

"I'll buy extra ink and paper."

"At least we don't have to worry about explaining our engagement to the town."

"I think they knew we were meant for each other."

"I think you're right. Even the goat knew."

Caleb grinned. "That is one smart goat."

He knelt and took her muddy hand between his own. "Anna Bishop, will you marry me?"

"Of course I will."

"Good."

"Now kiss me," she ordered.

He gladly complied. Their kiss was full of tender promise, a gentle assault on her senses.

"You don't play fair," she said.

"I know." He grinned.

She returned his smile. "Kiss me again."

Caleb decided then and there that it wasn't a bad thing to have a woman in charge, not a bad thing at all.

Epilogue

Three years later

Anna snatched her bonnet from the stand near the door. She checked her appearance in the mirror and swiftly tied the strings beneath her chin.

Caleb waited patiently, holding one-year-old Susan in his arms. "Don't worry," he said, "they can't start without you."

"Yes, but the mayor should at least be on time."

Women had won the municipal vote in Kansas that year and Anna had run for mayor the very next election.

She'd won by a landslide.

Caleb caught her gaze in the mirror. "We might even have time to stop by the new house and see what progress they've made."

"There's no time!" After Susan's birth, they'd realized their house was far too small for their growing family. "I heard Maxwell teasing you about the money. You're not annoyed, are you?"

"I rather enjoy being a kept man." Caleb grinned.

Anna rolled her eyes. Her father had left her more

money than she could possibly spend in a lifetime, especially considering their modest lifestyle. Figuring out ways to donate the surplus was a job in and of itself.

She adjusted her collar. "All right. I'm ready to cut the ribbon on Cimarron Springs' first ever salon for women only."

Caleb pecked her on the cheek. "I wonder who donated the money for the remodel of the old haberdashery."

Anna assumed an air of innocence. "I couldn't say. Although events turned out to be quite fortuitous. Since Mr. Phillips passed away last spring, Mrs. Phillips needed a source of income and a place to stay that accommodated Jane. The salon is the perfect solution."

She turned toward the door, but something in his expression stopped her. "What's wrong?"

"I wasn't going to tell you until after the ceremony, but you received a letter today."

Anna's chest tightened. "From the publisher?"

She'd spent the past two years writing letters and gathering stories, interviewing women and compiling their heroic journeys into an anthology. She'd sent off the manuscript months ago.

"I can't read it," she said. "I'll wait until this evening."

"Whatever you say."

She made it as far as the door and then stopped. "Hand it over."

Caleb complied, and she tore open the envelope, scanning the first few lines, then clutched the letter against her chest.

"They're going to publish my book."

Caleb grinned. "I never had any doubts."

She smothered him and Susan with kisses.

Caressing the back of her head, Caleb pressed his forehead against hers. "You are one extraordinary woman."

Anna smiled, her heart swelling with love, Susan squirming merrily between them. "I am one happy woman. Thank you for supporting me."

"Always," he said simply. "Always."

* * * * *

Florida author **Louise M. Gouge** writes historical fiction for Harlequin's Love Inspired Historical line. She received the prestigious Inspirational Readers' Choice Award in 2005 and placed in 2011 and 2015; she also placed in the Laurel Wreath contest in 2012. When she isn't writing, she and her husband, David, enjoy visiting historical sites and museums. Please visit her website at louisemgougeauthor.blogspot.com.

Visit the Author Profile page
at Harlequin.com for more titles.

COWBOY SEEKS
A BRIDE

Louise M. Gouge

What time I am afraid, I will trust in thee.
—*Psalms* 56:3

This book is dedicated to the intrepid pioneers who settled the San Luis Valley of Colorado in the mid to late 1800s. They could not have found a more beautiful place to make their homes than in this vast 7,500 feet high valley situated between the majestic Sangre de Cristo and San Juan Mountain ranges. It has been many years since I lived in the San Luis Valley, so my thanks go to Pam Williams of Hooper, Colorado, for her extensive on-site research on my behalf. With their permission, I named two of my characters after her and her husband, Charlie. These dear old friends are every bit as kind and wise as their namesakes. I also want to thank my dear husband of fifty years, David Gouge, for his loving support as I pursue my dream of writing love stories to honor the Lord.

Chapter One

July 1881

Randall Northam is a gambler. Randall Northam is a killer.

The words pulsed through Marybeth O'Brien's head, keeping time with the clatter of the iron wheels on the railroad track as the train propelled her inescapably toward her prospective husband. Until a few moments ago she'd thought his most notable quality was being the second son of a wealthy Colorado ranching family. But the lively young woman seated across from her had just imparted a vital bit of information Randall Northam's parents had left out when they'd arranged this marriage. And from the enthusiasm brightening Maisie Henshaw's face, Marybeth could see her story wasn't finished.

"Yep, he shot that thieving varmint right in the heart. Why, Rand can outdraw anybody." The red-haired girl elbowed her handsome young husband in the ribs. "Even me."

Dr. Henshaw chuckled indulgently, his expression

utterly devoid of censure, but rather, exuding only devotion for his wife. "You may have heard stories about how wild the West is, Miss O'Brien, but you will certainly feel safe with Rand protecting you."

"Just like me protecting you." Maisie chortled in a decidedly unladylike manner.

Her more refined husband nodded his agreement with a grin. "Well, we all have our talents."

Marybeth returned a weak smile while gulping down a terror she'd never felt as she'd made her plans to go to Colorado. She'd had some concern, yes. A great deal of doubt, of course. But never fear. In fact, the farther she'd traveled from Boston and the closer to her destination, she'd actually begun to look forward to meeting her prospective husband. If he turned out to be all that his parents and his own letters stated, she would reconsider her lifelong vow never to marry. But this disclosure about her intended changed everything and reaffirmed her determination never to be trapped in a miserable marriage, as her mother had been. She lifted a silent prayer of thanks for this encounter with the Henshaws and for finding out the truth about Mr. Randall Northam before meeting him.

Even as she prayed, guilt teased at the corners of her mind. She'd accepted her train fare from Colonel and Mrs. Northam, arguing with herself that perhaps Randall would turn out to be as kind, handsome and noble as his father, a former Union officer. If so, perhaps she could convince him to postpone the wedding until she found Jimmy. Surely, with two brothers of his own, he would understand her desperate desire to find her only brother who'd fled to Colorado eight long years ago to escape their abusive father. Finding Jimmy would not only reunite her with her only living relative, it would provide a means for her not to marry at all. That was, if Jimmy still had Mam's silver locket. With the key to a great treasure tucked inside, the locket would mean she could repay the Northams for her train fare.

"Don't you think so?" Maisie reached across and patted Marybeth's gloved hand.

"Wha—?" Marybeth felt an unaccustomed blush rush to her cheeks. How rude of her not to pay attention to her companions. "Forgive me. Would you repeat the question?"

"Now, Maisie, dear." John Henshaw bent his head toward his wife in a sweet, familiar way. "Miss O'Brien must be tired from her travels. We should give her time to rest so she will be at her best when she meets her future husband."

"Oh, I'm sorry." Maisie's pretty face crinkled with worry. "Would you like a pillow? A blanket?" She nudged her husband and pointed to the bag beneath his seat. "Honey, dig out that pillow I packed."

"Thank you. You're too kind." Marybeth accepted the small cushion, placed it against the window and rested her head, not because she wanted to sleep, but because she needed time to think. Although she hated missing the beautiful mountain scenery as the train descended the western side of La Veta Pass, she closed her eyes to keep Maisie from further talking. Again guilt pinched her conscience. This was no way to treat such kind people.

When they'd first met early this morning, the Henshaws had recognized their social duty to an unattached young woman traveling alone, just as several matrons and couples had all the way from Boston. Due to their protecting presence, Marybeth hadn't been accosted by a single man on the entire trip, although one well-dressed man in particular had stared at her rather boldly today when the doctor wasn't looking. He would have been more careful if he'd known Maisie was the one to watch out for. Marybeth wanted to laugh thinking about her new friend being a sharpshooter. If anything, she looked like a perfect lady in her fashionable brown traveling suit and elegant matching hat.

The moment the conductor had escorted her to the seat across from the Henshaws, Marybeth could see they were decent Christian people. Because they lived in the town where she would soon reside, she'd gradually told them more about herself, at last telling them she was Randall Northam's intended bride. Maisie had hooted with joy, announcing she'd known "Rand" all her life, and his sister, Rosamond, was her best friend. As if unfolding a great yarn, she told Marybeth about Rand's shoot-out over a card game in a saloon.

A gambler, a killer and, no doubt, a drunkard. This was the man she was expected to marry? Indeed she would not marry him, not in a hundred years.

Rand checked his pocket watch and then glanced down the railroad line toward Alamosa searching for the telltale black cloud of smoke from the Denver and Rio Grande engine. The wind was up today, so maybe tumbleweed or sand had blown over the tracks, slowing the train. Maybe a tree had fallen somewhere up on La Veta Pass and they'd had to stop to remove it before proceeding down into the San Luis Valley.

Rand chewed his lip and paced the boardwalk outside the small station, his boots thudding against the wood in time with his pounding heart. How much longer must he wait before the train arrived? Before his bride arrived?

He glanced down at his new black boots, dismayed at the unavoidable dust covering the toes. Hoping to look his best for his new bride, he brushed each boot over the back of the opposite pant leg and then wiped a hand over the gray marks that ill-advised action left. So much for looking his best. Where was that train anyway?

"Settle down, Rand." His younger brother, Tolley, half reclined on the bench set against the station's dull yellow outside wall. "If the train's going to be late, Charlie'll let you know." He jutted his chin toward the open window above him. Inside, Charlie Williams manned the telegraph, but at the moment no syncopated clickety-click indicated an incoming message. Tolley shook his head and smirked. "Man, if this is what it's like to get married, I don't want any part of it. Where's my cocksure brother today?" He patted the gun strapped to his side, clearly referencing the worst day of Rand's life.

"Could you just keep quiet about that?" He shot Tolley a cross look. After three years his brother still wouldn't let him forget the time Rand had been forced to kill a horse thief. Instead of understanding how guilty Rand felt about the incident, Tolley idolized him, even wanted to emulate his gun-fighting skills. "Don't say anything to Miss O'Brien except 'how do you do' and 'welcome to Esperanza.' Let me take care of the rest, understand?"

"Yes, boss." Tolley touched his hat in a mock salute. He glanced down the tracks. "Looks like your wait is over."

Rand followed his gaze. Sure enough, there came the massive Denver and Rio Grande engine, its black smoke almost invisible in the crosswinds, its cars tucked in a row behind it. Now his pulse pounded in his chest and ears, and his mouth became dry, just as it had before that fateful gunfight. Cocksure? Not in the least. Just able to hide his emotions under stress better than most people. At least most of the time. Today he couldn't quite subdue his nerves.

The engine chugged to a stop and sent out a blast of gray-white steam from its undercarriage. Porters jumped out, set stools in front of the doors and gave a hand to the disembarking passengers.

"Rand! Hey, Rand." Emerging from the second passenger car, Maisie Henshaw ignored the porter, practically leaped from the last step and ran toward him. Behind her, Doc Henshaw, toting a valise and his black doctoring bag, stretched out his long legs to keep up with his bride. Rand would never understand how these two very different people had gotten together, but it sure wasn't any of his business. Besides, anybody could see how happy they were.

Rand hoped his own imminent marriage would be just as happy. That would be an extra blessing on his road to redeeming his past. For three years he'd worked hard to live a perfect life by following every order, every wish of his parents, and taking on more than his share of chores to gain his older brother's respect. Now, if Miss O'Brien would have him, he would be marrying the young lady his parents had chosen for him. It made him feel as if he'd almost arrived at redemption. Almost.

Maisie dashed up and gave him a sisterly hug. "My, you're looking handsome. Any special reason you're all gussied up and out here waiting for the train?" She elbowed Doc in the ribs and chortled.

"Now, honey." His hands full, Doc gently bumped her shoulder with his own. "Let the man be."

"All right, all right." Maisie sniffed in mock annoyance. "But I'm in no hurry to go home." She marched over to the bench and plunked herself down beside Tolley. "Move over, kid."

Doc just chuckled at her antics. "Hello, Rand. It's good to see you." He sat next to Maisie.

Rand had only a moment to give his impromptu audience a scowl of irritation before their eyes all turned toward the train car. Maisie giggled and Tolley let out a low whistle. Rand followed their gaze. And nearly fell onto the bench beside them.

Slender and of medium height, the young lady had thick auburn hair piled high on her head, with a cute little brown-and-blue hat perched at the summit. Her sandy-colored dress—well, more suit than dress, and trimmed with dark blue bits of ribbon and such—hugged well-formed curves that he wouldn't let himself dwell on until after they were married. But it was her face that held his attention. Like a classical Roman statue of *Venus* he'd once seen in a magazine, her elegant beauty was flawless and her porcelain cheeks glowed with a hint of roses. He couldn't make out the color of her eyes, but she'd said in a letter that they were hazel.

Oh, mercy, she's even more beautiful than her picture. What did I ever do to deserve this prize? Nothing, that's what. It was all a matter of grace.

Thank You, Lord, for sending me such a lovely bride. That was, if Miss O'Brien would have him once he told her the truth about his past.

* * *

Foolishly putting off the inevitable, Marybeth had offered a silly excuse to the Henshaws for not following them right away. Maisie had teased about her shyness but hadn't forced the issue. The last passenger in the car, Marybeth had slowly moved toward the door where the conductor had given her a patient smile.

At last she emerged from the darkness, shielding her eyes from both the sun and the wind. A porter offered a hand and helped her to the ground. She pressed a dime—her last one—into his hand for the services he'd so diligently rendered during the trip. "Thank you."

As he bowed to her, a sharp whistle split the air. She located Maisie seated by the train station and pointing enthusiastically at a tall, broad-shouldered cowboy. He was dressed in a dark green plaid shirt, spotless black trousers and shiny black boots. While she couldn't see his face due to the broad brim of his light brown hat, his physique was certainly attractive, the sort that girls at her school always gushed over when the matrons weren't in the room.

Her gaze lit on the gun strapped to his belt and a shudder went through her. In traveling across the country, she'd noticed more than one cowboy wearing a gun. Another traveler had told her the weapons were necessary because of wild animals and maybe even train robbers. Yet how many of those cowboys had killed a man, as this one had?

He strode toward her with a firm gait and her heart pounded with fear…and a very odd thrill. What was wrong with her? She'd never been one to court danger. Indeed, she avoided confrontation at all cost.

"Miss O'Brien?" He tipped his hat to her.

Now she could see his face and her breath left her. When he hadn't sent a picture, she'd wondered if his looks were not particularly appealing. That was far from the case. In all of her twenty years, she had never seen a more handsome man, from his bright green eyes to his tanned, well-formed cheekbones and slender nose to his attractive, slightly crooked smile that revealed even white teeth. He even smelled good; a woody fragrance she couldn't quite identify. But it was those eyes, emerald green and reflecting the darker shade of his shirt, that held her attention, that mesmerized her.

"Yes, I'm Marybeth O'Brien." Her voice squeaked, but he had the good manners not to laugh. "Mr. Northam?"

"Yes, ma'am." He reached out to take her gloved hand. "Please call me Rand. We mostly go by first names out here. That is, if it's all right with you."

At his touch, a hot spark shot up her arm, turning to ice as it reached her neck. She couldn't stop a shudder, but again he didn't react. "Yes, that's fine." Somehow she managed to say the words. Somehow she managed to keep her knees from buckling.

For countless seconds they stood staring at each other. Marybeth tried to reconcile the idea of this young, incredibly handsome man being a killer, a gambler, a man exactly like her father. That thought shook her loose from her hypnotic state. Hadn't Da looked every bit the gentleman when he was sober? For the first time in her life she understood how Mam had been swept off her feet and right into a tragic, abusive marriage.

"Well—" She broke away from Rand's hold. "I have a trunk someplace." She looked around and spied it being unloaded from the baggage car. "There it is. Shall we?" She took a step in that direction.

"Yes, ma'am." Rand nonetheless gently touched her upper arm to stop her. "I brought my brother along to take care of that." He motioned to a younger version of himself. "Tolley, get yourself over here and meet Miss O'Brien… Marybeth, this is my brother Tolley."

The brothers' good relationship was evident in the boy's teasing smirk and overly polite address to her. "How do you do, Miss O'Brien? Welcome to Esperanza." From his singsong tone, she guessed he'd been coached.

"Very well, thank you, Tolley. I understand first names are the rule here, so please call me Marybeth." For some reason she felt no fear of him, despite the gun he wore. Did his easy smile and wide-eyed innocence hide a murderous spirit, too?

"Yes, ma'am." He shot a look at Rand almost as if seeking approval. "I'll take care of that trunk and see you later."

"Oh." Marybeth's heart sank as he strode away. She'd hoped the boy's presence would serve as a buffer between her and Rand. She looked up at Rand. "I—I was thinking…"

Again he touched her upper arm. Again a shiver raced up to her neck. "If you don't mind, I'd like for us to go over to Mrs. Williams's café for a bite to eat before I take you to your lodgings. That way we can start getting acquainted."

Marybeth's stomach answered for her with a slight rumbling. Heat flooded her cheeks. "Oh, dear. I guess you have your answer."

His smile held no censure. "Good. She has the reputation of being the best cook in Esperanza."

Marybeth accepted his offered arm—his very muscular arm—and they began their trek down the rutted street toward the center of town. Maybe this was best. She could break with him in public rather than in private. That way, if he was like Da, he wouldn't dare strike her. Da had always kept the abuse to the privacy of their shabby house so no one would see his true nature. Her only dilemma would be finding a place to stay afterward. Maybe that Mrs. Williams would help her. Maybe someone would. One thing was certain. Dr. and Mrs. Henshaw would be no help. From the admiring looks on their faces, it was obvious they thought Rand was nothing short of a hero.

Feeling the warmth of Marybeth's hand on his arm, smelling the fragrance of her lavender perfume, Rand adjusted his usual long stride to suit her shorter one. She had a dainty way about her that filled him with admiration. Most young ladies he knew tended to have a sturdier manner, although few were as tomboyish as Maisie and her sisters. He'd have to take particular care of this little gal until she became accustomed to Western ways. Pampering her would be his new favorite activity.

People along the street acknowledged him with a nod, a tipped hat or a wave, but no one interrupted their journey to the café. He knew they'd gossip about Marybeth and him, just as they had Nate and Susanna when his older brother was courting the Southern belle. He hoped their respect for the Northam name would inspire townsfolk to give him a wide berth so he and his prospective bride could get acquainted.

Prospective bride. That was how he'd thought of Marybeth ever since Mother had first written to him about her six months ago. Now that she was by his side, he was pretty close to dispensing with the "prospective" part. With his parents and sister extolling her character in their letters and saying they all agreed she was just the right gal to suit him, he felt as if he already knew her. They'd also written to say she would help to bring that element of refinement Dad hoped to add to the community.

Marybeth's letters had informed him that she liked music, liked to read, enjoyed cooking and housekeeping; the usual feminine qualities to make a man eager to go home at the end of the day. Her beauty was just a bonus. Not that he deserved any of it, of course. But maybe this was another example of God's grace toward an unworthy sinner.

"Here we are." He steered her toward Williams's Café and swung the door inward to let her enter first. The aroma of simmering chicken and freshly baked bread poured over them, whetting his appetite.

Before stepping over the threshold, Marybeth gave him a tremulous smile, causing his heart to bounce around inside his chest. The sweet little thing was skittish, bless her heart. Of course, he felt a bit nervous, too. Maybe by the time they finished dinner, they'd feel more comfortable with each other. Sharing a meal could have that effect on a person.

"Hello, Rand." Mrs. Williams, proprietor and chief cook, gave him a wave from the kitchen door. "Take any seat you like."

"Thanks, Miss Pam. Come over and meet my…meet Miss O'Brien." Stopping short of calling Marybeth his bride, Rand paused to hang his hat on the wall peg. He led her to a table beside the wide front window where both of them would be able to watch the passersby. It was also far enough away from the half dozen other customers to keep their conversation fairly private.

"Welcome to Esperanza, honey." Miss Pam walked across the recently enlarged dining room and held a floured hand out to Marybeth. Seeming to think better of it, she brushed the hand on her white apron and chuckled. "Oops. I just finished making dumplings to go with the stewed chicken, so let's not get any flour on those nice gloves."

"How do you do, Miss Pam?" Her smile warm and friendly, Marybeth seemed to catch on real quick to the casual way things were done out here, another attractive quality in Rand's mind. "Chicken and dumplings sounds wonderful."

"Miss Pam's are the best," Rand said. "Make that two."

"Coming right up." Miss Pam signaled Lucy, her waitress, before returning to her kitchen.

Lucy took their order for coffee. When she brought it, she gave Rand a surreptitious wink and then went about serving the other customers. Rand doubted the wink held any other meaning than teasing because Lucy and his best friend, Seamus, were courting.

As Marybeth removed her tan kid gloves, she glanced around the room and out the window, her shyness apparent. Rand gently captured one hand across the narrow table, hoping to likewise capture her gaze. Her long, slender fingers felt just right in his grasp, except for the tiny tremor in them. He gave her a reassuring squeeze.

"I'm glad you're finally here." Not the smartest thing to say, but all he could think of.

She looked startled. Frightened almost. The long trip

from Boston must have worn her down. "Where can I find a place to stay?" The way her gaze darted around the room, she reminded him of a rabbit trying to escape a dog pack.

Hadn't she heard his remark about lodging? Did she see something in him to cause her concern? Rand swallowed hard. If he didn't have such faith in his parents' choice, he would think this was all a mistake. Instead of being happy or even interested in being in his company, Marybeth almost seemed afraid.

Then it struck him. She knew. Someone, probably Maisie, had told her the one thing Dad had insisted was Rand's responsibility to tell her. Now she was frightened of him, and he had no idea how to go about soothing away her fears and assuring her of his constant efforts to live for the Lord.

There it was, the tiny hardening in Rand's expression that signaled the beginning of his anger. Oh, he'd find a way to cover it until they were alone. Then she'd pay. Just as Mam never knew exactly what had displeased Da, Marybeth had no idea what she'd done to anger Rand. Now his perfectly formed face was lined with a winsome sort of sadness, just like Da when he sobered up and felt ashamed for his brutality.

Rand cleared his throat. "We planned to have you stay with my brother and his wife, but Susanna's expecting her second— Uh-oh, sorry. Maybe where you come from, folks don't talk about such things."

Marybeth hid her surprise at his comment. Indeed, such matters were never discussed at Fairfield Young Ladies' Academy. However, in the lower class neighborhood where she'd grown up, people never held back when discussing the hows and whys of childbirth. Rand's concern for her sensibilities spoke well of him. It was a quality more in keeping with the man his parents had recommended to her so highly.

"I certainly understand why Susanna doesn't need company right now." She offered a little shrug to indicate a lack of concern, just the opposite of what she felt. Being in another woman's house could provide protection. "Perhaps a hotel?" She would have to take a job to pay for it, but she'd planned to do so anyway. Her purse was empty, and traveling to Wagon Wheel Gap to search for her brother, Jimmy, would require another season of earning the funds to do so.

"Another uh-oh." He smiled and grimaced at the same time, a wickedly attractive expression. *Oh, Lord, guard my heart against this man's charms.* "We don't have a hotel. My father plans to bring in a hotelier from back East, maybe even England. He's working on that and a lot of other things to build up the town. Of course that doesn't help us right now."

Before alarm could take hold of Marybeth, Lucy arrived with two bowls of steaming chicken and dumplings. Once again Rand took her hand. This time he bowed his head and lifted a short, sincere-sounding prayer of thanks for the food. Emotion churned through Marybeth's chest like a roiling sea. Da had prayed, too. Magnificent prayers in his lilting Irish brogue, prayers God would surely hear for their beauty. Yet he never changed, never improved his ways. She set aside the memories but would never permit herself to forget them, lest she end up like Mam.

"Can I bring you anything else?" The waitress gave Rand a simpering smile at odds with her tomboyish swagger. She was flirting with him, but from his friendly, "No, thank you," Marybeth could see he was oblivious to her attempts to get his attention. An odd sort of jealousy smote Marybeth. No, that was just silly. Not jealousy at all. Simply an awareness of the girl's bad manners in flirting with a man when he was in the company of another woman.

They wordlessly began to eat and Marybeth's appetite roared into command. If not for the two years spent at Fairfield Young Ladies' Academy, paid for by the ladies of her Boston church, she would shovel the delicious food into her mouth just as she had as a child.

"About where you're going to stay..." Lifting the shaker next to the salt, Rand added a healthy dash of pepper to his dinner. "Mrs. Foster is the local piano teacher and church organist, and she's got an extra room. She'll be mighty glad for the company because her husband died last year and she's still at loose ends. She's an older lady and a bit talkative, but kind as can be. I hope that meets with your approval."

The doubt and apology in his voice, along with his sorrowful wince as he mentioned the husband's death, gave Marybeth pause. He possessed all the outward trappings of a gentle, thoughtful man. But so had Da.

"It's very kind of you to arrange that, Rand." She offered a polite smile that hid her relief over not having to worry about lodging.

Confusion clouded his expression. "Did you think I wouldn't find proper lodging for you?" His tone held a note of injury.

"W-well." Her chest tightened into a familiar knot. Had she touched a nerve? Was he angry? "No, of course not. I mean, yes, of course you would."

He shook his head and chuckled. "Now that I think of it, when we were writing, I don't believe we addressed the topic of where you would stay." He gave his head a little shake. "An unfortunate oversight."

"Yes, that's it." The knot in her chest eased. "Just an oversight."

They'd almost finished their meal, so she'd best tackle the difficult subject hanging over them. That way, if he became angry, she could look for help. Perhaps Miss Pam. Or the plump older couple seated at a table in the corner. No, they were leaving. In fact, they were coming this way.

"Howdy, Rand." The man clapped him on the shoulder. "Who's this pretty newcomer?"

Rand introduced Marybeth to the Archers and said they lived south of town in the Bowen community.

"You've got yourself a fine catch, missy," said the woman. "Lots of girls around here have tried to lasso this boy since the day he first started shaving."

While the Archers laughed, Rand rolled his eyes in a charming way. "You folks have a nice day."

They took their dismissal in good humor and left. Once again the situation gave Marybeth pause. They obviously didn't fear Rand. Miss Pam and Lucy didn't, either. When had Marybeth decided he was her father come back to life? Maybe she didn't have to be afraid of him. Maybe she should dismiss her fears and give him a chance to prove himself.

"Are you ready to go?" Rand started to push back from the table.

"No." Trying to gather her thoughts, Marybeth took another sip of coffee.

"Oh." Rand settled back down. "You want dessert? Apple pie? Or Miss Pam's special elderberry pie?"

His sudden eagerness to please made Marybeth want to laugh, but what she must tell him was too serious for her to indulge in any such levity.

"No, thank you." She glanced out the window, where people walked to and fro on their daily errands. On the way here, she'd noticed many people giving Rand friendly waves. Like Miss Pam and Lucy, every single one appeared to admire him. Still, she must proceed with caution. "I have to tell you something." She lifted her coffee cup for another bracing sip.

"I was afraid of that." His face fell and his shoulders drooped with disappointment. "You won't marry me because I'm too ugly. There was a reason I didn't send a picture, you know."

Marybeth almost spewed coffee all over him, barely catching the liquid before it escaped her lips. Now she could see the mischief in his eyes that bespoke an awareness of his good looks without being excessively prideful, a rare quality. Most handsome men of her acquaintance strutted about, clearly proud of their appearance.

Once she regained her composure, she shook her head. "I'm afraid it's a bit more serious than that."

"Ah." The humor left his face but a gentle twinkle remained in his eyes. "Go on. You can tell me anything."

She would take him at his word, at least for now. Borrowing from her Irish legacy of masterful story-telling, she wove the "sad but true tale" of her family, punctuating it with a few well-placed tears and carefully leaving out several details. Eight years before, when her brother was only fifteen, he'd been beaten up by neighborhood bullies. Da had called him a coward for not standing up to the thugs, so Jimmy had left home and never come back. He'd written only one letter a year or so later, posting it from Del Norte, Colorado, and saying he was headed to Wagon Wheel Gap to do some silver prospecting. Now that their parents had died, the mention of which brought genuine tears to her eyes, at least for Mam, she knew she had to search for her only living relative before she settled down.

At this point she batted her eyes, sending a few tears down her cheeks, and then dabbed at them with a handkerchief and gave Rand a look that pleaded for understanding.

"I'm sorry to hear about your dad and brother not getting along." He shook his head and stared off with a thoughtful look. "Describe your brother to me."

Marybeth started. Could it be this simple? Was it possible that Rand knew him? "His name is Jimmy O'Brien." She couldn't keep the eagerness from her voice. "I haven't seen him since I was twelve years old. He was just a couple of inches taller than I was, so he may be about five feet, five inches now, if he takes after our father. He has red hair and hazel eyes." She searched her memory for other details, but none came to mind. She certainly would not mention Mam's silver locket, which she'd given him to keep Da from pawning it to buy liquor. Marybeth laughed softly. "And, as if you haven't already figured out, he's Irish."

Rand's frown of concentration intensified. "Does he speak with a brogue?"

"No." She shook her head. "We both worked hard to get rid of it so we could get better jobs." She had worked especially hard to speak without the brogue, hoping to find employment as a servant in an upper-class home, something a rich rancher couldn't possibly understand. "He did pretty well, and the ladies at my church were so impressed by my efforts that they sent me to Fairfield Young Ladies' Academy, where I met Rosamond." She bit her lip, hoping she didn't sound proud, wondering how much further to go. "I learned deportment, but I also learned typing and accounting skills." In her letters she'd mentioned the academy but not the training in office work.

"Typing." He scratched his head. "I've heard about those typewriting machines but haven't ever seen one. I did receive a letter written on one. Makes a real nice page, just like printing in a book."

She beamed a smile at him, encouraged that he didn't seem the least bit angry. "Yes. I'm hoping to find work, perhaps in a bank or for a lawyer."

"Work?" Now he frowned again, but still without anger. "But I'm responsible for your care. I've made arrangements with Mrs. Foster on the condition you would agree to live there until our wedding." His eyes narrowed. "Marybeth, please assure me that you didn't take advantage of my parents' kindness just so they would pay your train fare so you could find your brother."

"N-no, not at all." *Yes.* At least partly yes. "Please recall the part of our agreement stating that either of us has the right to cancel our wedding if we're not compatible."

"And in just forty-five minutes, you've decided we're not compatible?" The edge in his voice sent a shiver through her middle. "Seems you've already made up your mind." He raised his hand as if he wanted to hit something, and Marybeth prepared to duck. Instead he waved off the gesture and stared glumly out of the window.

To her surprise, instead of being angry he seemed wounded, even depressed, so much so that she felt sorry for him.

Could it be that he wasn't like Da at all? Could she trust him to help her find Jimmy? Despite being a gambler and gunfighter, maybe he had a core of decency she could learn to trust. But how could she really know for certain?

Rand wished he hadn't raised his hand that dismissive way, as he always did to show gunslingers that he wasn't planning to fight them, for the gesture appeared to have scared Marybeth. He turned to stare out the window to watch the traffic in the street. She hadn't even given him a chance. Maybe hadn't even intended to try. So much for his parents' and sister's harebrained idea of finding him a proper Christian lady to marry. He should have just married one of those nice girls who lived down in Bowen. There sure were enough of them to choose from. But Dad had wanted to bring fresh blood into Esperanza; ladies with fine manners like Mother's to help some of the wilder gals like Maisie improve their ways.

Thoughts of Mother always stopped him short. He raised a familiar silent prayer that the doctors at the Boston hospital would be able to find out what caused her breathing problems. Dad had been so anxious about her health that he'd left Esperanza, the community he'd spent the past thirteen years building, the town that looked to him for guidance for every important decision they made. Yet Dad had willingly made the trip

back East for Mother's sake. Rand longed for that same
kind of marriage, where the most important thing was
to take care of one another, no matter what the personal
cost might be.

His folks had taken his sister, Rosamond, along to
enroll her in the Boston finishing school Mother had attended as a young girl. There they'd met Marybeth, and
Mother had decided she was the perfect young lady for
Rand. Until today he hadn't cared much about those fine
manners Dad insisted the local girls needed to learn.
But after meeting Marybeth, he couldn't imagine marrying one of those cowgirls he'd grown up with. Still,
he was beginning to wonder how his folks could have
been so mistaken about Marybeth. Couldn't they see
she'd had another plan all along?

Rand had made a few plans of his own. He'd envisioned someone who could grow a kitchen garden *and*
a family and give him a little intellectual companionship on cold Colorado evenings. If he'd just married
one of the gals who always smiled so sweetly at him in
church, he wouldn't be sitting here feeling like a complete fool. But he also wouldn't have a bride who could
talk about something other than the price of cattle or
how the weather affected the crops.

Probably intent on listening to their conversation,
Lucy sidled up next to him and gave his shoulder a sisterly nudge with her elbow as she held out the coffeepot.

"You must be missing Seamus." He held his cup
while she poured.

Lucy shrugged. "If you see him, tell him I do miss
him." She sniffed. "Don't know why he has to be the
one up in the hills with all them cattle all summer long.
I don't have nothing to do on my days off."

Rand gave her a sympathetic smile. "He's the trail boss because he's the best man for the job. You can be proud of him for that."

"Humph. And what am I supposed to do while he's out there?" Lucy poured coffee for Marybeth and then took Rand's empty plate in her free hand. With a swish of her skirt that brushed fabric against his forearm, she headed back toward the kitchen.

Eyeing Lucy with a hint of disapproval, Marybeth put two lumps of sugar and a dash of cream in her cup, stirred and lifted the drink to her lips. Her graceful hands looked like white porcelain and her little fingers posed in refined arches as she held the cup. Beautiful, elegant hands, but not hands for a rancher's wife. What had his folks been thinking? This young lady was entirely too genteel.

Or maybe as she'd traveled farther west, she'd realized what she'd gotten herself into. Too bad he couldn't blame Maisie for this turn of events, but that wouldn't be fair. Even if she spilled the whole story, with her upbringing as a rancher's daughter, of course she'd be proud of his killing a horse thief.

Well, one thing was sure. With Marybeth making it clear they wouldn't be getting married anytime soon, if at all, he could postpone telling her about the fatal gunfight. He had no doubt Maisie had blabbed the story, so when they did get around to talking about it, he would have to reassure Marybeth that he wasn't proud of killing a man, no matter what other people thought. On the other hand, he was still responsible for her since she'd come all this way to meet him. Best get this all figured out.

"Now about that job you mentioned, how do you

plan on getting it?" He couldn't keep the rancor out of his voice.

She lifted her chin and gazed down her pretty little nose at him. "As I said, I plan to work for a lawyer or in the bank." She blinked in a charming, innocent way. "You do have a bank, don't you? I thought I saw one on our way here."

"Yes, we have a bank. But everybody knows that's a man's job. Besides, what makes you think Mr. Means is going to hire you?" Rand felt justified being a little cross. Not only was Nolan Means young, wealthy and good-looking, he kept trying to finagle his way into community leadership, something the Northam family carefully controlled to keep out unsavory elements.

Marybeth's hazel eyes flashed at his challenge. "I will have you know I am very good with accounts. Not only that, but with my typewriting ability, I will be a great asset. If Mr....Mr. Means, is it? If he doesn't need an accountant or secretary, I am certain some businessman in this growing town will be happy to employ someone with my skills."

Rand gazed at her, admiration mingled with annoyance. The girl had spirit, that was certain. But as he watched her, something else became evident in her bright hazel eyes—a look he'd seen in green gamblers who just realized they'd gotten themselves into a game with seasoned cardsharps. She had a secret, one that scared her. Why on earth did she think coming out West would solve her problems? But here she was, and despite her postponement—maybe even her cancellation—of the wedding, he had every intention of sticking to his plans to take care of her. A Christian man always kept his word, always saw to his responsibilities.

Bolstered with that thought, Rand scratched behind his ear and gave Marybeth one of his best "aw shucks" grins. "Well, Marybeth, I wish you all the best. And I will pray for your success."

Her eyes widened and she seemed to struggle a moment before answering. "Why, thank you, Rand. How very kind."

He shrugged. "I've been praying for you since last January when Mother first wrote to me about you."

"Oh." She looked down at her coffee cup. "Thank you."

He frowned. She seemed confused by his mention of prayer. Yet Mother had assured him she was a Christian. A real one, not someone who just went through the motions in church. Maybe she'd fooled them all. That meant he had more than one responsibility for this little gal. He had to take care of her *and* get her saved. He would take her to church every Sunday and let her hear some of Reverend Thomas's fine sermons. If he'd listened to those sermons when he should have, he'd never have killed a man, no matter how threatened he'd felt.

Another thing he could do for Marybeth was to write to the sheriff in Wagon Wheel Gap to see if he'd come across a man matching Jimmy O'Brien's description. Maybe if Rand found her brother, she'd forget working and decide to settle down with him. On the other hand, he needed to find out what she was hiding before he could marry her. That was quite a quandary, one the Lord would have to sort out.

"If you're done with your coffee, I'll take you over to Mrs. Foster's. She'll put you up until—" He shook his head. No longer could he think *until the wedding.* "Until you get things worked out."

He stood, pulled a half dollar out of his pocket and dropped it on the table to pay for their dinner, adding a nickel for Lucy's tip. When Marybeth continued to stare at him with some sort of unreadable expression, he sighed as he snagged his hat off of the peg.

"I guess I should ask if that's all right with you."

She gave him a tentative smile and her eyes seemed to glisten. "Yes, it's fine. Thank you. You're very kind, considering…"

Rand ducked his head to put on his hat *and* to hide a grin. Her eyes held that secretive look again, but this time with even more uncertainty. Maybe he had a chance with this pretty little lady, after all. And maybe his older brother could offer some tips on how to win a gal determined not to like him.

Chapter Two

"**S**hall we go?" Rand held out his arm and Marybeth set a hand on it.

Once again she could feel his muscles rippling through his fine cotton shirt. How nice it would be to depend upon such a strong man. But Da had also been strong before his final drink-induced illness, and his excellent physique had housed a deceitful soul. In fact, Marybeth had met few men, sturdy or weak, who kept their word. Was Jimmy any different, or had he become like Da? She'd prayed for years he hadn't fallen into such sinful ways, but she didn't hold out too much hope. After all, the American West was known for its lawlessness. Maybe Jimmy had chosen that path.

Even if he had, she was determined to find him and make him hand over the silver locket. Mam had told her it contained the key to a treasure that would take care of Marybeth all her life. Although Jimmy probably didn't know what lay hidden behind the tintype picture of their family, the locket still belonged to Marybeth. Of course she would share the fortune with him. Too bad Mam hadn't claimed the treasure herself and used it to escape Da and his abuse. Knowing him, he would have found her and forced her to turn over the money so he could gamble it away or use it in one of his get-rich schemes that always failed. The man had never known how to tell the truth or make a wise decision, other than marrying a good woman like Mam.

"It's not far, just six blocks." Rand glanced down at her high-top shoes, already covered with dust from the unpaved street. "But we can get a buggy if it's too far for you to walk."

His thoughtful gesture threatened to weaken her, so Marybeth forced her defenses back in place. "The wind has died down and it's a lovely day. Let's walk." She punctuated her cheerful tone with a bright smile. "Besides, Boston's a very hilly city and I walked everywhere there. This flat town is no challenge."

He chuckled—a pleasant, throaty sound. "If you're used to hills, I'll have to take you up in the mountains for a hike. That sure would challenge you." His teasing tone was accompanied by quick grin before a frown darted over his tanned face. "Of course we'd take a suitable chaperone." His hastily spoken addition showed once again his eagerness to please her.

Oh, how she longed to trust him. Yet how could she dare to when he hadn't even told her about that deadly gunfight Maisie was so proud of? When Marybeth spoke of delaying their marriage, his hurt feelings and disappointment had been obvious. Shouldn't he have bragged about the killing, assuming she'd regard him as a hero and change her mind? She'd been honest with him about her family, at least as close to honest as she'd dared to be, but he was hiding a very significant happening in his life.

"This is the street."

Rand steered her down a row of attractive two-story houses, several of which rivaled some of Boston's finer clapboard homes. One redbrick structure reminded her of Boston's older Federal-style mansions. Numerous houses were in varying stages of completion, adding to the picture of the growing community about which Colonel and Mrs. Northam had told Marybeth. Young cottonwood and elm trees lined the street, and several fenced-in yards boasted a variety of shrubbery and colorful flowers in the last blooms of summer.

"What a pretty town." Her words came out on a sigh.

"We like it." Rand smiled his appreciation of her compliment, and her heart lifted unexpectedly.

Peace hung in the air like a warm mantle, belying the town's Wild West location. Maybe Esperanza would be a good place to call home after she found Jimmy. It all depended upon the people and whether or not she fit into the community.

"Here's Mrs. Foster's house." Rand indicated a pretty brown house with a white picket fence, a stone foundation, a wide front porch whose roof was supported by slender columns, and gabled windows jutting out from the second floor.

A slender, gray-haired woman with a slightly bent posture bustled out of the front door. "Oh, here you are at last. Welcome, welcome." She descended the steps, holding the railing beside them, and pulled Marybeth into a warm embrace. "I'm so glad to meet you, Miss O'Brien. Welcome to Esperanza. Welcome to my home."

Tears flooded Marybeth's eyes. She hadn't been held in a maternal embrace in the four long years since Mam died, and oh, how she'd missed it. No formal introduction could have moved Marybeth as this lady's greeting did. She obviously possessed an open heart and generous spirit, just like some of the older ladies at her Boston church. "I'm so pleased to meet you, too, Mrs. Foster."

"Hello, Rand." The lady embraced him briefly and then looped an arm in Marybeth's and propelled her toward the stairs. "Come along, my dear. Tolley brought your trunk and carried it up to your room. If you need help unpacking, I'll be happy to assist you."

"Thank you." Marybeth glanced over her shoulder. Da never let Mam have friends, but Rand seemed pleased by Mrs. Foster's warm welcome.

Inside the cozy, well-furnished parlor, Mrs. Foster seated Marybeth on a comfortable green-brocade settee, waving Rand to the spot beside her. "You two sit right here, and I'll bring tea." She left the room humming.

"I sure am glad to see her so happy." Rand had removed his hat and placed it on a nearby chair. He brushed a hand through his dark brown hair and smoothed out the hat line. "She's been grieving for a long time. Probably will for the rest of her life." The hint of emotion in his voice revealed genuine compassion. "Having you stay here will be good for her."

Marybeth could not discern any ulterior motive in his words or demeanor. Once again she was confounded. Why would a gunslinger care about an old widow? "I'll be glad to help in any way I can." She eyed the piano. "That's a beautiful instrument. Do you suppose she would let me play it?" When Da wasn't around, Mam had taught Marybeth to play, using the piano in a neighborhood church. She'd gone to practice as often as she could, first to escape Da's anger, later for the sheer enjoyment of playing.

"I think she'd be pleased to hear you." Rand moved a hand closer to Marybeth's but pulled it back before he made contact, apparently rethinking the gesture. "I'd like to hear you play, too."

The intensity of his gaze stirred an unfamiliar sensation in her chest. Was it admiration? Oddly, traitorously, she hoped he did admire her. What girl didn't want to be appreciated?

"Well, I'd need to practice first. It's been a while since I played."

He seemed about to respond, but Mrs. Foster entered the room carrying a black-lacquered tray filled with all the necessities for a lovely tea. Rand stood, as any true gentleman would, until Mrs. Foster reclaimed her seat.

"Oh, my." He looked hungrily at the cake, the look every cook hoped for. "It's a good thing we didn't have any dessert at the café."

"The café!" Mrs. Foster blustered in an amiable way. "Why, I can outcook that Pam Williams any day." She raised her dark gray eyebrows and stared at Rand expectantly.

"Now, Mrs. Foster." He held up his hands in a gesture of surrender. "There's a reason I never volunteer to judge the Harvest Home baking contest or any other one. As a bachelor, I don't want to get in trouble with any of the many fine cooks we're so fortunate to have here in Esperanza. You don't know how much we depend on your good graces to have a decent meal from time to time."

He waggled his eyebrows at Marybeth and she bit back a laugh. It was their first moment of camaraderie, and it felt...*right*. Very much so. *Oh, Lord, hold on to my heart. Please don't let me fall in love with this man.*

"Humph." Mrs. Foster poured tea and passed it to her guests. If Rand weren't so used to Mother's Wedgwood china, he'd worry about breaking the delicate cup that was too small for his large hands.

Mrs. Foster served the cake and then focused on Rand. "Well, young man, you won't be a bachelor for much longer. Have you chosen your wedding date?"

He did his best not to choke on his tea. Mrs. Foster's question was understandable, but he hadn't had time to figure out how to tell folks the wedding was off. Besides, his family should hear it first and from him. The way gossip both good and bad traveled through the community, he'd get home and find out Nate and Susanna had heard all about the "postponed" wedding.

"I'm sure everyone knows how much planning a wedding requires." Marybeth sipped from her cup. "In fact, Maisie Henshaw tells me the church is planning to build an addition right after harvest, one that would accommodate large parties such as wedding receptions." She took a bite of cake. "Oh, my, this certainly is an award-winning recipe."

The smile she gave Mrs. Foster was utterly guileless, but Rand's chest tightened. Marybeth hadn't lied, but she hadn't told the whole truth, either. Of course, he still had some truth-telling to do, as well, so he mustn't judge her too harshly.

He noticed that Mrs. Foster's eyes narrowed briefly, as though maybe she hadn't been fooled by Marybeth's little diversion from answering the question. She didn't comment, however, just took a bite of cake. Food always provided a handy excuse for not saying something. Rand often used that ploy himself.

They passed several more minutes trading mundane information, as folks do when first meeting. Rand already knew everything Marybeth told Mrs. Foster, because she'd written it all in her letters. Too bad she hadn't felt inclined to warn him about her plans to postpone the wedding until she found her brother. Guilt smote him again. He should have written to her about the gunfight. Should have anticipated someone else bringing it up. He couldn't get over the idea that she already knew and that Maisie had told her. But what exactly did she know? What did she really think? These were things they needed to settle between the two of them, so he sure couldn't ask her those questions in front of Mrs. Foster. The dear old lady never hesitated to give her opinion on any topic under discussion.

Marybeth seemed weary from her travels, so Rand took his leave, promising to visit the next day.

As he walked toward town to see if Tolley was still around, a dull ache settled into his chest, replacing the growing joy he'd felt for weeks in anticipation of meeting and marrying Marybeth. This was no more than he deserved. What lady from back East would understand what he'd done? He didn't even understand it himself. Only his friends and neighbors proclaimed him a hero; only his younger brother wanted to copy his actions. He hated every memory of that fateful day and all he'd done that led up to it.

Shoving away those thoughts, he started his search for Tolley at Mrs. Winsted's general store. He remembered to pick up a packet of cumin and spool of white thread his sister-in-law, Susanna, had asked for, but didn't find his brother. Back out in the sunshine, he headed toward the livery and caught Tolley leading his saddled horse out of the stable.

"Say, shouldn't you be over at Mrs. Foster's wooing your pretty little bride-to-be?" Tolley's impish expression made Rand want to tweak his nose, as he used to when they were scrappy little boys.

"She's pretty tired from her travels." Rand tried to sound cheerful so Tolley wouldn't ask any more questions. "Did you order the rope from the hardware store?"

Tolley chortled. "Don't change the subject. Tell me—"

"Northam!" A well-dressed, black-clad man, gun strapped to his leg, stepped off the boardwalk and strode toward them. "Randall Northam."

Rand felt his dinner and Mrs. Foster's cake rise up in his gullet. Another gunslinger out to prove himself. Didn't he know better than to face two men? Tolley might be young and hotheaded, but he was a fast-drawing crack shot. *Lord, please don't let my brother get shot.*

He sighed. "I'm Randall Northam. What can I do for you, Mr.—?"

A sly smile crept across the man's face but his eyes remained as cold and deadly as a rattlesnake's. And surprisingly familiar. "Name's Hardison. Dathan Hardison. I believe you met my cousin Cole Lyndon about three years ago."

Rand went cold all over. Frozen cold in spite of the sunshine beaming down on his shoulders and the warm summer breeze fanning over him. If the man drew on him, he wouldn't be able to get his hand halfway to his holster. Somehow he managed to keep all emotion out of his face, a seasoned gambler's ploy. Except he wasn't a gambler. Not anymore. Nor was he a gunfighter, despite the gun at his side. But what could he say to the kin of the man he'd killed? *Lord, help me.*

"Yes, I 'met' Cole Lyndon. I'm sorry to say it was an unfortunate meeting." On the other hand, the no-good horse thief had robbed and beaten Susanna's father, leaving him for dead. The sheriff in Del Norte had said Cole had left a string of robberies and murders behind him. But no matter how often his friends called Rand a hero for outdrawing the wicked man, he'd never aspired to be an executioner. Never aspired to have every gunslinger from Montana to El Paso come gunning for him, risking his family and his town. So far he'd been able to talk himself out of another fight with humor or appeals to their better nature, even making a few friends of those who'd intended to face off with him. But revenge for injury to a man's family was entirely different. Trouble was, Rand knew he'd take it badly if anyone hurt Nate or Tolley. Especially Tolley, whose heavy breathing gave evidence of his rising temper.

"Unfortunate meeting. Is that what you call it?" Hardison's deadly cold tone hinted at imminent repayment for Rand's crime. The man glanced over his shoulder toward the Friday-afternoon crowds meandering along Main Street. He rolled his head and gave an unpleasant laugh. "Just wanted to let you know I'm in town." He slowly reached up to touch the brim of his hat in a mock salute, made as if to turn away and instead turned back. "Speaking of meeting, I almost had the pleasure of meeting a certain young lady from Boston on the train, but that sissified doctor and his cowgirl wife were playing nursemaid. I'll be looking for an opportunity to introduce myself to her."

Despite the horrifying pictures Hardison's words conjured, despite the sick feeling in Rand's gut, he sent up a prayer for grace. If this man hurt Marybeth... No, he wouldn't let Hardison rile him. "You'll find your sort of woman farther west, Hardison. Why don't you get back on the train tomorrow and head that way?"

He snorted and gave Rand a nasty grin. "Watch your back, Northam. We'll meet again."

"Yeah, well, you'd just better watch *your* back, mister." Tolley stepped slightly in front of Rand, his right hand poised to draw. "Why don't we settle this here and now?"

"Now, now, young'un." Hardison carelessly spat on the ground, but his right hand twitched. "Why don't you go home to Mama and let the men handle this?"

"Forget it, Tolley. Don't answer him." Rand half faced his brother but kept one eye on the gunslinger. "Don't say another word." He recognized the signs. Hardison had no plan to draw. At least not now. Part of his fun was stalking his prey to make them nervous.

"I'll be seeing you." Again Hardison touched the brim of his hat, turned his back on them and strode away.

"Why didn't you take him down?" Tolley pulled off his hat and slapped it against his leg, causing his horse to sidestep in alarm. "You're going to have to sooner or later."

"No." Rand gripped his brother's shoulder. "I made a deal with the Lord that I won't kill another man like I did Cole Lyndon." He'd do whatever was needed to protect his family and Marybeth, but never again would he kill someone to save his own life. Never again would he stare into the eyes of a man on his way to eternity, hopeless and without Jesus Christ because of him.

"Well, I didn't make that deal." Tolley glared after Hardison.

Rand swallowed hard as fear from his little brother gripped his belly. Why couldn't Tolley understand? He'd told him all about his guilt, about the horror he'd faced watching a man die by his hand. And now here was another consequence of his actions. Tolley just might get himself killed copying what Rand had done, maybe trying to protect him. No matter what it took, Rand had to keep his little brother—and Marybeth—out of trouble.

Chapter Three

Halting, discordant notes of piano music invaded Marybeth's senses and pulled her from a dreamless sleep. Mrs. Foster had said some of her students would have their lessons this afternoon, and this one clearly was a beginner.

Before Marybeth had lain down in the four-poster guest bed, her thoughtful hostess had brought a pitcher of hot water, but she'd been too tired to wash. Now, despite the tepid water, she freshened up from her travels, at least well enough to hold her until the promised Saturday-night bath. Her ablutions complete, she brushed the dust from her hair and wound it back into an upswept coiffure.

Still mellow from her nap, she studied her appearance in the dressing-table mirror, recalling with pleasure the way Rand had looked at her, how his gaze had lingered on her hair and then her eyes. His obvious admiration, gentlemanly in every way, would thrill any girl, as would his thoughtfulness.

Regret over her own behavior cut short her moment of joy. Perhaps she'd been hasty in her opinion of him.

Everyone she'd met or seen today regarded him highly. Perhaps she could open her heart to him, if only for friendship. He seemed interested in helping her find Jimmy, and even though he didn't approve of her working, surely he would understand her determination to support herself. When he came to take her to church on Sunday, she would ask for his help in finding a job.

She opened her trunk to lift out a fresh dress and then dug beneath the other garments for clean stockings. She caught a glimpse of white satin underneath it all and gulped back an unexpected sob. Mrs. Northam had insisted upon purchasing a wedding gown for her, and there it was packed in tissue. Shame brought an ache to her chest. She hadn't meant to lie to Rand's mother, at least not consciously. She'd merely grasped for an opportunity to search for Jimmy sooner than if she'd had to work for endless years to make enough money to come to Colorado. And now survival might force her to sell the beautiful satin gown. That would of course destroy her friendship with Mrs. Northam and Rosamond.

Marybeth shoved her emotions aside. Regrets and shame wouldn't do any good. Instead of waiting to see Rand on Sunday, she must get busy and solve her own problems. Today was Friday and most businesses would be closing soon. She must go back to the center of town and search for a job for which her skills suited her. At the least, she could locate the best places to apply on Monday. Once she changed out of her traveling ensemble and put on a black linen dress appropriate for office work, she grabbed her parasol and made her way toward the staircase.

As she descended, she smiled at the uneven three-four meter of the piano piece, which didn't quite obscure the melody of a Strauss waltz. Having had her own struggles to smooth out that same meter, she couldn't resist peeking into the parlor.

A dark-haired girl of perhaps twelve years sat ramrod-straight on the piano stool, her fingers arched over the keys. Mrs. Foster sat in a chair beside her, wearing a strained smile.

"My dear Anna, I don't believe you've been practicing enough this week."

"No, ma'am, I haven't." Anna sat back and crossed her arms in a rebellious pose. "I don't want to play piano. I want to learn to ride and shoot like Miss Maisie and her sisters."

"Laurie Eberly plays, Anna, and enjoys it very much."

"Humph. She's the only one."

While Mrs. Foster sighed, Marybeth ducked back out of sight and stifled a laugh. Oh, how she remembered the days of resisting Mam's lessons. Now she wouldn't trade her skill for the world. The memory of Rand's approval when she'd spoken of wanting to play caused a little hiccough in her heart. To reward all of his kindness, she would find out which songs he liked best and play them for him at the first opportunity.

"Well, my dear," Mrs. Foster said, "your brother insists that you learn, so let's try to get through this, shall we?"

After heaving out a loud sigh, Anna resumed her hesitant playing just as someone knocked on the front door.

Marybeth stepped into the parlor. "Let me answer that for you."

"Please do." The widow nodded her appreciation even as she frowned at Anna.

The front door boasted an oval window with an exquisite etching of wildflowers. Through the glass, Marybeth could see a well-dressed young gentleman, bowler hat in hand, gazing off toward town as he waited to be admitted. When she opened the door, he turned her way, stepped back and blinked in surprise. He quickly regained his composure.

"Ah. You must be Miss O'Brien." He gave her an elegant bow. "Welcome to our community. I am sure Randall Northam is happy at your safe arrival." He reminded her of the businessmen she'd seen at church back in Boston. Like some of them, he possessed plain patrician features that became more attractive when he smiled. "Please forgive my forwardness. I am Nolan Means, and I have come to escort my sister home."

It was Marybeth's turn to lose her composure. This was the banker Rand had mentioned. *Thank You, Lord!* Before she blurted out her amazement, along with a plea for a situation in his bank, her schooling in deportment took control. "How do you do, Mr. Means? Please come in. Anna is a charming child, and I believe her lesson is almost complete."

A sociable look lit his brown eyes as he entered the front hallway. "You have met her?" He chuckled. "How did she do today?"

Marybeth gave him a reserved smile. "I haven't met her yet, only observed her. I do look forward to making her acquaintance." How could she turn this conversation into a request to work at his bank? "She seems to be a delightful child who knows her own mind."

He chuckled again. "That is my sister, all right. And you are gracious to say it that way. Her schoolteachers have never known quite what to do with her."

The waltz ended with a poorly done arpeggio, and Mr. Means grimaced. "Am I wasting my money and Mrs. Foster's time?" he whispered.

She shook her head and leaned toward him with a confidential air. "I resisted my lessons at first, but my mother's persistence paid off in the end. Now I love to play. Give her a little more time."

"Would you be so kind as to tell Anna that? Perhaps it would encourage her to continue." He regarded Marybeth with a friendly gaze. "Are you a music teacher, too?"

She swallowed a giddy laugh. The Lord had surely arranged this opening. "Why, yes, but only as my second occupation. I recently completed secretarial training and hope to find employment." His arched eyebrows foreshadowed the question she didn't want to answer. "Rand and I haven't set a wedding date, and I do want to keep busy."

"Ah. I see." His changing expression revealed myriad thoughts: surprise, speculation, perhaps even interest. Yet his brief intense look stirred no emotion within her as Rand's had. In fact, she was relieved when his face took on a businesslike aspect. "Secretarial training, you say? Perhaps our meeting is fortuitous, Miss O'Brien. I have need of a new employee at my bank. Did you also study accounting?"

Somehow Marybeth managed to control her smile. "I did, sir." She assumed the professional posture her teachers had taught her. "As well as typing."

"Typing?" He stroked his chin thoughtfully. "This is indeed a fortuitous meeting. I have obtained one of those Remington Sholes and Glidden typewriters for sending out business correspondence, but I have not found anyone to hire who can manage a letter without errors. Perhaps you can help."

She gave him a slight bow. "If you're speaking of the improved 1878 model, I learned on that very machine."

"Well, then, Miss O'Brien." He reached out to shake her hand and she responded in kind. "If you will come to the bank at nine o'clock on Monday morning, we can discuss your employment. That is, if you are interested."

"Nolly!" Anna dashed into the front hall and flung her arms around her brother's waist. "Oh, do say I don't have to take lessons anymore." The sob that accompanied her plea sounded a bit artificial to Marybeth.

Wringing her hands, Mrs. Foster appeared behind her student. In that moment Marybeth realized the dear lady needed the income from these lessons. Losing a student might create a serious problem for her. All the more reason for her to secure the job at the bank so she could pay for her room and board. She could not remain this dear lady's guest forever.

"Now, now, Anna." To his credit, Mr. Means seemed not to notice Mrs. Foster's anxiety. Nor did he appear embarrassed by his sister's behavior. "We will talk about it later." He questioned Marybeth with one arched eyebrow. "As well as what you and I discussed, Miss O'Brien?"

She returned a nod, assuming he meant both Anna's lessons and the situation at the bank. Even if he decided she wouldn't do for the job, she would be glad to encourage the child to continue. That would be a small repayment to Mrs. Foster for her hospitality.

They took their leave and Marybeth turned to her hostess. "May I help you prepare supper?" She must keep busy until Monday to make the time pass quickly.

Mrs. Foster appeared to have recovered from her alarm, for she gave Marybeth a bemused look. "Nolan seems quite taken with you."

Marybeth coughed out a nervous laugh. She'd thought her demeanor was entirely proper. "Oh, I certainly hope not."

Mrs. Foster seemed satisfied with her answer. "Very well. Shall we get busy with supper? I thought chicken and dumplings would be nice." She beckoned to Marybeth then proceeded down the center hallway.

"That sounds wonderful." Grinning to herself, Marybeth complied. She couldn't wait to tell Rand about having the same supper dish Miss Pam had served them for dinner. The cooking rivalry between these two ladies clearly amused him, but following his example, she would praise her hostess's dish as nothing short of perfection.

Why had she so quickly thought of sharing such a thing with Rand? Perhaps because he'd been in her thoughts since last January and she'd often practiced what she would talk about with him. Even though she'd been uncertain about the marriage, she'd looked forward to making his acquaintance, perhaps even gaining his friendship. Now that she knew his true character, those goals seemed less appealing. What would he say when she told him she had found a job? What would he do?

Guilt and nervousness vied for control of Rand's thoughts as he drove toward town. Nate and Tolley had insisted they would take care of today's chores, but he still felt responsible for doing his share. It was all Susanna's fault. She and Nate were staying in the big house while his parents and sister were back East, and his sweet little sister-in-law had wheedled the truth out of him about Marybeth's reticence to marry right away. She'd insisted he must get busy courting.

"If Lizzy were feeling better, I'd say bring Marybeth out here today," she'd told him over breakfast. Rand's two-year-old niece had come down with a cold and had clung to her mother while she ate. "First thing next week, you have to do that." She'd encouraged her fussy baby to take a bite of toast, but Lizzy had refused. "How about a picnic? Today isn't too soon. Nate and I went on a picnic my second day here. His courage in facing down those Indians made him a hero in my eyes and went a long way toward winning my heart."

Nate had beamed at his bride's praise as he'd nudged Rand's arm. "Go ahead, brother. Rita can pack a basket while you get old Sam hitched up to the buggy. You can drive into town and surprise Marybeth. Ladies like to be surprised, don't they, sweetheart?"

Susanna had batted her eyelashes at Nate as if they were still courting. Rand admitted to himself that he'd like to have Marybeth look at him that way. Seated across the table, Tolley had just groaned.

"*Si*, Senor Rand." Rita, the family cook, had a little courting going on herself with one of the cowhands. "I'll have everything ready in fifteen minutes."

"Well," Rand had drawled, still uncertain. "I did promise Marybeth a hike in the mountains." He'd stirred a bite of griddlecake into a puddle of syrup on his plate. "I also promised we'd have a chaperone."

All eyes had turned toward Tolley, who'd shoved back from the table, shaking his head. "No, sir. Not me. I've got all those chores to do, yours and mine. Got cows to milk, stalls to muck out, mustangs to break, fences to check and a whole bunch of other stuff." He'd stood and started toward the door like a scared rabbit. "Helping with her trunk was one thing, but I refuse to play duenna while you two make eyes at each other. Find somebody else."

"But you'd look so purty in a lace mantilla," Nate had quipped.

Rita had giggled and Susanna had laughed. Tolley's response was to slam the back door on his way out.

Bouncing Lizzy on her lap, Susanna had said, "Why not stop by Maisie and John's and invite them along?"

So now Rand drove old Sam toward town with a large, well-packed picnic basket secured to the back of the buggy and a prayer in his heart that Doc and Maisie would be free today. If they weren't, maybe Mrs. Foster would go. Of course that would mean they couldn't go hiking because it would be too hard on the older lady, but they could go up to a meadow by the river. He couldn't decide which chaperone he preferred. Having either one hear his every word would only add to his nervousness as he tried to become better acquainted with Marybeth.

As if that wasn't enough indecision for a man to have, he also had to figure out what to tell her about Hardison. While Nate had advised him not to worry her with the gunslinger's threats, Tolley thought she ought to know what the man had said in regard to her. Rand usually took his cautious older brother's advice, and yet he couldn't entirely dismiss the idea that she should be on the lookout for danger. As peaceful as the Esperanza community was, as caring the folks were about one another, there was always a chance of getting bit by a sneaky snake in the grass.

At the Henshaws' two-story house several blocks from Mrs. Foster's, he found three waiting patients seated in the front hallway. He greeted them with concern over their health even as his heart took a dip. Obviously his friends wouldn't be able to get away for a picnic. Before he could leave, Doc came out of the surgery.

"You're just in time, Rand. You can give me a hand." Doc took him out the side door to a wagon, from which they unloaded a leather-topped oak examining table and carried it into the surgery.

With the new furniture in place, Doc eyed Rand up and down. "Now, what can I do for you? I should have asked you that before I put you to work."

"Say—" Maisie came in the room before Rand could answer "—shouldn't you be over at Mrs. Foster's house courting that pretty little bride of yours?" She punctuated her question with a wink, a rowdy laugh and a slap on his arm.

"Uh, yeah. That's where I'm headed." Why had he thought inviting them would be a good idea? Maisie had a good heart, and he loved her like a sister, but she also had a loose tongue. He wouldn't even waste time asking for sure if she'd told Marybeth about his past.

"But—" Doc said.

Not giving Doc a chance to finish, Rand made his escape, dashing back to the buggy and heading toward Mrs. Foster's house.

Pretty piano music came through the open front window and Rand paused to listen to the end of the song. If that was Marybeth, she wasn't bad, but not quite as good as Mrs. Foster. Of course she'd said she needed to practice, so he mustn't be too quick to judge.

When Mrs. Foster admitted him, however, he saw that Laurie Eberly was just finishing her piano lesson. At fourteen years of age, Maisie's next-to-youngest sister had a bit more musical talent than her four sisters, and she liked to sing. That was, when she wasn't batting her eyes at Tolley like all the other younger girls. No wonder his brother was skittish about courting with every young girl in the territory making eyes at him, and him not even ready to court. Rand had suffered through that same phase several years ago.

"Make yourself comfortable, Rand." Mrs. Foster waved him toward the settee as she started up the staircase. "I'll fetch Marybeth. I'm sure Laurie won't mind an audience, will you, dear?"

"No, ma'am. I'd love it." Laurie glanced over Rand's shoulder as if looking for somebody and then gave him a sisterly smile. "What's Tolley doing today? Busy at the ranch, I suppose."

"Oh, he's real busy." Rand had his own romance problems, so he sure didn't want to stir up anything that would annoy his younger brother. He sat, hat in hand, and realized his palms were sweaty. Who would have guessed courting could be so difficult?

"Maybe I'll ride out there after my lesson and visit Susanna." Laurie set her fingers on the keys and began to play a song Rand wasn't familiar with.

He couldn't figure out a way to discourage her from going out to the ranch and pestering Tolley, especially since Susanna probably would appreciate a visit. Like all of the Eberly sisters, Laurie would be a big help with the sick baby.

"Hello, Rand." Marybeth entered the parlor looking refreshed from her travels. Beautiful, in fact, with her pretty auburn hair piled high on her head and her eyes more blue than hazel today because of that blue dress. As he stood to greet her, his heart leaped into his throat. "I wasn't expecting you until tomorrow. Is everything all right?"

He had to clear his throat before he could talk. "Hello." Was that dismay or worry in her eyes?

"Now, Marybeth." Mrs. Foster stood by her with an arm around her waist. Their already comfortable relationship would encourage him if he weren't so nervous. "Can't a young man come calling unannounced?"

"Oh, yes. Of course." Marybeth seemed to force a smile. "How are you today, Rand?"

"I'm well, thank you." He felt the strain in his own smile. "And you?"

"Well, thank you."

They stared at each other for a moment until Marybeth looked down at her hands.

About now was the time when Maisie would slap his arm and tell him to speak up. Fortunately her little sister didn't seem so inclined. Laurie still sat at the piano, and even though she wasn't playing she didn't appear to be eavesdropping.

"I was wondering," he said, "if you would accompany me on a picnic—you and Mrs. Foster? We can go down by the river, enjoy the scenery and see what our housekeeper fixed for us. She's a great cook." He glanced at Mrs. Foster. "Of course, not as good as you, ma'am."

"Thank you, dear boy." Her beaming face showed how much she appreciated his words. How she must miss hearing her husband praise her cooking. "Rita is quite young, but she'll improve with a bit more experience." She looked between the two of them. "Thank you for inviting me to chaperone your outing. Unfortunately, on Saturdays, my teaching schedule and my organ practice for tomorrow's service keep me from accepting."

Was that relief he saw on Marybeth's face? Dismay wound through Rand's chest. Was she all that set against being with him? So much for Susanna's brilliant idea about courting.

Marybeth tried to hide her relief over Mrs. Foster's refusal. The last thing she wanted was to have the older lady present when she asked Rand how serious he was about helping her find Jimmy. Bless her kind heart, the lady was a gossip, as their late talk last night had revealed. She wasn't in the least malicious, but stated outright that folks had a right to know what was going on in their community. While Marybeth couldn't disagree, she didn't want her private business spread all over town and who knew where else. She must be the one who told Jimmy about Mam and Da being dead, an important piece of news she now wished she hadn't told Mrs. Foster. Yet how could she have kept it from her?

She scrambled around in her mind to think of a public place to go with Rand, a place where she'd feel safe or could walk away if need be. Perhaps that park she'd seen across from the church—

"If you need a chaperone, I'll go with you." Laurie lowered the fallboard over the piano keys and stood. "Before Maisie and Doc got married, I always tagged along to keep things proper." She gathered her music and put it in a leather satchel. "Since Tolley's busy and all, I can go fishing and see if the trout are biting."

She gave Rand a look Marybeth couldn't quite discern. "Sort of planned to do that anyway."

Relief and amazement struck Marybeth at the same time. The Lord was still guiding her life in His mysterious way. While Laurie fished, she and Rand could talk privately.

"That's real nice, Laurie." Rand gave Marybeth a doubtful look. "Of course, if you had plans…"

"Not at all." She must have sounded too eager, because Rand's sad expression turned upside down. Gracious, he was handsome when he smiled. Handsome when he frowned, too, but of course smiles were much better. "Just let me change into something more suitable."

It didn't take her five minutes to slip out of her plain blue gingham and into her brown traveling skirt and white shirtwaist. Mrs. Foster offered her the use of a broad-brimmed straw hat to protect her complexion from the sun, and she carried her parasol for extra shade and a shawl in case a breeze came up. In a short time, they were on their way north toward the Rio Grande.

Marybeth sat next to Rand in his buggy, with Laurie riding her horse alongside them. Each time they went over a bump, Marybeth's shoulder jolted against his upper arm, and she could feel the solid muscles beneath the blue plaid sleeve. How pleasant that might have been if they were truly courting. Or if he weren't wearing that gun strapped to his right leg. Did he always wear it, even to church? She'd find out tomorrow.

The road smoothed out north of Esperanza and they picked up speed. Marybeth gazed east across the wide, flat valley toward the Sangre de Cristo Mountains. On the left, the San Juan range appeared nearer. Was Jimmy someplace up there? Or was she on a fool's errand?

"Thinking about your brother?" Rand offered that lopsided grin that made her silly heart skip. Or maybe it was his insightful question that moved her.

"Yes." She looked away from him toward the east again and brushed at sudden tears, hoping he hadn't seen them. "After all these years, I can't believe I'm this close. At least close to where his letter came from. Is Del Norte far? That's where he mailed it."

"Not far." For some reason he gave a little shudder at the mention of the next town over. "It's a long day's trip there and back."

"You go there often?"

His jaw tightened. "Haven't been there in three years."

Her question had bothered him, but why? Did it have something to do with his killing a man? Should she press the issue or let it go? With Laurie now riding twenty yards ahead, her long red hair swaying with the movement of her horse, she wouldn't hear their conversation. Perhaps the time had come for Marybeth to tell him what Maisie had said. His response would reveal a great deal about his character.

Rand knew God was pushing him to tell her about killing Cole Lyndon. He'd planned to do so today, but had hoped for a more comfortable setting, like after they both had full stomachs.

"Three years. That's a long time for such a close town." Marybeth spoke simply, with no apparent meaning behind her words. "Especially since Mrs. Foster tells me Del Norte has more places to shop than Esperanza."

Had Mrs. Foster told her anything else? He'd better hurry or everyone in the area would blurt out their own version of the story about the worst day of his life.

"I don't go over there because I used to gamble, and I don't want to be tempted." Those were the words of a coward sneaking in the back door.

Marybeth eyed him with surprise and maybe a bit of worry. "Gambling? You *used to* gamble?"

"Yes, ma'am." He gave a little shrug, bumping her slender shoulder without meaning to. It made his arm buzz pleasantly, but how did she feel about it? From her frown, he guessed she was thinking about the gambling and hadn't even noticed. "I had a real bad experience the last time I played poker and decided it wasn't the best way to spend my time."

"Tell me what happened."

Still frowning, she narrowed her eyes and now he could tell for certain she already knew the answer.

He pulled in a deep breath and exhaled long and slow. This was so hard. Should he explain that the man he'd killed had bragged about robbing and beating Susanna's father and leaving him for dead? That the gold lying on the table between them had come from selling the old man's horses? That the man and his partner had already cheated at that very card game? That Rand and his pal Seamus were about to quit anyway? Excuses, all of them. If he'd had a lick of sense, he'd have just walked away from the table that day and found the sheriff. A sick feeling rose up in his gullet.

"I killed a man."

She barely blinked, just looked away from him toward the river ahead. "I see."

"Maisie told you, didn't she?"

Marybeth nodded, still not looking his way. "She said you're a hero because the man was a horse thief who'd done his own share of killing."

He shrugged again, this time taking care not to touch her. "That still doesn't excuse it. Instead of losing my temper, I should have let the law handle him."

She looked his way, tears rimming her eyes. "So you regret it." Not a question, a statement. Maybe she understood.

"I do. Deeply."

She set her long, gloved fingers on his forearm. This time her touch imparted an odd sort of reassurance. "Have you asked God for forgiveness?"

A grim laugh escaped him. "Every day."

"Then you must believe He has forgiven you."

Marybeth enjoyed the sweet smile that blossomed across Rand's handsome face. This had been an important moment for them because so far they hadn't had a chance to discuss their faith. Yet nagging at the back of her mind was the memory of Mam always forgiving Da, but Da never changing. Had Rand truly changed, or did he still have the kind of quick temper that would make him draw a gun and kill a man...or who knew what else? She would wait and see.

"Thank you." Rand squeezed her hand.

"For what?"

"For reminding me of God's forgiveness." He tugged the reins to the left to direct the horse down the path Laurie had taken. "Mother wrote that you're a woman of faith, and it's good to hear you speak of it." His gaze lingered briefly on her lips. To her relief, he made no move to kiss her.

They arrived at a small meadow beside the slow-moving river, so Marybeth would have to postpone asking Rand questions about his faith. She didn't think she'd done much to help him, but her words had obviously encouraged him. At the very least, it was an opening she could refer to later.

He jumped down from the buggy and loosely secured the reins around a slender young pine tree so his horse could help himself to the abundance of grass at his feet. Laurie had already dismounted and found a branch to use for a fishing pole.

"Aren't you hungry?" Rand called out to her.

"Sure am." Laurie continued to work with her pole. "I just wanted to get a line out in the water to see what's swimming by today."

"Suit yourself." Rand gave Marybeth a hand in stepping down from the buggy.

"What a lovely place." She breathed in the fresh, cool air of the shady meadow. Closer to the river she spied some wildflowers but didn't recognize what kind they were. Peace settled over her and she made up her mind to enjoy the day.

"Yep. It's real nice here. 'Course we have fish in the streams near our ranch, but the best trout come from the Rio Grande. That's why I like it." He walked to the back of the rig, untied the picnic basket and pulled a blanket from beneath it. Then he searched for a good spot to lay it out.

Marybeth hurried to his side. "I'll help you."

"No, ma'am. You're my guest today." Finding a shady spot, he moved a few rocks and branches out of the way. "I'll take care of everything."

Nonetheless, Marybeth reached for the blanket and

helped him spread it out. She started to follow him back to fetch the basket, but he stopped and gently gripped her upper arms. "You don't mind very well, do you? Now go sit down and let me manage the rest."

Despite his crooked grin and teasing tone, a shiver went through her. *No.* She would not feel this way. He was just being nice, just taking care of her, as any gentleman would. She tried to return a playful grin, but it felt too wobbly to be convincing. Turning from him, she did as he said and made herself comfortable on the old woolen blanket. Or as comfortable as one could be on the rough ground. She reached beneath the blanket and pulled out a few more rocks.

He returned with the basket just as she threw aside a large sharp stone. Instead of the charming grin she expected, his expression twisted into something she couldn't even describe. Fear? Anger? Because she'd moved a rock instead of waiting for him?

He slowly set down the basket, slowly pulled his gun from his holster and slowly pointed it straight at her. "Don't move, Marybeth. Don't move an inch."

The rattler was just pulling itself up into a coil not three feet from Marybeth's hand. Yet the fear written across her pretty face wasn't from the danger she hadn't even noticed. She was afraid of *him.* In spite of his confession, she still didn't trust him. But this was no time to sort it all out. She had minded his order and sat like a statue on the blanket, her widened eyes squarely focused on his gun.

Dear God, don't let her move. Let me kill the rattler without hurting her.

Gunfire exploded several yards to his left. Snake

parts flew in all directions. Rand's knees threatened to buckle. He glanced at Laurie, whose rifle bore a telltale curl of smoke around its barrel.

Now he was just downright annoyed. Saving Marybeth's life would have made him a real hero in her eyes. Yet honesty demanded that he hand the honors to a fourteen-year-old girl.

"Good aim, Laurie." He needed to downplay the situation, make it sound like an everyday occurrence to calm Marybeth's fears.

"Looked to me like Marybeth was in your way." Laurie shrugged as she returned her rifle to the leather holster on her horse's saddle. "I had a better shot from over here."

Rand nodded his agreement. "Let's see now. Shall we move the blanket to a nicer spot closer to the river?" Someplace far away from the dead snake. "I don't know about you ladies, but I'm as hungry as a bear coming out of hibernation."

He grinned at Marybeth about one second before she fell over on the blanket in a heap.

Chapter Four

Marybeth had never fainted in her life. She'd always refused to surrender to the frailties of the silly society girls she'd known at the academy. But now she found herself looking at the world sideways and trying desperately to reclaim reality. The first thing to register in her mind was Mrs. Foster's scratchy straw hat, one side now crushed between her face and the hard ground. Her eyes couldn't quite focus on two round brown objects in front of her: Rand's bent knees? Laurie's voice reached her through a dull roar inside her head. Or was the roar from the nearby river?

"I dunno, Rand. You sure you want to marry a gal who can't handle a little incident with a snake?"

"Hush. Don't be rude." He tugged on the ribbons holding the hat in place and moved it back from her head. "Marybeth?" His work-roughened hands felt gentle on her cheek. "Are you all right?"

Air. She desperately needed air. Dragging in the life-giving oxygen so scarce at this high altitude, she whimpered with relief as her lungs expanded. Oh, mercy.

What a baby she was. This was far from the most frightening thing ever to happen to her.

"'M fine." She tried to infuse the words with confidence, but they came out on a strangled whisper. This really must stop. She pushed herself up on one elbow, with Rand's support under her arm providing the strength she lacked. After another gulp of air, she expelled an awkward laugh. "Gracious." No other words came to mind, so she just looked up at Rand and gave him a tremulous smile.

He shoved his hat back from his forehead and returned the same, his relief obvious in his eyes. "Would you like a sandwich?"

His playful smirk sent a giddy feeling shivering through her. In spite of Laurie's impertinent question concerning her apparent lack of fortitude, his gaze bore no censure.

"Yes. Thank you." No, not at all. Not with her stomach twisting inside her at the memory of the gory snake remains.

Dismissing the dreadful sight from her mind, she placed a hand in his offered one and they stood as one. Once again she had to draw from his strength, this time to gain her footing, and now she couldn't look away from him. For untold seconds they stared at each other as she tried to read his soul, as her minister used to say. Unlike Da's darting, half-penitent looks, Rand's gaze held no deception, nor did any manipulation or anger emanate from his eyes' green depths. Only kindness and concern and sweet gentleness. Cautious trust welled up inside her accompanied by a sincere liking for this cowboy, this good, decent man. Surely he would help her find Jimmy. And while she had a lot more to learn about him, she might just think more about their marriage bargain. She quickly shoved aside that hasty, dangerous thought, replacing it with another. At least now she understood why Rand carried a gun. She might even get one herself if snakes were a constant danger.

Through the fog of her musings, she became aware of Laurie's soft giggle.

"Guess I'll move the blanket." The girl grabbed an edge and tugged, forcing Marybeth and Rand to break their visual connection and hop off onto the grass.

While Laurie gave the blanket a shake and dragged it to a shady spot several yards closer to the river, Rand stepped away from Marybeth to pick up the basket and offered her an arm.

"Miss O'Brien, would you do me the honor of accompanying me on a picnic?" He winked and waggled his eyebrows, probably trying to cheer her.

With a giggle of her own, or maybe it was a laugh of relief, Marybeth set her hand on his arm. She would show young Miss Laurie Eberly *and* Rand just how brave she could be by making as little of the snake incident as possible. "Why, Mr. Northam, I would be delighted."

At Marybeth's sassy response, Rand almost fell over in relief. *Thank You, Lord.* She might have fainted, but she got right back on her feet. More than that, as they'd stared into each other's eyes for those brief seconds, he could see her determination to overcome the incident. Was he flattering himself to think he'd helped in some way? Not that it mattered. This little city gal had spunk, and it made him all the more resolute to keep on courting her. Even if they didn't end up getting married, he wanted to be her friend.

Yet as he held her hand to help her kneel back down on the blanket, he remembered her real purpose in coming to Colorado was to search for her brother. Had she deliberately lied to his parents so they would pay her traveling expenses? He mustn't let her pretty face and nice manners hide a lying heart, something he refused to bring into his family.

How odd that in the past few years he'd fended off a half dozen local gals who'd tried to capture his interest, honest Christian girls he just didn't happen to care for enough to court. Yet the bride his parents had chosen for him could end up being a disappointment to them. He already felt a little disappointed that she hadn't inquired about Susanna's health today.

On the other hand, he couldn't imagine how it would be to have only one family member still living and yet not know where he was. Rand loved his brothers and sister more than words could say. Even when they fought or just disagreed, they were always there for him. Dad and Mother, too. From what Marybeth had said about her father, her family hadn't been blessed in that same way. Maybe if Rand learned more about her and them, he could unravel the mystery of her character.

One thing was sure. After he took Marybeth back to Mrs. Foster's house, he would start his search for Jimmy O'Brien by writing to the sheriffs in Wagon Wheel Gap and Del Norte. In fact, if he had a little more confidence in his ability to avoid temptation, come Monday morning he would ride over to Del Norte and speak to Sheriff Hobart in person.

Laurie took charge of the picnic basket and dug out

a sandwich to hand to Marybeth. "You ever go fishing?" She handed one to Rand before taking a bite of a third one.

"Ahem." Rand gave her a scolding look. "Shall we pray before we eat?"

Laurie had the grace to bow her head without protest, while Marybeth, who hadn't taken a bite yet, gave him an approving smile. "Yes, please."

After a quick argument with himself over whether to mention the snake, he decided the Lord deserved their thanks for keeping Marybeth safe. He should have prayed right after Laurie shot the varmint. Dad said a Christian man needed to take spiritual leadership in any situation when a minster wasn't present. Rand and his older brother tried to follow Dad's example now that he was away from home.

"Father, we thank You that Laurie shot the snake before it could cause any harm." No need to belabor the point, so he hurried on. "We thank You for this food and the hands that prepared it. And thank You for making this beautiful day for us to enjoy. In Jesus' name. Amen."

He opened his eyes to see Laurie chowing down, while Marybeth was staring at him with teary eyes… and a smile. A feeling as warm and pleasant as the day spread through his chest.

"Let's eat." He bit into the sandwich, and flavor burst in his mouth and set it to watering. "Oh, man," he said after he'd chewed and swallowed. "I don't know what Rita puts into her mystery sauce, but nobody can beat her roast beef sandwiches."

"Not even Mrs. Foster?" Marybeth raised one eyebrow and gave him a teasing smile.

"Shh." He held a finger to his lips. "Don't tell her I said that."

She gave him another one of those cute smiles and he felt a slight tickle in his chest that he couldn't quite identify. "I can see that cooking is a source of great competition among the ladies." Turning to Laurie, she said, "How about you? Do you like to cook?"

"Not much." Laurie shrugged. "It's more of a chore than fun. I'd rather be fishing." She glanced over at her pole, still stuck in the riverbank with its line trailing downstream. "Or breaking horses." A glint in her eye warned Rand that mischief was coming. "Do you ride? 'Cause if you do, I have just the horse for you. Name's Malicia."

"How kind of you." Marybeth's expression was pure innocence, except for a slight twitch of her lips, revealing to Rand that she wasn't fooled by Laurie's offer. "Unfortunately, I've never had the pleasure of learning to ride."

"Too bad." Laurie finished her sandwich and excused herself to tend to her fishing pole. When she was out of earshot, Marybeth rolled her eyes.

"Malicia, eh?" She laughed softly. "Malice? I don't need to speak Spanish to figure that one out."

Rand chuckled. "The Eberly girls don't have any brothers, so they have to do all the work around their ranch, including breaking horses and mucking out barns. They don't think much of women who can't keep up with a man. They do everything from herding cattle to cooking mainly because they don't have the luxury of being pampered like city girls."

The instant the words left his mouth, he knew his

mistake. Marybeth's eyes dimmed briefly and her lips pinched together into a grim line. "Hmm."

Before he could correct his mistake, Laurie whooped.

"Got a big one on the line." She gave the pole a little jerk to set the hook, struggled briefly with her unwilling prey and then pulled the large trout up on the grassy bank. "Will you look at that?"

Marybeth got to her feet, snatching up a knife from the picnic basket and striding toward the scene. "That's a fine fish, Laurie. Must be at least two pounds. I'll be glad to clean it while you catch another one."

Laurie stared at her briefly, gave Rand a quick glance and held out her still hooked catch. "Sure. Here you go." Her tone of voice was friendly, but her eyes held a challenge. Rand wanted to tweak her nose for being so contrary with this city girl who'd already shown a healthy bit of grit by dismissing the snake episode.

Marybeth deftly unhooked the squirming silver trout and plunked it down on the grass. With the skill of a butcher, she gutted it in no time, tossed the innards into the river and scraped off the heavy scales that marked it as a fairly mature fish. "Did you bring a creel?"

Her eyes already wide with surprise, Laurie gave a brief nod. "On the back of my saddle." She tilted her head in the direction of her horse.

Marybeth hesitated only two seconds before approaching the large gelding. After putting the fish into the wicker creel, she untied the basket from the saddle and carried it to the river, dunking it into the water as though she knew exactly what she was doing.

Laurie once again glanced at Rand and nodded her approval.

Rand lay back and rested his elbows on the woolen

blanket, content to watch the girls, whose coopera-
tive efforts suggested they were having fun catching
and cleaning the fish. Marybeth had surprised and
impressed him in a big way. In spite of her city upbringing, she didn't appear to be the least bit pampered, and
if he knew what was good for him, he'd better not make
any more remarks to suggest that she was.

Marybeth studiously avoided letting her face reveal
the triumph she felt over showing she wasn't afraid of
unpleasant tasks. Pampered, indeed. Maybe she couldn't
ride a horse or even feel comfortable going near the
large beasts beyond riding in a buggy. Yet before en-
rolling in the academy, she'd spent her entire life doing
whatever honest work she could find to survive in a
city not always kind to poor Irish immigrants. As to
the cooking competition of the local ladies, she had a
recipe or two she'd put up against the best of them. But
again, she'd learned at Fairfield Young Ladies' Academy not to brag, a challenge to anyone of Irish descent.
Her people had long been great storytellers and she'd
learned the art at her parents' knees.

"Where'd you learn how to clean fish?" Rand asked
later as they packed up to leave.

"In a Boston fishery when I was eight years old."
With a cool look, she dared him to think less of her for
her hardscrabble life.

Instead he nodded and grinned with seeming approval.
"I was mucking out stalls when I was that age. Don't
know which one's a harder job, but they're both pretty
messy." After securing the picnic basket to the back of
the buggy, he offered his hand to help her climb up.

"And smelly." She wrinkled her nose, which brought

the hoped-for laugh. "Boston Harbor usually stinks from all the fish and other seafood, and I wore the smell home with me every night. Not like this river. Everything here smells so fresh and clean. Even the fishy odor is mild and washed off my hands right away." She accepted Rand's help into the buggy and settled comfortably on the leather-covered bench. This moment of camaraderie encouraged her. He wasn't looking down his nose at her.

Maybe she should have trusted his parents enough to tell them everything about her childhood. They'd assumed she came from a middle-class home just because she attended a fine church and was a student at an academy for young ladies, but that was far from the truth. Yet Rand wasn't bothered by her working at a lowly job. Maybe he just didn't understand that only the poorest people took jobs cleaning fish at the fishery.

"I never thought about the smells of Boston." Rand settled beside her on the bench and grasped the reins. "I was born there, but we moved out here to Colorado when I was about ten, so I can't remember much about it. All I remember are the stories about the city's part in the American Revolution. My brothers and sister and I played Minutemen." His eyes took on a faraway look as if he were reliving those long-ago years. "Paul Revere's ride. Bunker Hill. Boston Tea Party."

"All the heroic events." She and Jimmy had also played those games with other children in their neighborhood. Better to reenact a war the Americans had won than the tragic Irish Rebellion her people had lost. Or the war that had been going on between the States during her childhood. Many a father hadn't come home from fighting for the Union, and her own da had suffered wounds that had plagued him until his death.

Rand nodded in response to her comment. "Heroics, yes. But being so young, I didn't appreciate the real history."

"Hey." Laurie had mounted her horse and swung him around toward the buggy. "You think Mrs. Foster would like these fish?" She held out the dripping creel.

"How thoughtful." Reaching out for the wicker container, Marybeth stifled the urge to dodge the river water flying about. She'd had much worse on her clothes working at the fishery. "I'm sure she'll enjoy them for supper."

"Well, if you two lovebirds can keep out of trouble, I'm going to ride on home." Laurie grinned at Marybeth and winked at Rand.

"Is that all right with you?" Rand asked Marybeth.

"Of course." If her teachers at the academy hadn't said ladies never winked, she'd have copied Laurie's impudent gesture. Winking at Rand might give him the wrong idea about her character, something she had guarded all her life.

"Go on." Rand waved his hand toward Laurie as if she were a pesky fly. "Git. And tell your pa I said hello."

"That's not all I'll tell him." The girl kicked her horse into a gallop, laughing as she rode away.

Marybeth wanted so badly to act shocked by the girl's cheeky behavior, to pretend that she herself was some fine lady who'd grown up with fine manners in a fine home. But she couldn't put the cat back in the bag, not after gutting fish and admitting she'd worked in the fishery. Yet neither did she have to revert back to the hoydenish behavior of her childhood in the slums, where both women and men had to be feisty and tough to survive.

The buggy rolled along in a syncopated pattern accompanied by the rhythmic squeak of the leather seats, the jangle of the harnesses and the clip-clop of the horse's hooves on the hard-packed ground. Reminded of an old Irish tune, Marybeth found herself humming along.

"Go ahead and sing." Rand shot her one of his charming grins before turning his eyes back to the road ahead. "I may even join in."

She eyed him, enjoying the cut of his strong jaw, high cheekbones and straight nose. If looks were all that counted, he'd be an easy man to love.

"Go on." He nudged her arm with his elbow and gave her another grin.

At least a month had passed since her last solo in front of her Sunday school class, so she took a moment to clear her throat and get back into the rhythm of the horse's gait.

"'While on the road to sweet Athy, hurroo, hurroo. While on the road to sweet Athy, hurroo, hurroo. While on the road to sweet Athy, a stick in me hand and a drop in me eye, a doleful damsel I heard cry, Johnny I hardly knew ye.'"

Caught up in the song and feeling a bit reckless, she infused her words with the Irish brogue she'd worked so hard to lose. To her delight, Rand whistled along in harmony. Before she realized what she was singing, she warbled, "'Where are your legs with which ye run when first you learned to carry a gun? Indeed your dancing days are done. Oh, Johnny, I hardly knew ye.'"

Rand quit whistling, and if she wasn't mistaken, released a quiet sigh. Regret filled her. Did the song about the Irish Rebellion remind him of his own gun battle, which clearly still bothered him, despite others considering him a hero? She stared out across a wheat field almost ripe for harvest. Why hadn't she chosen a different song? But once again, she couldn't put the cat back in the bag.

Rand wished he hadn't let the song get to him. After all, he'd insisted that she sing, and she did it very well. Yet when would he be able to put his gunfight behind him, to stop wishing he'd never "learned to carry a gun" and just enjoy life? In the back of his mind, he knew Dathan Hardison's appearance in Esperanza was part of the problem.

Lord, I need Your help. It's not fair to Marybeth for me to get all melancholy like this. He straightened his shoulders and inhaled deeply of the fragrant wheat field on their left. Soon it would be harvest time, a time that promised survival through the coming winter. Before the geese flew south or the passes were blocked by snow, he needed to survive this winter of his soul.

"I've been trying to think what's wrong with that song." He forced cheer into his voice.

"Oh?" She turned sad eyes in his direction.

"And I've figured it out. It's all about sorrow." He enjoyed the way she blinked in confusion.

"Of course it is. Poor Johnny comes home from war maimed and unable to care for his wife and child." She bit her lip as if sorry she'd said that.

"That's where you have it all wrong." He smirked. "This is the version we sang when our Boston boys— *and* my father—returned from fighting in the South."

He launched into a spirited song with the same melody. "'When Johnny comes marching home again, hurrah, hurrah. When Johnny comes marching home again, hurrah, hurrah. The men will cheer and the boys will shout; the ladies they will all turn out. And we'll all feel gay when Johnny comes marching home.'"

By the time he reached the hurrahs, she'd joined in singing with a gusto that matched his own. As the buggy rolled across Main Street toward Mrs. Foster's Pike Street home, they were both laughing together like old friends.

"If it's not too bold of me to say, we make beautiful music together, Miss O'Brien." He salted his words with a bit of the Irish brogue he'd learned from his friend Seamus.

"Aye, that we do, Mr. O'Northam." Her merry mood gave her face a pretty glow. "Do you play an instrument of any kind to accompany us?"

"No. I never had the time to learn." And regretted it now. Was it too late to take up the guitar or accordion, the instruments that had always attracted his interest?

"I'll just have to teach you. Then you can leave ranching behind and go on the road as an entertainer."

Now he let out a hearty guffaw. What a delightful young lady. He could spend the rest of his life getting to know her. If she would have him.

A glance down the street cut his joy short. Dathan Hardison leaned casually against a post in front of Winsted's General Store, his arms crossed and his hat tipped back from his face as he chatted with Mrs. Winsted. The widow's posture was nothing short of sociable, meaning Hardison was worming his way into her good graces. Maybe Rand and his brothers were wrong not to warn folks in the community about this man's reason for coming to town.

Forcing his attention to the road ahead, he also forced a smile he didn't feel. "I'll come by Mrs. Foster's at ten o'clock tomorrow to escort you to church." He could hear the strained, almost authoritarian note in his voice, so quickly added, "That is, if you'd like."

The flush of high-spiritedness faded from her face and she gazed off with a frown, as though the idea didn't particularly appeal to her. Once again, caution reined in his growing affection for her. If she balked at going to church, how could he commit his life, his love, to her?

Rand's mood had shifted so quickly that Marybeth stared down Main Street to see what had caused it. The pleasant scene betrayed nothing unusual, just an ordinary Saturday afternoon with people going about normal business. Perhaps he was just temperamental—not a good sign. Oh, she'd dispensed with the notion that he might be abusive like Da, but she wouldn't marry a man with a temper or even habitual cross moods. She refused to be like Mam, always hurrying to cheer Da when he came home in a bad humor just so it wouldn't get worse. How often she herself had tried to make things right in their home, to no avail.

Rand cleared his throat, recalling her from her musings. "You did plan to go to church tomorrow, didn't you?"

She detected a note of irritation in his voice and that habitual urge to make things right crept into her chest. She tamped it down and gave him a saucy grin. "I'll not be needing you to keep me on the straight and narrow, Mr. Northam. I'm well and good dedicated to it myself."

She tossed her head and sniffed. "In fact, Mrs. Foster tells me she goes over to the church early to make sure everything's in fine fettle for the services, so I'll be going along with her and setting out the hymn books."

Her impertinent tone must have pleased him, for he gave her one of his attractive smirks. "And maybe I'll just be showing up to help you set them out. What would you think of that?"

She tapped her chin thoughtfully with her forefinger. "Hmm. I might just be able to stand your company, providing you don't get all bossy and try to tell me how to go about it."

"Why, Miss O'Brien, I would na dream of it."

Their merry mood restored, she enjoyed the rest of the ride down Pike Street to Mrs. Foster's house.

"Won't you come in?" she said as he handed her down from the buggy.

"I'd like that very much, but Nate didn't give me the whole day off. I still have chores and Tolley won't take kindly to my leaving them all to him."

He held her hand a little longer than was proper, but for some reason she didn't mind. Gazing up into his green eyes, edged as they were with dark lashes, she thought once again how easy it would be to fall in love with this man, if looks were all that counted. If nothing else, today she'd learned he would keep her safe. That was worth a great deal.

"I should go in." She tugged her hand free and retrieved the creel from the floor of the buggy, where grassy water formed a small puddle. "Oh, dear. I hope that doesn't leave a stain."

"Aw, nothing to worry about. It won't take a minute to wash it out." He took the creel from her and offered his arm. "Let's take these fish around to the back door so they won't drip water through the house."

"As if I hadn't thought of that very thing." Seeing he really wasn't so eager to get to those ranch chores, she found herself in no hurry to lose his company.

"O'course ya did." His Irish brogue was entirely entertaining and she rewarded his remark with a laugh.

As they strolled along the flagstone walkway toward the backyard, Marybeth took in the scent of the roses planted in narrow beds against the two-story house. She hadn't had a chance to see the outside of the house and found it entirely charming. "How lovely to have roses growing right here. We never had—" She stopped short of saying "anything so grand at our house." Despite her admission that she'd worked in the fishery, she still didn't want to admit to him how poor her family had been, so she finished with "A knack for growing flowers." Or decent soil in which to grow them.

"Maybe Mrs. Foster can show you her gardening methods. If not, Susanna can. She's done a fine job of keeping up the flower garden at our house while Mother's back East."

"And when do you suppose I'll be introduced to this Susanna?" In truth, Marybeth wasn't certain she wanted to meet the young lady or at least not form a friendship with her. She'd had very few intimate friends in her life, and if she got too close to Rand's sister-in-law, she feared it would make it all the harder not to become a part of his family.

"She may come to church tomorrow if Lizzy feels better."

"Poor baby. I'll be praying for her." Marybeth adored children. In spite of her determination not to get close to his family, if she didn't have her appointment with Mr. Means on Monday morning, she might ask Rand to fetch her out to the ranch so she could help Susanna take care of the wee colleen.

Oh, dear! With Rand's teasing her in an Irish brogue, hers was returning like a rekindled fire, one she must stamp out right away. In Boston, the Irish garnered little respect, and she refused to invite such treatment out here. Not that anyone in the Northam family had disparaged her background. Brogue or not, with a name like O'Brien she could hardly fool Rand's parents, and they'd been more than kind to her. A twinge of guilt stirred within her. More than kind, indeed, if they wanted her for their son. It was nothing short of an honor to be regarded in that light. But was Rand as honorable as his parents?

Once at the back stoop, Rand handed her the creel and gazed at her, a half smile on his lips. He tipped his hat back, bent forward and placed a kiss on her cheek. "Until tomorrow."

He strode away, whistling, and disappeared around the corner of the house, leaving her standing there, fish in hand and a longing in her heart for Sunday morning to arrive very soon.

Chapter Five

"Thank you, Marybeth." Mrs. Foster ran a damp rag over the oilcloth that covered the kitchen table. "You've helped me so much. Bringing home those delicious trout for last night's supper and cooking them, and now washing breakfast dishes."

"You're very welcome." Marybeth put the last dish away and draped the damp tea towel over the rack at the end of the kitchen cabinet. "I believe everyone should help out, no matter what the work is." Just because Rand might be at the church didn't mean she was in a hurry to get there. Truly, it didn't. Never mind how much she'd enjoyed his company yesterday. Nineteen hours and a restless night of sleep had restored her senses.

Last night she'd dreamed about Jimmy, dreamed Rand had found him and brought him to her right here at Mrs. Foster's. Only, when she'd dashed out the door to greet him, he looked more like Da than her jolly brother. Older, bent with care, tortured eyes, darker hair shot through with gray. Surely that couldn't have happened to Jimmy. He was only twenty-three.

So she shook off the nightmare, mainly because she

didn't put too much stock in dreams. Still, she couldn't help but wonder what changes she would find in her brother.

"We'd best hurry over to the church." Mrs. Foster shoved a clean dust rag into the satchel containing her music and bustled out of the kitchen toward the front door, with Marybeth close behind her. "I always like to dust the pews and windowsills and sweep a bit before people begin to arrive. Our pastor is a single young man, and without a wife to help him, he has to do everything himself. So until he finds a suitable bride, we older ladies try to keep the dear man well fed and his clothes mended."

From her landlady's maternal tone, Marybeth imagined a pudgy, sweet-faced little man whose sermons kept his flock comfortable in their pews. On the other hand, if he was the bossy type, perhaps he would urge her to marry Rand right away. As she and Mrs. Foster walked up Pike Street toward the church on Main Street, her anxiety grew. The last thing she needed was a pushy preacher telling her how to live her life.

Contrary to the impression Mrs. Foster had given her, Reverend Thomas was a tall, rather handsome and well-built young man with kind eyes devoid of any high-handedness. If she didn't know better and he weren't wearing a fine black suit, she would have assumed he was a cowboy.

"Welcome, Miss O'Brien." The minister shook her gloved hand and gave her a slight bow. "I understand you and Rand will be setting a date soon. I hope you'll permit me the honor of joining you two in marriage." His warm smile, Southern inflections and the jolly glint in his eyes caused her to like him right away, even as his words made her heart sink.

"Oh. Hmm." She glanced at Mrs. Foster, who was already dusting the pews. "I understand you're building an addition to the church, so we'll probably wait until it's finished so we can have our reception there." Now she sounded as gabby as her landlady.

"Ah, very good." Reverend Thomas retrieved a broom from the cloakroom and began to sweep dust and leaves across the floor toward the front door. "I've always advised couples to get to know each other fairly well before marriage."

Relief filled Marybeth as she reached for the broom. "Please let me do that."

He released it without argument. "Thank you. I do want to go over my sermon notes one more time before the service." Without another word he strode up the center aisle and disappeared through a side door.

Marybeth had just finished sweeping the last of the dust down the front steps of the church when Rand arrived on horseback. His gaze landed on her and he reached up to touch the brim of his hat. "Howdy, Marybeth." There was a sweet, shy note in his voice that sent her heart into a spin. In fact, she was feeling a bit shy herself, as though they hadn't seen each other just yesterday. Oh, bother. Where was her resolve not to become attached to him?

"Hello, Rand."

Gracious, he looked handsome and capable as he dismounted and secured his horse to a railing under a nearby tree. His black suit, white shirt and black string tie added to his attractive appearance. When he turned and gave her that crooked smile of his, it was all she could manage to scurry back into the church before she gave her heart away on the spot.

No, no, no. She would not fall in love with his good looks. Hadn't the minister just said a couple should get acquainted before marriage? She'd been here only two days. Despite knowing Rand's parents for a brief time in Boston, she simply had too much to learn about their son before letting herself fall in love. Most important was whether or not he would keep his word about helping her find Jimmy. No matter how long it took, he must do that before she would even consider loving him enough to change her lifelong determination not to marry.

Entering the building, he removed his hat and ran a hand through his hair to get rid of the hat line. She'd already come to love and expect the gesture. "Howdy, Mrs. Foster. I'm here to help. Don't tell me you ladies have all the work done."

"You can help Marybeth set out the hymnals." Mrs. Foster nodded toward the cloakroom.

"Yes, ma'am." He turned to Marybeth, his grin still in place. "You first."

She scooted past him and into the narrow room where churchgoers could hang their hats and coats. Rand settled his wide-brimmed black felt hat on one of the four-inch pegs. It was a fine new chapeau, probably kept just for Sunday and special events. His light woolen suit also appeared to be of the finest quality. How many men could afford such a wardrobe? Rand's wife would probably never want for anything, except maybe the freedom of a single life. Mam had been imprisoned by her marriage, by Da's moodiness and temper.

At the end of the small cloakroom sat a three-shelf

bookcase covered with an old sheet to protect the hymnals from dust. She removed and folded the material while Rand scooped up a handful of the books. As his arm brushed hers, a pleasant feeling shot up her neck. From his quick intake of breath she guessed he hadn't minded the contact, either.

"Sorry to bump you that way. It's a little tight in here." He gave her an apologetic smile before making his way out to the sanctuary.

"It's all right," she whispered to his back, not trusting herself to speak out loud. What were these feelings he caused? Why did she wish he'd kiss her on the cheek again, as he had yesterday afternoon? She'd never felt this way toward any man.

Rand took several deep breaths as he headed toward the front pew. It might be Sunday, and he might be in church, but he'd had an almost overwhelming urge to plant a kiss on Marybeth's ivory cheek right there in the cloakroom.

The moment he'd ridden up to the church and seen her busy at work with that broom on the front steps, his chest had swelled with pride and appreciation not only for her beauty, but for her willingness to help, whether the work was sweeping a church or cleaning a fish. It was a bit too soon to say he was in love, but he had a feeling it wouldn't be long before he handed his heart to the lovely Miss O'Brien on a silver platter. It took some doing to remind himself that he still needed to discern her character and find out whether she'd lied to Mother and Dad.

She cut short his concerns when she brought a stack

of hymnals to the front and set them down. "How many should we put in each pew?"

He surveyed the wooden benches he'd helped to build nine years ago, ten on the right and ten on the left, each of which held six or more adults or an assortment of children. "Three ought to do it. Folks don't mind sharing, and we need to be sure everyone can see one. Reverend Thomas has a habit of choosing at least one song nobody knows just so we can learn more of them."

Chuckling in her feminine way, she disbursed the books down one side while he took care of the other. "Are all of the pews filled on a Sunday morning?"

"Pretty much." A mild sense of pride in his community brought a grin to his lips. Before he'd gotten right with the Lord, how often had he slept through Reverend Thomas's excellent sermons? Some cowboys still nodded off from exhaustion, but at least none from drunkenness. Dad had forbidden alcohol in the town he was building, and everyone who'd settled here agreed. There were plenty of saloons in the nearby towns to attract men who wanted to waste their money after the sun went down on payday.

Marybeth seemed right at home in the church. After she finished with the hymnals, she went down front to stand by Mrs. Foster and hold one of the books open as the older lady practiced at the pump organ. Sometimes Rand wondered how old Mrs. Foster could manage to pump with her feet and play at the same time, but she seemed to do it with ease. He recalled the husbandly pride beaming from Captain Foster's face on Sunday mornings over his wife's skillful playing. Rand couldn't wait to hear Marybeth take to the keyboard. No matter how well she played, he'd praise her efforts.

At the end of the hymn Marybeth gently closed the book. "Would you like me to help you during the service?"

"Thank you, my dear, but I've promised Laurie she could do it. She treasures the responsibility."

Promise. Rand had forgotten all about telling Marybeth how he'd kept his promise. As soon as she joined him in the center aisle, he offered his most charming grin.

"By the by, I almost forgot to tell you that I wrote letters about your brother to the sheriffs of Del Norte and Wagon Wheel Gap. Took them over to the general store and slipped them through the mail slot. Mrs. Winsted will see that they get out tomorrow afternoon."

Marybeth gripped his forearm with surprising strength and gazed up at him with the prettiest smile he'd ever seen. "Oh, Rand, thank you so much." Her eyes glistened with unshed tears. The strength of her emotions nearly undid him. "This means the world to me. You just can't imagine how much."

No, he couldn't. His family had always surrounded him, even at his worst. What must it be like to be alone in the world and searching for a long-lost brother? He placed a hand over hers and gently squeezed. "If Jimmy O'Brien is anywhere in the San Luis Valley, we'll find him."

She nodded but pursed her lips and didn't say anything more. He could tell she was having trouble reining in her emotions, and he had a little difficulty holding on to his own. But having a sister had taught him how to deal with women's tears. Sort of. Right now he longed to pull Marybeth into his arms to comfort her, just as he would Rosamond if she was all weepy.

Unfortunately the Archers and several other families were entering the church and beginning to fill the pews. For the past three years Rand had done all he could to maintain a spotless reputation, and he sure didn't want to damage Marybeth's before folks even met her, so he just patted her shoulder.

"Where would you like to sit?" He was glad to see her bright smile return.

"Where does your family sit?"

"Just about any place. We don't have special pews. The preacher put an end to that when a cranky older member chased a poorly dressed young couple out of a pew he'd claimed as his own. They were new to the community, and we never saw them here again. Later the preacher said they'd joined a church down in Waverly. These days we all try to welcome anybody who comes through those doors, no matter how they're dressed or what they look like."

"Oh, my." Marybeth's eyes had widened as he told the story and now she nodded thoughtfully. "That's what the second chapter of James teaches, isn't it? We're not to be a respecter of persons."

Rand eyed her with a new appreciation. If she knew the scriptures that well, it sure did say something good about her character.

They slid into the third row on the left just as Tolley and Nate entered the church. Rand waved them over, pride surging through his chest at the idea of introducing Marybeth to his older brother.

Marybeth's pulse began to race at the prospect of meeting more of Rand's family. There was no mistaking the resemblance between Rand, Tolley and the tall man with him. She could find no fault in any of their similar features, yet somehow Rand's face appealed to her, whereas his brothers' did not. Maybe it was that crooked boyish grin.

"Marybeth, you've met Tolley. Here's our older brother—"

"And warden," Tolley quipped.

Rand shot a scolding look at him. "Our older brother, Nate," he finished.

"Hello, Tolley. How do you do, Nate?" Marybeth reached out to shake his hand. "I'm so happy to meet you. Did Susanna have to stay home with baby Lizzy?"

Her simple question seemed to please Nate. Behind his regretful smile, pride in his wife and baby girl glinted in his eyes as he shook her hand. "I'm mighty glad to meet you, too, Marybeth. And thanks for asking about my girls. Yes, they'll have to stay home for just a few more days. Lizzy's getting better, and Susanna's eager to meet you, so they'll be coming to town by Wednesday or Thursday, I'm sure."

The friendly warmth in his gaze made Marybeth regret her earlier doubts about meeting Susanna. What a dear, good family they all were. What would it be like to be accepted as a part of it? Would she even know how to act? Or how to feel accepted?

Mrs. Foster started to play quietly on the organ and people began to settle into their places. Rand moved down to the end of the pew, and she followed him, while the brothers filed in after her. Seated between Rand and Nate, Marybeth felt the power of their well-built physiques. Though a bit intimidated, she also had never felt so safe and protected.

Reverend Thomas welcomed everyone to the service and then announced the hymn. Rand held out the hymnal for her as they joined in a rousing "Onward, Christian Soldiers." Standing between the two brothers, Marybeth could hardly suppress a laugh. While Rand's pleasant baritone provided an admirable bass harmony just as it had yesterday, Nate's enthusiastic efforts weren't even in the same key. Or any key, for that matter. If she did decide to marry into this family, she was glad her husband would be the one who could carry a tune.

Marry? Husband? The words stopped her. She'd always vowed never to have a husband, and here she was thinking of marrying Rand. But how could she not look favorably on him when he'd kept his promise about writing those letters? When he'd stood here not ten minutes ago and promised to find Jimmy, if he was to be found anywhere in this great valley?

Lord, what am I going to do? Maybe the minister's sermon would have an answer for her. After all, when she'd prayed about accepting Colonel and Mrs. Northam's offer to pay her train fare to come west, hadn't the minister in their church preached that very Sunday about Abraham being called out of his homeland to a new land of his own? She'd taken that as a sign she was to begin her quest to find Jimmy. But it didn't mean she had to marry Rand. Did it?

As the hymn ended and the congregation took their seats, Rand sensed that same unease in Marybeth he'd noticed from the first. Although she seemed happy to be in church and certainly enjoyed the singing, if her smile was any indication, her mood had grown sober at some point during the hymn. He doubted it was Nate's poor excuse for singing that caused her sudden change, but he couldn't imagine what had brought on that furrowed brow.

Reverend Thomas announced a meeting of the deacons after the service, so that meant Rand would be staying. He was sitting on the church board while Dad was out of town. The preacher also mentioned the ladies' fund-raising quilting bee on Thursday. Rand hoped Marybeth would consider attending the bee so she could become friends with the other ladies at church. If she could see what a fine community Esperanza was and how genuine the people were, maybe she'd decide marriage to him wouldn't be so bad. He hoped and prayed that would happen, even as his concerns about her truthfulness whispered a word of caution to his mind.

After a few other announcements and another hymn, during which the offering was taken, the pastor moved to his place behind the pulpit just as the church door banged open. Although Rand's parents had taught him to keep his attention on the preacher no matter what happened at the back of the church, he couldn't help turning around to see who the noisy latecomer was.

Hardison!

Rand's first instinct was to reach for his gun. But this being Sunday morning, he'd left it in his saddlebag in deference to the preacher's wishes about no guns being brought into the church building. Everyone honored that wish, except maybe Maisie and her sisters, who probably carried derringers in their reticules. Right now Rand wished he'd stuck his sister's small firearm in his pocket. Then again, he never imagined Hardison would dare to complete his threats right here in God's house.

Tolley shot him a look and a nod, but Rand frowned

and shook his head. They wouldn't chase the man out, not after his speech to Marybeth about this church welcoming everyone to its services. He prayed he wouldn't have to eat those words.

Before he could figure out what to do, Hardison whipped off his hat and gave the preacher a nod. "Sorry," he whispered, sounding as though he meant it.

"Welcome, friend," the preacher said. "We're glad you're here."

Hardison walked around to the window end of a back pew and slid in next to Susanna's father and stepmother. He gave them a friendly smile, one so sincere that Rand almost believed it. Apparently, Edward MacAndrews did believe it because he shook hands with Hardison, while his wife, Angela, returned a maternal smile.

Rand's insides twisted at the deception. What was this man doing here? After threatening Rand and his family and Marybeth, why would he intrude on this holy time?

On the other hand, Reverend Thomas seemed pleased at the intrusion, perhaps even a little bit more invigorated than usual. He read the scripture passage from Psalm 119. "'Wherewithal shall a young man cleanse his way? By taking heed thereto according to Thy word.'"

Ordinarily, Rand would sit up and take notice. Since killing Hardison's cousin, he'd tried diligently not only to listen carefully to each sermon but also to cleanse his way of every possible sin. But it was no sin to protect those he loved, those he was responsible for, was it? He'd been assured by friends and family that it had been a righteous execution of a killer, yet he still couldn't reconcile himself to being the executioner.

The preacher went on. "'With my whole heart have I

sought Thee. O let me not wander from Thy command-
ments. Thy word have I hid in my heart that I might not
sin against Thee.'"

Only by force of his will could Rand take in the lesson from the sermon. Had he truly been seeking God
with his whole heart these past three years? When was
the last time he'd worked on memorizing passages that
spoke to him? Despite knowing it was wrong to judge
people according to their wealth or position or clothing,
he hadn't known that verse about not being a respecter
of persons was in the book of James. He would have to
look it up when he got home. This morning he'd been
so eager to get to town that he'd forgotten his Bible,
another lapse.

As Reverend Thomas always did, especially when a
stranger attended services, he ended his message with
the gospel. He explained how Jesus' death on the cross
paid for everyone's sins, no matter how bad a person
was. All a man had to do was to reach out and accept
the gift, just like a birthday present. He spoke of Christ's
resurrection as the promise to all believers that they
would one day be in Heaven with Him.

Usually, Rand loved to hear the simple gospel that
had turned his life around three years ago, especially the
way Reverend Thomas delivered it. The preacher didn't
pound the pulpit, nor did he holler or pour shame and
condemnation on his congregants, like some preachers
Rand had heard as a boy. Like Jesus, Reverend Thomas
led them like a flock.

If he weren't so concerned about Hardison, he would
let the message settle over him like a warm blanket to
chase away the chill of guilt that often plagued him. Instead he prayed for God's protection on everyone in the

congregation because he had no doubt the gunslinger would do something to disturb the peace in this holy room.

Sure enough, just as the preacher finished his invitation to anyone who wanted to accept Christ's free gift of salvation, Hardison stood and walked to the front, brushing invisible tears from his cheeks as he walked.

While others whispered "Praise the Lord" or "God bless him," Rand ground his teeth. Even Tolley seemed more puzzled than disbelieving. But Rand would believe the gunman had been converted when Mount Blanca crumbled into sand and spread across the Valley floor.

Marybeth blinked in wonder as a man strode up the aisle toward the preacher. Her Boston church didn't have altar calls, but Rosamond had told her about them. How wonderful that during her first visit to this place of worship a man became convicted of his need for Christ and was willing to make his new faith public.

The pastor invited him to kneel and then knelt beside him and put an arm around his shoulders while they prayed. As she watched them stand and the pastor introduce Dathan Hardison to the congregation, she realized he was the man who had stared at her so boldly on the train. At the time she'd felt very uncomfortable under his leering perusal and more than a little grateful for the companionship of Dr. and Mrs. Henshaw. Perhaps now that he'd become a Christian, this man would behave in a more seemly fashion toward ladies. At least his expression bore signs of repentance, for which she could only rejoice.

She glanced up at Rand to share this joyous moment, only to see a scowl on his face. A quick glance at Nate revealed less hostility, but still a decided lack of approval. Impatience and annoyance swept through her. A man had just come to the Lord. Why would they not be pleased? This was the first real flaw she'd seen in the entire Northam family's character. What other disappointments would they hand her in the coming days?

On the other hand, Nolan Means, seated across the aisle with his sister, Anna, wore a pleased, even interested, smile. That spoke well of the banker. Maybe he would befriend Mr. Hardison. She had an idea Rand and Nate weren't planning to.

After church, Rand excused himself from walking Marybeth back to Mrs. Foster's, telling her he had a deacons' meeting to attend. "I'll leave you in Mrs. Foster's capable hands." He gave her that cute smile of his, but the troubled look in his eyes conveyed another feeling altogether. "She'll get you safely home."

As if she couldn't get herself safely back to the house. But she wouldn't challenge him about that. "Is everything all right?" Maybe she could get him to explain his disapproval of Mr. Hardison.

He gently squeezed her forearm. "Nothing for you to worry about. Just church business." His attention now on Nate, he seemed in a hurry to get away from her for the first time since they'd met.

Fine. If he wouldn't share his concerns with her after she'd told him so many of hers, then so be it.

"Well, I'll bid you good day." She edged past the brothers and joined her landlady down front by the organ. "Your music was lovely, Mrs. Foster. It certainly put me in the mood for worship." And Rand just ruined it all.

As she shook hands with the minister on her way out

into the summer sunshine, she decided to let her negative feelings go, as Mam had always urged her to do. That had been Mam's way to survive her miseries, but Marybeth had never quite mastered it.

Mrs. Foster introduced her to several people, including Susanna's father and stepmother, Mr. and Mrs. MacAndrews, who welcomed her as if she were already part of their extended family. Maisie and Doc made sure she met the rest of the Eberly family: the parents, of course, and sisters Beryl, Georgia and Grace, who at twenty years old was half a head taller than her own father. Laurie gave Marybeth a wave and now was busy with the other girls her age, probably waiting for Tolley to emerge from the church.

All in all, Marybeth felt the warmth of Christian love around her. Several men surrounded Mr. Hardison and chatted with the new convert as if he were an old friend. When he glanced her way, he smiled and tipped his hat but made no move to approach her. That spoke well of him. No doubt he would wait for a proper introduction, as a gentleman should. She would forgive and forget his inappropriate stares on the train.

Mr. Means spoke to Marybeth briefly and reminded her of their appointment tomorrow morning. As if she could forget it. A job at the bank was exactly what she needed to support herself and to keep her from being forced to marry Mr. Randall Northam, with all of his changing moods.

After Marybeth and Mrs. Foster left, Rand stayed in the pew to talk with his brothers about Hardison before the deacons' meeting.

"Everybody believed his act," Tolley said in an urgent whisper. "We need to expose him for what he is."

"Hang on, brother." Nate blew out a long breath. "I'd be one of those who believed him if Rand hadn't told me his name and described the encounter you two had with him." He looked toward the door, where the last few church members lined up to shake hands with the preacher on their way out. "Besides, who's to say he wasn't convicted of his need for the Lord during the preacher's message? It was one of his best sermons, and that's saying something."

The familiar nudge of conviction for his own sins stopped Rand's protest before he could give voice to it. He wished he'd listened more intently to the preacher's words when he was younger.

"Another thing." Nate went on. "We don't want to alarm the townfolks or take a chance on turning them against a new Christian. That is, if he's sincerely converted."

"You weren't there when he threatened Rand." Tolley scowled at his oldest brother. "Tell him, Rand."

"No sense repeating what I told him Friday night." Rand saw Reverend Thomas and the other deacons returning to the sanctuary. "Nate, can you stick around until after the meeting? Maybe we can ask the preacher what he thinks."

"Sure." Nate set a hand on Tolley's shoulder. "Would you mind riding back to the ranch and making sure Susanna and Lizzy are all right? And say I'll be a little late for dinner?"

Tolley shrugged off his hand. "'Course not. Won't mind at all. No, sir. Not me. I'm old enough to be your errand boy but not old enough to sit in on a meeting with the men." He marched up the aisle, snatching his hat from the cloakroom and clapping it on his head as he exited the church.

Rand cast a rueful look at Nate. "We've got to let the boy grow up someday."

"Maybe." Nate shrugged. "When he cools that temper down a bit."

Rand nodded. Nate had fought his own battle with a strong temper and with God's help had won. Now he had a cool head and steady hand, which was reason enough for Dad to leave him in charge of the ranch. Rand was glad to leave the authority to him, something he couldn't have said three years ago when he'd chafed under his older brother's authoritarian ways.

Which was why Rand had been more than a little surprised when Dad had left him, not Nate, in charge of the family's church responsibilities. Especially considering that the deacon board was, in effect, the town council, until Dad returned and organized the setting up of an official city government. So far Esperanza and the surrounding community had grown peaceably on their own, with good people moving in every week, folks taking responsibility where they saw a need, and no one stirring up trouble. Until Hardison.

"All right, men." Reverend Thomas waved the seven deacons and Nate to their seats in the two front pews. "Let's make this short and sweet. Mrs. Foster's invited me to dinner, and I don't want the fried chicken to get cold."

While the other men laughed, a jealous itch crept into Rand's chest. He refused to let it bite him. The preacher would never intrude on another man's territory. Still, he wished he were the one having dinner with Marybeth and her landlady. To ease his own mind, he'd need to stop by the house on his way home to see whether Mrs. Foster had opened her home to Hardison. She or someone else usually fed newcomers…and strays.

After a prayer for the group to make wise decisions, Reverend Thomas beckoned Rand to the front. "What's on the docket today?"

Rand had overcome his nervousness at leading older men several months ago. They all had come to respect him, and of course they all respected the Northam name. Today, however, the specter of Dathan Hardison and his dead cousin hung over him as he dug notes out of his shirt pocket. Only willpower helped him get through the bits of business.

In the end, the men decided that enough children now attended the church to warrant the establishment of a formal Sunday school, so once the addition was built, they would have to line up some teachers with Bible knowledge. The ladies' fund-raiser was a priority for their support, so Rand urged the men to let their wives participate. Finally, citing the scripture about caring for aged widows, Rand encouraged the board to offer Mrs. Foster some payment for her faithful organ playing, her being a widow lady with no family nearby to take care of her and only piano lessons and her husband's pension from the war to live on. All measures were passed unanimously.

"Well, if there's nothing else, we can dismiss the preacher to his fried chicken." Rand made a final note on his scrap of paper about Mrs. Foster and stuck it back in his pocket.

"Actually, I do have something else." Nolan Means

stood in the second pew and leveled a benign look at Rand. "If I may?"

Rand gave him a short nod. "Sure. You want to come up here?" Dad had warned him that bankers often liked to take over the leadership of a town simply because they had money. Despite their own wealth, Dad insisted the Northams would not rule the town, just try to lead it with the Lord's help. Rand didn't know Means well at all, but he'd keep an eye on him.

"No, thanks. I can speak from here." The banker, around twenty-four years old and impeccably dressed in his black suit and white linen shirt, glanced around the group. "As you all may know, the new bank is my first to manage under my uncle's backing."

Rand found it interesting that the man seemed surprised by his own statement, much as he himself had been surprised by Dad's faith in him.

"Of course, I want to make it a success," Means went on. "Which keeps me on my knees." He chuckled and the other men joined in. "I know Esperanza is a fine town, but I'm concerned about outsiders, especially those riding through on their way to the silver fields. Not that I expect a robbery, but it's always a possibility."

When several men murmured their surprise, he hurried on. "I believe it's time our town hired a sheriff, someone full-time to watch out for our interests."

"Not a bad idea," Edgar Jones, the barber, said. "Mrs. Winsted next door to me tells me she's been missing small things from the general store. Mostly candy, so it's probably mischievous boys, but other items, too, that can slip easily into a pocket. The presence of a lawman in town would discourage such shenanigans."

Again the other men murmured their concerns.

"I think Mr. Hardison might be a possible candidate," Means continued. "I spoke to him after church, and he told me he has had a long history with the law."

Rand almost choked over Hardison's wily words. Until this moment he'd been willing to listen to Means, but this was going too far. He opened his mouth to tell these fine men exactly what Dathan Hardison was up to. Even cool, calm Nate frowned and moved forward on the pew as if he were about to stand in protest.

"Hold on." Reverend Thomas stood beside Rand. "Let's not load so much on a new convert. Let me disciple him for a while." The look in his eyes told Rand he had a deeper meaning behind his words.

Means started to voice his protest when old Charlie Williams stood next to him, his mountain-man hackles raised like a grizzly bear's.

"The Colonel said he'll hire a sheriff when he comes back. We'll wait for him on this." While the other men talked all at once, Charlie gave Rand a curt nod, as if to say, "Don't lose control, boy."

Suppressing a grin, Rand raised his hands over the hubbub. "All right, all right." When he had their attention, he said, "Charlie's right. We'll wait for the Colonel, but in the meantime, I'll write to him about our concerns. Will that be enough for you all?"

That promise seemed to settle everyone down. "All right. If there's nothing else, this meeting is adjourned."

Nolan Means didn't exactly look pleased, but his expression held no anger. If he really had concerns about a bank robbery, they most certainly would have to address the matter.

After the other men left the church, the preacher released a long sigh. "We dodged that bullet, didn't we?"

"What?" Rand and Nate chorused together.

The preacher chuckled. "Friends, I don't consider myself as wise as Solomon, but I do know a real conversion when I see one. Unfortunately, Hardison will have to go a long way to prove he's redeemed before I believe him." His eyes exuded a pastoral sadness that spoke well of his character.

Rand and Nate exchanged a look.

"Is it time to tell him the whole story?" Rand asked his brother.

"Be my guest," said Nate.

As Rand unfolded the tale of Hardison's threats to Reverend Thomas, the weight of fear he'd felt on his chest for the past three days seemed to lift a few notches. But he couldn't help thinking Hardison had a hidden agenda that included more than just revenge for his cousin's death. Why didn't he just confront Rand for a shoot-out? Why was he trying to inveigle his way into the close-knit community of Esperanza?

Chapter Six

"I'll answer the door." Marybeth removed her apron and laid it over the back of a kitchen chair.

"Thank you, dear." Fork in hand, Mrs. Foster turned a chicken leg in the frying pan and brushed a sleeve over her damp forehead. "This will be done in just a few minutes, so have the preacher take a seat in the parlor."

Anticipating a pleasant dinner with Reverend Thomas, Marybeth made a quick trip through the dining room to be sure the table was still properly set. Last evening she and Mrs. Foster had polished the silver and set it out with the gleaming rose-patterned china. Crystal goblets awaited tea now stored in the icebox—iced tea for a Southern gentleman—and white linen napkins lay beside the plates on the white damask tablecloth.

Pleased to see her landlady's cat had not gotten on the table and disturbed the settings, Marybeth hastened to the front door. Through the oval etched-glass window, she saw the preacher was not alone. Rand! Her heart skipped and her hand trembled as she opened the door.

"Good afternoon, gentlemen. Please come in." She

stood aside to let them in. *Oh, bother.* Her voice was shaking, but due to which of these men? Until this moment she'd been too busy helping Mrs. Foster to be nervous. Of course she'd felt a little concerned about the preacher because he might ask too many questions about her wedding plans…or lack thereof. But Rand's appearance also made her a bit nervous. Why had he come?

Both gentlemen greeted her as they removed their hats and stepped over the threshold. The preacher hung his hat on the walnut hall tree beside the door, but Rand stood just inside.

"I can't stay," he said in answer to her questioning look. "I just wanted to be sure you and Mrs. Foster got home all right." She could see the relief in his eyes, but for what?

"Of course we did." She glanced at the preacher. "It's just a short walk. What could happen in three blocks in this lovely, peaceful town?"

The men traded a look, which both irritated her and made her feel good. She dismissed the irritation born of her desire, her *need* for independence. Rand's obvious relief over her safety touched her. Once again, she could see he wanted to take care of her, an admirable quality she could not disregard. Even as she thought it, she also remembered all those cozy feelings could be a trap from which she would never escape.

"Probably not much would happen on a Sunday." Rand turned his hat in his hand. "I guess I just wanted to see you again. I won't be able to visit you until late tomorrow morning. Ranch chores, you know." He gazed down at her with those gentle green eyes, and her pulse stuttered.

"Oh." She glanced at Reverend Thomas, whose benign expression showed interest without being intrusive. It also convicted her. Should she tell Rand about her appointment at the bank? Her mouth took over before her mind decided. "I may not be here."

He blinked. And frowned. "Where will you be?" The crossness in his voice reminded her that his moods changed quickly. Too quickly, and for no apparent reason.

"Why, I... I—" She shouldn't lie. *Must* not lie. "I have an appointment with Mr. Means at the bank. A job interview." She ended breathlessly so he wouldn't bark out another question.

But now his expression changed from cross to worried. He traded another look with the preacher before gazing at her again. "What time is your appointment?"

"Nine o'clock."

"Maybe I'll ride into town about then and walk you over to the bank."

"I could walk her over for you, Rand," Reverend Thomas said. "That way you could complete your chores without worry."

Marybeth felt the urge to stamp her feet like one of her spoiled classmates often did back at the academy. Growing up, she'd never had the luxury of expressing her feelings so strongly. "What's the matter with you two? I can walk to the bank by myself."

Maddeningly, they traded another one of those paternalistic looks. Finally the preacher said, "She'll be fine. I'll make sure."

"All right. If you insist." Rand placed his hat on his head. "I'll come by the bank and walk you home." He turned toward the door and then back to her. "I should say 'may I come by to walk you home?'"

The annoyance in his tone and expression struck Marybeth's funny bone, and she couldn't stifle a laugh. "You won't know what time."

He raised his fists to his waist. "Then I'll just sit outside the bank until you come out."

The preacher laughed. "I think he has you there, Marybeth. Why not let him escort you home?"

She cast him a saucy grin she hoped didn't seem irreverent. "Oh, very well. I suppose I'll be finished with the interview by ten o'clock. Or ten minutes after nine, if it doesn't go well." *Lord, please let it go well.*

"Good. I'll be waiting outside the bank at ten minutes after nine." Rand frowned. "I don't mean to say I hope it doesn't go well. Actually, I do hope it doesn't—"

"Quit while you're ahead, Rand." The preacher chuckled.

"Good idea." Rand gazed at Marybeth for another long moment. Then he spun on his heel and marched out the door and down the steps.

Good manners demanded that she turn her attention to Reverend Thomas, but she would much rather watch Rand ride away. Gracious, he was a good-looking man. A determined, capable man. She had no doubt whatsoever that he could accomplish anything he set his mind to.

Which stirred up no little concern inside her. While those were good qualities when it came to his finding Jimmy, she wasn't so sure she wanted them turned her way if he decided he was going to marry her.

"I could not be more pleased with your skill, Miss O'Brien." Mr. Means stood beside Marybeth's chair and bent over her shoulder watching her progress as she copied a handwritten letter using the Remington Sholes and Glidden typewriting machine. "I cannot see a single error in your transcription."

"Thank you, sir." She smothered a wide smile that might reveal how violently her heart had skipped at his compliment. She felt not the slightest attraction to the man, but his easy manner suggested he would be a pleasant employer for whom to work. "Would you like to try dictation?" Her fingers itched for the challenge.

"Hmm." He stared off as though considering the matter. "No, better not. You see on this page—" he held up the handwritten letter she'd just copied "—how many times I scratched out my words when better ones came to mind. No need to waste paper." He reached out as though to pat her shoulder but then seemed to think better of it. "I will be delighted to sign and send this letter to my uncle in New York. He went to a great deal of trouble to acquire and send this machine for the bank, so it will give him great satisfaction to finally receive a letter written on it."

"Very good, sir." Marybeth rolled the bar to release the sheet and handed the letter to him.

"Will you be able to start work right away?" He studied the typed page with interest as he spoke.

"Today?" She could hear the giddy squeak in her voice, but he had the good manners not to laugh.

"If you can. I have several letters I would like to send out with today's three o'clock post."

Once again her heart skipped. Rand's letters asking the two sheriffs about Jimmy would go out this afternoon, too. How long would it take them to reach their destinations and answers be returned? If she didn't keep busy, she'd find herself fretting over the situation.

"I'd be happy to start today." She ran her hand over the corner of the polished oak desk where she would be assuming her duties. Nearby stood a dark walnut hat rack that held her hat, gloves and reticule. It also could serve as an umbrella stand, but Mrs. Foster told her the San Luis Valley had very little rainfall. Coming from Boston, Marybeth found that quite remarkable.

"Good. I'll write those letters and bring them to you. In the meantime, would you go over to the café and fetch me a pot of coffee?"

He was still looking down at the letter, so could not have seen her shock. She quickly schooled her face back to a pleasant, professional smile.

So it was true, what she'd learned in her secretarial training. Ladies who worked as secretaries must also serve coffee and tea and whatever other refreshments their bosses required. Never mind their advanced training, they were still just maids with extra skills.

"Of course, Mr. Means. Would you care for cream and sugar?"

He glanced up at her, not seeming really to see her. "Yes, please. And perhaps one of Miss Pam's pastries. She knows the ones I like."

"Very good, sir." Marybeth put on her hat and gloves before proceeding out the front door of the stone bank. She carried her reticule, although it held no money. Surely, Mr. Means didn't expect her to pay for the coffee and pastries. She would tell Miss Pam to put the cost on the banker's account.

"It's about time." Rand leaned against the bank's hitching post, arms crossed and hat low over his eyes. "It's almost eleven o'clock. What were you doing in there?"

"Rand." She gasped softly. She'd forgotten all about his offer to walk her home. But his cross tone of voice cut short her regret. "Well, if you must know, Mr. Northam, I've just been hired to work at the bank. I start today."

"Is that so?" He pushed his hat back to reveal those appealing green eyes filled with disappointment and a dash of annoyance. Marybeth steadied her swaying emotions. She would not let him change her course.

"Yes, it is." She tugged at her gloves and stepped off of the boardwalk into the dusty street. Which only served to remind her of how tall and well formed he was. She huffed out a cross breath over her own ambivalence. "Now, if you'll excuse me, I have an errand to run."

He gave her a mischievous grin. "Ah, I see. You're the new errand boy. What happened to the typewriting job?"

She could feel her temper rising, but she wouldn't give him the satisfaction of seeing it. "Why, you're entirely mistaken. Mr. Means is delighted with my typewriting skills. While he writes some letters for me to transcribe, I'm fetching us a pot of coffee and some pastries."

As she walked away from him, guilt smote her. Mr. Means hadn't said anything about coffee for *her*. She'd often told half-truths to Da to keep from getting hit, yet Rand hadn't done anything to deserve such treatment. Nor did she think the Lord approved of such deceptions. Before she could turn around and tell Rand the truth, he fell into step beside her.

"I might just have one of those pastries myself." To her chagrin, he offered her his arm. "Nobody makes them like Miss Pam, but don't tell Mrs. Foster I said that."

She couldn't very well let him walk along beside her with one arm bent and sticking out, so she set her hand on it. Mercy, he had powerful muscles. "You know, Mr. Northam, I've looked up and down this street and I can't see any reason why I need your protection as I walk around town."

"Maybe not." He gave her that devastating smile. "But I just want to make certain everybody knows you're taken."

She stopped in the middle of the street and glared up at him. "I most certainly am not *taken*." Staring up that way, she felt her hat slipping off the back of her head and reached up to catch it, bringing a low chuckle from Rand. "Now, if you'll excuse me, I need to complete my errand and get back to work." She started to march off in a huff when he gently gripped her upper arm and turned her back.

"Do you mind?" She wanted to struggle against his hold, but that would make a scene to shame them both.

"Now that you mention it, I do mind." He tipped his hat back again. "Marybeth, you don't need to do this. You don't need to work at a job while we're searching for your brother."

The pain in his eyes cut into her, yet not so deeply as to change her mind. "But I want to, Rand. I want to earn my own livelihood, not be supported by you. How would that look if we end up not getting married?"

He winced visibly, stared off and then slowly returned a sad gaze to her. "All right. But I'm going to walk you home every day. And the preacher is going to be watching out for you when you walk to work in the morning."

Something in his voice held a warning she could not easily dismiss. "Why? What are you not telling me?"

Again he stared off, but this time he seemed to study the numerous people going about their business on the street. "I don't want to worry you, but you have a right to know. There are always unsavory elements passing through Esperanza on their way to the silver mines. Not all prospectors are dangerous, but some like to prey on the unsuspecting. Some transients get their prospecting stake by robbing good people as they travel west. They cause havoc and then disappear before anyone can call them to account for it or even know who they are."

"Oh." Marybeth knew well which parts of Boston held that same danger. She'd lived in a poor, rough neighborhood but had known of rougher areas closer to the waterfront. "Very well. I accept your offer to escort me home each day." She started to turn away but instead set a hand on his arm. "Thank you, Rand."

Relief blossomed across his tanned face and that charming smile appeared again like sunshine. "Now, let's get Mr. Means his coffee before he fires you."

His teasing tone lightened her mood considerably. "Humph. You didn't see how pleased he was with my typewriting. Why, I'm going to be indispensable to him. You just wait and see, Mr. Rand Northam."

His chuckle held a hint of ruefulness. "I don't doubt that for one second, Miss O'Brien, and that's what worries me."

Rand might have continued to argue with Marybeth about her job if he hadn't noticed the pride and self-respect just being hired had already given her. He didn't understand why any lady would want to earn her own living when she could get married and have a husband to provide for her. Yet something in Marybeth's past must have left a hole in her heart that needed to be filled up. She'd made it clear he wouldn't be able to do that, which stung a little. A lot, actually.

Still, if she needed this job to bolster her spirits, he couldn't object. Maybe she was like Tolley, who still felt the need to prove himself. In fact, Rand knew that feeling himself, and all too well. Further, Marybeth was right that folks wouldn't think too highly of either of them if he supported her and they ended up not getting married. She didn't need to know he was paying her rent. Mrs. Foster had promised not to give away their little secret. The old dear might talk about many of the happenings in town, but she also could keep a secret if asked to.

So he'd learned a few things about Marybeth today that might help him if their relationship continued to move forward. She had something in her past still affecting her, and because of that, she needed to prove herself. Also, she wasn't hard to persuade about a matter if he gave her good enough reasons. He hadn't lied about dangerous transients passing through, but saw no reason to warn her specifically about Hardison.

Best of all, she looked awful cute when she got riled. He'd have to play that to his advantage. In the most innocent way, of course.

Her workday ended at four o'clock and Rand made sure he was waiting outside the bank door, leaning against the hitching rail as he had that morning. He hadn't seen Hardison during either trip to town, and the preacher said he hadn't, either. For a man who'd been so broken up about his own sin the day before, the gunslinger didn't seem to be in any hurry to learn about how to live the Christian life.

When Marybeth emerged from the bank, Rand straightened, swept off his hat and gave her a deep bow. "My, my, Miss O'Brien, you sure must have an easy job 'cause you look fresh as a daisy, just like you did this morning." Earlier he'd forgotten to compliment her, which Nate had told him was an important part of courting.

"Humph." She stuck her pretty little nose in the air. "Don't think you can sugarcoat your obvious disdain for my job, Mr. Northam. I'll have you know I've been busy all day—"

"Fetching coffee all day? Are your feet tired? I can hire a rig to drive you home."

"Oh, you." She smacked his arm and strode off down the boardwalk.

With a laugh he caught up and fell into step with her, having to shorten his long stride considerably to do so. "How was your day, Marybeth?"

She shot him a sweet smile. "Very exhilarating, thank you very much. I love typewriting almost as much as I love playing the piano."

"Mmm. Glad to hear it." Glad to see the sparkle in her eyes even though he hadn't put it there.

"Why, thank you." She rewarded him with another of those smiles.

Oh, mercy, how he wanted to plant a kiss on her pretty ivory cheek. When he'd done it before, she hadn't objected. Maybe he would when they reached Mrs. Foster's front porch. Or maybe he'd at least ask her permission. Yes, that was the idea. Make sure she didn't mind before he started acting like he could kiss her anytime he wanted to. In the meantime he wanted to stay on her good side, and he knew just how to do it.

"I checked with Mrs. Winsted over at the general store," he said. "She made sure my letters got on the train headed over to Del Norte. Sheriff Hobart will have his in the morning. The other letter will take another day or so to get to Wagon Wheel Gap by stagecoach, depending on roads and bridges." He inhaled deeply after that long speech and enjoyed the delight on Marybeth's face.

"Oh, Rand, thank you again. I won't be able to sleep tonight wondering what the sheriffs will have to say. This is so exciting." She executed a happy little skip and then put a dainty gloved hand to her lips and resumed her more sedate pace. "Goodness. What will people think if they see me hopping down the street?"

Rand chuckled. "I would hope they'd think you were happy to be with me." *As happy as I am to be with you.*

She looped her arm in his as they turned down Pike Street. "I am, Rand. Just be patient with me, will you?"

From the bright look in her eyes, he believed her, and he'd do all he could to be patient, to give her all the time she needed to decide she liked him enough to consider marrying him.

They reached Mrs. Foster's front porch where he walked her up to the door. When she paused before going inside, Rand removed his hat and cleared his throat.

"Marybeth, I don't want to presume anything, so I'm asking your permission to…well, I'd really like to give you a peck on the cheek."

"Why, Mr. Northam, I don't recall you asking permission the last two times you kissed me. Why so shy all of a sudden?" Merriment danced in her eyes. Was her happiness due to being with him or his writing letters about her brother or her good day at work?

"Well…" He drawled the word out slowly. "Nate got after me for kissing you without asking, so I thought I should ask this time."

Suddenly serious, she blinked, and her eyes reddened just a little. "That's very sweet of both of you. It makes me feel…very special."

"You are." Now he knew one more thing about her: she didn't know what a fine lady she was. Maybe over time he could remedy that. "Well?"

She laughed. "Oh, all right. Just a quick kiss."

He did make it a quick one. Then he let out a whoop, jumped down the front steps and barely felt his feet touch the ground all the way back to the livery stable to pick up his horse.

"Do not be nervous, Miss O'Brien." Mr. Means stood off to the side as Marybeth took her place in the teller's cage. "You have watched Mr. Brandt for two days now, so you know what to do."

She gave him a shaky nod just as the bank's front door opened, jangling the bell that hung above it. She turned a smile toward the customer but had to force herself to keep it in place. The leering man from the train. She hastened to remind herself he was also the one who'd prayed with Reverend Thomas in front of the whole church last Sunday.

Removing his hat, he approached the cage wearing a smile of his own. "Good afternoon, ma'am." He glanced around the area and seemed to notice Mr. Means in the background. "Good afternoon, sir." Now he settled a pleasant gaze on Marybeth, one devoid of any impropriety. Without the leer, he wasn't bad-looking, though in no way could he compare to Rand.

Rand, who would be coming soon to escort her home from work. She'd enjoyed their walks back to Mrs. Foster's these past few days. It always made her days even more pleasant. First, though, she had work to do.

"Good afternoon, sir." She swallowed hard. Her first time to help a bank customer! "How may I help you?"

"I'd like to open an account, if I may." He reached into his nicely pressed black frock coat and pulled out a leather wallet that looked new.

"Of course, sir." Marybeth reached into a drawer for a ledger, a small booklet in which she would record the deposit. She turned to the front page and dipped her pen into the inkwell. "What name, please?"

"Dathan Hardison." He bent forward to watch her write, but the bars of the cage kept him from coming too close. Still, she caught the pleasant scent of his shaving cologne. He spelled out his name as she carefully printed it on the page.

When the ink dried, she turned to the first lined page. "And how much will today's deposit be?"

He pulled some large bills from the wallet, along with a handful of five-dollar gold coins from his trousers' pocket, and shoved it all through the small opening below the bars. "Three hundred and eighty-five dollars."

Marybeth did her best not to gasp. That was a small fortune. Maybe there was more to Mr. Hardison than she'd thought. Maybe he'd come to Esperanza to open a business. "Very good, sir," she said in a monotone voice that mimicked Mr. Brandt's.

She counted the money, put it in the drawer and recorded the amount in his ledger, adding her initials beside the figures. Before handing the booklet to him, she also wrote the amount in her teller's ledger. "This booklet will serve as your receipt, Mr. Hardison. Whenever you wish to make a deposit or withdrawal, be sure you bring it with you."

"Yes, ma'am." He gave her a friendly smile that included Mr. Means. "Begging your pardon, ma'am, but would it be too forward of me to ask your name?"

To her relief, Mr. Means stepped forward. "Good afternoon, Mr. Hardison. Permit me to introduce you to my new assistant, Miss O'Brien. Miss O'Brien, this is the gentleman who joined the church on Sunday."

"Oh, yes, of course." Marybeth thought her response sounded better than saying right out that she recognized him. "How do you do, Mr. Hardison?"

"Miss O'Brien." He gave her a gentlemanly bow before turning his attention to Mr. Means. "If I may, I'd like to make an appointment with you regarding some business matters."

"I happen to be free right now." Mr. Means stepped over to the locked door leading out of the teller's cage. "Miss O'Brien, you may close up here now." He gave her a meaningful look and she returned a nod. "I shall see you tomorrow morning."

"Yes, sir."

While her boss exited the tiny chamber and relocked it from the other side, she gathered the deposits of the day, counted them and made sure they matched the numbers in the ledger. After initialing the entries, she carried everything to the unlocked safe in the darkened back corner of the room. Mr. Means hadn't given her the combination to the safe, which was fine with her. He'd left it open, however, so she put everything inside, closed the heavy door and spun the dial to secure the money.

Satisfied that she'd done everything properly, she took the key hanging at her waist and unlocked the teller's cage, exited and relocked the door. Finally she untied the leather strap from her belt and dropped the key in the lockbox outside Mr. Means's office. After a last look around the wide bank lobby, she went to her desk to retrieve her hat and gloves.

How proud she felt of her first four days of work. In addition to typewriting the letters Mr. Means had written, she'd learned the duties of a teller so she could take Mr. Brandt's place when he went to dinner or perhaps became ill. Marybeth had learned his wife was expecting a happy event, so he would need some time off for that. She would be more than pleased to fill in for him any time Mr. Means asked her.

Wouldn't Da be amazed that a daughter of his could handle money so impartially, never once thinking of stealing it for her own use? Marybeth lifted a silent prayer that Jimmy had taken after Mam, not Da, in regard to money. As for Marybeth, she had decided the best way to avoid temptation was to regard the bills as pieces of paper and the coins as bits of metal. The only money she wanted was what she earned and what Mam had left to her. If Jimmy still had that locket, the two of them would be set for life and never have to depend on anyone else.

Outside in the afternoon sunshine, Rand waited in

his usual spot. When he straightened and gave her that wonderful smile, she felt a twinge of guilt over her recent thoughts, and even more so when he stepped over and bowed, one hand behind his back.

"Marybeth, I don't know how you do it. A long day at work, and you still look as fresh and pretty as one of my mother's roses." To emphasize his words, he pulled a bouquet of red and white roses from behind his back. "For you."

"Oh, Rand, what a lovely surprise." She took the flowers and breathed deeply of their sweet, heady scent. "Thank you."

She took his offered arm and they ambled down the boardwalk under a sunny sky. Happiness bubbled up inside her such as she'd never known. Yet she couldn't decide whether it was being with Rand or having a successful day at work.

"That's not my only surprise for you today." He gave her a smug grin that threatened to undo her giddy heart.

"Indeed? Well, then, surprise me again."

"First of all, Susanna's waiting at Mrs. Foster's to meet you."

"How nice." Marybeth's pulse quickened. Would his sister-in-law like her? Would they become friends? "Is the baby well? Did she come, too?"

The questions appeared to please Rand, because his grin broadened. "She did. Say, do you like children?"

"Yes, I do. Very much." Of course she would have to marry to have children of her own. Maybe she'd have to settle for enjoying other people's children. "I'm looking forward to meeting Lizzy."

"She's a sweetheart."

As they turned down Pike Street, Marybeth started

to ask Rand what her next surprise was. Before she could speak, a rider came along beside them.

"Good afternoon, folks."

Marybeth shaded her eyes and looked up into Mr. Hardison's smiling face. At least it seemed like a smile. With the sun behind him, it was a little difficult to tell. When she started to greet him, Rand stopped beside her, his posture suddenly stiff and his shoulders hunched up.

She shuddered. There he went again with those changing moods of his. When Da's shoulders used to hunch up like that, there was sure to be a brawl. What was it about Mr. Hardison that set Rand off this way? If they fought, she would walk away and refuse to speak to either of them ever again.

Chapter Seven

Rand ground his teeth and moved between Marybeth and Hardison. What a cheap trick to pull, coming up on them on horseback to give himself an advantage. If he wanted to kill Rand, why not just bushwhack him and then run off to Texas or someplace? He swallowed hard, knowing he had to answer the man.

"Afternoon, Hardison." His hand under Marybeth's elbow, Rand resumed his walk and continued to guide her down the street.

"Mind if I tag along with you folks?" He reined his horse a little closer to Rand's right side, making it impossible for him to draw his gun if he needed to protect Marybeth.

"If you hadn't noticed, we're busy having a private conversation, so, yes, I do mind." Rand kept his eyes straight ahead.

"Ah. Then I won't interrupt you." He gave a throaty chuckle that seemed to hold a hint of a threat. "I'll leave you to it. Good day, Miss O'Brien."

The jangle of reins and clip-clop of hooves gave evidence that he'd turned back, but the oily, familiar way he addressed Marybeth sent an icy shiver down Rand's back.

"Where did you meet that—" Rand glanced down to see her disapproving frown. He met it with one of his own. Instead of saying "polecat," as he felt inclined to, he finished his question with, "man?"

"He came into the bank today. Mr. Means introduced us." Her defensive tone did nothing to calm Rand. Had he merely been a customer or was Hardison seeking her out? Worse, was she somehow attracted to the well-dressed gunslinger? He didn't ask her any of those questions because he didn't want her upset when she met Susanna.

"Well, I suppose if you had a proper introduction, it's all right." Far from it, but Rand wouldn't tell her. He'd stick with the plan he, Nate and the preacher had come up with and just watch the man. Only trouble was that Hardison wasn't doing what they expected, which was calling Rand out at some inconvenient moment when a lot of people he cared about could get hurt. The gunslinger was weaseling himself into the good graces of those people. Even Miss Pam had remarked out of the blue that the "new Christian" ate at her café three times a day. Rand knew she was glad for the business, and he supposed even polecats needed to eat. He also had no idea of how to figure out what Hardison's next move would be.

They were about to arrive at Mrs. Foster's house, so he decided to warm the coolness between him and Marybeth. Only one thing was sure to work. "I hope Lizzy's not down for a nap so you can see her at her best. When she first gets up, she can be a little cranky."

His ploy worked because Marybeth looked up at him and her eyes brightened. "I wish we'd stopped by the general store and bought some candy. That's a sure cure for crankiness."

He gave her a smug, teasing grin. "All taken care of." He retrieved a small brown paper sack from his trouser pocket and handed it to her. "You can give her one of these lemon sticks, and she'll be your best friend."

"Aren't you clever?" Marybeth peeked inside the bag and then tucked it into her reticule. Her smile of appreciation eased Rand's concerns considerably.

He still couldn't imagine why she seemed friendly to Hardison. The man was years older, probably in his midthirties. While he was well-dressed and could put on proper manners, he didn't seem to have anything to recommend him to a young girl. Or maybe Rand was misreading her reactions. Other than his mother and sister and the Eberly girls, he didn't have much experience with women, and he didn't understand a single one of them.

How would Marybeth react if he just plain out told her Hardison was out for revenge and they all needed to be careful around the man? Of course he wouldn't without first talking to Nate and Reverend Thomas. But he sure would like to gain her trust. Maybe the letter in his pocket would help him do that. He hadn't opened Sheriff Hobart's reply yet because it was his third surprise for her. He thought she'd be pleased if they opened it together. A prickle of excitement spiked inside his chest. Yes, reading the letter together would be just the thing to gain Marybeth's trust and maybe make her real happy in the bargain.

"Here we are." Rand kept his hand cupped under Marybeth's elbow as they climbed the steps and approached the front door.

She could hear ladies' voices coming through the open front window, and her nervousness returned. Not that it had completely disappeared or been helped by the encounter with Mr. Hardison. She couldn't understand why Rand disliked the man.

Now, as he smiled down at her, his hand still under her elbow, an odd and slightly thrilling thought popped into her mind. Was Rand jealous? Was he concerned that because she'd put off their marriage, she might find some other man to care about, to marry? Indeed, that must be it. Her heart gave a little twist at the thought. As kind as he'd been to her, he deserved to know she would do no such thing. Maybe if she revealed her nervousness over meeting his sister-in-law, he would forget all about their encounter with Mr. Hardison.

"Stay close to me." She leaned toward him and spoke in a whisper. "I do so want Susanna to like me."

"How could she not like you?" The way his face brightened and the gentle squeeze on her arm assured her she'd said just what he needed to hear. But unlike the manipulations she'd used on Da to avoid his tempers and beatings, this was a good thing. Now a pleasant warmth flooded her chest, and somehow she liked Rand all the more for it.

He opened the door and nudged her over the threshold and into the parlor. "Good afternoon, ladies."

Mrs. Foster and her guest set down their teacups and rose to greet them.

"Wan!" A darling little blonde girl in a pink calico dress toddled toward Rand, her hands reaching out. "Up, up."

"Hello, little dumpling." Rand lifted her to the ceiling and the child rewarded him with squeals and giggles.

Then he lowered her and nuzzled her neck, bringing more squeals.

Marybeth thought her heart would melt on the spot. This big, strapping cowboy playing with a baby and obviously adoring her. She'd never seen a man so taken with a child.

Rand settled the baby on his left hip and beckoned Marybeth forward. "Good afternoon, Mrs. Foster. Susanna, this is Marybeth, my..." His pause caused the room to go silent...and yet another thread of guilt to wind through Marybeth. He'd almost introduced her as his bride-to-be, yet he had the good manners to respect her wishes in that regard.

"You don't have to tell me who this is." Susanna rushed over and grasped Marybeth's hands. "This is Marybeth O'Brien. I would know you anywhere from Rosamond's description. She's written all about you." Shorter by several inches, she stood on tiptoes and kissed Marybeth's cheek. With blond hair a little darker than her daughter's, Susanna was a true beauty, even more so because she was expecting and had that maternal glow many women took on when a baby was on the way. Her soft Southern accent only added to her charm. "Welcome to Esperanza. We all hope and pray you'll love it here."

The warmth of her greeting soothed away Marybeth's concerns and brought tears to her eyes. "Thank you. How could I not love this town? Everyone's been so kind."

Susanna tugged Marybeth over to the settee. "You sit down. I'll make a fresh pot of tea."

"No such thing." Mrs. Foster picked up the silver tea

tray. "You two girls sit down and get acquainted, and I'll fetch more tea." She looked at Rand. "Coffee for you?"

"Tea's fine. Thank you, ma'am." He sat in the chair nearest Marybeth, the baby still content in his arms. "If you haven't figured it out yet, this is Lizzy."

"How do you do, Lizzy?" Marybeth reached out her hand.

Lizzy turned away and burrowed her face in Rand's shoulder. He gave Marybeth a significant look, glancing down at her reticule, where she'd hidden the candy. She leaned over toward Susanna and asked in a whisper, "May I give her a lemon stick?"

Susanna's enthusiastic nod caused her blond ringlets to bounce, adding to her charm.

Marybeth caught Lizzy's eye. Then, with lavish gestures, she opened her reticule and pulled out a lemon stick. She made as if to put it in her mouth just as Lizzy's hand shot out.

"Me."

"Oh, do you want this?"

She nodded solemnly.

"Mama, may she have it?"

"Why, yes, she may."

"Here you are, Lizzy." With great ceremony, Marybeth presented the candy.

Lizzy's eyes sparkled as she grasped it and stuck it in her mouth.

While Susanna instructed her baby in how to say "thank you," Marybeth glanced up at Rand. The sweet, intense look in his eyes almost took her breath away. Approval? No, more than that. But surely not love, either, after knowing her less than a week. Yet she basked in the glow of that look through her entire visit with Susanna and late into the evening.

Only after she went to bed did she remember he'd hinted that he had more surprises. Apparently he'd forgotten all about it, too. Or maybe it was the candy. Surely it was too soon to have letters back from the sheriffs about Jimmy. Either way, she'd enjoyed being with Rand and meeting Susanna and Lizzy. It wouldn't be too hard to feel at home with this family. Except that she desperately longed to find her brother, the only family she had left in the world. Until she learned the truth about Jimmy's whereabouts, even if he'd gone to Mexico or California or who knew where, she would never have peace.

Rand had driven Susanna halfway home in the buggy before he remembered the letter. She needed to get home to put Lizzy down for her nap and start supper, so he couldn't very well turn around and go back to town. Maybe it was best this way. If Sheriff Hobart had bad news, he could find a way to tell Marybeth without her going into shock.

After supper and evening chores, he went to his room to read the letter. Sure enough, it was a disappointment. The sheriff hadn't seen any short, wiry, red-haired Irishmen in the area over the past seven or eight years. The lawman was well-known for his memory of faces, names and happenings, so Rand took his word without hesitation. Somehow he'd have to tell Marybeth, and the sooner the better.

Cautioned by the way things had turned out on Thursday, Rand opened his mail right away on Friday. The letter from the sheriff of Wagon Wheel Gap said he couldn't recall anyone of Jimmy's description. Irishmen, yes, but none with such bright hair, short stature and no brogue. He added that he'd been there less than a year and so would ask the old-timers if they knew anything about a Jimmy O'Brien.

Rand's heart ached for the disappointment Marybeth would experience when he gave her the news. But it wouldn't be fair to her if he put it off.

At four o'clock he met her at the bank and invited her to an early supper at Williams's Café. "I went by Mrs. Foster's and told her I planned to ask you out. She said it was all right with her as long as I brought you home before dark." He gave her a smile he didn't really feel, but it seemed to work.

"Thank you, Rand. I understand Miss Pam fixes roast beef on Friday nights, so this will be a fitting end to a wonderful week."

They walked the block and a half to Williams's Café, speaking to several people as they traveled. Marybeth had met some of them at church and some at the bank, so introductions were few. In a way, Rand felt a little jealous that he hadn't been the one to introduce her, but in another way, he was proud that everyone seemed to like her…and especially that she seemed to like everyone. Maybe that was why she had been pleasant to Hardison. She'd never made an enemy.

Seated across the table from him in the café, she looked as pretty as a picture. Before he could give her the bad news about the letters, she spoke.

"Rand, I've noticed this town doesn't have a saloon. In all of the stories we've heard back East about the Wild West, it seems there's always a saloon where the troubles begin." Her innocent, trusting gaze bored just a bit deeper into his heart.

"That's because my dad and the other founders of the community voted to keep spirits out." He tried not to sound too proud, as though he'd been responsible for the decision. After all, he'd ridden over to the saloon in Del Norte plenty of times to play poker, and look where it had gotten him. He'd killed a cardsharp whose cousin now wanted revenge. "We want people to feel safe and be safe here in Esperanza." And if they weren't safe, it was his fault.

"No liquor." The wonder in Marybeth's voice and eyes was something to behold and resembled her expression just after she'd been rescued from the rattlesnake, as though she couldn't quite believe it. "That's remarkable."

"I suppose." Rand shrugged. "If more towns adopted that law, there'd be a lot less wildness to the Wild West."

She laughed, and he detected a note of relief in it. He wanted to ask what that was all about, but Lucy approached the table to take their order. They'd have to talk about it later because he had an idea it meant something significant to Marybeth.

"You're looking mighty fine this afternoon, Rand." Lucy stood close to him, her skirt brushing against his shoulder. "What can I get for you, sweetie?" He wished she wouldn't be so familiar with him, but the poor girl was still missing Seamus, so he'd tolerate it for now.

"Two roast beef dinners." He looked at Marybeth. "That is, if you'd like the same?"

She didn't so much as glance at Lucy. "Yes, thank you." The chill in her voice rivaled a winter wind off of the San Juan Mountains.

As the waitress moved away from the table, Marybeth finally slid a look at her departing form through narrowed eyes and her pretty lips formed a disapproving pucker. To her credit, she didn't say anything, but Rand had an idea she wanted to. He'd best move the conversation on to the letters, no matter how hard it would be to disappoint her.

Reaching across the table to give her hand a squeeze, he cleared his throat. "I heard back from the sheriffs."

Hope lit up her face like sunshine, but she must have noticed his frown, because that hope quickly vanished, replaced by reddened eyes. "They haven't seen him." Her voice broke.

He shook his head, emotion blocking any words of sympathy he might try to speak.

"Oh, Jimmy, where did you go?"

Her forlorn tone broke his heart and he didn't have much at hand to cheer her. Just one thing came to mind.

"Is it possible your brother changed over the years?"

"I don't think so." Her frown deepened. "He was always a younger version of our father, except he had Mam's red hair. I wish I still had the letter he wrote from Del Norte. Maybe the postmaster over there would remember him." She stared toward the café door as if she wanted to go right now and find out.

"Say, that's a good idea." He liked anything that might encourage her, and he hadn't even thought of the postmaster. Or, in this case, the postmistress of many years. She would have been the one to handle the letter, and maybe Marybeth's brother just never crossed paths with Sheriff Hobart. The only other possibility, one he'd refused to give much thought, was that maybe Marybeth had made up the whole story. Maybe she didn't even have a brother. But that didn't make any sense. Why would she have agreed to come out to Colorado, not even wanting to get married, if there was no Jimmy O'Brien?

He tried to dismiss the notion, yet he couldn't resist testing her. "Tell you what. How about we ride over there tomorrow and find out?" As much as he hated to return to the town where he'd killed a man, he had to find out the truth about this matter. He'd always known he'd have to go back if he had a good enough reason. This seemed to be it.

Again, her face lit up like sunshine. "Could we? You said the other day it's a full day of travel to go both ways. If we left early, would we be back before dark?"

Her eagerness dispelled his suspicions. It also reminded him that she didn't ride. They'd have to take the buggy, which would make the trip slower.

More time in her company. More time to prove to her that he might make a pretty good husband, after all. Of course they'd have to take a chaperone. He'd ride over to the Eberly place to see if any of the sisters was free to go along.

Saturday brought sunshine and warmth with just enough of a breeze to make the trip to Del Norte pleasant. Their picnic basket once again tied to the back of the buggy, Marybeth sat beside Rand, with Beryl Eberly perched on a makeshift seat behind them. The hilly scenery and an occasional fluffy cloud floating over the distant San Juan Mountains only added to the enjoyment of the ride. Hope and excitement filled Marybeth's heart. Perhaps today they would learn where

Jimmy had gone. But even if they didn't, she would be grateful to Rand for trying to find her brother.

She could hardly believe his generosity and that of his neighbors in helping her search. Truly this community was a warm, wonderful place to live. Not like Boston, where the Irish were still fighting for respect. Here no one blinked or frowned upon hearing her last name. In fact, she'd met several folks with Irish names, though none of them from Ireland itself, just second-or third-generation Americans. While she and Jimmy had been born in the old country, they'd come to America when she was a baby and he was not quite five years old. Da had come for the opportunity to better himself, or so he'd always said. But Mam, in one of her weaker moments when his cruelty had beaten her down, had revealed Da had left behind many debts.

Shoving aside bitter memories, Marybeth leaned back in the buggy to enjoy the ride. They traveled a fairly wide and well-worn road, which Rand told her had been an Indian trail, a path for prospectors and finally a stagecoach route extending all the way to Wagon Wheel Gap. Each time she heard the name of the mining town far up in the mountains, her heart skipped. On another day, would Rand take her that far if they learned Jimmy had gone there? Or would she have to purchase a stagecoach ticket and go on her own? It would be some time before she could afford to do that.

For today, she would use the fourteen-mile trip each way to become better acquainted with another Eberly sister. Beryl was the middle sister and somewhat quieter than Maisie and even Laurie. Still, with a little coaxing, Marybeth was able to persuade her to describe the various plants and trees they passed.

"Up in those hills—" she pointed south of the road "—those are aspen. They turn yellow in the fall and look real pretty fluttering in the wind. Farther down you can see the piñon trees." She indicated a grove of tall, bushy trees that appeared to be evergreen. "They bear nuts that are right tasty. We gather them in the fall and use them for baking."

"Don't tell anybody I said this—" Rand waved a hand toward the picnic basket "—but Beryl's the best cook in the whole Eberly clan."

While Beryl snorted, grinned and gave his arm a shove, Marybeth bit back a laugh. Rand needed to be careful with all of his compliments about the cooking of his various female friends. If those women ever got together and compared his praise, probably none of them would invite him to a meal again. And if they were all such fine cooks, what would he say about her skills if they got married?

Oh, dear. That thought was occurring entirely too often these days, and she'd only known him a week, not counting the six months they'd been writing back and forth. If she didn't watch out, she'd find herself more than liking him. She'd fall mindlessly in love with him, and then where would her search for Jimmy be?

They reached the outskirts of Del Norte in good time due to dry roads and no headwinds. Rand drove the horses off the trail to a shady spot under the tall cottonwoods that grew along the Rio Grande. If Marybeth was going to get more bad news, better to hear it on a full stomach. Beryl had kindly offered to prepare the picnic, and she'd packed a fine basketful, with chicken sandwiches, potato salad, pickles, apple crumb cake and cold coffee.

Not for the first time, Rand wondered whether Marybeth liked to cook. She hadn't been bothered by his compliments to other ladies' cooking, which could mean either she had confidence in her own skills or she'd never learned and didn't care to. He wasn't sure how that would work out if they married. All the women he knew, especially ranch gals, were pretty jealous about their cooking, so he was always quick to praise their efforts.

Odd the random thoughts he had about Marybeth. What kind of music did she like, other than hymns and Irish folksongs? Did she like Christmas as much as he did? Would she feel trapped being a ranch wife like a few local women he knew? Or would she be like Susanna and find her calling in having her own home and children to care for? At least now he knew she loved children. Lizzy had been won over by a lemon stick, but Marybeth had been won over by his niece's sweet baby ways. Did she want to have a few children of her own? Not a question he could ask until he'd won her heart.

As he lifted her down from the buggy, he couldn't help but notice her nervous glances around the site, so he gave her hand a squeeze.

"Looking for snakes?" Beryl quipped with a grin.

Rand wanted to throttle her, but Marybeth laughed. A shaky sound, but still a laugh, which showed her spunk. He liked that.

"Yes, indeed. I suppose Laurie told you all about our encounter last Saturday."

"Yep." Beryl untied the picnic basket. To Rand, she said, "You want to get the blanket?"

They settled down, offered a prayer and began to eat, making quick work of the picnic and saving some in case they got hungry on the trip back to Esperanza.

On the road again, they headed toward town. Rand saw in the corner of his eye that Marybeth was twisting her hands nervously. He prayed she wouldn't be disappointed this time. Prayed that this mysterious Jimmy O'Brien had somehow made an impression on someone who would remember him all these years later.

He made a quick stop at the sheriff's office, mainly to let the lawman know he was in town, but also to tell him about Dathan Hardison and his threats. Hobart had been more than good to Rand after the shooting, refusing to charge him with a crime and insisting he take reward money that had been offered for Cole Lyndon, dead or alive. He'd also suggested it might be a good idea not to come back to Del Norte for a while. Rand wasn't sure three years was a long enough while, but for Marybeth's sake, it would have to do. Concerned that some unsavory sorts might be in the jail cells, he left the girls in the buggy and entered the office on Grand Avenue.

"Come on in, Rand." The sheriff seemed glad to see him, offering his hand and a warm pat on the shoulder. "I'm glad you came by. Have a seat." He waved Rand to a chair in front of his desk. After the usual polite inquiries about each other's families, the sheriff said, "I shouldn't have been in such a hurry to answer your letter the other day. After thinking on it, I do recall some redheaded cowpokes coming through town from time to time."

Rand felt a happy little kick in his chest, but he cautioned himself not to get too excited. Jimmy wasn't a cowpoke; he was a prospector. Marybeth had been adamant about that. "That's some memory you have there."

Hobart grimaced and scratched his head. "Not what it used to be. I don't think I can add anything. If a man doesn't have a distinctive scar or maybe an accent of some sort, it's hard to pin down a memory of him."

Rand nodded. "We thought we'd go over to the post office to see if Mrs. Sanchez remembers anything."

"Good idea." Hobart grimaced again. "I should have asked her myself and saved you a trip." He shuffled some Wanted posters on his desk. "Let me know what you find out."

"Yessir, I'll do that." Rand wouldn't tell him he was more than happy to have another full day with Marybeth. More than happy to help her search for her brother. "Say, while you're looking through those posters, do you have anything on a Dathan Hardison? He's a cousin of Cole Lyndon."

Frowning, the sheriff eyed him. "Cole's kin, eh?"

Rand nodded and gave him a brief account of Hardison's actions in Esperanza, including his threats and his so-called conversion, which even had the preacher suspicious.

The sheriff scanned the papers on his desk and then dug an envelope filled with more Wanted posters from his drawer. "These are new. Help me take a look." He gave half of the pile to Rand.

They sorted through the heavy paper sheets, some with photographs, others with drawings of men, most wanted dead or alive. Rand didn't recognize any of them as Hardison.

"Nope, nothing here." Hobart scratched his chin. "If

he committed a crime, he could have done it under a different name. Or he could have served his sentence."

"I suppose." Rand glanced out the window at the girls. Marybeth was making good use of her fan, so she was probably getting too hot. "Let me know if you hear anything, would you?"

"Sure thing." Hobart grunted. "I'll send out some queries and see what I can come up with."

"Much obliged." After taking his leave of the sheriff and setting aside his concerns about Hardison, Rand reported to the girls about Hobart's retrieved memories of red-haired cowboys. As he expected, Marybeth's pretty hazel eyes lit up with hope.

"Thank you, Rand." She clasped his arm as he drove the buggy farther down Grand Avenue to the general store, where the post office was located.

Despite the momentary hope he'd felt in the sheriff's office, as they drew closer to their destination, he had a sinking feeling this was all a waste of time.

Marybeth could barely contain her excitement. As hard as she tried to quiet her giddy emotions, she couldn't subdue her hopes. Even the bright, sunny day seemed to portend good news.

The streets were crowded with all sorts of people, both men and women, both decent community folks like those in Esperanza and some ruffians very similar to the worst she'd seen on Boston's waterfront. Rand explained that Del Norte was the stopping off place where prospectors on their way to the silver fields bought their gear. He said those men were pretty much harmless.

"On a Saturday, you can tell the difference between the cowboys and the prospectors." He nodded toward a rowdy group of men. "Those are the cowboys. They're here to waste their hard-earned pay. That's why they're cleaned up and in their best clothes." He snorted his disgust and shook his head. "Now that fellow over there, he's a prospector." He indicated a dusty traveler. "You can tell by his clothes and his sharp-eyed look. He'll be buying his gold pans and picks over at the general store before heading farther west right past Del Norte Peak." He pointed toward a mountain that rose above the town.

Marybeth studied the landmark, whose highest valleys still bore remnants of snow. Was Jimmy somewhere beyond that peak? Did he look like this shabbily dressed man so clearly determined to change his fortunes? If only her brother knew he held the key to enough treasure to take care of them both. That was, if he still had the locket.

"Here we are." Rand reached out to hand her down from the buggy.

Back in Boston, buggy rides had been few and far between. Yet after only a few times out with Rand, Marybeth was becoming more adept at getting in and out of the conveyance without tripping on her skirts. She still needed to take his hand to step down, and his strong grasp sent a pleasant shiver up her arm. Only when he gently squeezed her fingers did she realize she was shaking. A quick look up into his gentle eyes calmed her and sent more agreeable feelings churning through her chest.

Oh, my. How will I ever keep hold of my heart when it seems to have a mind of its own? Yet how could she not respond to his kindness? His sacrifices for her sake? Mrs. Foster had told her how much work it took to run a ranch. With Rand neglecting his duties to help with her quest, she must at the very least be grateful. *Grateful enough to marry him?* She was far from ready to answer that question.

Beryl had jumped down from her perch and now waited on the boardwalk. Unlike Laurie, she didn't smirk or send teasing grins their way. Of course, she was a couple of years older than Laurie and thus more mature. Her restraint was both admirable and much appreciated.

"Shall we go in?" Rand offered an arm to both Marybeth and Beryl.

Beryl's face grew a bit pink beneath her freckles. Maybe she wasn't used to gentlemanly manners. Marybeth had learned how to receive such graces only two years ago at Fairfield Young Ladies' Academy, so she understood how the younger girl felt. If she could help Beryl and her sisters, including the irrepressible Maisie, learn about the finer customs of society, it might in some small way repay their kindnesses. After Marybeth inquired about Jimmy, she would offer to help Beryl shop for some feminine fripperies.

They entered the general store and Beryl's eyes lit up. Instead of perusing the aisles of fabric, laces and ladies' hats, however, she strode away toward the guns and saddles, the heels of her riding boots thumping on the wood flooring. Marybeth caught herself before laughing out loud at her own foolish thoughts about Beryl. Being a true cowgirl, maybe she didn't want to purchase fripperies or to learn social graces.

"The post office is that little room in the back." Rand indicated a sign above a small area similar to a teller's cage. "Looks like the postmistress is in." He gave a gentle tug on Marybeth's arm.

Her pulse quickened, especially when she saw the woman's gray-streaked hair. Surely she'd been around long enough to recall Jimmy.

"Howdy, Mrs. Sanchez." Rand gave her a charming grin, and her expression brightened.

"Señor Randall Northam, how good to see you." She leaned forward with her forearms on the counter. "The people of Del Norte, they still speak of your heroics in ridding our town of those evil men. You know how grateful we are, *sí*?"

Rand gave what seemed like an involuntary shudder. "Thank you, ma'am." He cleared his throat. "This is Miss Marybeth O'Brien from Boston."

The woman acknowledged Marybeth with a friendly smile. "I have met a certain Señor O'Brien. Perhaps you are related?"

Chapter Eight

Rand felt his jaw drop, while Marybeth yipped like an excited puppy.

"You've met Jimmy? You know my brother?" She looked about ready to jump through the bars separating her from the postmistress. "Oh, please tell me where he is."

From the way Mrs. Sanchez drew back, Rand was pretty sure it wouldn't be that simple. He put a bracing arm around Marybeth's shoulders. "Hold on, sweetheart." Oops. Better not let that slip out again until she really was his sweetheart. "Ma'am, was it recent when you met him or sometime in the past?"

The lady shook her head. "Oh, very long ago." She gave Marybeth a compassionate smile. "I have the excellent memory, but this one, he was easy not to forget by anybody. Hair the color of autumn sunsets, same color *la barba y bigote* just beginning, like he was trying to look older." She chuckled in her deep, throaty way. "James O'Brien. He came in the store many times wanting to mail his letter, but changing his mind. Fi-

nally he gave it to my late husband. It was to go to—"
She gasped softly. "To Boston. Did you receive it?"

Marybeth swayed and Rand tightened his hold on
her. "Yes," she said on a sob. She looked up at Rand,
her eyes brimming. He guessed she couldn't speak, so
he'd best do it for her.

"We appreciate your information, Mrs. Sanchez. By
any chance, do you have any idea where Jimmy went
after turning the letter over to you?"

"*Sí, naturalmente.* He go to the silver fields up there."
She waved toward the west as if brushing away a pesky
fly. "Carlos, my husband, God rest his soul, he tell the
boy he should be the cowboy. Not like those." She batted a dismissive hand toward the front of the store just
as some cowpokes walked by the display window. From
their swaggering, staggering steps, Rand surmised they
were already in the midst of their Saturday night cel-
ebration, even though it wasn't much past two o'clock
in the afternoon. "Go to *el rancho del buen hombre*, the
ranch of the good man like Colonel Northam or George
Eberly. Work for him, Carlos tell him. It is good life."
She shook her head, sadness emanating from her maternal eyes. "What can you do when the young ones refuse
the wise advice? No, this one buy his mining supplies
and go west. We see him no more."

"Well, then." Marybeth straightened, a smile brightening her face and making it even prettier. "I'll just have
to go to Wagon Wheel Gap. Thank you, Mrs. Sanchez."

Her reaction to the news both surprised and worried
Rand, but he gave her an encouraging nod anyway. For
his own part, he couldn't be more pleased to find out for
certain Jimmy O'Brien actually existed. Now he had to
decide just how far to go in helping Marybeth find him.

Wagon Wheel Gap wasn't a place for a lady. If Nate agreed to it, maybe Rand and a couple of hands could go up there once the cattle came down from summer grazing in the mountains and the hay was in. He'd keep that to himself, though. No sense in putting ideas into Marybeth's head. No sense in stirring up hope too soon. Or stirring up any hope at all. After almost eight years, would O'Brien still be prospecting? Any sensible man would give up after all that time and take up a more realistic occupation.

On the way back to Esperanza, Marybeth found the day even brighter and the wild Colorado scenery even lovelier than when they'd traveled west that morning. Speaking with someone who actually knew Jimmy, knew where he'd gone, gave her hope beyond all her expectations. Although more than seven years had passed since Mrs. Sanchez had last seen him, Marybeth had no doubt her determined brother would still be searching for silver or gold or whatever valuable minerals the San Juan Mountains had to offer. If he'd already struck it rich, surely he would have contacted Mam, would have come to rescue her and Marybeth from Da.

The thought sobered her. Jimmy would be heartbroken when he learned Mam was dead. If he was still the loyal, caring person she remembered, he'd also grieve for Da, but more for his wasted life than his demise. Marybeth prayed he hadn't followed their father's habits, either the drinking or the everlasting search for quick riches. She thought, not for the first time, of prospecting as exactly that, a quick riches scheme. She added a prayer about the locket. If he'd sold it to buy his mining supplies, that would be the end of that. They'd both be working hard to survive for the rest of their lives. For her it wouldn't be quite so bad. She could marry Rand.

The thought shamed her. It wouldn't be fair to Rand if she married him just to get a husband to provide for her. Wouldn't be fair to her, either. At least Mam had loved Da, and Marybeth couldn't think of settling for anything else. That was, if she had to marry. Which she prayed would never happen.

"What's going through that pretty head of yours?" Rand gently elbowed her arm. "Are you pleased with what we found out?"

She looked up at him without answering for several seconds. Should she tell him what was in her heart? That she could not bear to postpone the trip to Wagon Wheel Gap? She would have to earn enough money for the stagecoach fare, food and lodging. It would take a while, even with the generous salary Mr. Means paid her. If she asked Rand, would he take her now? She couldn't bring herself to do it, not when she had no plans to marry him.

"Well, are you pleased?" Rand repeated.

"I'm sorry." She couldn't even tell him how sorry she was. She hadn't missed his slip in calling her "sweetheart" back at the post office. He wouldn't think she was so sweet or that she even possessed a heart if he knew how disloyal her thoughts were. "Yes, I'm more than pleased. Thank you so much for today."

"Glad to do it."

He gave her his cute, crooked grin, and her traitorous heart warmed dangerously in his favor. Oh, how she wanted to tell him everything. Well, not everything, but more about Jimmy. More about her growing-up years.

About Mam and Da. About why finding her brother was more important to her than marriage.

She couldn't very well discuss those things with Rand while Beryl sat at their shoulders. Maybe they could talk more once they delivered their chaperone to Maisie's house in town, where she would spend the night.

Marybeth glanced back to engage the girl in a more general conversation. But Beryl's head was propped on one arm against the top of the leather seatback, her wide-brimmed hat pulled low over her face and her newly purchased, pearl-handled six-shooter safely tucked in its wooden box and clutched close to her chest. Yet even with her steady breathing indicating she was asleep, Marybeth couldn't tell Rand about the things eating at her soul until they were completely alone.

They rolled into Esperanza just as the sun ducked behind the San Juan range and lengthening shadows spread darkness across the San Luis Valley like an ocean's rising tide swept over the seashore.

Rand turned off of Main Street onto Clark Avenue where the Henshaws lived. Beryl awoke just as they reached her sister's two-story house. Or so it seemed. Maybe she'd been awake the whole time. Or maybe that was Marybeth's own guilty conscience, which took for granted that everyone bent the truth in some way or another from time to time.

Leaving Beryl to explain the success of the day to Maisie and Doc, Rand and Marybeth made the two-block trip to Pike Street. As they traveled, Marybeth tried to summon the courage to tell Rand all that was in her heart, yet she found her moment for complete truthfulness had passed. Mrs. Foster met them at the door and insisted Rand must join them for a light supper.

Perhaps it was for the best. If she told Rand everything, she'd lose any semblance of control in the situation, and she might lose Rand's friendship. He certainly wouldn't keep helping her if she told him right out she didn't plan to marry him, maybe never had. At this point, she really couldn't say herself what she'd felt back in Boston. All she'd known then was that Colonel and Mrs. Northam had offered to pay her fare to Colorado. And not just any place in that new state, but the very area where Jimmy had gone. How could she not accept their offer? Yet now her guilty feelings diminished her joy over the day's revelations.

Despite her drooping spirits, she managed to smile and chat during supper, bringing Mrs. Foster into the circle of those celebrating her good news. Afterward, she saw Rand to the door. "Thank you for everything. I had a lovely time, and not just because of what Mrs. Sanchez told us." As she said the words she knew they were true. She'd become more than accustomed to his company; she honestly enjoyed it. If she did lose his friendship, the loss would be devastating.

"I had a good time, too." Even in the dim lantern light, his attractive smile stirred traitorous emotions in her heart. "I'll meet you at the church in the morning." He squeezed her hand. "We'll each choose a side of the church and see who can set out the hymnals faster."

Here he was again, making even the simplest task more fun. "I'll accept that challenge."

He bent forward but pulled back and questioned her with one raised eyebrow and a comical smirk.

She huffed out an indulgent sigh. "Yes, I suppose you may kiss me." She couldn't contain a giggle over his silliness.

This time his lips made contact just a wee bit closer to hers rather than farther up her cheek, and once again her heart lilted. As he donned his hat, his knowing grin and waggle of his dark eyebrows suggested he knew how he'd affected her. If she truly was going to stay in control of her future, she really must stop reacting to him this way.

Satisfaction filled Rand over the events of the day, and he whistled as he drove home. He could tell Marybeth liked him, liked it when he kissed her on the cheek. One of these days he'd kiss those pretty, tempting lips and hope she liked it even more.

On second thought, he'd better postpone such plans until he found out what she was hiding from him. He could still see it in her eyes, the way she'd seem about to tell him something but then back off. Maybe she'd trust him more if he made that trip to Wagon Wheel Gap and located Jimmy. If he could reunite her with her brother, surely that would put an end to whatever was bothering her. Then he could court her in earnest.

He chuckled to himself. Remembering the fairy tale he'd read to Lizzy a few nights ago, he pictured himself as a knight courting a princess. To win her hand, he'd have to go on a quest to a distant location and bring back a particular treasure. What a fine story, one his friend Seamus would appreciate. But Seamus was up in the mountains with the cattle, and if Rand told his brothers, they'd never let him live it down.

* * *

After a lovely church service the next day, Marybeth visited with several people whom she'd met at the bank, including Mr. Hardison.

"How was your first week at the bank, Miss O'Brien?" His warm smile and courteous tone made her wonder again what Rand found so offensive in the man.

"Very enjoyable, thank you."

"Then you'll continue working there?"

"Why, I suppose so."

She started to add that she'd stay because Mr. Means was a pleasant employer, but across the churchyard, she saw the three Northam brothers coming their way. Rand's expression was nothing less than hostile. As before, she guessed he was jealous, yet this time she found no pleasure in it. Would he start an argument, a fight, right here in front of the church?

The three brothers were still a few yards away when Susanna hurried over and put an arm around Marybeth's waist. "You're coming out to the ranch for dinner, aren't you?"

"How do, Mrs. Northam?" As Mr. Hardison tipped his hat, he didn't seem to notice Susanna's warning glare sent toward her husband and his brothers. "A mighty fine sermon today, don't you think?"

"I would agree, sir. 'Blessed are the peacemakers' are words we all should heed." Her lilting accent carried the same Southern inflections as Reverend Thomas's. "Now, if you'll excuse us." She turned Marybeth away from the gentleman and urged her toward the grassy lawn where the smaller children were playing tag. "I spoke to Mrs. Foster and she doesn't mind sparing you for the afternoon. Do say you'll come."

Marybeth looked back to see whether Rand and his brothers had actually accosted Mr. Hardison, but the minister had beaten them to it. Reverend Thomas must have said something witty, because Mr. Hardison was laughing. With trouble averted, Marybeth gave her attention to her new friend. Her potential sister. The thought stirred a dormant longing within her. Having a sister meant having a confidante, another woman to share joys and secrets with, as Marybeth had had with Mam. As she'd just begun to with Rosamond back at the academy.

"I'd love to come." Yes, she did want to go, wanted to be with Rand and his lovely family, wanted to see this Four Stones Ranch he was so proud of. Putting aside questions about his dislike for Mr. Hardison, she joined the Northam entourage heading south from town.

The men rode horseback, following the ladies in the buggy. While Susanna drove, Marybeth found herself the center of Lizzy's attention. The child must have decided she was a worthy friend even without the bribe of a lemon stick, for she rested in Marybeth's arms as if she had always done so.

In return, her sweet scent and childish babble charmed Marybeth and stirred a longing to have her own child to pamper and cuddle. She imagined any child of Rand's would be a fine-looking boy or girl. If she didn't marry him, the privilege of bearing said child would belong to another woman. She found the thought more than a little annoying. Then she was annoyed at herself for being annoyed. She mustn't be a dog in a manger, not wanting the hay and not wanting another animal to have it, either. Yet the thought of stepping aside so another woman could have Rand's attentions grated inexplicably on her heart.

With the Northam cook off for the day, Susanna and Marybeth put together a simple but substantial dinner of sandwiches, potato salad and pickled vegetables. Afterward, Rand took Marybeth on a tour of the house. To her amazement, the roomy two-story abode had a ballroom on its north end where, Rand told her, the family enjoyed entertaining their neighbors for just about any special occasion they could come up with. With his parents back East, he'd been put in charge of the annual Christmas party.

"That's almost five months away, but Susanna's expecting about that time, so I'll need some help." He questioned her with a hopeful look.

"Of course." The words came out before Marybeth could stop them. But then, she would enjoy helping a friend throw a party. A little baking, planning a few games, handmade decorations, maybe a gift exchange. "I'd love to."

His grateful grin stirred agreeable feelings that were becoming all too familiar. Only by forcing her thoughts to Jimmy could she keep her mind in charge of her heart. More or less.

"Would you like to see the property?" His face exuded familial pride.

"Very much." She might as well look around at what she was giving up by not marrying him.

Rand took her by the hand and led her out the front door to the wide, covered porch. To the west, the San Juan Mountains stood out starkly against a rich blue sky on this bright, cloudless day. She could envision watching glorious sunsets from the nearby rocking chairs, a restful end to a hard day of work.

He took her down the front steps onto the neatly trimmed green lawn spreading beneath the shade of four elm trees. Everything seemed to be in full bloom, including the flower beds at every corner of the large house. Marybeth inhaled a deep breath, enjoying the clean, fresh scent of country living.

"It's so beautiful, Rand."

He beamed at her praise. "We like it."

Northam land stretched as far as the eye could see to the north, south and east. Beyond the fence bordering the house's front lawn lay a vast field of lush uncut green grass waving in the late summer breeze.

"I never imagined the place would be this big." Marybeth could scarcely take it all in. "What's growing in that field?"

"That's alfalfa hay." For a moment Rand studied the field with a critical eye. "When it's ready for harvest in another month, we'll winnow it into rows, fork it into wagons and store it in the barn. It'll feed Northam horses and cattle through the winter."

Rand explained that their drovers would herd the steers to market over the mountains, and the cattle left behind would be brood stock for the next year.

"Come autumn, this is a pretty busy place. While the men take care of the cattle and harvest the hay, the womenfolk harvest their kitchen gardens and preserve the produce. Everybody on the ranch has an important job to do."

"So much work." A sliver of understanding opened in Marybeth's mind as she recalled Da's complaints about how hard it had been back home in Ireland to bring sustenance out of the ground. He'd hated being a farmer.

"Yep." Rand's fond gaze, untouched by any such complaint, took in their surroundings. "But well worth it." His gaze remained unchanged as he turned to look at her. "It's a good life."

What did she sense in his look and tone? Pride, with a hint of wistfulness, if that was even possible? Did he hope she would see his home and land with the same deep affection? At a moment like this she was all too close to saying she'd like to be a part of his family's "good life" here on Four Stones Ranch.

Forcing away words that would forever trap her, she considered her options. While she couldn't tell him the whole truth, she could strike a bargain with her conscience. Without telling him of her aversion to marriage, she would make sure he understood why she must postpone making plans for a shared future.

"I can't thank you enough for taking me to Del Norte yesterday." She looped an arm in his as they walked around the corner of the house toward the back, where an enormous barn dominated the scene. "It will take some time before I can earn enough money to make the trip to Wagon Wheel Gap, but I do have to go there and search for Jimmy." She offered him an apologetic smile. "Rand, please understand that I can't think of getting married until I find him." She swallowed hard as sudden tears threatened to undo her. "Or find out what happened to him."

"I do understand." He looked ahead, his face stoic, all smiles gone. "And I hope you understand my side of things. If there was any way I could take time off and go there now, I'd do it. But my brothers have been managing the ranch without my help for over a week now, and I've got to do my share."

"Yes, of course." Another rush of emotion surged up inside her, choking off the words she wanted to say. Lest he misunderstand her tears, she directed her gaze toward the great barn. "What a large structure. It's almost as big as Boston's Faneuil Hall." Not really, but still very large.

Rand's doubting frown, peppered with a healthy dose of humor, put an end to Marybeth's tears. "Faneuil Hall, eh? While that's a mighty complimentary comparison, I do think your memory is a bit off. Even after all these years, I remember how huge that place was. Three stories, isn't it?"

"Not to mention the attic and tower."

"Which, I notice, you *did* mention." His teasing chuckle dismissed the last of her sadness.

With him being so agreeable, why not just tell him everything? Confess it all and see how he took it. Before she could form the right words, four black-and-white dogs emerged from the barn, yapping and barking, and charged toward them. Terror gripped Marybeth and she grasped Rand's arm, thinking they would dash back to the house.

"Hey, there, you little scalawags." Instead of sharing her fear of the dog pack, he knelt and let them clamber all over him. They licked his face, nipped at his ears and vied for the best place in his attention.

Now she could see they weren't in the least bit dangerous like the dog packs in Boston, but merely half-grown puppies. While she couldn't fully share Rand's enthusiasm, she did pet one sweet-faced dog that insisted upon including her in the melee.

"Aren't you a cute one?" She had little experience with dogs, but this one seemed to like being scratched behind the ears, much like Mrs. Foster's cat. The puppy wagged its tail and licked her hand and turned around in a circle before coming back for more, tangling itself in her skirt.

"I think you've made a friend." Rand stood and beckoned to her. "Now that they've inspected us, I think they'll let us into their barn."

Inside were at least a half dozen cats, maybe more, but it was the dogs that garnered Rand's attention. "Would you like one of them? Maybe as a watchdog?"

She stifled a laugh when she saw his sober frown. "Why would I need a watchdog?"

"Might be nice to have one to bark a warning when somebody comes to call."

Somebody like Mr. Hardison? She wouldn't ask for fear it would stir up trouble. "Let me ask Mrs. Foster."

"Good idea." He picked up the hefty puppy that had been so friendly to her. It seemed a bit more aggressive than the others in demanding attention. "Maybe we'll just take this little gal with us when we go back to town. Once Mrs. Foster sees her, she'll say yes."

"You don't think that's presumptuous?" Marybeth copied the way Rand scratched the dog's head and received another friendly lick in return. What fun it would be to call it her own.

"Nope. In fact, I'm sure Mrs. Foster will like her." Rand ruffled the puppy's fur as he set her down. "She can always say no."

"Is the puppy old enough to leave her mother?"

"Oh, sure. They've been weaned for months. The mother is up in the hills with the cattle, along with her own mother. She and her brothers were our first litter and are old enough to be working dogs now. The men are trying to train them to help with herding." He shook his head and clicked his tongue. "One of my father's projects that didn't go as planned. The man he brought over from Europe to train the dogs found out about some gold strikes near Denver. He packed up and took off without a word." Rand huffed out a sigh of disgust. "Out here a man's word is everything. If there's anything I hate, it's when somebody backs out on an agreement, even when it's just a spoken promise. This man had actually signed a contract but broke it."

Marybeth managed to maintain an interested expression, but once again all the joy went out of her. Even though Rand didn't know it, she'd broken the agreement she'd made with his parents. Would he actually hate her when she told him the truth? It was no less than she deserved, but somehow she couldn't bear the thought of losing his friendship. To have those piercing green eyes filled with contempt for her rather than kind regard.

But was marriage the only way to keep his good opinion?

"Miss O'Brien, I am more than pleased with your work." Mr. Means stood beside Marybeth's desk reading a letter she'd just typewritten for him. As always, his countenance was a pleasant but professional mask. "I will sign it, and you can take it to Mrs. Winsted for posting when you go out for dinner." He turned away then back again, and she could not miss the warmth in his gaze. "I have been thinking… That is, I was wondering—" To her shock, he tugged at his collar and swallowed hard, almost like an awkward young boy. "May I take you to dinner at Williams's Café today?"

During her secretarial training, Marybeth had learned that some employers might attempt to take advantage of their secretaries. She could not think Mr. Means, a church deacon, would do such a thing. Still, as she and her fellow students had been taught, she kept in place a pleasant but professional facade. "Thank you, sir. I usually go home for dinner, and I should do so today so I can make sure Mrs. Foster is managing our new puppy without any difficulties." A simple ploy and not really necessary. Her landlady had been delighted with the puppy and together they'd named her Polly.

"Ah." Disappointment clouded his brown eyes. "Forgive me. I did not mean to—"

In an instant she knew her mistake. He hadn't meant to make an inappropriate offer at all. "Perhaps tomorrow?"

A smile lit his entire face. "Yes. Tomorrow." He strode away to his office with an almost jaunty gait.

Oh, dear. The last thing she needed to do was to incite the interest of another man. What would Rand say? Yet Mr. Means was her employer, and she mustn't offend him, either.

At noon, after posting his letter, she hurried out of Winsted's general store to go home for dinner. In her haste, she bumped smack into Mr. Hardison, sending him back a pace or two. He caught her upper arms in a powerful grip and righted her before she could fall to the boardwalk or even cry out.

"There now, Miss O'Brien." Courteous as always, he bowed and tipped his hat. "You must be in a hurry. May I be of assistance?"

"What? Oh, I mean, I don't believe so. Do forgive me for not watching where I was going." She inhaled deeply, taking in the scent of his expensive cologne, and started to move on. To her chagrin, he fell into step beside her.

"If it's not an intrusion, I beg the privilege of escorting you to whatever your destination might be."

"Please don't bother." She gave him a quick and, she hoped, dismissive smile.

"No bother at all, dear lady. Esperanza may be a quiet town, but one never knows when outlaws will ride through and stir up trouble."

"Very well. Thank you." She prayed Mrs. Foster would not invite him in for dinner. That would be more than she could expect Rand to tolerate, yet if it happened, she would have a hard time keeping it from him.

"Miss O'Brien, please don't think me impertinent, but I would be honored if you would accompany me on an outing this coming Saturday. We could take a picnic out to a scenic spot I've found in the foothills."

Had he been hiding in the bushes yesterday afternoon when Rand brought her home? He'd invited her to do the very same thing. "Thank you, sir, but I have unchangeable plans for Saturday." Despite his nice manners, she would *not* offer to go with him another day, as she had with Mr. Means. Juggling two gentlemen was already going to be a challenge she'd never expected or ever hoped to encounter.

At the house Polly lay in a furry ball on the front porch. She perked up as they approached and bounded down the stairs. Last night the little darling had slept on Marybeth's bed, and they'd already formed a sweet bond.

"May I see you to the door?" Mr. Hardison offered

his arm just as Polly grabbed his trouser leg in her teeth. "Hey, you mangy mutt. Quit that."

Instead she tore at the cuff, growling and twisting as if she were tearing at some sort of prey. Just as Mr. Hardison reached down to strike her with a clenched fist, Marybeth snatched the puppy up, heavy as she was, and pretended to scold.

"Why, you silly little doggy. What's got into you? Don't bother the nice man." The nice man who now wore a dreadful scowl much like Da used to wear when he was in a temper. Marybeth took a deep breath. "Why, Mr. Hardison, she's just a puppy who needs a bit of training." Or so Rand had told her. "If she damaged your trousers, I will mend them."

His eyes narrowed and Marybeth stepped back with another deep breath. Would he strike her instead of Polly? Her terror must be obvious, for his expression quickly relaxed. "I'm sure my trousers will need no repair, Miss O'Brien. If they do, the Chinese laundry will mend them." Now his smile turned oily. "I wouldn't like to see those pretty hands engaged in such labors." With another tip of his hat, he bowed away. "You and I will have our outing at another time."

Was there an edge of a threat to his statement? Her throat closed in fear and no words emerged to contradict him. Right now she would like nothing more than to rush into Rand's strong arms for comfort.

Yet back at work, as the afternoon progressed, she convinced herself it wouldn't be wise to further prejudice him against Mr. Hardison. After all, Mr. Means's years of banking gave him more insight into people's characters than a rancher's years of chasing cattle. Her employer spoke of loaning Mr. Hardison the money to start a new business. Just because he had a temper, just because certain of his traits reminded her of Da, that didn't mean Marybeth should be afraid of him. Did it? After all, she had no plans to deepen her acquaintance with the man.

Only when she stepped out of the bank at the end of the day did she realize her folly in thinking she could hide her encounter with Mr. Hardison from Rand. As he had every day last week, he was leaning against the hitching post, waiting for her, and the stormy look in his eyes sent a shiver through her middle rivaling the worst fears she'd had growing up.

Chapter Nine

The instant Rand saw the startled look in Marybeth's eyes, he regretted his anger. After all, it wasn't her fault Hardison had accosted her. Still, he was just a bit miffed over her attitude toward the gunslinger. If Lucy from the diner hadn't told him about the encounter, would Marybeth have done so? He straightened and took a step toward her, offering a stiff smile, which was all he could muster at the moment.

"Afternoon, Marybeth. Did you have a good day?" He stepped up on the boardwalk and offered his arm.

She hesitated briefly before accepting it. "It had its good and not-so-good moments." As they began to walk, she looked straight ahead.

"Yeah, me, too." How would he get her to tell him about Hardison? Certainly not by being angry, so he forced a chuckle. "The other pups kept looking for the one you took. I tried to tell them she's found a better home, but since she's the alpha dog in the litter, they're sort of at loose ends." Thinking about the dogs helped to improve his mood. "Those crazy critters trailed me all over the ranch today while I was trying to get my chores done."

Marybeth's laugh sounded real. "Well, you be sure to tell them Polly's already made herself at home and doesn't miss them at all."

She glanced up at Rand with a sweet smile and something pleasant kicked inside his chest.

"Polly, eh? Not a very bold name for a watchdog."

"I wanted to call her Roly-Poly, but Mrs. Foster said she'd outgrow her puppy fat soon, so the name wouldn't make sense. We settled on Polly."

They shared a laugh over that but then Marybeth sobered and sighed. "In fact, she's taken over. You'll be fortunate if she lets you in the house."

Rand wanted to make a smart-alecky quip, but something in her voice cautioned him. "Care to explain that?" Lest he'd sounded too demanding, he added, "I mean, she was my dog until yesterday. If she misbehaved…" They'd reached the end of the boardwalk and he helped her step down onto the dusty street, where they continued their walk.

"Let's just say it was one of my not-so-good moments. When I went home for dinner, Mr. Hardison insisted upon accompanying me." She looked up, her gaze clearly questioning him.

"Humph" was all he could manage to say as relief crowded out the last of his ill feelings. For one crazy moment right after Lucy told him what had happened, he'd wondered if Marybeth and Hardison had been in cahoots all along. They'd arrived on the same train, so it was possible. Now his conscience questioned why he'd become so suspicious of her. And when would he get over thinking she was less than honest with him?

"Humph? That's all you have to say?" Marybeth removed her arm from his and stalked ahead. When he caught up and gently snagged her arm again, she shot an accusing glare his way. "He made me uncomfortable, Rand. I know Mr. Means is doing business with him, but… Oh, dear. That's confidential bank business. Please forget I said it."

"Already forgotten." Not by a long shot, but he wouldn't tell her. If Means didn't have any more discernment than to work with a man like Hardison, maybe Dad had better find another banker for Esperanza while he was back East. "Not the part about your feeling uncomfortable, of course. Did he do anything…eh, rude?"

"No. Well… No. He did ask me to go on a picnic on Saturday. I told him I had plans." She shot him another of those odd looks, like she was still hiding something. "He said we'd have our outing another day. I should have told him that was not likely to happen."

Rand felt her shudder, a vibration so small he wouldn't have noticed if they hadn't been arm in arm. "Something did happened, Marybeth. I can tell."

To his shock, she giggled in her cute girlie way. "Oh, yes, something happened. Polly came out to meet us and nearly tore the cuff right off of his trousers."

Rand burst out laughing. "Smart dog. Now aren't you glad I insisted that you take her?"

Marybeth rolled her eyes. "Yes, Rand. You were right. It's good to have a watchdog."

They'd reached Mrs. Foster's house all too soon and he didn't want to leave her. They had so much more to discuss and not just about Hardison. He sensed she was opening up to him little by little. Maybe it was time to ask her some deeper questions about her life so he could understand her hesitancy to marry him and at the same time answer his own concerns about what she was hiding.

He tried to stifle an idea that had occurred to him yesterday as he'd shown her around the ranch, but it was an honest concern for any rancher. Susanna and Rita would have a hard time getting the kitchen garden harvested all by themselves, and the food was necessary to get the family and hands through the winter. It sure would be nice if Marybeth could become a part of the family, live at the ranch and help the girls out. Yet it was hardly a reason for rushing either of them into a marriage that could end up being miserable for both of them.

As they walked toward the house, he saw Polly on the porch. The pup's ears shot up and she raced down the steps, practically falling all over herself. He knelt to gather her in his arms, but Polly had eyes only for Marybeth. Her new mistress squatted and cooed silly words, stirring an odd sort of jealousy in Rand. He wouldn't mind if Marybeth cooed silly words to him.

"Do you have to hurry in?" To emphasize his question, he climbed the steps, sat on the top one and patted the spot next to him. Through the open front window the aroma of beef and onions, probably a stew, set his mouth to watering. Mrs. Foster made the best stew and biscuits. Of course that was next to Miss Pam and maybe Rita's mother, Angela.

"Well…" Marybeth glanced at the door. "It's Mrs. Foster's turn to send supper over to Reverend Thomas, but she always gives me a few minutes to relax before I help in the kitchen. I suppose I can sit with you for a little while."

"Good, because lots of people pass by this time of day, and everybody can see I'm here, and you're with me."

She settled down on the step and gave him a teasing smirk. "As if everyone didn't already see you walk me home every day."

"That's right. Maybe I'd better ride into town and walk you to dinner, too, so certain people won't—" He'd started to say "try to horn in on my territory," but calling her his territory might offend her.

"Don't do that, Rand." She set one perfect, gloved hand on his sleeve and lightning shot up his arm clear to his neck. If she noticed the way he shivered with enjoyment, she was too much a lady to remark on it. "After seeing all the work you have to do at the ranch, I don't want to take any more of your time."

Her sweet smile and warm gaze only added to the pleasantness of the moment. Oh, to come home to that every day. Suddenly unable to talk, he coughed to clear his throat. Now if he could just clear his mind and come up with some way to open the discussion. Polly chose that moment to wiggle in between them and lay her head on Marybeth's lap.

"She sure has taken to you."

He reached out to scratch behind Polly's ears at the same moment Marybeth did. Their hands bumped and they shared a grin and then fell into a rhythm of petting the furry little rascal.

"Rand, I—"

"Marybeth, would you mind—"

They began at the same time. Both stopped.

"You go ahead." He encouraged her with a nod. Maybe if she opened up on her own, he wouldn't have to ask questions she might find nosy.

"Thank you." Her warm response hinted at a growing trust. At least he hoped so.

She sat there for a bit, gazing out across the street toward a newly finished house, but seeming not to see it. In her gaze, her expression, he saw something familiar, but he couldn't quite capture the memory. Maybe she was becoming so much a part of his life that her features were burned into his thoughts. He certainly did dream about her every night; a welcome change from his nightmares about killing a man and being stalked by his cousin. He shoved aside thoughts of Dathan Hardison. If the gunslinger so much as looked at Marybeth in the wrong way, Rand would make sure he never did it again.

Lord, no. Not that blinding, killing anger. Please don't let me go back down that path.

Last night Marybeth had sorted out exactly how much she wanted to reveal to Rand. If he took her family history well, maybe he would understand when she told him she'd never wanted to marry and still didn't. Even if he didn't understand, she still had her job and could still save enough money to continue her search for Jimmy. The thought didn't please her as much as she'd hoped, but it was all she had. Forcing a sunny tone, she began.

"Back in Ireland, my father was a farmer, so I wasn't surprised to see how much work goes into ranching. Unlike you, Da hated working the land and raising sheep, probably because he wasn't very successful at it." She sighed, unable to maintain her false cheer. "So he sold the farm and brought us over here to Boston. Because he didn't have training in any other work, he had to take menial jobs. Mam worked as a housemaid, and Jimmy learned his way around the city at six years old so he could be a messenger boy. We rented a house in a poor neighborhood where a lot of other Irish folk live."

There. Now Rand knew her family had been poor. Yet his intense gaze held only interest, no censure. Encouraged, she went on to the worse details.

"Da had a couple of bad habits, which didn't do anything to help." She inhaled to gain courage to say words she'd never spoken to another living soul. "He drank and he gambled."

Rand winced slightly, maybe remembering his own gambling days. She hadn't meant to hurt him, so she hurried on.

"He was always trying to get money the easy way. I'm not sure, but I think he may have worked for some dishonest men. No matter whom he worked for, when he got paid, he would lose the money in a card game or buy whiskey until the money was all gone." She forced herself to say the next words, the very worst she could tell him about her childhood. "Drunk or sober, he beat all of us. He also took Mam's and Jimmy's earnings, even sold the furniture until there wasn't a stick that still belonged to us just so he could gamble." She'd intended to keep aloof from her sad tale, but she ended on a sob.

Rand set his hand on her back, right smack in the center where it felt so good, so comforting. "You don't have to go on."

Sniffing, she retrieved a handkerchief from her reticule and dabbed away tears. "Let me finish." At his nod, she braced herself with another deep breath.

"Do you remember when I told you Jimmy and I worked hard to get rid of our Irish brogue? We wanted to move up, to become respectable, so we could get better jobs. We decided to attend church and listen to the minister and try to talk like him." She grinned at the memory. "It was sort of a competition, and I think I did a little better than Jimmy. He always said it wore him out, made him have to think too hard. But really, he was pretty good at imitation." Rand was probably getting tired of the story, so she decided to cut it short.

"Anyway, after Da beat Jimmy one too many times, he left home to come out here. Mam died four years ago, and Da lasted until about three years ago when the whiskey finally took him. I found a job and kept going to church. I loved learning about God's fatherly love, because I sure hadn't received any from my da." She shook her head, determined not to dwell on that subject.

"The church ladies were very kind and two years ago offered to send me to Fairfield Young Ladies' Academy where I could learn proper manners and, if I wanted to, secretarial skills. When your parents brought Rosamond to the academy last January, she and I became friends, and for some peculiar reason, all three of them seemed to think you and I would suit each other. I can't imagine why." She bit her bottom lip before finishing. "I may have learned proper manners and got rid of my brogue, but that still doesn't change my rough upbringing, my family's poverty. It's a part of who I am and who I'll always be."

She gazed up at him to gauge his reaction, especially her last comment. Even through her tears, she could see compassion and kindness and maybe even a hint of affection in those green eyes.

He grasped her hand and gently squeezed it. "I disagree with you. You've worked hard to overcome a dif-

ficult upbringing. You've got spirit and a healthy dose
of ambition." He shoved his hat back, leaned toward her
and touched his forehead to hers in an endearing gesture
that brought more tears to her eyes. "Overcoming hard-
ship is the American way, so don't apologize for things
that aren't your fault. You don't have anything to be
ashamed of. Stand tall." He pulled back and gave her a
teasing grin. "At least as tall as a little gal like you can."

She choked out a laugh and a sob at the same time.
This wasn't at all what she'd expected. Why hadn't she
trusted him sooner? Maybe she could finish it all right
now and see what came of telling him the complete
truth. Before she could speak, he stood and tugged her
to her feet.

"Come on. Stand tall and be proud of all you've accomplished. There are so many paths you could have
taken, but you chose a life of faith and following the
Lord. My parents saw and admired that in you."

"So you don't think they'll ever regret arranging—"
She couldn't bring herself to refer to their proposed
marriage. "For me to come out here? I mean, once they
learn the truth about my background?"

Rand gave her another one of those teasing grins that
tickled her insides. "My father was a Union officer, and
he knew every detail about the men who served under
him. Not only that, but he grew up in Boston. I have no
doubt he knew much more about you than you think."

Horror gripped her, but only briefly. She'd often
been hungry, had even been forced to sleep in an alley
sometimes, but she'd never fallen into such despair as
to demean herself to survive. Early on, she'd seen what
happened to such girls. Colonel Northam could ask anyone who'd known her and learn of her spotless reputa-

tion. In fact, as Rand said, he probably had. The thought both reassured and unnerved her at the same time.

"Hello, Rand." Mrs. Foster emerged from the house wiping her hands on a tea towel. "Will you stay for supper?"

"No, thank you, ma'am. I need to get back to the ranch." He brushed a kiss over Marybeth's cheek. "And I need to speak to the reverend on my way out of town. Why don't I deliver his supper to him?"

Disappointed to see their conversation end, Marybeth had no choice but to let him go. The rest of her story would have to wait for another day. Maybe. She'd never spoken so honestly with anyone before, and she wasn't sure she'd have the courage to take that last step of truthfulness and confess she'd never really planned to marry Rand. It was one piece of information Colonel Northam wouldn't have found out because she'd never told anyone. What would the Northams think of her then? What would Rand think of her?

After washing the supper dishes and cleaning up the kitchen, Marybeth sat at Mrs. Foster's piano and practiced a few of her favorite hymns. She also tried some new ones. Her landlady sat nearby in an overstuffed chair, busy with her knitting. On the top of the piano, Pepper, the black-and-white cat, lounged indifferently, his eyes occasionally straying in Polly's direction. From her spot on the floor by Mrs. Foster, Polly also eyed the cat. The moment the puppy had entered the house, she'd made it clear she expected to be in charge. Pepper, being a rather docile feline, had objected to the idea only briefly before realizing his ability to climb out of reach made him impervious to Polly's aggression. Marybeth thought for certain she saw a smirk on the cat's face.

After only a week and a few days of living here, she'd come to love this homey scene each evening. With the added amusement of the animals, she thought she could live this way forever. That was, after she found Jimmy. Of course she wouldn't mind visits from Rand, and the more the better. But she wouldn't keep him from courting other girls once she told him of her determination to remain unattached. The thought caused a stew in her stomach that had nothing to do with Mrs. Foster's fine cooking.

She turned the pages of the hymnal and found a song she didn't know so she could practice her sight reading. Before her fingers touched the keys, a knock sounded on the front door.

"I'll go." If it was Mr. Hardison, she'd simply have to tell him she would prefer not to receive him. If he truly was a gentleman, he would accept her decision.

Through the etched-glass window in the door, she made out the figure of Mr. Means. Even though the porch was deeply shadowed, Marybeth could see a bouquet of red roses in one hand, his hat in the other, and her heart sank. She had to let him in. How could she refuse to see him and still keep her job? Opening the door, she pasted on her most professional smile, though this clearly was not a business call.

"Good evening, Mr. Means. What a surprise." She stood back so he could enter. "Do come in."

"Thank you, Miss O'Brien." As he had earlier, he seemed a bit awkward, almost charmingly so. How could a wealthy, nice-looking young man be so unsure of himself? "I hope you will not mind my calling at this hour, but my gardener just cut these roses, and I thought of you."

"Oh, how nice. But you shouldn't have." Really, really shouldn't have. He knew she'd come to Esperanza as Rand's supposed bride. Had he seen her reticence to set a date and decided to court her himself?

Polly ambled over and sniffed Mr. Means's shoes and pant legs, causing Marybeth no end of concern. But the gentleman reached down and let her sniff his hand.

"Hey, there, little boy. What a fine little fellow you are." He ruffled her fur and patted her head.

Unfazed by his mistake regarding her gender, Polly licked his hand.

"Please join us in the parlor." Marybeth waved a hand in that direction. "I'll get us some tea. Or coffee, if you prefer."

"Tea, please." He hung his hat on the hall tree and followed her into the room.

Mrs. Foster bustled over to greet him, even as she questioned Marybeth with a look. "I'll get a vase and the tea. You youngsters sit down." She took the roses and disappeared through the dining room door.

Marybeth chose a chair rather than the settee, and Polly settled on the floor beside her. "It was very thoughtful of you to bring the roses. Their fragrance will fill the house."

"Yes, it will." He tugged at his collar and glanced around the room as if looking for something to talk about. "When did you get the dog?"

"Rand gave her to me yesterday."

"Rand. Of course. And it is a female. My mistake." He smiled at Polly and said no more.

Marybeth knew it was her place to keep the conversation going, but what on earth should she say to him? Mrs. Foster rescued them both by coming back with the tea tray.

"Now, dear," she said to Marybeth, "while you pour, I'll put the roses in a vase."

After she returned and placed the filled vase on the coffee table, she managed to coax some conversation from Mr. Means by telling him of Anna's improvement on the piano in her last lesson.

"Thank you." He shrugged in a self-conscious way. "We all know how important such accomplishments are for a young lady if she is ever to fit into society and make a suitable marriage. It is difficult enough to rear my sister out here in the West when the only examples she has are cowgirls such as the Eberly sisters." He grimaced as he glanced at Marybeth and Mrs. Foster, almost as though he expected them to voice their agreement to his obvious distaste. When they remained silent, he went on. "So of course when you arrived, Miss O'Brien, I saw immediately hope for Anna. Would I be too forward if I asked you to give her lessons in deportment? I shall pay you, of course, beyond what you earn at the bank."

"I, well…" Marybeth almost bit her tongue to keep from rejecting his request out of hand. No, indeed. This was entirely fortuitous. More pay meant her trip to Wagon Wheel Gap would happen sooner than she ever could have dreamed. And if this was the only reason for Mr. Means's visit tonight, his only reason for asking her to dinner earlier in the day, she had nothing to worry about. "I'd be delighted, sir. When would you like for me to begin?"

"I would be honored if you would come to our house

for supper Saturday evening so you and Anna can get better acquainted." His broad smile and warm gaze seemed a tiny bit more familiar than before, though not inappropriately so.

"Of course. I would like that."

Only after she saw him out the door did she recall her plans to go on a Saturday picnic with Rand. Now what was she supposed to do?

Gripping a picnic basket in one hand, Rand held Marybeth's hand with the other as they inched across a fallen log over Cat Creek. The day couldn't be more beautiful. Except for a few little white clouds over the San Juan range, the sun shone with its usual brilliance, and just the right amount of breeze kept everybody cool. Of course it never got too hot here in the foothills, so he hoped she would be comfortable. At least physically comfortable.

She hadn't seemed relaxed with him since last Monday evening, even though he'd done his best to show her that a background in poverty was nothing to be ashamed of. Yet for the rest of the week when he walked her home, she'd been fidgety and didn't ask him to stay and chat. When he asked if Hardison had bothered her again, she assured him she hadn't seen the man other than when he came into the bank to speak to Mr. Means.

Not that he'd been too worried about the gunslinger. Reverend Thomas had promised to keep an eye on Marybeth as she walked to work in the mornings and during her dinner break travels. For a man of God, the preacher was no sissy, so that set Rand's mind at ease.

Once they'd crossed the creek, Rand glanced back to be sure the rest of their party made it across. Tolley, three of the Eberly sisters and Reverend Thomas each took a turn balancing on the makeshift bridge without any problems. Maybe the preacher could figure out whether Rand was doing anything to annoy Marybeth, because he sure couldn't figure it out himself.

"What a beautiful view." A bit breathless, Marybeth gazed out across the San Luis Valley.

"You doing all right?" Rand set down the basket and studied her face.

"Very well, thank you." She inhaled deeply. "I'm still getting used to the altitude. I never understood what people meant when they said mountain air is thin. Now I know."

"Well, you just sit down." Rand hurried to lay out the blanket Beryl had brought. "We'll pass out the fixings." Maybe all this week she'd been reacting to the air, not to him. She'd just needed her rest after working all day.

"Do let me help." She resisted his attempt to seat her.

"Let her help, Rand." Grace, the second oldest of the Eberly sisters, set down her own basket. "She'll be fine. A little work never hurt anybody."

If anyone would know, it was these sisters, who'd done men's work all of their young lives. "All right, then."

"Say, when do we eat?" Tolley, always hungry, eyed the baskets with interest.

"Just hold your horses, cowboy." Laurie had carried three leather rifle sheaths from the buckboard. "Let's have our shooting competition first." She set the sheaths on a large flat rock, unsnapped them and pulled out the firearms. "Who's first?"

Rand had forgotten all about this part of their plans. He shot a quick look at Marybeth and was relieved to see the interest in her eyes. While the others decided the order in which they'd shoot, she sidled up to him, and his pulse kicked into a gallop.

"I'd like to learn how to shoot." She blinked those pretty hazel eyes at him, and he found his own breathing a bit difficult.

"Since when, Miss City Gal?" He somehow managed to inject a note of teasing into the question.

"Since two weeks ago when we had an encounter with a rattlesnake." She answered in the same tone, which tickled him to no end.

While the Eberly sisters sent approving looks her way, Rand and the other men laughed. They quit laughing when she pulled a Remington double-barreled Derringer from her reticule.

"I bought this yesterday. Will you show me how to use it?"

"Yes, ma'am. I'd be happy to." Pride swelled in his chest over Marybeth's determination to fit into Western life. She'd make a mighty fine helpmeet if he could just win her heart. Of course he'd feel a little better about it if she'd sought his help in choosing the pocket pistol, but he'd have to let that pass. She was pretty independent and he didn't want to discourage that quality in her.

Using pinecones, rocks and empty tin cans they'd brought along, the party spent the next hour or so in competition. At the end of it all, Grace and Rand tied, with not a single miss, no matter what they shot at. Marybeth didn't join their contest, but Rand was pleased that she did learn to keep her eye on the target and not flinch when she pulled the trigger of her tiny firearm.

Later as they finished off their picnic with rhubarb pie smothered in fresh cream, Rand pondered how to keep the party going. With Marybeth looking to him for her shooting lessons, maybe he could teach her his favorite game for winter evenings.

"How about we head back to the ranch and play checkers? We can have supper there."

For some reason, Marybeth gave a little start and bit her lower lip. Before he could ask why, Beryl piped up.

"Aw, you just want to show off, Rand. Everybody knows you can even beat the Colonel at checkers."

"I'd sure like to come, Rand," the preacher said, "but I still have a few things to do in preparation for church tomorrow."

"Sorry, Rand," said Grace. "We have chores to do. Maybe another time."

At that, Marybeth sighed with obvious relief.

Which gave Rand something more to ponder. Was she getting tired of his company? Or did she have other plans? Neither idea made him the least bit happy.

Marybeth had never faced such a dilemma. After a pleasant Saturday evening with Mr. Means and Anna, she felt obligated to sit with them in church the next morning. Yet while she and Rand passed out the hymnals, guilt caused a dull ache in her chest. She should tell him about the previous evening, but the words wouldn't come. Now, if her employer invited her to join him and his sister, what would Rand think? Would he still help her find Jimmy, or would he decide she was fickle and have no more to do with her? Above all, she didn't want the two men to see each other as rivals for her interest when she was trying very hard not to care too much for Rand.

As if she could see Marybeth's predicament, Susanna came to her rescue, just as she had last Sunday with Mr. Hardison. Accompanied by Lizzy, who flung herself into Marybeth's arms and insisted upon being picked up, Susanna put a hand on her waist and directed her to the pew near the front where Rand and his brothers were seated.

"You must come out to the ranch for dinner again today," Susanna whispered just as Reverend Thomas stood to speak.

With the entire service to decide how to answer, Marybeth settled on the excuse that Mrs. Foster could not do without her. In truth, the older lady had decided to make two more bedrooms available for boarders. With Marybeth gone the day before, this Sunday afternoon was the only time she could help her landlady. She would wait to tell Rand her Saturdays would also be taken from now on, for that was when Anna would have her lessons in deportment.

After the service ended Rand and Tolley hovered around her like mother birds, undoubtedly to keep Mr. Hardison away. They needn't have worried. The well-dressed businessman stood just beyond the churchyard chatting with Lucy from the diner. Marybeth found the pairing rather odd due to his well-spoken ways and Lucy's less-than-ladylike flirting. Surely there was no accounting for tastes.

When Marybeth told Rand about her plans for the day, he couldn't hide his disappointment. While it was admirable for her to help Mrs. Foster, he renewed his suspicion that she was hiding something. On the other hand, even if she was, he had a secret of his own, and fair was fair.

After the cattle came down from summer grazing and the steers taken to market, he and Tolley planned to head up to Wagon Wheel Gap to look for Jimmy O'Brien. If the weather turned bad and snow kept them from traveling over the mountain trails, they'd go first thing come spring. He understood Marybeth's eagerness to search for her brother, but Colorado weather could turn deadly in a very short time, killing horses and men. With all the dangers they'd face, he just couldn't let her go with them. She hadn't seen Jimmy in eight years, so a few more months shouldn't make that much difference.

He could just picture the way her sweet face would light up when she saw her brother again, and he sure did want to be the one who arranged that reunion. Then maybe she'd tell him all of her secrets. Then maybe she'd decide marrying him wasn't such a bad idea.

Waiting for spring would take a lot of patience, a trait to which he couldn't lay much claim. The last time he got impatient about his lot in life, he'd ended up killing a man. This time he wouldn't force the issue. But he would pray like crazy for the snow to hold off so he could bring Jimmy home to Marybeth before Christmas.

Chapter Ten

As she'd hoped, Mrs. Foster gained three additional boarders. Homer Bean, the new clerk from Mrs. Winsted's general store, took one room while he saved money to bring his wife and children from Missouri. In the other room resided the Chases, an elderly couple whose house up by Rock Creek had burned down. They needed a place to stay until their sons built a new one. None of the three could be expected to help with the household chores, so Marybeth and Mrs. Foster had extra cooking and cleaning.

After work each day Marybeth hurried home to help with supper, cutting short her time with Rand. Despite their usual banter, plus an occasional bit of jolly singing, not once did she feel as close to him as she had that Monday evening in August. With him being busy on the ranch and her being busy on Saturdays with Anna, their only other times together were Sunday mornings when they passed out hymnals. Marybeth missed him, missed being with his family, but with some effort, she was able to subdue such feelings by thinking of her quest to find Jimmy.

Due to Mr. Means's generosity, Marybeth's bank account had grown faster than she'd ever dreamed. By late September she had almost enough money to make the stagecoach trip to Wagon Wheel Gap. So far, she hadn't found the courage to tell Rand of her travel plans. From his comments about the volume of ranch work done in the autumn, she knew he wouldn't be able to go with her until after October. By then the stagecoach might not be running due to bad weather and deep snow. But she couldn't wait until spring, not when Jimmy might be so close.

Somehow she must summon the right words to tell Rand about her plans. While she was at it, she should probably tell him of her plans not to marry. Earning her own living had given her a self-confidence she'd never before experienced. How could she hand over the control of her life to a husband who would have the legal right to take her earnings, tell her what to do and even beat her if he felt the urge?

She reminded herself Rand wasn't like that, wasn't at all like Da. He never tried to tell her what to do. He never displayed a violent temper or threatened her. But after being married for any length of time, what husband wouldn't take charge? She doubted even Rand would let her continue to work, to have her own money with no one to answer to about how she spent it. No, marriage just wouldn't work for her. And she had one idea of how to show Rand she wouldn't make a good wife for a rancher.

With the church's annual Harvest Home only a few days away, she picked the last of the tart green apples growing on Mrs. Foster's tree. She made a pie with not enough sugar and a bottom crust so thick it would

remain undercooked. She left the cinnamon out altogether. This would be her entry in the pie contest. Next,
she would nominate Rand to be one of the judges. With
all of his compliments to other ladies about their cooking, he'd made it clear he considered this an important
issue. Once he tasted her entry, he'd think twice about
wanting to marry her.

Fork in one hand, pencil and paper in the other, Rand
stood in line with the two other judges as they moved
down the table tasting each of the nine pies and writing
down a score. Whoever nominated him to judge had
no idea how much he disliked the idea of comparing
one lady's cooking to someone else's. As a bachelor, he
didn't want to hurt anybody's feelings, especially when
each of the ladies had fed him at one time or another.
Reverend Thomas seemed to have no such concerns.
He enthusiastically moved from pie to pie, acting as
though each one was the best he'd ever tasted before
he wrote down a score.

Only one good thing might come out of the situation for Rand. The judges weren't supposed to know
who baked each pie, but Marybeth had hinted that hers
might just be resting on a blue-striped tea towel. He
knew Mrs. Foster was a bit jealous of her kitchen, so
Marybeth had been relegated to helping the older lady
and hadn't had much chance to practice her own skills.
Today he'd finally taste something she made. It would
be a challenge to judge it impartially because he was
sure she'd earn a perfect score.

Or so he thought. The instant he put a big forkful of
the tart, undercooked apples and greasy, congealed crust
into his mouth, he wondered how he'd even manage to

swallow it. How had the preacher done it? Or Bert the blacksmith, the third judge? Yet both men had moved on to the next entry without any reaction.

Rand's eyes began to water as he chewed. Forcing the bite down his throat, he took a gulp of water from one of the cups the committee had provided for each judge to sip between entries. He blinked, and there before him stood Marybeth, a sweet, expectant smile on her pretty face. He answered with a nod and a shaky grin before writing down her score, a two on a scale of one to ten. Even that was generous.

Fortunately the next pie flooded his mouth with flavor, erasing the sour taste. He recognized Miss Pam's handiwork in the flaky crust, perfectly done apples, spicy cinnamon and just the right amount of sugar. He'd had her pies often enough to know she rated a score of ten on just about everything she cooked.

He couldn't fault Marybeth for her lack of cooking skills. She'd probably never had the opportunity to learn. Once they married, if they married, Susanna and Rita would teach her everything she needed to know.

Marybeth could hardly keep from laughing at poor Rand's expression as he bit into her pie. While the preacher and the blacksmith had taken small bites, probably saving room for the feast they would enjoy later in the day, Rand had forked up a huge mouthful. When he gave her a smile, weak as it was, guilt pinched her conscience. It was a mean trick to pull on him. On all of the judges. But if it accomplished her purpose, so be it.

Now that the judges had tasted all of the entries, other folks crowded around to finish off the pies, and Marybeth hurried to remove hers from the table. Unfortunately, Mr. Means reached for the pie tin just as she did.

"A little bird told me you baked this one." He served himself a large portion and took up his fork.

"Wait." How on earth would she stop him?

"Are you concerned I will ruin my dinner?" He chuckled. "We have two hours before it will be served." With that, he took a bite. His eyes widened and he grimaced. After swallowing, he chuckled again. "Well, Miss O'Brien, I admire you for entering the competition. My hope for Anna…and for you…is that you will always have someone to cook for you, as every well-bred lady should."

Such a charming, albeit two-edged comment. "Thank you, sir. I'll admit it would be a nice way to live." With that, she whisked the pie away and dumped it into a pail where all leftovers not fit for people were collected for pig food.

Rand promised himself he'd never judge another food contest again. Now how was he going to face Marybeth? Of course no one knew exactly what score each judge placed on each pie, only who won the first three places once the scores were tallied. The blue ribbon went to Miss Pam, with red going to Rita's mother, Angela. Mrs. Winsted took home the yellow and seemed more than pleased to receive it. But when Rand happened to see Marybeth's pie in the pigs' slop bucket, his heart ached for her, and he found a stick to stir the slimy mess until it was unrecognizable.

After a horserace, which Tolley easily won with his reckless riding, and a potato sack race, which the Barley twins won, dinner was served under the cottonwoods surrounding the church. Once Reverend Thomas said grace, Rand looked around for Marybeth and nearly bumped into her coming around the corner of the building.

"There you are." She gave him a sweet smile and nodded toward the folks lining up at the long makeshift tables where the food had been laid out. "Shall we join the crowd?"

His heart hitched up a notch at her use of "we" with its implication that she took for granted they'd eat together. So she wasn't avoiding him, something he'd worried about since she'd started spending her Saturdays with Anna Means. "Sure thing."

As they filled their plates, he considered whether or not to bring up the pie competition, at last deciding he should, but carefully. "I'm sorry your pie lost out to Miss Pam's. Year after year, nobody can beat her."

Instead of being upset, as some other contestants had been, she giggled in her cute way. "I always won the typewriting contests at the academy. I don't need to win everything."

All the tension Rand had felt for the past two hours dissolved. "Well, I can tell you another thing you've won."

They settled down on a blanket spread on the grassy lawn. "What's that?" The sweet look in her eyes gave him hope that today they could restore the closeness they'd enjoyed weeks ago.

"My—" He couldn't say she'd won his heart. It was too soon to say he loved her, especially when he still thought she was hiding something. "My utmost admiration, that's what."

"You're very kind, Rand." For some reason she grew

pensive, staring down at her plate and stirring her food yet not eating. She inhaled a deep breath and blew it out. "I have something to tell you."

Her tone warned him this would be bad news, and his heart hitched in a completely different way. "Go on."

"I've been saving my money, and I'll have enough to go to Wagon Wheel Gap by the middle of October."

Rand gaped at her. Nothing could have surprised him more. "You don't mean you're going by yourself." He could hear the harshness in his own voice but couldn't rein it in. "And you already know I can't go with you until after we've taken the cattle to market."

"Yes, I do mean I'm going by myself."

Rand's appetite vanished and he set down his plate as anger took over. "How do I know you'll come back?" He hadn't meant to blurt that out, and regret immediately filled him, especially when she leaned away from him with a gasp.

"Why would you ask that?" Her eyes widened as if she was afraid, and he wanted to kick himself. "Of course I'll come back after I find Jimmy or find out what happened to him."

He believed her, but he still couldn't let her go. "Wagon Wheel Gap isn't a safe place for decent ladies, especially traveling alone."

She huffed out a sigh of impatience. "I traveled all the way across the country by myself. Decent people always look out for young ladies traveling alone."

Rand also sighed. Deciding on a ploy he'd hoped never to use, he glared at her. "All right, you can go. That is, after you pay my family back for your train fare from Boston."

Tears flooded her eyes and spilled down her cheeks,

and his heart ached for her. But he couldn't, mustn't, relent. Her expression hardened and then grew haughty. "Very well, Mr. Northam. I will repay you. Of course that means I won't have enough money to search for my brother right away, but you knew that."

She jumped to her feet. "I have no idea why you're being so unreasonable when I'm so close to having my dream come true. I thought you understood what finding Jimmy means to me. But since you don't and since you won't help me, I believe this sets a pattern for any woman who marries you." She huffed out a breath, stared off for a moment and then bent over him with her hands fisted at her waist. "Please do me the favor of not forcing your company on me again. Do not come to the bank to walk me home. Do not meet me at the church to pass out hymnals. Do not—"

"All right then." He stood, towering over her in a posture mimicking hers. "I'll leave you alone just as soon as you repay that train fare."

"Oh!" She stomped her foot. "You're being so unreasonable." She started to turn away, but he took hold of her arm. Finally after all this time, he figured out what her secret was, just as he'd suspected from the first.

"You never did plan to marry me, did you?"

Eyes filled with guilt and defiance were the only answer she gave him. He released her and she spun around and stalked away.

With every step she took away from him, Rand's heart shattered just a little more. He'd tried to protect her, but he'd said all the wrong things. Worst of all, at last he knew for certain what she'd been hiding all this time. Now he just had to figure out what else she'd kept from him and from the good people of Esperanza.

* * *

Marybeth knew she should stay and help the other ladies clean up after dinner, but she couldn't bear to run into Susanna and Lizzy or any other member of the Northam family. Once Rand told them about their conversation, they all would turn against her, just as he had. Nor had Marybeth missed the smirk on Lucy's face. The waitress had been sitting several yards away and obviously had heard the argument. Well, now she could flirt with Rand all she wanted, even though she was supposed to be sweethearts with Rand's friend Seamus. Or maybe Mr. Hardison was her beau now. Marybeth never bothered to keep up with gossip.

She found Mrs. Foster and told her landlady she wasn't feeling well, which wasn't a lie. As never before in her life, she was truly heartsick over ending her friendship with Rand. The three-block walk home seemed to take forever. With each step, the truth about how wrong her deception had been hammered deeper into her soul. Yet Rand wasn't without his faults. He might not be brutal like Da, but he was just as controlling. She would never be able to live with that. They were better off without each other.

At least he followed her order not to come early for church the next day. While Mrs. Foster practiced her hymns on the pump organ, Marybeth dusted the hymnals and placed them in the pews. Even though she knew her actions helped out, it wasn't as enjoyable as when she and Rand raced to finish first, each placing the books just so in each row as part of their merry competition.

The sanctuary began to fill and she saw him approaching through the front door. Before panic could set in, she saw Anna and Mr. Means move into a pew and asked if she could sit with them. Both seemed pleased with the arrangement. On the other hand, Rand's scowl, Susanna's concerned gaze and Lizzy's confusion were hard to ignore. Nor was she helped in the slightest by Reverend Thomas's sermon on the thirteenth chapter of First Corinthians. Love might suffer long and be kind, but look at what that kind of love had gotten Mam. A life of misery.

After church Marybeth declined her employer's invitation to Sunday dinner, explaining she needed to help Mrs. Foster. Although that was true, her aching head and heart were the real reasons she had no wish to spend the day with anyone except Rand. She told herself she'd simply grown used to him, even fond of him because of his kindnesses. Yet another thought would not let her be. Was it possible she loved him? She'd never been in love, never even dreamed of it because of her parents. Mam's unshakeable love for Da had kept her imprisoned in an unhappy marriage, something Marybeth vowed she'd never accept for her own life.

Another voice whispered to her that Susanna and Nate appeared happy, even blissful, after three years. Mrs. Foster often reminisced about her late husband's tender devotion to her, and her tear-filled eyes made it clear she still grieved for him. Maisie and Doc Henshaw, as different as two people could be in personality and upbringing, seemed wildly happy. Pam and Charlie Williams were like comfortable old shoes together, both wearing age lines that turned up in constant smiles. Was it possible Marybeth and Rand could find that same sort of happiness?

No, she just couldn't take the risk. Until she found

Jimmy, she would not place herself under the authority of someone as bossy as Rand Northam. Maybe not even then.

Despite all of her internal arguments against caring for him, she still felt the sting of disappointment when he wasn't waiting for her after work the next day. Annoyed with her own obvious contradiction, she stalked off down the boardwalk, the heels of her high-top shoes thumping against the wood in a most unladylike sound.

She stepped down onto the dusty street and came near to colliding with Mr. Hardison, who seemed to appear from nowhere.

"Say, young lady." He laughed softly as he gripped her arms and steadied her. "You and I keep bumping into each other."

"I'm so sorry, Mr. Hardison. I wasn't paying attention." She pulled free from his light grasp and continued her trek home.

He fell in beside her. "Where's Mr. Northam today?"

From his tone, one would think they were old friends. Maybe the animosity was only on one side. Still she wouldn't discuss Rand with a man he disliked.

"Lovely day, isn't it?" She gave him a bright smile to soften the rebuke of not answering his question.

He laughed again. "I understand. Yes, it is a lovely day when I have the privilege of escorting a beautiful young lady home."

The very idea! Heat raced up her neck and she stopped to face him. "Is that what you're doing, sir? Because I don't recall your asking or my granting permission for such a privilege." She never should have let him walk her home those weeks ago, for he seemed to think that gave him the right to do so anytime.

Hand on his chest, he blinked, frowned and tilted his head in a charming, clearly abashed manner. "Do forgive me, Miss O'Brien. I didn't mean to be presumptuous." He exhaled a wounded sigh. "Surely you know I've been admiring you from afar. If Mr. Northam doesn't realize what a prize you are, he's making a serious mistake. Someone is going to steal you away from him."

Marybeth huffed out a sigh of her own. She was not some sort of prize to be given to the highest bidder or stolen from someone who owned her, but she wouldn't contradict him again. He wasn't a bad man. In fact, from all she'd heard at the bank and at church, he was beginning to fit into the Esperanza community. According to Mr. Means, he was making plans to build a hotel or some such business.

"Yes, of course I forgive you." She resumed her walk. "And, yes, you may escort me home. Today." She hoped he understood this was not to be a standing arrangement.

"I'm truly honored." After a few moments of walking in silence he said, "Forgive me, but I couldn't help overhearing your, eh, discussion with Mr. Northam on Saturday. Something about you wanting to go to Wagon Wheel Gap and find someone named Jimmy? Mr. Northam seemed very much against your plans."

Marybeth's head ached from a long day at work and not eating enough dinner. What did it matter if the whole town knew about her missing brother? Somewhere in the back of her mind, she wasn't sure she'd seen Mr. Hardison sitting near enough at the picnic to hear her argue with Rand. And if he had been, hadn't he heard her order Rand not to come see her again?

No matter. It would feel good to talk about Jimmy. She gave Mr. Hardison a shortened version of her reason for coming to Colorado to search for her brother, taking care not to say she'd never intended to marry Rand. In any event, for the past two days, that idea had begun to sit sour in her stomach. But again, maybe Mr. Hardison didn't hear the part of the conversation that included Rand's accusation.

"Why, my dear, you should have told me about your brother sooner." He beamed as if she'd given him a gift. "Why don't you let me help you make that trip? Why, I'd even escort you there. What would you think of that?"

Hope sprang up inside her so fast that she couldn't speak for several moments. In that brief time, serious reservations crept in. Apart from Rand's dislike of this man, she had her own responsibilities to think of. She must honor Rand's wish and pay him back and then save more money for the trip.

Even beyond that, she could see God's hand in delaying her trip. Just today Mr. Means had explained more about banking during harvest time. With crops and herds sold, more people would be making deposits, even investments. For those whose crops had failed, loans could be granted to see them through the winter. Her employer needed her, and if she deserted him after all of his generosity, her integrity would be in shreds. He'd never rehire her and never give her a recommendation. Like Rand, he would lose all faith in her. Worse than that, she would be just like Da, who'd never even tried to be responsible.

"Well, what do you say?" Mr. Hardison jolted her from her thoughts. "Shall we make that trip before the snows block the roads?"

She cast a demure look his way. "You're very kind to offer, but I can't leave now. Mrs. Foster and Mr. Means both depend upon me."

"Maybe it's time you looked out for yourself, my dear."

Confiding in this man had been a mistake, as were her kinder thoughts toward him. He'd addressed her twice as "my dear" in an almost suggestive way. This time it grated on her nerves. Before she could comment, Reverend Thomas strode toward them from a side street. To Marybeth's shock, he wore a gun strapped to his leg. Even on their picnic to the foothills, he'd been unarmed.

"Hello, folks. How are you two on this fine day?"

Mr. Hardison answered with little enthusiasm, but Marybeth felt nothing short of relief at seeing the preacher.

"I'm well, Reverend." She soon found herself walking between the two men as they neared her home. "Are you coming to discuss next Sunday's hymns with Mrs. Foster?" She could think of no other reason for him to continue accompanying them, but she hoped he'd see her into the house.

"Ah, you've made an excellent guess." He laughed in a nonchalant way. "Do you suppose if I stick around long enough, she'll invite me to dinner?"

"If she doesn't, I will." Marybeth glanced up at Mr. Hardison. "How about you? Have you met Mrs. Foster's new boarders, Mr. Bean and the Chases? We have the nicest discussions around the supper table. The Chases have some exciting stories about settling here in the Valley right after the war."

His responding smile was more of a grimace. "Thank

you, my dear, but I already have plans. Perhaps another time?"

"As you wish." If he called her "my dear" one more time she would correct him in no uncertain terms.

He left them at the front gate, but Marybeth didn't relax until they entered the house and closed the door. "Oh, my. You came along at just the right time."

"Uh-huh. I couldn't get away as soon as I'd planned, but it worked out just fine. The Lord's will is never late."

"You planned?" Her voice rose a few notches above normal, so she quickly added, "How very thoughtful."

This sounded very much like some sort of collusion with Rand. Was he now trying to control her life through other people? Instead of anger, a feeling of being protected warmed Marybeth's heart. She hadn't resisted the help and protection of the church ladies back home in Boston. Why should she object to the decent people of this community looking out for her? If not for her desperate need to find Jimmy, she could easily sit back and enjoy that protection, as long as no one tried to control her.

As for Reverend Thomas's planning to walk her home, how could she fail to appreciate it? With men like Mr. Hardison roaming this town, she would do well to encourage him. Nothing in his demeanor suggested anything other than pastoral concern.

Everyone in town must have heard about her falling-out with Rand. The next day, several unattached men lingered at her desk or at the teller's cage when she took Mr. Brandt's place on his dinner hour. At the end of the day, as she donned her straw hat and white gloves, Mr. Means exited his office and approached her desk.

"Miss O'Brien, I have been sitting in my office this

past hour trying to think of a reason, an excuse, actually, for asking you a rather impertinent question." He cleared his throat and tugged at his collar. "I could think of nothing other than my wish to continue in your company. Therefore, if you would not find it disagreeable, may I have the honor of seeing you home?"

Was this more of Rand's collusion? No, he wouldn't ask her employer to watch over her, not when he'd exhibited a bit of jealousy toward the man on more than one occasion. Marybeth had never received so much attention in her entire life. While it should be flattering, she only felt uncomfortable. But Mr. Means's company was certainly preferable to Mr. Hardison's.

"I would enjoy that very much, Mr. Means."

"Nolan. Please call me Nolan outside of banking hours."

His eyebrows arched as if he was seeking her agreement, which gave her no choice but to say, "Yes, of course, Nolan. And you must call me Marybeth."

As they walked, a cool autumn wind cut through her light shawl and threatened to blow off her straw hat, and grit sprayed over them, preventing conversation. Halfway home, they passed the preacher, who tipped his hat and kept walking in the other direction.

Appreciation and understanding swept through Marybeth, and the tears stinging her eyes had nothing to do with the sand blowing into them. God's servant, Reverend Thomas, was indeed keeping an eye on her, just like the angels mentioned in the book of Hebrews who ministered to Christians and kept them safe. When he didn't join Mr. Means and her in their walk toward Mrs. Foster's, she assumed he approved of Mr. Means... Nolan. Which was a good thing, wasn't it?

* * *

In late October, Rand watched as his drovers herded the last of the steers off the property and up the trail toward La Veta Pass. Maybe next year he and Nate could convince Dad to send the steers in boxcars to the Denver market so they'd be more likely to make it over the Pass before the first snows hit. They'd argued it was a much safer, easier mode of transport than driving the critters through the long, dangerous mountain passes. In previous years they'd lost too many steers, whose market value surpassed by a long shot the cost of sending the herd by train. But Dad held out for the old ways, still not entirely trusting trains for such a valuable cargo. So now the drovers faced countless nights sleeping on the cold ground and always having to watch out for wolves and grizzly bears on the lookout for an easy meal.

Their best cowhand, Seamus O'Reilly, told Rand and Nate he planned to stay in Denver for a while. Seems he'd come down from summer grazing to find Lucy sporting with another man, so he needed some time away to heal. He'd heard about a camp meeting to be held in the city by some preacher from back East, so after the cattle were delivered, he planned to herd the cowhands in that direction to keep them out of trouble. He promised to be back at the ranch by Christmas. After a summer in the mountains, he deserved the time off.

Rand understood how Seamus felt, but he hadn't wanted to burden his friend with his own woman troubles in the middle of sorting out the cattle. Nor did he tell him about Hardison. Knowing the Irishman, he'd want to take care of the gunslinger before he left town. As much as Rand needed to confide in someone, he figured he and his friend would have time to talk on the way to Denver. Being out under the stars had a way of making men open up to each other.

Rand had just begun to pack his gear when Nate announced he'd be taking the trip instead.

"Sorry, brother," Nate had said over dinner a few nights earlier. "I just got a letter from Dad today. I'm going to Denver. You stay here and see the church addition gets started."

After losing Marybeth, Rand had felt like he'd been kicked for a second time. Since that fatal card game three years ago, he'd been trying to live a perfect life, trying to do everything in his power to make his family proud of him. Did his father think he couldn't be trusted to get the money from the cattle sale safely home? Did Dad think he'd gamble it away, as he used to gamble away his own pay? Or maybe get into a gunfight in Denver, where countless cowboys would be congregating in the worst areas of town?

He wouldn't argue with Nate or try to usurp his authority, but watching that last steer being driven off the property without him sure did stick in his craw. His commiseration with Seamus would have to wait.

After his long morning of work, he ambled over to Williams's Café for some pie. Maybe Marybeth would be fetching coffee for that pompous banker. The last he'd heard from her, she'd sent Tolley home with a deposit slip and a cryptic note stating she had transferred the cost of her train fare into the Northam account. Nothing else. No mention of missing him or wanting to see him. Of course he didn't blame her. After his harsh accusation, why would she want anything to do with him?

That didn't stop his chest from aching every time he

saw her, especially when she was with Nolan, the man who walked her home every day, the man who sat next to her in church and who probably had her over to his fine house for dinner all the time. All the things Rand wanted to do. He couldn't even bring her flowers because none grew on the ranch in this cold weather. Yet Nolan's gardener managed to keep hothouse flowers on the pulpit most Sundays, so the banker probably gave some to Marybeth, too.

Reverend Thomas had told him about her uncomfortable encounter with Hardison back in September. Apparently the gunslinger had gotten the message she didn't want his company, but that still didn't mean she was entirely safe from him. On the other hand, now that Nolan was courting her—Rand couldn't think of it any other way—he doubted Hardison would make a move on her. Not when the gunslinger was so busy trying to convince the good people of Esperanza he was an upstanding businessman. He had some nefarious plans up his sleeve like the extra ace his cousin Cole used to cheat with, but Rand hadn't seen him do a single thing to indicate what those plans might be.

He hung his hat on a peg in the café and eyed the pies in the new glass pie safe sitting on the sideboard. Miss Pam sure was making her restaurant nice with such fancy touches. Settling in the back corner, he hoped no one would spot him and put to words the questions their faces asked every time he was in town. Everybody knew Marybeth had come out here to marry him. Now that she'd won all of their hearts, they probably wondered what terrible thing he'd done to lose her to Nolan.

"What'll it be, Rand?" Miss Pam greeted him with a sweet smile that held no such censure. "I just baked apple and peach pies this morning, and I still have a slice of elderberry left over from yesterday."

"Let me finish off that elderberry. I'll take home a slice of peach pie for Susanna."

"It's real nice of you to take care of her while Nate goes shopping for furniture." Miss Pam blinked, as if her own words surprised her. "Oh, dear. Now don't you go telling her what I said. Nate made me promise to keep it a secret."

As she hurried off to get his pie, Rand leaned back with a grin. So it wasn't a lack of trust in him that sent Nate to Denver in his place. Dad probably hadn't even sent a letter, at least not one concerning who was to deal with the cattle buyers. Nate would do a fine job, as always. Plus he and Susanna did need more furniture for when they moved back into their own house after Mother and Dad returned from Boston.

When Miss Pam brought the pie, he noticed extra whipped cream topped it, and he chuckled. "With that bribe, you can be sure I'll keep your secret." Not that he would ruin Nate's surprise. In fact, he'd do everything he could to keep his sweet sister-in-law occupied until Nate came home.

That evening over supper, he quizzed her about her Southern upbringing, her favorite recipes and several other subjects on which he already knew her thoughts. While he searched his mind to come up with something else, Susanna laughed in her musical way.

"Rand, you can quit beating around the chokecherry bush. If you want my advice on how to win Marybeth's heart, just ask me."

"Hold on." Tolley scooted his chair back and picked up his dishes. "If you're going to talk about mushy stuff, that's my cue to go do evening chores." He shuddered comically and made his way toward the kitchen.

Susanna laughed again. "One day that boy's going to discover girls, then Katie bar the door." She leveled a gaze on Rand that was decidedly maternal, although he was a year older than she. "Now let's talk about you, brother dear. We've all been busy with harvest and getting the cows off to sell, but don't think I've failed to notice you're not courting anymore."

Rand looked down at his empty plate, over Susanna's head and then at the kitchen door Tolley had just exited. "After three years of being in this family, you should know it's not the cows we sell, but the steers."

"Don't change the subject." Susanna pasted on what seemed like an attempt to look stern, but her sweet face just looked prettier. Nate was one blessed man to have her. "What happened between you and Marybeth?"

The warm concern in her voice soothed something deep inside him. Maybe he didn't need Seamus, after all.

He told her the whole story, including his early suspicions about Marybeth and how, when they'd argued, she hadn't denied his accusation of never planning to marry him.

"Trouble is, now that she's told me she doesn't want to see me anymore, I realize how much better I could have handled the situation. And I don't have any way to fix what I broke."

"So you do want to fix it?"

He choked out a mirthless laugh. "Sure do. This is killing me."

"Well, sometimes love feels that way."

"Love?" He shook his head. Then nodded. "I guess I

do love her. We have some things to work out, but after sorting through it all these past few weeks, I don't see why we can't."

"Neither do I. That girl's only fooling herself if she claims not to love you. You just have to get together and talk about it." Susanna's blue eyes twinkled like they did when she had a surprise for Lizzy. "Now pay attention. Two weeks from this Saturday, we're holding the meeting about the church addition. The ladies are going to make it a box social to raise money. With crops in and cows—*cattle*—sold, we're hoping everyone will feel generous and make big contributions."

Rand scratched his chin. "Sis, did you just change the subject, or does this somehow pertain to Marybeth and me?"

"Silly boy, of course it pertains to the two of you. You can buy Marybeth's box, and she'll be required to sit with you. It's the perfect opportunity for you to apologize and get all of this nonsense straightened out."

"Right. Apologize." Rand took a deep gulp from his coffee cup. Did he care enough about Marybeth to eat her awful cooking? The question had no more formed in his mind than his heart leaped up and slapped him broadside on the head. Of course he could, along with the crow he'd need to eat as he apologized.

After the sting of realizing she'd never planned to marry him had worn off, he'd admitted to himself she had plenty of reasons to remain single. If he could just tell her how much he admired her for her loyalty to her brother, how much he'd like to build a loving family like his in which that sort of familial love made everyone feel secure and appreciated, maybe he could change her mind.

But only if he won her basket. Bidding against the banker, who could afford to employ four servants, a gardener and a groom for his horses might cost Rand his entire share of the income from this year's cattle sale. Could he do that and still look Dad in the eye and claim to be reformed and responsible? What if his parents found out about how she'd deceived them and decided she wasn't worthy to be a member of the family?

It was a chance he'd just have to take.

Chapter Eleven

He lost! Just when he thought his eight-dollar bid would win Marybeth's box, Nolan jumped to the new ten-dollar limit set by the committee this year. They'd cited last year's sad event when one love-struck cowboy sold his saddle to buy his girl's box, only to have her marry someone else the following week. Nobody could say the people of Esperanza were insensitive to the limited funds of cowhands…or to their broken hearts.

To hide his disappointment, Rand tipped his hat to the banker. It wouldn't do for a Northam to show poor sportsmanship. Then, waiting to bid on the next box, he hunched down in his thick woolen coat to ward off the cold November wind blowing through the churchyard.

They could have held the proceedings in the sanctuary, but some folks thought that would be as irreverent as the moneychangers whom Jesus threw out of the temple in Jerusalem. Even though the fund-raiser was for the church, out of respect for those views, Reverend Thomas said they'd set up the tables outside on the brown lawn. But these folks were a hardy lot, used to Colorado winters, so there were few complaints.

The four unattached Eberly girls had each prepared dinners sure to hold some mighty fine cooking, so he'd bid on Grace's box. As nice-looking as her sisters, she'd grown tall and awkward and had no beau, so he'd do the neighborly thing and have dinner with her. But the preacher beat him to it, so Rand moved on to the next sister. Beryl's and Laurie's boxes were also snatched up by eager bidders. Rand ended up with twelve-year-old Georgia, named for her father when it became apparent no son would be born to George and Mabel.

So much for Susanna's plan for him to make up with Marybeth. Instead he was stuck with a child who was more interested in talking to another girl than to him. So he ate by himself and stared across the churchyard at Marybeth and Nolan chatting up a storm. Didn't those two talk to each other enough at work?

He wanted to think this was all a part of God's plan. Maybe the Lord didn't intend for him to win Marybeth's heart. After killing a man, maybe he wasn't fit to have a sweet, pretty wife. But if she married Nolan, it would be mighty hard for Rand to stay in the same community and watch her have a happy family life with someone else.

When Rand had actually bid on her box, Marybeth's heart had skipped with hope, and she'd prayed he would win it. She'd missed him so much and longed for a chance to beg his forgiveness for taking advantage of his family. But after their bitter parting at the Harvest Home, she'd assumed he'd never want to see her again. He certainly hadn't tried to, had certainly minded her orders to stay away. Maybe his attempt to win her box was a sort of peace offering, one she gladly would have accepted.

Nolan's bid of ten dollars brought a gasp from the crowd then applause. Of course a wealthy banker would think nothing of contributing that amount to the church building fund. No doubt he would donate a great deal more over time, as would the Northams.

Yet as they sat there in the cold, she couldn't think of a single thing to say. With Nolan walking her home from work each day, they didn't have much left to talk about other than the weather. The topic turned out to be his favorite as he waxed eloquent about how different the moist cold of New York was from the dry cold of Colorado. She could only smile and nod and wish her employer would cease courting her. Yet if she rejected him, he might dismiss her, and then where would she be? On the other hand, encouraging him was no less a lie than failing to tell Rand the truth about not wanting to marry.

How foolish she'd been to accept Colonel and Mrs. Northam's offer to pay for her train fare in exchange for her marrying their son. In addition to being dishonest, it proved she wasn't trusting the Lord to help her find Jimmy.

But here she was, and she no longer owed the Northams any money. Now, if she could just keep her employer from taking his courtship as far as a proposal, maybe she could find a way to encourage Rand to resume their relationship. He'd taken the first step by bidding on her box. She would pray for an opportunity to return the favor. This very evening, she would write him a bread-and-butter note thanking him for his bid. If he didn't take the bait, she'd understand.

After Nolan escorted her and Mrs. Foster home, however, her landlady suffered a bad chill and took to her bed. Marybeth made chicken soup and bread and fed the boarders before taking a tray upstairs to Mrs. Foster. The dear lady's cough rattled in her chest, just as Mam's had in her final illness. Terrified, Marybeth sent Homer Bean to fetch Doc Henshaw, and indeed the diagnosis was pneumonia.

"Keep out as much of the cold air as you can," Doc said as he applied the mustard plaster he'd concocted in the kitchen to the older lady's chest. "Keep her sitting up as much as possible, and set a teakettle to boiling in the fireplace. The steam will put moisture in the air, which should help her breathe." The young doctor gave her an encouraging smile. "Can you do that?"

"Yes, of course." Marybeth had done all of these things for Mam, yet they hadn't saved her. After Doc left, she tended to each detail and then knelt beside her landlady's bed and prayed she wouldn't die.

In that moment something shifted inside her, and God's immediate path for her became clear. Instead of being so desperate to find Jimmy right away, when he might not wish to be found at all, she would turn her attention to this dear woman who'd opened her heart and home, becoming like a mother to Marybeth. In effect, her family. How could she do any less than stay by her side and see to her needs, whatever they might be? If it meant giving up her job, so be it. As far as Jimmy was concerned, she would go to Wagon Wheel Gap as soon as the snows melted in the spring.

Rising from her prayer, she felt an odd pinch of irritation toward her brother. Why hadn't he contacted her all these years? Why hadn't he sent another letter or even come home to Boston to see how the family had fared in his absence? If he'd done his duty by them, she never would have had to come searching for him.

What a silly thought. She was glad to be here in Esperanza. Glad to be taking care of Mrs. Foster. As to her deceiving the Northam family, well, the Lord would have to straighten that out in His time.

She stuffed rags around the rattling windows and closed the green-velvet drapes for an added layer of protection against the icy night wind. The upstairs hearth didn't have a cooking arm, so she found a small cast-iron grate to set the teakettle on close to the fire. She brought her bedding to Mrs. Foster's room and slept on the chaise longue to be near the invalid and to keep the fire going.

Sometime during the course of a long night, she remembered the note she'd planned to write to Rand. That would have to wait. Maybe if the other boarders pitched in to help, she could write to him tomorrow. As far as attending church was concerned, she trusted the Lord would understand that she couldn't leave Mrs. Foster alone.

In the morning, to her dismay, the Chases announced they would leave after church to stay with one of their sons, despite cramped accommodations that must be shared with seven grandchildren. Marybeth's next disappointment came from Homer Bean. After filling the wood box in the kitchen, he told her he would find other lodgings so she wouldn't have to cook for him. He did promise to keep the wood box filled and to bring anything they needed from the general store. She supposed she should be grateful for whatever assistance he could give, but she couldn't help but feel a bit stranded. Whom would she send in case of an emergency?

With the other boarders gone, Marybeth scrambled to think of ways she could help her landlady. As far as she knew, Mrs. Foster's income would now depend solely on the piano lessons, so Marybeth would teach the students. If she could find someone to sit with Mrs. Foster during the day, she could still work at the bank and use her salary to make the house payments. If the monthly amount exceeded what she made, surely Mr. Means would grant an extension. Perhaps Mrs. Foster, being a Union army officer's widow, received a pension from the government. Marybeth wouldn't ask because discussing money might distress the dear lady. She knew only one thing. Whatever it took, she was determined to lift every burden from this woman who had been so kind to her.

Even though Marybeth hadn't withdrawn her orders for him not to visit her, Rand decided to speak to her after church. If she agreed to let him visit, he would remind her of her promise to help with the Northam family Christmas party. He'd remind her that Susanna would have her baby in another month, so she wouldn't be able to perform the hostess duties. If he could persuade Marybeth to help, maybe that would open the door to more conversation and even a restoration of their friendship. Maybe even courtship. He would try real hard not to rush that last part.

In a jolly, hopeful mood, he arrived at church early to renew their competition in passing out the hymnals. Reverend Thomas had just completed that chore and gave him the sobering news that Mrs. Foster was gravely ill.

"When I visited a short while ago, she looked mighty poorly." The preacher frowned and shook his head. "Doc's more than a little concerned, but thank the Lord, Marybeth's doing her best to take care of her."

Rand's heart sank. "Do they need help?" He cast around in his mind to think of what could be done. Susanna couldn't even make it to church these days, and of course in her condition, she had no business nursing a sick person. Surely other church ladies could help, such as elderly but spry Mrs. Chase, who was right there in the house. "Maybe I should go over there and check."

"You could, but why not wait until after the service. I'd like for us all to pray for Mrs. Foster."

As anxious as he was to see how Marybeth was coping, Rand couldn't disagree. He managed to sit through the service, thankful for Laurie Eberly's somewhat competent organ playing. The girl had only played piano before, so her efforts on the double keyboard were greatly appreciated. The preacher delivered a short sermon and then the entire congregation joined in prayer for the dear lady.

Afterward, Rand told his brothers he'd follow them home later. He made his way to Mrs. Foster's just in time to see Mr. and Mrs. Chase leaving the house, valises in hand.

"Can't stay and be a burden on that poor lady." Mr. Chase's wide-eyed look bespoke more fear than concern.

Rand couldn't fault them. They'd suffered a lot when their house burned down. That sort of loss could shake a man's soul and make him fear more tragedies.

Rand had been to the house so often it seemed like a second home, so he didn't bother to knock. Marybeth must have heard him because she emerged from the kitchen and came down the center hallway. For a moment he thought she was going to rush into his arms. He'd have gladly let her. Instead she drew back.

"Rand." She brushed loose strands of hair from her face with the back of flour-covered hands. "What can I do for you?" No smile accompanied her words. Did she prefer not to see him? Or was she just worried about Mrs. Foster?

"What can I do for *you*, Marybeth? Name it and it's done."

Now a hint of a smile touched those smooth, plump lips he'd so often wanted to kiss.

"Please make sure everyone knows Mrs. Foster's illness isn't catching, so her students can come for after-school piano lessons beginning at four-fifteen each weekday and all day Saturday. As soon as I'm home from work, I'll be teaching them until she's back on her feet."

He could tell she'd already made a plan, probably during a long, sleepless night, if the tiny dark smudges under her eyes were any indication. How would she manage to work at the bank and teach piano lessons in addition to caring for Mrs. Foster? He wouldn't question her, though.

"I'll spread the word. Anything else?"

A tiny sigh escaped her. "If there's a lady who can sit with her while I'm at work, that would be…wonderful." She breathed out that last word on another sigh, and he longed to take her in his arms. Instead he crossed them to keep the temptation from overpowering him.

"Maisie Henshaw, of course." He should have thought of her before. Maisie and her sisters were in the thick of things no matter what was happening in the community.

Marybeth laughed softly, wearily. "Of course."

"I'll go right over there and ask her, but I've no doubt she's already planning to come by today with Doc."

With those details taken care of, he stood gazing into those shadowed hazel eyes. Right then and there, he knew he loved her with all his heart. She could have moved out like the others. Could have done a lot of things to ensure her own ease and interests. But she'd stayed to help an old widow who couldn't do a thing for herself. That bespoke a deeper character than he'd given her credit for after realizing she'd never planned to marry him. He'd forgive her and forget all of that. The Lord knew well and good how many times Rand had needed forgiveness in his life.

This wasn't the time to talk about it, though. Nor was it the time to ask if she would still help with the Christmas party. In fact, if Nate and Susanna agreed, he'd cancel the whole thing because he sure couldn't do it all by himself. An event like that took a lot of planning and work, and he'd never paid attention to how Mother and Rosamond did it all.

He sure hoped his parents wouldn't be disappointed in him for failing to continue a family tradition, their annual gift to the town they'd founded. The children in the community would especially miss it, and so would their parents. He was disappointed enough in himself. This was just another failure to add to his list. How could he even think of courting Marybeth if he kept on letting people down? What kind of husband would he make?

* * *

He came to offer help. Until that moment Marybeth hadn't realized how utterly bereft she'd felt after the other boarders moved out. Through a sheen of tears, she watched Rand leave, enjoying the view of his manly form as he strode out the front gate, leaped into the saddle on his brown-and-white horse and rode away at a gallop.

Other than being grateful for his help, she wasn't quite sure what all had happened just now, but clearly Rand no longer hated her for her deception, if he ever had. No, his eyes had held more tenderness, more admiration, than she'd ever seen in them before. Maybe in time they could patch up their friendship, if nothing more. She had to admit that when he'd entered the house and walked down the hall toward the kitchen, she'd experienced a jolt of happiness. How would it be to have him come home to her every day? Maybe marriage—to the right man, of course—wouldn't be such a bad thing.

She had little time to ponder such ideas because she must finish kneading the small batch of bread she'd started and set some stew meat and onions to browning. Even if Mrs. Foster couldn't eat anything besides a little broth, it was always important to have food prepared in the larder.

Maybe Rand would come back to help later today and she could serve him some of her stew. She could imagine him hesitating to take a bite, but not wanting to be rude, he'd give it a try. That would take care of any memories of under-baked apple pie he might still have.

There she was, thinking of him again. As if he'd ever been far from her thoughts. Funny how those few minutes as they'd stood in the hallway could banish her exhaustion and give her strength to carry on.

Mrs. Foster needed almost constant care, and Marybeth could only catch a few short intervals of sleep. Maisie and Doc came later in the afternoon for a short while. Then, after a second long night with little rest, Marybeth welcomed Maisie back as she prepared for work.

"Don't you worry about a thing." The lively redhead, Marybeth's first acquaintance here in the San Luis Valley, plopped down in a chair beside Mrs. Foster's bed and pulled her knitting out of a tapestry bag. "I'll be right here, and Doc will come by a couple of times today."

Glad to have something besides sickness to focus on, Marybeth touched the tiny white wool garment coming into shape on Maisie's needles.

"Oh, Maisie, are you—"

A hint of sorrow flickered briefly in the other girl's eyes. "No, no. Not me. This is for Susanna's baby."

"Well, I know she's going to love it." Marybeth's heart went out to Maisie, married nearly a year and still no blessed event loomed on her horizon. How difficult it must be to watch her husband deliver babies all over the area and yet not be able to give him one of his own.

Would Marybeth fare any better once she and Rand...*if* she and Rand married? Although she'd postpone her search for her brother to take care of Mrs. Foster, she still couldn't bring herself to marry anybody until she knew what had happened to Jimmy.

She bundled up in her brown woolen coat and plowed into a headwind all the way to work. By the time she arrived at the bank, her face stung and her toes had no feeling at all. As she entered the building, Mr. Brandt called a greeting from the teller's cage as he counted the ready cash into the drawer. Returning a smile, Marybeth warmed herself for a moment beside the potbellied stove in the center of the lobby.

Mr. Means emerged from his office and hurried over to help her take off her coat.

"I didn't expect you in today, Marybeth, eh, Miss O'Brien." He hung the coat on the coatrack beside her desk.

"Thank you." She removed her gloves and unpinned her hat and placed it above her wrap.

"How is Mrs. Foster?"

"Doing poorly, but Maisie's with her today." She looked at her desk. "Do you have any letters for me to typewrite?"

"Actually, since you're here, I do. Let's go in my office and I'll give them to you."

She followed him into the well-appointed office and waited while he shuffled papers on his desk.

"I must tell you, Marybeth, I am not pleased to see you staying at Mrs. Foster's while she is ill. You could fall ill yourself, and I could not bear to see that."

Marybeth felt a flush of heat creep up her neck, dispelling the last of the chill she'd gotten on the way across town. How could he, a church deacon, be so heartless in regard to a dear elderly lady—the church organist who gave them all so much joy with her music? His sister's piano teacher!

Marybeth sent up a quick prayer not to answer her employer harshly and then spoke in her most matter-of-fact voice. "Thank you for your concern, Mr. Means. Doc says it's unlikely anyone will catch it. In fact, I'm going to continue giving piano lessons for her, so you can send Anna over on her usual day."

"Ah. I see." He had the grace to look abashed. "I suppose by Friday we will know whether that is an acceptable idea."

Marybeth softened her inward criticism. She couldn't blame him for being cautious. Like her, he and Anna had lost their parents to illness, maybe even pneumonia. She hadn't asked for details when he'd told her they'd died. Yet she certainly understood his devotion to his little sister, for she would do anything to protect Jimmy…if she just knew where he was.

On the other hand, she believed with all her heart that people had a responsibility to others in the community who weren't part of their family.

With Mrs. Foster so needy, she just hoped the citizens of Esperanza felt the same way.

Chapter Twelve

On Thursday, Rand hurried his mare into the livery stable, dismounted and shut the doors. If today's wind was any indication, this would be a bitter winter. Not unusual for Colorado, of course, but still unwelcome. Eager to get his business taken care of, he glanced around the large building.

"Ben, you here?"

"Coming." Ben emerged from the side room that served as his office and sleeping quarters. "Just finishing up with another customer." He tilted his head toward the man behind him.

Hardison! Rand's hand twitched, as it always did when he saw the gunslinger. The man hadn't caused any trouble during the months he'd been in Esperanza, but he'd never failed to shoot a sly grin in Rand's direction when no one else was looking. That was enough to make Rand practice his draw every chance he got, praying the whole time he'd never have to use it.

"Rand Northam." Hardison reached out as though they were old friends. With Ben looking on, Rand had no choice but to shake hands with him.

"Hardison." Rand gave him a brief nod and then turned to Ben.

"Haven't seen you for a while," Hardison said. "How's that pretty little gal of yours? Last time I was over at the bank, she seemed to be real happy working there." The leer on his face was unmistakable, as was the threat inherent in his tone.

Rand swallowed a sharp retort. Returning threat for threat wouldn't protect Marybeth. Best to divert him, make Hardison think she didn't mean too much to him. "Didn't you hear? Miss O'Brien and I called it quits at the church fund-raiser." He snorted out a phony laugh, even as his stomach tightened. "We were so loud, I would have thought everybody heard us." He handed his reins over to Ben, who led his mare to a stall. "That's the way it goes sometimes."

"Well, then." Hardison's eyes narrowed and his grin widened, giving him the look of a weasel. "You won't mind if I step in and court the little lady myself."

Rand forced a shrug. "Can't think she'd be interested in your sort." He walked toward the door. "Ben, I'll be back in an hour or so."

"Hold up." Hardison followed him out into the wind. Once the door was shut behind them, he set a hand on Rand's shoulder, again as if they were friends. "Y'know, Northam, folks around here are real nice. They've taken to me just fine and respect me as an upstanding citizen. It'll be a shame to let them all down by killing you. Of course, when you draw first, what's a man to do? He's got to defend himself."

Rand jerked away from the gunslinger's hand. If he didn't have important business at the bank, he'd have done with Hardison right now. *Lord, help me. I can't bear to kill another man.* "Don't hold your breath. I don't plan to draw first on anybody. Never have, never will."

Hardison said something more, but his words were lost in the wind. Rand had already turned away and begun his trek toward the bank. He couldn't let anything stand in the way of today's errand. Last night he and Tolley had decided to pay off Mrs. Foster's house, something they knew Dad would approve of. Captain Foster had taken a bullet for Dad during the war and never really recovered from the injury. In spite of that, he'd come out to Colorado to help Dad build this town, and his death last year had grieved everybody in Esperanza.

In the center of the bank lobby, a fire roared in the new potbellied stove, offering warmth to customers and workers alike. Marybeth sat at her typewriting machine copying a letter on the desk beside her. He hadn't seen her since Sunday and was glad to see she appeared rested. She looked up and gave him a quizzical smile. Rand thought his heart might melt on the spot.

"Mr. Northam, how nice to see you."

Mr. Northam? When had she decided to stop calling him Rand? Maybe that was best, though, considering what he'd said to Hardison.

"Same to you, Miss O'Brien." He held back a familiar smile. Maybe it was best to start backing away from her now.

"Rand." Nolan came out of his office with his hand extended. Here was someone Rand didn't mind shaking hands with, even if he was a bit pompous. Even if he obviously had an interest in Marybeth. "What can I do for you today?"

"Just a little bit of business." He nodded toward the other man's office.

"Sure. Come on in." Once inside the room Nolan stepped behind his desk and waved toward a chair. "Have a seat. Would you like some coffee?" He indicated a steaming pot on the small, square woodstove in the corner.

"No, thanks." Rand waved away the offer but liked what he saw. Now Marybeth wouldn't have to fetch coffee from Miss Pam's café on days like this. "We want to pay off Mrs. Foster's house loan."

Nolan's jaw dropped, and he blinked. After a moment he seemed to recover. "That is very generous of you. Are you sure your father would approve?"

A blast of hot anger shot up Rand's neck, but he pulled in a calming breath. "In the Colonel's absence, my brothers and I are in charge of ranch business, including finances." He referenced his father's title for effect, and it worked. Nolan sat up a bit taller.

"Ah, well, then. Never let it be said this banker turned down money." His laugh was a bit strangled, and he chewed on the edge of his lip. "I am certain you have the say-so, but just to protect the two of us, I would like to have one of your brothers sign the transfer of funds with you."

"That's reasonable." Not really, but he wouldn't argue. "Tolley and I are working fence the rest of this week. Nate's in Denver, but he'll be back any day now. Two of us can come back in next Monday."

"Now that we have it settled, I have a question." At Rand's nod, Nolan continued. "Would I be stepping on anyone's toes, namely any Northam toes, if I hosted a Christmas social at my house?" While he chuckled,

Rand's heart sank. "I know your family hosts a large event each year but—"

"Go ahead." Rand jumped to his feet. Just what he needed. In spite of what Nolan had said about stepping on toes, the pompous city boy was muscling in on Northam territory. Dad had warned him about that. Said if a banker became the town's social leader, the poorer folks would be left out. "Just remember to invite the whole community. Especially the children."

"Children?" Nolan tilted his head, clearly puzzled. "You cannot be in earnest. I really cannot have children running around in my house. We have too many delicate vases and figurines and works of art. Why—"

"Do what you think is best." Rand clapped his hat on his head and stalked out of the room. Somehow he would find a way to give the children a party. Maybe he and his cowhands could finish the addition to the church by Christmas in spite of the weather.

With a brief nod to Marybeth, he stepped out onto the street. Over in front of Mrs. Winsted's general store, Hardison stood watching him. A shudder coursed through Rand that had nothing to do with the biting wind, and a sad truth sank into his chest. Even if he never had a showdown with Hardison, there would always be someone after him who would use Marybeth to goad him. She would always be in danger. If he truly loved her, and he did, he would stay far away from her and let her marry the priggish banker. The thought made him sick to his stomach.

"Is there anything else I can do for you?" Marybeth lifted the supper tray from Mrs. Foster's lap and set it on the bedside table.

Sitting up in bed for the first time in almost a week, the elderly lady wheezed out a cough before answering. "No, dear. Not right now. Do you think Anna will come for her lesson?"

"Yes, she will. Mr. Means said he would bring her over at five, which is—" she checked the watch pinned to her shirtwaist "—in five minutes."

"Oh, dear. You'd best hurry down." Despite her words of dismissal, she grasped Marybeth's hand with fragile fingers. "I can't tell you how much I appreciate all you're doing. What would I have done without you?"

To hide an unexpected burst of emotion, Marybeth leaned down and placed a kiss on one pale, wrinkled cheek. "I'm just happy to see you feeling better. Now, before I go, shall I hand you a book or help you lie down?"

"I think I'm up to reading my Bible." She nodded toward the holy book on the table.

"Very good." Marybeth placed it in her hands, adjusted the lamplight and carried the tray downstairs.

Just as she emerged from the kitchen, shadowy figures appeared beyond the window in the front door. She hurried to greet Anna and Nolan.

"How is Mrs. Foster?" Nolan still looked skeptical about being in the house.

"Much improved, as I told you this morning." She gave Anna an encouraging smile. "Are you ready for today's lesson?"

Something akin to a pout appeared on the girl's face, but she quickly replaced it with a smile. Marybeth had taught her that a lady was always gracious, even when she was displeased. Apparently her lessons in deportment were being taken to heart. "I suppose."

"Go warm up your fingers, Anna." Nolan gave his sister a gentle nudge toward the parlor. "I would like to speak to Miss O'Brien."

As the girl left them, Marybeth gave him an encouraging smile. "Let me assure you that while my methods are a little different from Mrs. Foster's, I don't think I'll completely spoil her playing."

"That does not concern me." He gave her a shy smile and rolled his bowler hat in a nervous gesture. "I thought I should tell you...that is, would you please inform Mrs. Foster that her house loan will be paid in full? After Monday, she will not owe the bank another penny."

Marybeth stepped back as tears welled up. "Oh, Nolan, that's wonderful." She moved closer and gripped his arm. "She's been so worried about her bills, and now, thanks to you, she can set her mind at ease. This is sure to help in her healing."

"But I—"

Unable to stop herself, Marybeth reached up and placed a quick kiss on his cheek. "Oh, my. I'm so sorry. Please excuse me."

Color flooded his face, and he put a hand on the spot her lips had touched. "I cannot permit you to give me the credit, not even for a moment." He shuffled his feet, ever the schoolboy around her. "The Northam family is responsible for this charitable act. That is why Rand came to the bank last Monday. He will return this coming Monday to complete the transaction, so Monday morning I will have you typewrite the papers for him to sign."

Rand did this! What a good, kind, generous man. Hope sprang up in her heart. If he would do that for Mrs.

Foster, he surely would keep his promise to Marybeth and help her find Jimmy. And once that was done, she would be a hundred kinds of foolish if she didn't marry him. Strangely, that thought no longer dismayed her, nor did it feel like an obligation. In fact, she felt her heart lighten at the prospect for the first time since she'd met his parents in Boston.

On Sunday morning, Mrs. Foster felt well enough to be left alone so Marybeth could attend church. Just as Marybeth expected, the dear old lady's health had improved significantly after she learned of the Northams' generosity. Marybeth couldn't wait to tell Rand the results of his remarkable gift and to thank him on behalf of her landlady.

To her surprise and disappointment, he didn't come early to help her distribute the hymnbooks. After their chat last Sunday, she thought they'd begun to heal their friendship. She managed to complete the task before practicing on the little pump organ, so different from the massive pipe organ at her home church in Boston.

After she'd played the opening and offertory hymns, she sat in a chair beside the organ rather than having to choose between Rand and Nolan. If Rand noticed, his face betrayed no emotion. Nolan gave her a fond smile that almost seemed proprietary. She resolved not to make eye contact with him again during the service.

With the weather being colder and most of the cattle gone to market, more cowhands attended church, so the sanctuary was filled almost to overflowing. Some of the men had to stand against the back wall. At first Marybeth thought Reverend Thomas's sermon would be addressed to them, for he once again spoke on the passage in Psalm 119:9. "'Wherewithal shall a young man cleanse his way? By taking heed thereto according to Thy word.'" The preacher went on to urge the congregation to study and memorize the Scriptures. "For only when we hide God's word in our hearts do we have the spiritual resources to know His will and to keep from sinning against Him."

His words pricked Marybeth's conscience. Surely the Lord meant this sermon for her. How long had it been since she'd memorized a Bible verse? Before guilt could consume her for her neglect and for her sinful deception of Rand's parents—her sin that was ever before her—the minister went on.

"But when in our human weakness we do fail to keep His Word, 1 John 1:9 tells us, 'if we confess our sins, He is faithful and just to forgive us our sins, and to cleanse us from all unrighteousness.' If you find yourself in the midst of a sinful way of life…" He paused and looked around the room to take in every congregant. "Stop now. Confess your sins. And let our Lord Jesus Christ cleanse your heart and fill you with His peace."

As always, he invited anyone who wished to come to the Lord to leave their seats and come forward for prayer. Or, if they preferred, he would be happy to meet with them in private.

Marybeth played the final hymn, watching in the corner of her eye as Rand and Tolley left the sanctuary. Once again disappointment struck. Was he ignoring her? What had happened since that sweet moment the previous Sunday when he'd come to ask how he could help her care for Mrs. Foster? In fact, he'd been a little brusque last Monday when he'd come to the bank. Maybe he'd decided she wasn't worth waiting for. If so, he might not keep his promise to help her find Jimmy. After all of his kindnesses to others, that would be the cruelest cut of all.

Due to a light snowfall that threatened to get worse, Rand and his brothers spent most of Monday making sure the cattle had enough shelter and hay, especially the expectant cows who would deliver their calves come January. By midafternoon, Rand was as restless as a cat at milking time. Finally he and Tolley were able to saddle up and head to town. He could postpone signing the papers to pay off Mrs. Foster's house loan, yet for some reason he felt the need to show Nolan his word was good.

"I don't want to forget the peppercorns Rita asked us to get." Tolley nodded toward the general store. "Can't have her fixin' steak without fresh ground pepper. Can we do that first?"

"Fine with me." Now that they were in town, Rand relaxed a little. The bank wouldn't close for another hour.

They found Grace and Beryl Eberly inside the store doing a bit of shopping, too. They traded the usual information about their cattle and their families and the threatening snows, even though they'd chatted about the same things yesterday before church. Once Tolley had the peppercorns tucked in his pocket, Rand stepped toward the door.

As he reached for the glass doorknob, Laurie burst in, bringing with her a hail of powdery snow. "Grace, Beryl, come quick. The bank door's locked and something's going on in there."

Rand's heart seemed to stop. "Marybeth."

Tolley and the girls gave him a brief look before they drew out their guns and headed for the door.

"Hold on." Rand's heart now hammered in fear, just as it had three years ago when he knew Cole Lyndon had meant to kill him. "You can't just go over there waving your guns. If the bank's being robbed, we have to be careful or somebody's going to get shot."

"Come on, Rand." Tolley shoved his gun back in his holster. "You know who it is. Tell 'em." He jerked his head toward the girls and Mrs. Winsted, who'd grabbed her own rifle from behind the counter. The clerk, Homer Bean, watched the proceedings wide-eyed.

In that moment Rand could see how foolish it had been to keep this a secret from the townsfolk. How could he have made the mistake of thinking Hardison was only after him? The man was a criminal, just like his cousin. A killer and a thief. He'd aim to hurt as many people as possible.

"Dathan Hardison's been threatening me since he arrived in town. His cousin Cole Lyndon is the man I killed…" After all this time, he still nearly choked as he said it. "He wants revenge."

Grace Eberly snorted. "I had a feeling he was no good."

"Too much of a charmer." Mrs. Winsted checked her Winchester to be sure it was fully loaded. "Always trying to sweet talk me like I was some green girl."

"All this yammering doesn't solve the problem." Tolley headed for the door again.

"Hey." Grace caught his arm. "I've got a plan."

Rand's own mind was spinning with wild imaginings about what the gunslinger would do to Marybeth, and it would be his fault. At twenty years old, Grace had a good head on her shoulders, so he gave her a curt nod. "Let's hear it."

Marybeth watched the light snowfall through the bank window. In another hour she could go home and prepare supper for Mrs. Foster. This had been a quiet day of work. Other than typewriting the contract for the Northams, she'd had little to do. Perhaps the weather was keeping people at home.

Mrs. Foster would be so pleased to know she now officially owned her house as of today. That was, if Rand and one of his brothers arrived before closing time. She had to admit to herself that her heart had skipped a beat each time the door opened, only to dip with disappointment as the person entering wasn't Rand.

In spite of all that, she had another delightful bit of news to give her landlady. This morning Doc had sent a boy to fetch Mr. Brandt because Mrs. Brandt had safely delivered a baby girl. Nolan had generously given the new father the rest of the day off, so Marybeth had taken his place behind the bars of the teller's cage.

"I wonder where those Northam boys are." Nolan emerged from his office reading the time on his pocket watch. "They must be held up by the weather."

Bristling at his reference to the Northam men as "boys," she inwardly scoffed at the idea that a little snow would prevent Rand from keeping his word. Well, at least for Mrs. Foster. If he wasn't even speaking to Marybeth, she doubted he would still want to search for Jimmy, snow or no snow.

The door opened with a jangle of the bells above it, and her foolish heart once again suffered disappointment. Instead of Rand, Mr. Hardison and another man entered, and she didn't like the look in either man's eyes. When the newcomer locked the door and pulled a gun from his holster, a wave of dizziness swept over her. They'd come to rob the bank.

Just outside her cage, Nolan stiffened. "Gentlemen, what can I do for you?" His voice was tight, but she sensed no fear in him.

Mr. Hardison had the nerve to laugh in a malicious way. "Did you hear that, Deke? Mr. Means wants to know what he can do for us."

The other man, dressed in shabbier clothes and sporting a ragged beard and long, greasy hair, laughed in a coarse way that sent a sick feeling through Marybeth's stomach. "Jest tell 'em we came to make a withdrawal."

Mr. Hardison snickered. "That's right. Now, Mr. Means, if you'll just unlock the door to the money room, we'll get along just fine."

"As you wish." Nolan took the duplicate key from his pocket. Instead of unlocking the cage door, he tossed it through the bars to Marybeth. "No matter what happens, do not let them in there. Remember your training."

"Yes, sir."

If he could be brave, so could she. As he'd taught her, she scooped up the cash in the drawer and hurried over to the safe. Before she could close and lock it, or even put the money inside, a shot rang out, startling her so badly, she tossed the cash into the air. The flutter of bills and the sound of coins clinking on the marble floor would have been comical in any other circumstance. As it was, all she could do was stare at the open safe, frozen in fear.

With the sound of the gunshot still reverberating

throughout the lobby, she slowly turned, terrified at what she would see. She choked out a breath of relief that Nolan had not been shot. Instead Mr. Hardison held him around the neck and pressed his gun against the captive's temple. A red welt caused by the just-fired weapon's barrel had already spread around the point of contact. Even so, Nolan simply stared at her, his eyes soft with care, his jaw clenched.

"Now, missy, you just open that door before anybody gets hurt."

"No," Nolan choked out, only to receive a tighter tug on his throat.

Trembling as she never had in anticipation of Da's worst beatings, she gazed sadly at her brave employer. "I can't let him murder you."

Nolan's eyes reddened, and he gave her as much of a nod as he could.

Her hands shook so badly she could barely get the key into the lock. Once she turned it, the man named Deke shoved the door open and thrust her out. She spun around to catch her balance on something, anything, but failed and crashed to the floor, her head striking a hard object as she went down. Pain roared through her and spots swam before her eyes. For a moment her world went black. She'd been in this position before, and as before, a primal craving for survival gripped her.

She forced herself into awareness. *Lie still. Force yourself to relax. Pretend to be unconscious. If he thinks you're dead, he'll leave you alone.* Mam had taught her this lesson well. Now her mind reached for something more.

Her face was turned away from the shuffle of feet and grunts of a struggle. Was Nolan trying to fight off the robbers? She prayed he would simply let them take the money. She slowly opened her eyes just a slit and saw the coatrack had been overturned. Her reticule and the loaded Derringer within it lay too far away, but her hat, along with its long, sharp hatpin, was inches from her right hand.

"Get the money bag." Mr. Hardison's voice. "Fill it." He must be talking to Nolan.

More scuffles. More grunts. She moved her hand a half inch. When no one stopped her, she reached for the pin, wrapped her fingers around it and drew it into concealment against her wrist. Now there was nothing left to do but lie here and pray for an opportunity to thwart the robbers. For all the lessons Mam had taught her, fighting back was one she'd failed to impart.

Rand knew he should just go to the bank, break down the door and have it out with Hardison. But that would double the risk to Marybeth. If she died because of him, he would never forgive himself. Against his better judgment, he must participate in Grace's crazy scheme.

Being the second oldest after Maisie, Grace had outgrown her whole family, even George. At maybe five feet, ten inches tall, taller in her high-heeled riding boots, she often walked with stooped shoulders as though she was trying to hide from the world. Today, however, she threw those shoulders back, held her head high and marched across the street to the bank, while Beryl and Laurie trailed behind through the deepening snow, talking and laughing as if they were out for a summer stroll.

More guilt plagued Rand over letting these girls lead this rescue, for he had no doubt both Nolan and Marybeth needed to be rescued. But the Eberly girls had been raised to face anything the Wild West threw at them. They'd been deeply offended when Rand had tried to talk them out of helping and argued that their family's money was in that bank, too.

In case Hardison was watching, Rand and Tolley walked in opposite directions and then each circled back to creep close to either side of the bank's double front doors. With Mrs. Winsted and Homer Bean sounding the alert to other townsfolk, he could count on more help coming soon. Rand prayed as he never had before that no one would be killed today. And if someone had to be, he asked the Lord to let him be the one.

Once he and Tolley were in place, Grace banged on the door. "Hey, Nolan, open up. We need to make a deposit."

Beside her, Laurie and Beryl continued to chatter and giggle, something as far from their natural behavior as a cow jumping over the moon. So far, the act was going just as planned.

Through the fog in her mind, Marybeth heard someone banging on the bank's front door. "Hey, Nolan, open up. We need to make a deposit."

Grace Eberly's voice! *Lord, no. Please don't let anyone else get involved.*

"Let her in." Mr. Hardison spoke, probably to that horrid Deke person.

"No." Nolan's voice sounded hoarse. Did Mr. Hardison still have an arm around his neck?

"Shut up." Mr. Hardison added a curse Marybeth hadn't heard since her father died.

Slowly she turned her head just in time to see Mr.

Hardison approach to yank her to her feet. "Now you listen and listen good, missy. If you don't want your friends shot dead, you act like there's nothing wrong." He turned to Nolan. "You got that?"

Nolan nodded and Marybeth did the same.

A loud click indicated the lock had been turned. "Come on in, ladies."

Deke's weasel-like invitation sickened Marybeth, but the odd way the sisters were acting sent a strange little thread of hope through her. None of them ever giggled or minced around like silly girls trying to catch a man's attention. Why were they doing it now?

"Gracious me," Grace said. "Who's this?" She gave Deke a wide grin and gave Mr. Hardison an expectant look. "You gonna introduce us?"

Marybeth could hardly hold back a laugh at the harried expression on the man's face. "Uh, sure. Deke, the Misses Eberly. Ladies, Deke." His expression grew grim. "Now, about that deposit. Deke, hold out the bag."

"What!" Grace glanced at her sisters and spoke with exaggerated horror. "Why, they're robbing the bank. Who'd have ever guessed that such a nice gentleman as Dathan Hardison would rob a bank?"

"And with such a greasy, slimy partner," Laurie quipped.

"Now, see here, you little brat, I'll—" Deke stepped toward Laurie with one hand raised, but before he reached her, she ducked away.

In that moment Rand and Tolley burst through the front door, guns drawn. At the same time the Eberly girls drew theirs.

"Watch out!" Nolan cried.

Already holding his gun, Mr. Hardison fired at the

girls. Someone screamed in pain. The gunman aimed at Rand. Without a thought, with all her might, Marybeth swung her right hand back and stabbed the hatpin into the gunman's upper arm, which was all she could reach. With a howl of pain worthy of a banshee, he dropped the gun and flung her down on the floor. Another gunshot. More screams. Then utter chaos as the bank filled with townspeople, all armed and ready to put an end to the robbery.

Within seconds Mr. Hardison and his cohort were tied up with rope provided by Mrs. Winsted. Deke howled in pain over a gunshot wound to his leg. Mr. Hardison held his injured arm and glared at Marybeth with murder in his eyes.

Nolan gently helped her to her feet. "Are you all right?" He brushed a hand over her temple and showed her the blood on his fingers. "You're hurt."

"I can't even feel it." She let him pull her into a comforting embrace, though his arms were not the ones she longed for. Not ten feet away, Rand gazed at her, frowning. He turned away, clearly with no mind to do that comforting himself. "Oh, Nolan, it was so horrible. Thank the Lord you're all right." Thank the Lord that Rand and Tolley and the Eberly sisters were all right, too.

"You were very brave. I am very proud of you." He breathed out a laugh of relief. "Everything is all right now. Everyone is all right."

All right. All right. She heard the phrase echo throughout the room as everyone confirmed their friends' well-being. Yet sobs from the other side of the lobby proved them all wrong. Marybeth and Nolan made their way through the cluster of people to where Grace and Laurie knelt on the marble floor weeping. Across Grace's lap lay Beryl, her eyes closed, her face white as a sheet and a dark red stream of blood staining the front of her blue plaid shirt.

Chapter Thirteen

Wavering between fear and rage, Rand paced the hallway outside Doc Henshaw's surgery. He stopped from time to time to give Laurie and Grace an encouraging hug. Beyond the surgery door, Maisie helped her husband as he tried to save Beryl's life.

Tolley had gone out to the Eberly ranch to tell her folks what had happened. They would arrive soon, if their buggy could make it through the snow. Mabel no longer rode horseback, but she'd probably make the effort for one of her daughters.

Charlie Williams had tended the wounds on Deke's leg and Hardison's arm. Now the two outlaws were trussed up like Christmas turkeys and stuffed like baggage into the cargo room at the train station under the watchful care of Charlie, Mrs. Winsted and two upstanding cowboys.

Rand couldn't have been prouder of the way the courageous townsfolk had come together to stop the robbery. Nolan's courage had surprised him most, but he supposed bankers lived with the possibility that they could be robbed. No wonder he'd wanted to hire a sheriff. Too bad he hadn't seen through Hardison sooner.

Once Dad heard about the robbery attempt, he'd no doubt say it was indeed time to hire a lawman for the town and build a jail, too. Until then, the closest law was Sheriff Hobart over in Del Norte. The townsfolk all agreed they needed to escort the prisoners into Hobart's care until the circuit judge came to the area. They'd elected Rand to lead the posse, but he refused to go until he knew whether Beryl would survive. If she didn't, Hardison and Deke would get their due. A long jail term for attempted robbery would be nothing compared to being hanged for murder.

Despite the successful thwarting of the robbery, Rand couldn't help the flash of annoyance sweeping through him. He'd prayed that if someone had to get hurt, it should be him. The preacher would no doubt tell him God was still in control, but Rand would have to think on that for a while. The Eberly girls weren't the dainty sort of female, but they still deserved respect and protection, as all women did. He'd gladly take a bullet for any one of them.

The face of one dainty girl who'd been just as brave as the sisters came to mind. Rand had been sick with fear when he saw Marybeth in Hardison's clutches. Yet she'd struck the man with her hatpin just as he was about to shoot Rand. Brave girl. She'd saved his life. But when everything got sorted out, it was Nolan's arms she'd sought. Or maybe Nolan had just reached out to her before Rand could. He'd probably never know.

Though it grieved him, this was probably for the best. Even with Hardison in custody, someday somebody else would come gunning for Rand and would try to make a reputation for himself. He couldn't risk Marybeth's life again, not when she'd come so close to being killed. Best to let her go so she could marry someone like Nolan and live in a nice house in town with servants to do all the work. He reluctantly dismissed his fond images of her living on the ranch because there she'd be doing chores as even well-off ranch women did. Like Mother and Rosamond. Like the Eberly girls, who were too much like sisters to interest him in a romantic way.

The door to the surgery opened, and Maisie emerged, her bloodstained white apron a frightening symbol of her sister's tragedy. She rushed to gather her other sisters in her arms.

"She's hurt bad, but she's gonna make it." While the three of them wept together for joy, Doc came out looking tired but pleased.

"Hardy stock, these girls." He emitted a broken laugh. Or maybe it was a sob of relief.

Rand couldn't speak over the emotion welling up inside his own chest. *Thank You, Lord.*

Until that moment he hadn't realized how much he'd wanted to kill both Hardison and his partner for their evil deed. He didn't know whose bullet had hit Beryl because both of them had fired several shots. And both of them had had murder in their hearts or they wouldn't have fired in the first place. With all the bullets flying around, only the grace of God kept more of them from finding a target. God truly was in control, just as the preacher always said.

Until Marybeth sat beside Mrs. Foster's bed to tell her about the robbery, she'd managed to hold on to her emotions. After the amazing people of Esperanza had come together to imprison the two crooks, Nolan had asked Marybeth to visit Anna and explain why he would be late coming home for supper. Anna had taken the news with remarkable stoicism for a twelve-year-old. It was the Meanses' housekeeper who'd struggled to maintain her composure. Marybeth had felt the need to sit with both of them until the older lady calmed down. Once they'd received word Beryl would survive, she'd made her way home along the snow-covered streets.

Now in the presence of her landlady, she felt her own self-control slipping. After relating the afternoon's events as gently as she could, she laid her head on her friend's lap and let the tears flow. Mrs. Foster caressed her hair and murmured comforting words. Soon a soft rumbling in Marybeth's ear alerted her to her duty. She sat up and dried her damp cheeks.

"Well, now that that's all done, I'll go fix us some supper." She forced a brightness she didn't feel into her tone. "We have some of last night's shepherd's pie left over. Does that sound good?"

"It sounds very fine indeed." Sympathy and understanding shone from Mrs. Foster's eyes. "And if you want to talk some more, I would be happy to listen."

Their supper warmed, Marybeth brought it to the bedside so they could eat together. Mrs. Foster consumed a few bites before putting down her fork and regarding Marybeth with a searching gaze.

"My dear girl, when are you going to marry Rand Northam?"

Marybeth gulped down her bite and took another. At last she put aside her tray. "Rand no longer wants to marry me."

"What nonsense." Mrs. Foster barked out a harsh

cough, but the deathly rattle no longer reverberated through her chest. "I've seen that boy's eyes when he looks at you. He loves you. And when a Northam falls in love, it's forever."

Marybeth shook her head. "After he realized I came out here with no intention of marrying him, I think he decided I didn't deserve his love. He's been ignoring me these past few days, and I don't blame him."

"He may be trying to guard his heart. That's understandable. But if you ask for his forgiveness, I have no doubt he'll give it."

Hope flickered briefly inside her but then died. Even before they'd all discovered Beryl had been shot, Rand hadn't tried to comfort her after her ordeal. He'd left her to Nolan, which had cut her deeply, not to mention how much it complicated matters. By accepting Nolan's calming embrace, she may have given both men the wrong impression about where her affections lay. But how could a person control an emotional reaction in the aftermath of chaos?

She would do as Mrs. Foster suggested. She'd go to Rand and ask forgiveness. Yet even if he gave it, even if he proposed to her, she simply could not marry him until she learned what had happened to Jimmy. Too much of her life, too much of her heart, had been invested in finding her brother. She couldn't give up until she looked on his face…or his grave.

On Tuesday, after the six men in the posse had packed warm clothes and provisions for a trip of uncertain length, Rand fetched the outlaws' horses from the livery stable, paying their bill with money from Hardison's pocket. Nolan, ever the gentleman, informed

Hardison that his deposit would be safe in the bank until he needed it. Charlie Williams suggested they should make sure it wasn't stolen before giving it back to the outlaw.

In high spirits, and ignoring the complaints of their wounded prisoners, the group rode out of Esperanza, some hoping, others praying, they would be back by the end of the day, or at least by Wednesday. Although the snow had stopped and the sun had steamed off a goodly portion of it, a surly bank of dark clouds hovered above the mountains at the north end of the Valley. None of the men wanted to be stuck in another town due to the snow because it might be weeks before they could return home.

Heading west on the rolling trail, they were slowed by deep drifts the sun couldn't reach, so it was late afternoon before they arrived in Del Norte. They found Sheriff Hobart in a sad state, coughing and wheezing and unable to lift his head off the pillow on the cot beside his desk. Fortunately he had no prisoners at the time.

"My deputy quit last week," he said when he could catch his breath. "A couple of you men will have to stay and keep watch over these scalawags until the judge comes."

Rand groaned inwardly but straightened his shoulders. "This is my responsibility. I'll stay." He couldn't wait to see the last of Dathan Hardison, but wait he must. "Sheriff, you'd best go home so your wife can take care of you." He didn't like the old man's gray pallor and prayed he could whip this sickness.

Between coughs, the sheriff wheezed out, "I need to deputize some of you men first."

They'd decided Frank Stone and Andy Ransom, both unmarried cowboys, would stay to help Rand. The sheriff managed to say all the right words, receive their pledges to uphold the law, and pass out three silver badges before collapsing back on his cot.

While Rand and two others kept an eye on the prisoners, now locked safely behind the iron bars of the jail cells, the other three men helped Hobart get home. When they returned, they brought a fresh loaf of bread and a steaming kettle of stew to go along with the ever-present coffeepot on the jailhouse's potbellied stove.

On Wednesday, those who were leaving got an early start in hope of beating the storm now moving south across the Valley. As the day darkened and snow began to fall, Rand's spirits sank. His family would be all right. Beryl was on her way to recovery. But in all the chaos, he and Tolley hadn't managed to sign the papers to pay off Mrs. Foster's house. Worse still, in his absence, Nolan could court Marybeth all he wanted to.

Rand hadn't had much chance to think about his decision not to court her anymore, but here in this desolate jailhouse over the next few days he began to think he'd made a mistake. In front of him was a stack of Wanted posters bearing the faces of men who'd made the wrong choices in life, just like Dathan Hardison and Cole Lyndon. Just like Deke Smith, whose simpleminded countenance belied his evil soul.

Rand didn't want to reach the end of his own life with any more regrets added to his grief over killing a man. As the days wore on, he realized he would always regret not trying to win Marybeth's heart. He'd be honest with her about the risk of being married to a man whom other gunslingers might want to outdraw and then let her decide whether or not to take that risk. For his part, he'd be downright foolish not to find out whether she would prefer him over Nolan.

Risk was a part of life. After the war Rand's parents had risked their future to come out to an untamed territory and start building a new life far from the safety of Boston's upper class into which they'd both been born. George and Mabel Eberly and Captain and Mrs. Foster had done the same. In Del Norte he saw many people risking everything, including their lives, as they set off for the mountains to look for silver and gold. In Rand's view, Marybeth was worth far more than any material wealth. And she'd risked everything to come West in search of her one remaining family member.

Love and admiration for her flooded his heart, his mind. How he wished he could go right now and find Jimmy O'Brien and bring him home to her for Christmas. Then maybe she would feel free to marry him. And, oh, how he wanted to marry her. But responsibility demanded that he stay to see this matter to an end. Even if Nolan won her heart in his absence.

In the meantime he regretted not having made arrangements with Mrs. Winsted to purchase some Christmas presents for the children of Esperanza. Before he could even send up a prayer that Nolan would change his mind and let the children attend the party, he noticed Andy Ransom seated across the jailhouse whittling on a piece of wood. As it took on the shape of a wooden soldier, Rand's burden eased. This was the Lord's answer even before he prayed. They would carve wooden toys, soldiers for the boys and tiny baby dolls for the girls. That would be just the thing to keep his mind off of Marybeth.

Who was he trying to convince? She would always be at the forefront of his thoughts. If she married Nolan in his absence, Rand would never be able to stay in the San Luis Valley.

For the rest of the week after the robbery, Marybeth didn't have to report to work until midmorning because Nolan shortened business hours due to the snowstorm. By Friday, the early December sunshine brightened the landscape and even gave a suggestion of warmth for most of the shorter daylight hours. Marybeth was grateful when Nolan dismissed her at three o'clock so she could purchase some provisions at Mrs. Winsted's general store on the way home.

As Nolan helped her put on her coat, his hands lingered on her forearms for a few seconds. "May I bring Anna for her usual piano lesson this afternoon?"

"Of course." She stepped away from him, trying not to give offense for the abrupt movement by picking up her hat and pinning it in place. While she doubted she'd ever have to use that long hatpin as a weapon again, it certainly had come in handy the previous Monday.

"After that, if you do not mind, may I speak with you?" He dipped his head in his shy way. "Since you've assured me Mrs. Foster is much better now, perhaps Anna can visit with her."

Marybeth secured her dark blue woolen scarf around her neck and then tugged on the matching mittens her landlady had knitted for her during her convalescence. As much as she wanted to deny Nolan's request, perhaps it was time to settle this matter. Even if the man she loved never spoke to her again, she certainly wouldn't play with the affections of her employer. "Yes, of course." Manners required her to add, "Perhaps you could stay for supper."

Mild alarm flitted across his pleasant face. "Well, um—"

Her confusion was brief, followed by amusement. He'd eaten a bite of her pie at the fund-raiser and probably shared Rand's concerns about the quality of her cooking. She would not correct him. "Of course, if you have other plans for the evening, I understand."

With the matter settled, she made quick work of her shopping and hurried home to prepare supper. Even if Nolan didn't wish to eat her cooking, Mrs. Foster always praised whatever she prepared.

Perhaps affected by the attempted robbery and the mortal danger her brother had faced, Anna had practiced diligently all week, as proved by her competent if not brilliant playing. She made her way through Brahms' "Lullaby" and Luther's "A Mighty Fortress is our God" with very few mistakes. Still, as she gathered her music at the end of the lesson, she whispered to Marybeth, "Did Grace Eberly really shoot the bank robber?" The wonder and admiration in her eyes revealed that her longing to be a cowgirl had not lessened.

Marybeth gave her a solemn nod. After all the details had been sorted out, Grace received the credit for taking Deke down, shattering one of his legs. The man would be fortunate if he ever walked normally again.

Marybeth didn't want to think about the damage she herself had done to Mr. Hardison. She shuddered at the memory of how her hatpin had dug deep into his upper arm and then raked downward after he'd knocked her to the floor. According to Charlie Williams, she'd managed to stab his upper arm in just the right spot to render the entire appendage useless. The thought had sickened her until several people commented that the now former gunslinger would never be able to draw a gun on anybody again. Although she cringed at the thought of hurting anyone so badly, perhaps the Lord had allowed it to stop the killer. After all, the Bible related the story of how a shepherd boy named David had killed the evil giant Goliath.

With Anna upstairs, Marybeth sat in the parlor sipping tea with Nolan, who seemed to forget why he'd lingered. He chatted about his gardener, who always managed to keep the hothouse warm enough so his flowers continued to bloom. "It is remarkable to have fresh flowers year-round in such a cold climate." He went on to describe additions he'd planned for his house and asked if she had any suggestions for improving his property. Then he thanked Marybeth for calming his housekeeper after the robbery. "Mrs. Browder could not say enough about how poised you are." He took a sip of tea and eyed her over his cup. "That is a very high compliment coming from an Englishwoman."

Marybeth could only smile and nod and wonder where this all was leading.

Nolan set down his cup and saucer and inched closer to her on the settee. "Marybeth, it cannot have escaped your notice how much I admire you. I fully understand that you came to Esperanza to marry Randall Northam, but it appears to me…and to others…that your plans have changed." His eyes glowed with fondness and he chewed his lower lip briefly. "If that is true, I hope you will not find this question inappropriate."

Marybeth's heart dropped. Surely he would not propose. Before she could stop him, he went on.

"As you may have heard, the Northam family usually holds a Christmas party for the community. In the absence of Colonel and Mrs. Northam, and with the Northam family's blessing, of course, I will be hosting a formal dinner and social at my house on Saturday evening, December 17. You may have already noticed Christmas Eve is the following Saturday, and I thought some people may want to stay home the night before Christmas. Hence my choice of that date. You are invited, of course. And in addition, would you do me a great favor and teach Anna about her duties as a hostess?"

So he didn't plan to propose. Marybeth withheld a sigh of relief. "Yes, of course." Rand's party was to be on Christmas Eve, so there would be no conflict. That was, if he returned from Del Norte in time. "I would be happy to help Anna and you with the party."

He seemed relieved, as well. Had he doubted she would help? "I plan to invite the leaders of our entire community." Now he took on his shy look. "I have not had the chance to tell you of my plans for the future, but perhaps you will find them interesting. It is clear to me that Esperanza requires more leadership, and at the party I will propose that we have an election right away. Further, I will put myself forward as a candidate for mayor."

She supposed every town needed a mayor, but why was he telling her of his ambitions?

"Of course, in that position, I will need a wife, a helpmeet, as the scriptures say, to stand by my side as a leader among the fair ladies of our town." He coughed softly. "I can think of no one but you who would fill that office to perfection."

For a moment she could only stare at him. Then an idea came to mind. "I'm honored, Mr. Means." She must step back from the familiarity of using his Christian name. "However, I believe you deserve a wife who has moved in higher social circles than I have. You should know that I come from very humble beginnings. My parents were poor immigrants and died in poverty." She would not reveal Da's drunkenness or gambling unless Nolan became persistent. Besides, Rand knew all of these things and had made it clear none of it mattered to him.

Nolan chuckled. "Poor beginnings do not mean anything in America. My father was also an immigrant. He simply managed to build a fortune where some could not." He leaned over and grasped Marybeth's hand. "Due to your finishing school training, you have all the grace and dignity of the most elegant society ladies I knew in New York. Any man of intelligence would be proud to have you by his side. Would you do me the honor of becoming my wife?"

There it was, the unwanted proposal. Yet in no part of this discussion had he spoken of love, for which she was glad. It made turning him down much easier. She pulled her hand free from his grasp.

"Mr. Means—"

"Nolan, please."

She sighed. "Nolan. I admire you, too, but that's not enough for me. I want…*need* to be in love with the man I marry."

"But that can come in time, as it did in my parents' marriage."

"It's too late." She injected as much firmness as she dared into her words. "I'm already in love with someone else." Now if she could only confess her feelings to the object of that love.

Nolan's shoulders slumped. "Yes. Of course. Randall Northam."

"Yes."

He chewed his lip again. "I hesitate to ask this, but will you still help Anna with our Christmas social?"

"Of course I will." How interesting, even comical, that he took her rejection so easily. Whom would he pursue now? One of the uncultured Eberly girls? Another comical thought.

The circuit-riding judge rode into Del Norte on December 14. Within two days he pulled a drunken lawyer away from his gambling over at the saloon, summoned a jury of upright citizens—all of whom remembered Cole Lyndon—conducted a trial and received the verdict. Dathan Hardison and Deke Smith were found guilty of attempted robbery and attempted murder. As soon as the north pass cleared in the spring, they would be escorted to the prison in Canon City, where they would spend the next thirty years. In the meantime, Frank and Andy agreed to stay on as deputies so Rand could return home.

As he carefully packed the carved toys and his few belongings into his saddlebags, Hardison taunted him from his cell. "I'll get out, Northam, and when I do, I'll be gunning for you. You just keep looking over your shoulder. And I've got plans for that little gal of yours, too. She owes me for what she did to my arm."

Eyeing the limp appendage hanging at the man's side, Rand considered several responses before deciding on the best one. He stepped closer to the cell and leveled a hard stare on Hardison. "Word is a lot of men die in prisons. Sickness. Murder. So-called accidents. You need to be planning what you're going to say to the Almighty when you leave this earth. Did you ever listen to a word Reverend Thomas preached while you were sitting there pretending to believe in Jesus Christ? I hope so. You need to be thinking about Him and what He did for you."

Hardison's curses followed Rand out the door, along with poor, stupid Deke's cackling laugh. These past few weeks had reminded him of the kind of men he used to gamble with, and he couldn't get away from these two fast enough.

The weather smiled on his travels on Saturday, December 17, and he arrived in Esperanza just after the sun ducked behind the San Juan Mountains. He rode directly to Mrs. Foster's house, determined not to let another day pass without proposing to Marybeth or at least getting her permission to court her. To his disappointment, no one was home, so he rode over to Main Street. With Esperanza having no night life, only a few people walked the streets. Lucy was just emerging from Miss Pam's café. After she closed and locked the door and turned toward her home, he reined his horse in her direction.

"Hey, Rand." The usually talkative girl didn't seem too eager to chat, but continued on her way. No doubt she was still ashamed of throwing over a good man like Seamus and taking up with a scoundrel like Hardison.

"Hey, Lucy." He dismounted and fell into step with her. "Where is everybody? The town's even quieter than usual of an evening."

She shrugged. "Most of 'em are probably over at

the banker's mansion." Pulling her thin shawl tighter around her, she cast a wistful look in that direction, though the house was several blocks away and not visible from where they were. "He's having a party."

"Ah. Right. The Christmas party." Rand had forgotten this was the day Nolan had picked for the event. That's where Marybeth and Mrs. Foster were. His heart dropped into his stomach like a rock as he realized what this meant. Marybeth had chosen Nolan, and that was that.

Lucy seemed as depressed as Rand. He'd known her all her life and couldn't just ride away with her about to cry. "Why aren't you there?"

"Me?" She burst out with a bitter laugh. "Mr. Banker man only entertains Esperanza's *elite* citizens. He didn't even invite my ma, and she's as good as anybody in this town."

Not invite the town's best seamstress, a dedicated member of the church? What was the matter with Nolan? In the gray illumination of twilight, Rand could see tears glistening on Lucy's cheeks. He wanted to encourage her but had to be careful so she wouldn't misunderstand his intentions.

"Well, don't feel bad. As the preacher might say, we're all elite in the Lord's eyes. Scripture says when we belong to Him, we're chosen and accepted."

She gave him a soft smile not at all like her usual flirting ones. "Thanks, Rand. Good night." With a wave over her shoulder, she turned down her street.

Now his own words came back on him. Chosen and accepted. Maybe not by Marybeth, but by the Creator of the Universe, the Savior of whosoever believed in Him. Rand couldn't lightly dismiss the ache in his heart, yet he would seek the comfort of the One who offered the peace that passed understanding. He would also pray that Mother and Dad would come home soon so he could explain to them in person why he'd be leaving the San Luis Valley forever.

Out at the ranch, Nate welcomed him home and gave him the news that he and Tolley had taken care of paying off Mrs. Foster's home. Susanna added that Tolley had gone to Nolan's party tonight to represent the family. That was fine with Rand. His younger brother needed a healthy social life. Right after the shooting, right after seeing Beryl nearly die, he'd admitted to Rand that he'd lost his interest in gaining a reputation as a gunslinger. That had eased some of the guilt Rand still felt over killing Cole Lyndon.

"Say, I almost forgot." Nate shoved back from the kitchen table where they'd just finished supper. "You have a letter from Wagon Wheel Gap. I'll get it." He picked up a burning kerosene lamp and moved toward the door.

Pulse pounding in his ears, Rand followed his brother down the hallway to Dad's office. "Did you read it?"

Nate glowered at him briefly. "I don't read other people's mail." He shrugged. "Besides, if it's bad news, I knew I wouldn't be able to hide it from Susanna, and she wouldn't be able to keep it from Marybeth. With the baby due any day now, she's a bit emotional." He grinned, clearly not bothered by his wife's changing moods.

Rand grunted. "Right." He sat at Dad's desk and slit open the envelope, pulling out the folded page. At the first words, sorrow gripped him for Marybeth's sake.

Dear Mr. Northam,

Have located grave marker for one Jimmy O'Brien.
Date of death, September 14, 1876.
  Wish I could give you better news.
Yours sincerely,
Archie Doolittle, Sheriff
Wagon Wheel Gap, Colorado

Rand handed the letter to Nate then folded his arms across the desk and rested his forehead on them. How could he tell Marybeth? How could he bear to see her heart break?

"Lord, have mercy. He's been dead for over five years." Nate gripped his shoulder. "What are you going to do?"

"I don't know." Rand raised his head and scrubbed his hands over his eyes. "I was looking forward to going to church tomorrow." In spite of his dread at the idea of seeing her with Nolan, he longed for the comfort of an hour of worship with fellow believers. "But how can I look her in the face? She'll know something's wrong right away. What do you think—?"

Urgent knocking on the door interrupted him. "Señor Nate, come quick. Señora Susanna, she needs you."

Nate bolted out the door, with Rand right behind him. In the kitchen Susanna leaned back in a chair, her hands pressed against her protruding belly.

"Nate, honey, it's time."

Nate knelt beside her. "Let's get you upstairs, darlin'." He shot an expectant look at Rand, his eyes asking the question he didn't voice.

"I'll go for Doc." Tired as Rand was, he would do anything for his sweet sister-in-law.

While Nate tended Susanna and Rita took care of

little Lizzy, Rand retrieved his tan oilcloth duster from the closed-in back porch and then headed to the barn to saddle a fresh horse.

He had no doubt Doc and Maisie would be at Nolan's party. Would it be possible to get their attention without seeing Marybeth? If he did see her, what would he say? Just a week before Christmas, how could he destroy all of her hopes of ever reuniting with her brother? The best thing would be to completely avoid her, no matter how much he wanted to talk to her.

Chapter Fourteen

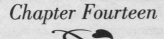

Marybeth guided Anna around the spacious drawing room to greet each guest, giving hints as to what the girl should say to each one from the ideas they'd rehearsed. As they moved away from their short chat with Doc and Maisie, Anna sighed...again.

"I know everybody here. I know what they did today and what they think of the weather. Why do I have to ask these silly questions?" The now-thirteen-year-old crossed her arms and huffed out a sigh.

"Because Nolan wants you to learn how to be a gracious hostess." Marybeth had worked hard to absorb the lessons at Fairfield Young Ladies' Academy. Teaching them to Anna reinforced them in her own mind. "You must practice so it's second nature. You can appreciate that, can't you? You never want to be caught not knowing what to do or say."

Another sigh. "I suppose not." Anna's face brightened. "There's Tolley Northam. What should I say to him?" She giggled. "Can I tell him how much I like the way those big green eyes of his light up when he wears that gray shirt?"

Just like Rand's. Marybeth stifled a smile. One day soon she'd be able to tell him she admired more than his eyes. "Only if you want to make him uncomfortable."

"That'll be half the fun." Anna took a step in Tolley's direction. "All the girls like to torment him just to see his face turn red."

Marybeth caught her arm as gently as she could. "Save that for another day and—"

A small commotion at the drawing-room door cut her short. "Come, Anna. It's your responsibility to learn what's going on so you can smooth over any unpleasantness."

They approached a cluster of people gathered around... Rand! Marybeth's heart leaped into her throat. He must have returned home in the past couple of hours, because Tolley had told her earlier his brother was still in Del Norte. She left Anna and shoved through the crowd, for the moment dispensing with the manners she'd worked so hard to learn. She did manage not to cast herself into his arms, but her whole body trembled with wanting to do just that.

"Is Doc here?" Rand appeared exhausted and a bit unkempt. Dark whiskers on his handsome face suggested he hadn't shaved for several days, yet he looked wonderful to Marybeth.

Doc and Maisie approached from the other direction, already donning their wraps.

"Is it Susanna?" Maisie pulled on her leather gloves while Doc retrieved his black bag from a nearby table.

"Yes." Rand's gaze lighted on Marybeth and he gave her a brief nod.

Her heart jumped again but then sank when he didn't offer a smile or other greeting. Maybe it was time to be a little more like Maisie and Anna. She stepped over to him.

"Hello, Rand. It's good to see you back."

Maisie and Doc swept past him, and he started to follow them. "Good night, folks."

"Rand—" She couldn't let him go without asking him to come see her. That was, if he still cared for her.

He turned back just as Nolan stepped up beside her and snaked his arm around her waist. "Good evening, Rand. We are glad to see you back. When it is convenient, Marybeth and I would like to hear all the news about Hardison."

Glaring at Nolan, Rand plopped his hat on his head. "Sure thing." He disappeared into the hallway. Seconds later the front door slammed.

Marybeth spun around to face Nolan. "Why did you do that?"

"My dear, you cannot blame me for trying to discourage the competition." He put on his shy face and for the first time she could see it was all an act. Further, his "my dear" sounded entirely too much like Dathan Hardison.

Mindful of several people watching, especially Anna, she smiled, leaned close to his ear and whispered in her sweetest tone. "But, *dear* sir, as I thought I'd made quite clear to you, there is no competition. There is no *we*. And since you refuse to hear me, I will be going home now."

His possessive smile drooped slightly. "May I at least have one dance before you leave? Please do not embarrass me in front of my company."

Every instinct shouted "no." Every lesson she'd

learned at Fairfield Academy insisted she must comply. "Very well."

Yet as they twirled around the drawing room to Mrs. Foster's slightly rusty Strauss waltz, Marybeth chanced to glance out the front window. There stood Rand in the light streaming through the glass, his hands shoved into the pockets of his long coat, his shoulders hunched, his eyes on her. Before she could lift a hand to hail him, he turned and strode away.

The wind slicing around the edges of Rand's oilcloth duster wasn't nearly as sharp as the pain in his heart. He spun away from the mansion and nailed shut the door of hope he'd briefly opened when he knew he'd see Marybeth this evening, after all. Maybe the Lord planned it this way so he'd finally get it through his head that she wasn't for him. With all of her fancy training back East, no wonder she preferred to marry a banker. He tried to console himself that a ranch wife should know how to cook, but his heart answered that he would eat anything she prepared and love it because it came from her hands.

Back home for the second time this evening, he set aside his troubles and kept Nate company in the ballroom, the farthest spot in the house from poor Susanna's cries. She was a brave little gal, but even a cow sometimes bawled when dropping a calf.

To keep Nate's mind off of his wife's suffering, Rand showed him the toys he'd brought home. "Frank and I carved the rough shapes, and Andy finished up the details. He's got a real talent."

"Those are really something." Nate turned a four-inch toy soldier over in his hands and then picked up one of the smaller doll babies. "I know Lizzy will love to have one of these. Maybe Susanna can sew little blankets for them when she's up and about." He gazed around the ballroom he'd built just over three years ago for their parents' twenty-fifth wedding anniversary. "You know, being in here makes me want to give the Christmas party, after all. We could do it next Saturday, this one just for the children. If all goes well…" He glanced up toward the other wing of the house as though trying to see Susanna through the ceiling and walls.

Rand patted his brother on the shoulder and sent up another prayer for the little mother and her coming baby. A party was a good idea. Maybe it would be just the thing to help him forget Marybeth. Mother always said doing for those less fortunate helped a person get over his own troubles. He'd speak to the preacher about the party after tomorrow's church service.

Around three in the morning Maisie came downstairs and invited them to come see the newest member of the Northam family, a healthy baby boy with a head full of the signature dark brown hair. Susanna was already sitting up, looking tired, happy and every bit as healthy as her son. Nate wiped away tears of relief and. happiness before embracing the two of them.

A bit emotional himself, Rand let the happy event soothe away some of his sorrow over losing Marybeth. He fell into bed for a long, deep sleep, only to wake up around noon on Sunday and realize he'd missed church. He offered an apology to the Lord, but he figured the Almighty had mercifully let him sleep so he wouldn't have to see Marybeth sitting with Nolan. After all, a man could only take so much heartbreak.

* * *

Worn out from the previous night, Mrs. Foster stayed home from church to recuperate. Although several other ladies could have taken her place at the organ, they'd all urged Marybeth to play the hymns. They didn't have to ask twice. Now she wouldn't have to sit with Nolan, nor would she have to explain to Anna why she wouldn't be sitting with them anymore. She would, however, smile at Rand to let him know she would welcome a chance to talk with him. If he didn't approach her after the service, she would chase him down before he could mount his horse and ride away.

To her disappointment Tolley was the only member of the Northam family present at church. During announcement time, he revealed the good news of Nathaniel Junior's birth. He also said that since the church addition wasn't quite finished, his family would be holding a Christmas party for the children of the community the next Saturday, Christmas Eve. Several ladies volunteered to bring food and help through the week, as well as with the event itself.

Marybeth loved the idea of the party. This would be the perfect opportunity to show Rand how well she could cook. If that didn't restore his interest in her, nothing would. The thought of failing to win him sobered her, yet she couldn't be entirely depressed about helping out. At least she'd get a chance to see Lizzy and the new baby.

After the service, the ladies gathered at the back of the church to decide when each would take a meal out to Four Stones since Rita would be too busy helping Susanna with the children to do all the cooking. Marybeth volunteered to go on Saturday. That would give her time to plan and prepare her best recipes. It would also give her time to come up with Christmas gifts for the Northam family. She knew exactly what she would give to Rand.

On Friday afternoon Seamus and most of the cowhands returned home from Denver, all of them better off after their extended stay at the camp meeting. Seamus's faith in the Lord had already been as solid as the Rock it was founded upon. Now his entire countenance, bearded though it was, glowed with an inner peace and joy. Some of the other hands had seen the Light and been converted. Of the fifteen drovers who'd taken the herd north, only three decided the seedy section of Denver was more to their liking than being preached to. Sorry to hear about the reprobates, Rand and Nate agreed the three had never been happy in a town with no saloon and no liquor.

After the men cleaned up from their travels, the trail cook fed them supper in the bunkhouse, during which Rand told them all about Hardison's attempted bank robbery. Later Rand took Seamus to the ballroom to show him the decorations for the next night's party.

"If you're not too worn out, maybe you could help me finish trimming the tree in the morning."

"I'm your man." Seamus plopped down on a sturdy settee and laid his head back against the antimacassar protecting the green velvet upholstery from just such actions. In his absence he'd let that beard grow out, the long, bright red whiskers contrasting sharply with his shoulder-length dark auburn hair. "I don't suppose you've seen Lucy while I've been gone."

Rand sat in a nearby chair, pleased for a chance to

finally talk with his friend. "I saw her last Saturday. She looked pretty miserable." He explained about the party at the Meanses' house.

"It's a shame he treats folks that way." Seamus got a faraway look in his eyes. "Y'know, Rand, a while ago when you told us about what happened with that scoundrel she took up with, instead of being angry, I felt sorry for her. I believe with all my soul the Lord's forgiven us for that shooting over in Del Norte. He's forgiven me for a whole lot more I've never told you about. I'd be a hypocrite if I didn't forgive her for misjudging Hardison. From what you said, I guess he put on a pretty good show that could turn any girl's head. What would you say if I rode into town tomorrow and invited her to the party?"

Rand thought for a moment as more of his own guilt sloughed away. "I'd say you're right about forgiving others as we've been forgiven. Go ahead and invite her."

"Now, tell me about your little gal. You never did tell me her name." Seamus seemed to have lost some of his Irish brogue, but the accent had always come and gone depending on the situation. Tonight he sounded more like a regular cowboy, probably from hanging around with the other men for so long. "When are you two getting hitched?"

Rand blew out a long sigh. "She's not my girl anymore. She took that job at the bank and Nolan Means started courting her. While I was in Del Norte guarding Hardison, he won her over." And just as Seamus forgave Lucy, he needed to forgive her for breaking his heart.

Seamus sat up and reached over to grip Rand's shoulder. "I'm sorry to hear that."

"Thanks." Annoyance cut into his self-pity. "Let's

talk about something else. Can we count on you to stick around and work for us another year, or do you plan to become a circuit-riding preacher?"

Seamus chuckled. "Nope. No preaching for me. But during the camp meeting, the Lord convicted me about some things I've done. I have some business to attend to back in Boston before I make any promises here."

"Boston? I thought you were from Philadelphia."

Seamus hung his head. "I guess I should come clean about a few things in my past."

"You don't need to do that." Rand gave his friend's arm a little shove. "It's all forgiven, remember?"

"Yes, but I still need to reconcile with my family, at least Mam and my sister, Marybeth. Even my da, if he's still alive...and sober."

Rand nearly passed out on the wave of shivers running through him. "Jimmy O'Brien."

Seamus jumped to his feet. "How did you know my real name?"

Rand could only stare at his friend, unable to speak. Now he didn't have to tell Marybeth her brother was dead. It might be too late to win her heart, but at least he could give her the Christmas present he'd so desperately wanted to.

After making certain Mrs. Foster was as well as she claimed, Marybeth slid her perfectly baked apple pie from the oven and placed it in a towel-lined basket. The cast-iron pot full of Irish stew sat in a wooden crate by the front door beside one sturdy leather case and a canvas bag full of presents, all ready to be carried out when Doc and Maisie came to fetch her.

Excitement and nervousness vied for control of her

emotions, with excitement winning the moment the Henshaws arrived in the late afternoon. In the backseat of their surrey sat the three young daughters of the Chinese couple who operated the laundry at the edge of Esperanza. The girls' coal-black eyes were round with wonder, as though they thought perhaps a mistake had been made in their inclusion in today's festivities. Having grown up Irish in Boston, Marybeth knew all too well about such doubts. She gave the girls a warm smile as she climbed into the back and took a seat beside them. Soon they were on their way south toward Four Stones Ranch, singing Christmas carols as they went.

Several other wagons traveled in the same direction. Mrs. Winsted drove her supply wagon filled with children and young people who joined in the singing once they were in earshot. Among the passengers, Marybeth saw Lucy, whose contrite demeanor for the past month had gone a long way to restoring her reputation. Marybeth decided she would make friends with the girl this very evening. After all, they'd both been taken in by Mr. Hardison's charming ways. Marybeth had just seen through his façade.

The singing made the trip seem faster and soon the buggies and wagons turned down Four Stones Lane. At the house Marybeth helped unload the smaller children. With many hands available to take the food and presents inside, she carried only one item in her hands, the leather case holding the gift she'd bought for Rand at Mrs. Winsted's general store.

The presents had cost all of her savings, yet she'd enjoyed buying them. Over the past few days an abiding sense of peace had overcome her in regard to Jimmy. Winning Rand's love was more important to her now, especially since her brother might not still be in Wagon Wheel Gap or even Colorado. Besides, as long as Nolan didn't dismiss her for refusing his courtship, she could save more money for the trip. If he did discharge her, the Lord would show her what to do next.

Now, looking up at the lovely two-story house where Rand had grown up, she could no longer doubt this was where she was supposed to be. Love for her cowboy welled up inside her as she climbed the steps onto the wide front porch. But would he even want to see her after Nolan's possessive behavior last Saturday? Maybe not, because it was Nate and Tolley who welcomed the guests at the front door and sent them through the parlor to the ballroom. Rand wasn't there, either. Disappointed, Marybeth set the round leather case near the Christmas tree.

Across the room Susanna sat in an overstuffed brocade chair holding her new son. Marybeth joined the other ladies cooing over the beautiful baby boy. What a fine head of dark hair he had, just like his da. Just like his uncle Rand. Amidst the hubbub, she couldn't help but wonder how she would react when she saw him. More important, how would he react when he saw her?

"Now, you don't want to give her apoplexy." Rand had been worried since last night trying to figure out the best way to reunite Seamus and Marybeth. "Maybe you should stay here until I can talk with her and slowly introduce the idea that we may have found you."

Seamus, usually a calm man, paced the dining-room floor, stopping from time to time to grab a bite of beef or chicken or a cookie from the food-laden table. "This morning I had a hard time not telling Lucy about all of this. A harder time not riding over to Mrs. Foster's to find Marybeth. But I didn't want to spoil your surprise." He chuckled and his hazel eyes shone brightly in the light from the crystal chandelier hanging in the center of the ceiling. "I sure hope the girls will be friends 'cause they're gonna be sisters." He stroked his long red beard thoughtfully.

Rand's emotions slowed considerably at the thought of his friend's upcoming marriage. Just this morning, Seamus and Lucy had mended their fences. He had no such chance with Marybeth. He tried without success to summon up some of the joy he'd felt over being able to reunite her with her brother. Yet all he could think about was watching her dance with Nolan last week.

"Well, go on." Seamus gave him a little shove. "See if she's in that last group of folks who just came in."

Rand's knees shook as he approached the ballroom. There across the wide space Marybeth knelt beside Susanna, her face filled with sweet admiration for Junior. It sure would be nice to have her look at him that way. He squashed the dream. It would never happen.

He stepped down into the room just as she turned his way. To his surprise, that sweet smile broadened and she hurried through the crowd to meet him.

"Hello, Rand." She sounded a bit breathless, exactly the way he felt. Her hazel eyes twinkled brightly. Why hadn't he ever noticed how they resembled Seamus's?

"Hello, Marybeth." His pulse pounded in his ears. She seemed mighty glad to see him. That could only be good. Did he dare to revive his dreams about her?

"Before you say anything, I have something for you." She grabbed his hand and tugged him toward the Christmas tree. Lifting up a leather case with a red bow on it, she shoved it into his hands. "This is a concertina. I can teach you how to play it, and I'll play piano. We can sing together like we did that first Saturday after I arrived. That is, if you want to."

As he took the shiny new music box from its case and examined it, understanding swept through him. This was her way of saying she wasn't engaged to Nolan. That the two of them had a chance. "A concertina? Wow." How had she known he'd always wanted to play one but just hadn't had the time to learn? "These are pretty expensive." Maybe as much as ten dollars with the leather case, a lot for a young lady of limited means to spend.

She shrugged. "I had some money saved up."

"Sure. For your trip to Wagon Wheel Gap." Yet she'd spent it on him. That made the gift all the more price-less.

Again she shrugged. "I'll save some more while we wait for spring."

Stunned, Rand could only gaze at her for several moments. She'd postponed her most precious dream so she could give him a present. Nothing in the world could proclaim her feelings for him any better than that. Now he must give that precious dream back to her. He carefully put the concertina in its case and set it back under the tree. "What would you say if I told you there's no need to go up there?"

Her happy expression dimmed a little. "I have to go, Rand, just to find out for myself whether Jimmy's up there." She put a hand on his arm. "You can understand, can't you?"

"I can." He couldn't keep his news any longer. "I've found your brother."

Just as he'd feared, she swayed toward him, her face pale. He caught her before she went down and steadied her.

"Don't worry, darlin'. He's alive and well." Rand chuckled nervously. By now everyone in the room was watching them. "'Scuse us, folks." He put an arm around Marybeth's waist and propelled her out to the parlor through the front hallway and into the dining room. "Marybeth, this is Seamus O'Reilly, once known as Jimmy O'Brien."

She stared in disbelief. "But—"

"Mary, me sister dear." Seamus put on his brogue and held out his arms. "Come give your brother a welcome kiss."

"It is you! It is! Oh, Jimmy!" She dashed across the room and threw herself at him, bursting into choking sobs. Seamus shed a few happy tears, too.

As much as he wanted to comfort her, Rand stood back and let them have their reunion. Grateful she'd never have to see the sheriff's letter about the grave bearing her brother's name, he would let Seamus tell her what he'd been up to all these years.

"So after those miners put a price on my head, I gave all my poker winnings to the undertaker to help me fake me own death. We even put up a wooden grave marker. After that, I hightailed it out of town, took the name Seamus O'Reilly and became a cowboy." Jimmy gave Marybeth a rueful grin, his eyes filled with shame. "You'd think after watching Da gamble away all of his money, I'd have better sense. But it took that shoot-out in Del Norte to complete the job."

Marybeth had just about cried out all of her tears, but

emotion still churned within her. "If only Mam could see you now. So tall and handsome. And with dark hair. I guess all the red sank down to that impressive beard."

He chuckled. "It's a good thing I changed over these past few years. None of the miners ever recognize me when we happen to cross paths. O'course, not many of 'em venture this far from the mining fields. They're all so wild to strike gold or silver, I suppose Jimmy O'Brien is long forgotten."

"But never forgotten by me. Never." Marybeth couldn't stop a fresh flood of tears. Finally regaining her self-control, she needed to settle one last thing in her mind. "Do you still have Mam's locket?"

"I do." Jimmy tugged at a silver chain around his neck and produced the beloved piece of jewelry. "It's been a great comfort to me over the years, making me think of Mam as it did, God rest her sweet soul." He blinked away a tear. The news of her death had devastated him. "You can have it now. Maybe it'll do the same for you." He managed to tangle the chain in his beard, but with her help, he undid the clasp and put the inch-and-a-half oval locket in her hands.

She turned it over and over, studying the finely etched floral design. She looked at Rand, sitting by so quietly, so patiently, through their long conversation. If she opened the locket and found the key to the treasure Mam had promised, how would it affect their relationship? Did she still wish to be wealthy and independent? To never have to marry or be under a husband's rule?

Somehow those dreams no longer mattered. Rand had proved himself to be far different from Da. Far different from every man she'd ever met. Her heart welled up with love for him and she had her answer. Randal

Northam was treasure enough for her. That was, if he would still have her.

She placed the locket back in Jimmy's hand. "Mam put it in your care. You keep it."

Jimmy blinked in surprise. "But don't you want to look inside? To see the wee picture of the four of us in happier times?"

"I do." Rand took the locket from him. "I want to see *wee* little Marybeth before she grew up to be so sassy." He unclasped the lock and folded out the two sides. There in a tiny framed picture sat Mam, Da, Jimmy and herself, just as they'd looked fresh off the boat from Ireland. "Aw, such a pretty baby." He sent her a teasing grin that made her heart jump. "You've grown up to look just like your beautiful mother. Or should I say your mam?"

"And here's the best part." Jimmy retrieved the trinket and revealed a second opening behind the picture. "Mam always said this was the key to a great treasure. After all I've been through, I know 'tis true." He placed the locket back in Marybeth's hands.

Inside the second frame, written in delicate script, were the words "What time I am afraid, I will trust in Thee. Psalm 56:3."

Wonderment filled Marybeth such as she'd never known. Now at last she understood what real treasure was. Not gold. Not independence. Not even Rand's love. But rather, faith in God, her heavenly Father. Mam had trusted in Him through all the miseries, all the beatings, all the fears. And these many years, Marybeth had been just like Da, gambling on obtaining material wealth to make her happy. Despite her belief in God, she hadn't

fully trusted Him for her future. Yet He had been pre-
paring the happiest of *earthly* treasures for her: Rand.

"Jimmy, I want you to have this." She gave the jewelry back to him. "When you find your true love, you
can give it to her." She blinked. "Oh, dear. You're this
Seamus person Rand's been telling me about, so *Lucy*
is your—" It was one thing to be friendly to Lucy, but
could she stand to see Mam's precious locket hanging
around the girl's neck? Well, if her brother loved Lucy,
she supposed she could, too.

"That, she is." Jimmy beamed and his eyes twinkled.
"And I'd best be getting over to the ballroom so she and
I can visit before this party's over." He stood and pulled
Marybeth up into his arms, placing a kiss on top of her
head. My, he'd grown so tall and strong, no longer the
slight boy Da had so cruelly abused. "Rand, if I leave
my sister to your care, will you behave yourself in a
proper manner?"

"You can count on me." Rand rose and shuffled his
feet in a charmingly shy way, so different from Nolan's
deceitful attempts at the same.

Jimmy opened the dining-room door and the sounds
of laughter and singing wafted in from the ballroom.
He gave Marybeth a wink before leaving her alone with
Rand.

"Marybeth, would you—?" Rand began.

"Rand, I wonder—"

They both stopped. For her part, Marybeth's entire
being tingled with emotion and anticipation.

"You first." She must give him a chance to say the
words his bright green eyes were already speaking.

"Ladies first." His grin sent her heart spinning. "I
insist."

"Oh, all right. But just know I'm not going to be one of those mousy little wives who always gives way to her husband." That didn't come out right. Of course she would honor and obey her husband. So she added, "At least not without some discussion."

"Well, now, Miss Sassy, exactly whose wife are you planning to be?" He stood tall, crossed his arms and gave her a long look, as though trying to appear severe. He didn't succeed.

Subduing the giggle trying to escape her, she ambled over to the side table where the desserts were laid out. "I thought maybe yours. But you have to pass a test."

His puckered his lips as though smothering a grin. "And that is?"

She took a small plate from the provided stack and dug a triangular server into her apple pie. "You have to prove your love for me by eating an entire slice of the pie I baked."

His smothered smile became a grimace, which he tried to hide with a cough. "Sure thing, darlin'." He slowly, reluctantly, closed the space between them and accepted the offered plate. With a sigh and an apologetic shrug, he took a bite she could only call dainty. His eyebrows arched. His eyes widened. He blinked.

"My, my. This is the most delicious apple pie I've ever eaten, bar none." He ate another, larger bite. When he'd practically gulped down the entire piece, understanding spread across his handsome face. "Back at Harvest Home, you knew exactly what you were doing, didn't you?"

"Sure did." She sampled the pie. Should have put in a bit more cinnamon, but this wasn't at all bad. "Just wait until you taste my Irish stew."

"I hope I don't have to wait much longer." Rand set down his plate and grabbed her around the waist. He lifted her from the floor and spun her around. She squealed with delight, throwing her arms around his neck and wishing he'd never let go. When at last he set her down, he cupped her face in his hands. "Miss Marybeth O'Brien, may I kiss you?" His husky voice overflowed with emotion.

Joy bubbled up inside her, making it just as hard for her to speak. "Mr. Randall Northam, I do wish you would."

"But I mean may I really, truly, kiss you?"

Now she understood. Not a brotherly peck on the cheek. Not a sweet kiss on her forehead. But a kiss smack on her lips promising her all the good things to come. "Oh, yes, Rand, me love, you may."

And so he did.

Chapter Fifteen

After Christmas the men of Esperanza took advantage of every sunny day to complete the church addition. With winter slowing down many ranch duties, Rand had time to supervise the building project, which would benefit the entire community. As nice as it was to have the ballroom at the Northam house, folks in town needed a place to gather so they didn't have to travel so far for special events.

Rand enjoyed working with his hands. Seeing the structure take shape gave him a sense of satisfaction as nothing else he'd ever done. Every board he sawed, every nail he hammered, meant the church would soon have rooms for Sunday school. And none too soon.

At the Christmas Eve party, Nate had read the Christmas story from the Bible. With Susanna seated nearby, baby Nathaniel in her lap, Lizzy standing beside them, Nate had then talked about how special every baby was. Yet as much as he loved his son and daughter, he reminded everyone that the most special baby ever born was baby Jesus, the Son of God, because He had come to save His people from their sins. The children listened quietly, their eyes full of wonder, partly because Nate had a gift for storytelling, partly because some of the children were hearing the story for the first time.

Yep, they sure did need Sunday school, and Nate would make a very good teacher. Funny how a man who could make his drovers quake in their boots could speak so gently to the little ones, yet still capture their attention, just like Dad.

Rand would gladly take on the job of teaching the older boys. He'd make sure they knew all about his careless attitude toward life at their age and how it had caused him nothing but grief. Maybe he could keep them from following in his footsteps. As always, that thought reminded Rand of Tolley and his turnaround after the shooting. It was the one good thing to come out of the bank robbery.

As the days passed, Rand's former feelings of failure and inadequacy faded away. Like Tolley, instead of admiring him for killing a dangerous outlaw, his neighbors now followed his leadership in building the church addition. He didn't ever expect to completely be free of the guilt over killing Cole Lyndon, but he'd come to a place of peace with the Lord about it. It was time to move on and take his place in the community, with his beloved Marybeth at his side.

So Rand set a fast but careful pace for the men, urging them to give as much time as possible to the completion of the addition. For his part, he was there every day. It didn't hurt that the first social event to take place after the building's dedication would be his own wedding reception.

On a Saturday in late January 1882, Marybeth and Lucy stood in the cloakroom at the back of the sanctuary, both dressed in white. Lucy wore Susanna's three-year-old wedding dress, let down a few inches to accommodate her greater height. Marybeth wore the satin gown her future mother-in-law had bought for her last spring in Boston.

Although Marybeth would have been pleased to have Colonel and Mrs. Northam at the wedding, she couldn't wait for spring to become Mrs. Randall Northam. All fences had been mended, including her relationship with Lucy. Even Nolan wished her well and admitted his affection for her was no match for Rand's obvious devotion. He proved the truth of his sentiments by providing white roses from his hothouse for the bridal bouquets.

Attending Marybeth and Lucy were Laurie and Beryl Eberly, each dressed in a new blue gown made by Lucy's mother. Beryl had survived the gunshot wound, and her color, while still a bit pale, promised full recovery.

Also recovered was Mrs. Foster, who now played Richard Wagner's "Bridal Chorus," signaling the time had come for the brides to make their grand entrance. Nate offered an arm to each girl, and they proceeded down the aisle toward Rand and Seamus. Tolley stood up with his brother, and Wes, another longtime Northam cowhand, stood beside Seamus. Marybeth thought her red-bearded brother presented a very fine picture, but surely no groom had ever been as handsome as clean-shaven Rand in his new black frock coat, white shirt and black string tie.

Her heart overflowing with love and joy, tears clouding her vision, Marybeth traded a look with her soon-to-be sister. Lucy's blue eyes shone bright in the morning sunlight streaming through the east windows.

Did any bride ever remember saying her actual wedding vows? Before Marybeth knew it, Reverend Thomas had pronounced the two couples men and wives, and Rand was kissing her right in front of the whole congregation. Everyone burst into applause, something she'd never witnessed in her more formal Boston church. Her Fairfield Young Ladies' Academy training notwithstanding, she much preferred the relaxed and homey feel of Esperanza Community Church. Here no one looked down on her for being Irish.

The reception hall in the new church addition was festooned with evergreen garlands. Two tables laden with presents, each with a three-tiered cake baked by Miss Pam in the center, awaited the bridal couples. In the corner, a trellised arbor decorated with white silk roses provided the perfect spot for wedding pictures.

Lucy and Seamus posed first for the traveling photographer, whose large black camera served as a source of great interest to the children. The young man promised to take a picture of them all together if they would just stand safely away while he worked. He ducked under the black cloth and held up the lighting pan. As the magnesium powder flashed, the children shrieked with delight. Next, Rand took his seat beneath the arbor, and Marybeth stood just behind him, her lace-gloved hand on his shoulder. Again the powder flashed and again the children shrieked. Marybeth had to blink several times to clear her vision.

By late afternoon the reception dinner had been served by the ladies of the church, the presents opened and the cakes cut and eaten. Now Marybeth longed to be alone with her beloved. Standing behind the table that held their gifts, she stood on tiptoes to whisper in his ear. "Can we slip away without anyone seeing us?"

He cast a furtive glance around the room. "I did hear mention of a shivaree, but that would be later on this evening." He chuckled. "Funny how I was annoyed with Nate for skipping out after his wedding so we couldn't do the honors for him and Susanna. Now I'm hoping we can escape it." He tugged her to his side and gazed down at her, love shining in his eyes. "You ready to go?"

"Oh, yes. More than ready." She noticed a few ranch hands huddled together in another corner and occasionally glancing her way. Nothing terrified her more than the idea of being carried away from Rand now or ever. "How are we going to get away without being noticed?"

"Slip out into the hallway and hide in the second room on the right. I'll enlist Tolley's help. He owes me." He placed a quick kiss beneath her ear that sent delightful shivers down her neck.

In the Sunday school room, she found her woolen shawl among the other coats and wraps and flung it around her shoulders. She waited by the window until Rand came around with his horse. Why hadn't he brought a buggy? He knew she'd never ridden. Yet once he helped her out through the window, placed her in the saddle and then swung up behind her, she felt safe and secure in his arms. Circling around the church, they rode south of town. The sun was near setting by the time they passed Four Stones Lane and continued south.

"Where are we going?" Marybeth called over her shoulder.

"Nate and Susanna said we could stay at their house until Mother and Dad return. After that, they'll move back in. I plan to start building our own place right away."

With its columned front porch and numerous windows, the pretty one-story white house looked homey and inviting. Rand shoved open the front door and carried her inside. He set her down in the center of the charming little parlor, lit a kerosene lamp and started a fire in the stone fireplace.

"Susanna promised to send over some provisions from the big house." He led Marybeth to the well-stocked kitchen. "Looks like we could hole up here for weeks without anybody knowing where we are." He checked the cast-iron cookstove. "Needs wood, but there's a pile by the back door."

Lamp held high, he showed her the rest of the house, including three bedrooms. Baby Nathaniel's nursery was equipped with brand-new mahogany furniture Nate had bought in Denver after the cattle drive. Lizzy's room had dainty feminine furnishings. Marybeth could hardly wait to decorate such rooms for her own little ones.

Next, Rand took her to the master bedroom, a spacious and well-appointed chamber. He set the lamp on an oak chest of drawers, from where it cast a warm light on the bright quilt covering the four-poster. Heat rushed to Marybeth's cheeks as she considered the implication of standing in this room with her new husband.

"Now that you've had the tour, did you get any ideas for our house?" Rand tucked his thumbs through his belt loops and leaned back against the door jamb. "I'll build whatever you like."

"Well, right at the moment, I wasn't exactly thinking about our house." She gave him a saucy grin.

He blinked those big green eyes in mock astonishment. "Why, Mrs. Northam, are you thinking what I think you're thinking?"

"Why, I don't know, Mr. Northam." She giggled. "What do you think I'm thinking?"

Instead of answering he gathered her in his arms and leaned down to deliver another one of those heart-stopping kisses. She did her best to answer in kind.

Then he froze. "Do you hear that?"

"Rand, don't tease." She tried to capture his lips again.

"Wait. Shh. Listen."

Sure enough, discordant sounds reached her ears from afar, growing closer by the second.

"Oh, no."

"Quick. Put out the lamp. I'll douse the fire." He hurried away from her toward the parlor.

After turning down the lamp wick, she followed close on his heels through the darkened house. He raced from window to window, locking them and closing draperies. Outside the noise had grown to a loud cacophony of rattles, bangs, gunfire, whooping and who knew what else.

Marybeth grabbed her new husband's arm. "Oh, Rand, don't let them take me away from you. Please."

"Take you away?" Even in the dim room, she could see his tender expression. He pulled her into a secure embrace. "They won't do that, darlin'."

"They won't force their way in?"

He chuckled. "No. We don't do it that way around here. They'll just keep us awake all night. Unless they decide we're not here."

Relief swept through her and she leaned into his chest. "I hope they didn't see the smoke from the fireplace."

"Maybe they missed it in the dark."

From the noise still resounding through the walls, she was fairly sure they hadn't.

"Even so," he said, "they'll smell the smoke."

Marybeth chewed her lip for a moment. "Do you suppose if we feed them, they'll go away? I could make some soup."

"It's an idea."

She spied his concertina beside the settee. "And we could sing to them."

His broad shoulders slumped. "I've been too busy to practice."

Now she giggled. "With a little warm-up, I think my fingers will remember a couple of songs."

He laughed with her; a deep, throaty chuckle that tickled her insides. "Shall I invite them in?"

"Why not? I'll fix some coffee to warm them up and then start the soup."

Within a few minutes the Eberly sisters, the Northam brothers, the other newlyweds Seamus and Lucy, and numerous cowboys and townspeople had crowded into the parlor and kitchen. Lamps were lit, fires were stoked in the hearth and kitchen stove and soup bubbled in a cast-iron pot.

As the laughter and merriment swirled around her, Marybeth couldn't regret this interruption of her wedding night. After all, she was now a part of a wonderful community. All of these people accepted her, loved her. Like Rand's love for her, this was a treasure greater than any she'd ever dreamed about.

And she could live with that.

* * * * *

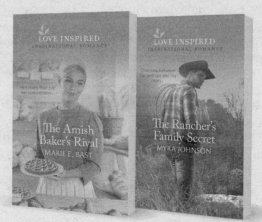

SPECIAL EXCERPT FROM

🍃

LOVE INSPIRED
INSPIRATIONAL ROMANCE

When Susannah Peachy returns to her grandfather's
potato farm to help out after her grandmother is injured,
she's not ready to face Peter Lambright—the Amish
bachelor who broke her heart. But she doesn't know his
true reason for ending things…and it could make all the
difference for their future.

Read on for a sneak peek at
An Unexpected Amish Harvest *by Carrie Lighte.*

"Time to get back to work," Marshall ordered, and the other men pushed their chairs back and started filing out the door.

"But, *Groossdaadi*, Peter's not done with his pie yet," Susannah pointed out. "And that's practically the main course of this meal."

Marshall glowered, but as he put his hat on, he told Peter, "We'll be in the north field."

"I'll be right out," Peter said, shoveling another bite into his mouth and triggering a coughing spasm.

"Take your time," Lydia told him once Marshall exited the house. "Sweet things are meant to be savored."

Susannah was still seated beside him and Peter thought he noticed her shake her head at her stepgrandmother, but maybe he'd imagined it. "This does taste *gut*," he agreed.

"*Jah*. But it's not as gut as the pies your *mamm* used to make," Susannah commented. "I mean, I really appreciate that Almeda made pies for us. But your *mamm*'s were extraordinarily *appenditlich*. Especially her *blohbier* pies."

"*Jah*. I remember that time you traded me your entire lunch for a second piece of her pie." Peter hadn't considered what he was disclosing until Susannah knocked her knee against his beneath the table. It was too late. Lydia's ears had already perked up.

"When was that?" she asked.

"It was on a *Sunndaag* last summer when some of us went on a picnic after *kurrich*," Susannah immediately said. Which was true, although "some of us" really meant "the two of us." Peter and Susannah had never picnicked with anyone else when they were courting; Sundays had been the only chance they had to be alone. Dorcas, the only person they'd told about their courtship, had frequently dropped off Susannah at the gorge, where Peter would be waiting for her.

"Ah, that's right. You and Dorcas loved going out to the gorge on *Sunndaag,*" Lydia recalled. "I didn't realize you'd gone with a group."

Susannah started coughing into her napkin. Or was she trying not to laugh? Peter couldn't tell. *How could I have been so* dumm *as to blurt out something like that?* he lamented.

After Lydia excused herself, Peter mumbled quietly to Susannah, "Sorry about that. It just slipped out."

"It's okay. Sometimes things spring to my mind, too, and I say them without really thinking them through."

It felt strange to be sitting side by side with her, with no one else on the other side of the table. No one else in the room. It reminded Peter of when they'd sit on a rock by the creek in the gorge, dangling their feet into the water and chatting as they ate their sandwiches. And instead of pushing the romantic memory from his mind, Peter deliberately indulged it, lingering over his pie even though he knew Marshall would have something to say about his delay when he returned to the fields.

Susannah didn't seem in any hurry to get up, either. She was silent while he whittled his pie down to the last two bites. Then she asked, "How is your *mamm*? At the frolic, someone mentioned she's been…under the weather."

I'm sure they did, Peter thought, and instantly the nostalgic connection he felt with Susannah was replaced by insecurity about whatever rumors she'd heard about his mother. Peter could bear it if Marshall thought ill of him, but he didn't want Susannah to think his mother was lazy. "She's okay," he said and abruptly stood up, even as he was scooping the last bite of pie into his mouth. "I'd better get going or your *groossdaddi* won't let me take any more lunch breaks after this."

He'd only been half joking about Marshall, but Susannah replied, "Don't worry. Lydia would never let that happen." Standing, she caught his eye and added, "And neither would I."

Peering into her earnest golden-brown eyes, Peter was overcome with affection. *"Denki,"* he said and then forced himself to leave the house while his legs could still carry him out to the fields.

Don't miss
An Unexpected Amish Harvest *by Carrie Lighte,*
available September 2021 wherever
Love Inspired *books and ebooks are sold.*

LoveInspired.com

LOVE INSPIRED

INSPIRATIONAL ROMANCE

UPLIFTING STORIES OF FAITH, FORGIVENESS AND HOPE.

Join our social communities to connect with other readers who share your love!

Sign up for the Love Inspired newsletter at **LoveInspired.com** to be the first to find out about upcoming titles, special promotions and exclusive content.

CONNECT WITH US AT:

Facebook.com/LoveInspiredBooks

Twitter.com/LoveInspiredBks

Facebook.com/groups/HarlequinConnection

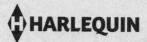

HARLEQUIN

Heartfelt or thrilling, passionate or uplifting—Harlequin is more than just happily-ever-after.

With twelve different series to choose from and new books available every month, you are sure to find stories that will move you, uplift you, inspire and delight you.

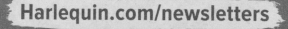